The Caine Prize for African Writing 2013

A Memory
This Size
and other stories

Emmanuel,
Thanks for
coming out!
— Tope Folarin

The Caine Prize for African Writing 2013

A Memory This Size
and other stories

JACANA

New Internationalist

The Caine Prize for African Writing 2013

First published in 2013 in Europe, North America and Australasia by
New Internationalist™ Publications Ltd
Oxford OX4 1BW
www.newint.org
New Internationalist is a registered trademark.

First published in 2013 in Southern Africa by
Jacana Media (Pty) Ltd in 2013
10 Orange Street
Sunnyside
Auckland Park 2092
South Africa
+2711 628 3200
www.jacana.co.za

Individual contributions © The Authors, 2013.

Cover art © Michael Salu.

Design by New Internationalist.

Printed by TJ International Ltd, Cornwall, UK
who hold environmental accreditation ISO 14001.

British Library Cataloguing-in-Publication Data.
A catalogue record for this book is available from the British Library.

Library of Congress Cataloguing-in-Publication Data.
A catalogue record for this book is available from the Library of Congress.

New Internationalist ISBN 978-1-78026-119-5
Jacana ISBN 978-1-4314-0838-2

Contents

Introduction

Selected from 96 stories from 16 African countries, this anthology contains the five stories from the 14th annual Caine Prize shortlist. For the first time two of the writers who participated in the most recent Caine Prize workshop appear on the shortlist and there are an unprecedented four Nigerian entries.

The Chair of Judges, art historian and broadcaster Gus Casely-Hayford, summarized the shortlist as 'outstanding African stories that were drawn from an extraordinary body of high-quality submissions'. He added: 'The five contrasting titles interrogate aspects of things that we might feel we know of Africa – violence, religion, corruption, family, community – but these are subjects that are deconstructed and beautifully remade. These are challenging, arresting, provocative stories of a continent and its descendants captured at a time of burgeoning change.'

The 2013 shortlist comprises:

- Tope Folarin (Nigeria) 'Miracle' from *Transition,* Issue 109 (Bloomington, 2012)
- Pede Hollist (Sierra Leone) 'Foreign Aid' from *Journal of Progressive Human Services,* Vol. 23.3 (Philadelphia, 2012)
- Abubakar Adam Ibrahim (Nigeria) 'The Whispering Trees' from *The Whispering Trees,* published by Parrésia Publishers (Nigeria, 2012)
- Elnathan John (Nigeria) 'Bayan Layi' from *Per Contra,* Issue 25 (Philadelphia, 2012)
- Chinelo Okparanta (Nigeria) 'America' from *Granta,* Issue 118 (London, 2012)

Joining Gus Casely-Hayford on the panel of judges are award-winning Nigerian-born artist, Sokari Douglas Camp;

author, columnist and Lord Northcliffe Emeritus Professor at UCL, John Sutherland; Assistant Professor at Georgetown University, Nathan Hensley; and the winner of the Caine Prize in its inaugural year, Leila Aboulela. Once again, the winner of the £10,000 Caine Prize will be given the opportunity of taking up a month's residence at Georgetown University, as a Writer-in-Residence at the Lannan Center for Poetics and Social Practice. The award will cover all travel and living expenses. The winner will also be invited to take part in the Open Book Festival in Cape Town in September 2013.

This book also contains the stories that emerged from this year's Caine Prize workshop, which was held in Uganda for the first time. On the shores of Lake Victoria we assembled 12 talented writers at the Garuga Beach Resort Hotel where we were surrounded by spiders, fat on swarms of lake flies, whose webs cocooned all the surrounding foliage. We are immensely grateful to Beatrice Lamwaka and Hilda Twongyeirwe for helping us to find Garuga and to Goretti Kyomuhendo for all her useful advice. Three of the writers who took part were shortlisted in 2012 and four were local Ugandan writers; the others hailed from Nigeria, Kenya, Malawi, Zimbabwe and Botswana. During 10 days of peace and quiet the workshop participants write, read their work to each other, discuss and critique each story. They were guided by Veronique Tadjo (Côte d'Ivoire) and Pam Nichols (South Africa), who are both based at the University of the Witwatersrand in South Africa. The only breaks included a visit to St Mary's High School in Kisubi where writers spoke to 150 boys about the workshop and read from their work in progress. Later that evening we launched the *African Violet* anthology at the Barn Steakhouse in Kampala with our co-publishers FEMRITE and the help of the British High Commissioner Alison Blackburne and the British Council country director Peter Brown.

We now have seven African co-publishers and continue to be committed to making Caine Prize stories available to read all over the continent. We are delighted that we have agreed co-publishing arrangements with 'ama Books in Zimbabwe, who join the long-standing partnerships we already have with Jacana Media in South Africa, Cassava Republic in Nigeria and Kwani? in Kenya and last year's additions of FEMRITE in Uganda, Sub-Saharan Publishers in Ghana, and Bookworld Publishers in Zambia. The anthology is now available as an ebook supported by Kindle, iBooks and Kobo and we are continuing to develop our partnership with the literacy NGO Worldreader to make the first nine award-winning stories available free to African readers via an app on their mobile phones.

The principal sponsors of the 2013 Prize were the Oppenheimer Memorial Trust, the Booker Prize Foundation, Miles Morland, Weatherly International plc, China Africa Resources plc and CSL Stockbrokers. The DOEN Foundation primarily supported the workshop in Uganda and support was also received in kind from the British Council, FEMRITE and the African Writers' Trust. The British Council and Commonwealth Writers, a cultural initiative of the Commonwealth Foundation, and the Lennox and Wyfold Foundation also gave valuable support. Kenya Airways and the Beit Trust both provided travel grants for workshop participants. There were other generous private donations, and vital help in kind was given by: the Royal Over-Seas League; Bodley's Librarian; the Rector of Exeter College, Oxford; the Royal African Society; Marion Wallace of the British Library; Stephanie Newell and Ranka Primorac of ASAUK; Jacqueline Auma of the London Afro-Caribbean Book Group; Tricia Wombell, Coordinator of the Black Reading Group and Black Book News; the Southbank Centre. We are immensely grateful for all this help, most of which has been given regularly over the past years and without which the Caine Prize would not be Africa's leading literary award.

Lizzy Attree
Administrator of the Caine Prize for African Writing

Caine Prize 2013
Shortlisted Stories

Miracle

Tope Folarin

OUR HEADS MOVE SIMULTANEOUSLY, and we smile at the tall, svelte man who strides purposefully down the aisle to the pulpit. Once there, he raises both of his hands then lowers them slightly. He raises his chin and says *let us pray*.

'Dear Father, we come to you today, on the occasion of this revival, and we ask that you bless us abundantly, we who have made it to America, because we know we are here for a reason. We ask for your blessings because we are not here alone. Each of us represents dozens, sometimes hundreds of people back home. So many lives depend on us, Lord, and the burden on our shoulders is great. Jesus, bless this service, and bless us. We ask that we will not be the same people at the end of the service as we were at the beginning. All this we ask of you, our dear saviour, Amen.'

The pastor sits, and someone bolts from the front row to the piano and begins to play.

The music we hear is familiar and at the same time new; the bandleader punches up a pre-programmed beat on the cheap electronic piano and plays a few Nigerian gospel songs to get us in the mood for revival. We sing along, though we have to wait a few moments at the beginning of each song to figure out what he's playing. We sing joyful songs to the Lord, then songs of redemption, and then we sing songs of hope, hope that tomorrow will be better than today, hope that, one day soon, our lives will begin to resemble the dreams that brought us to America.

The tinny Nigerian gospel music ends when the pastor

stands, and he prays over us again. He prays so long and so hard that we feel the weight of his words pressing down on us. His prayer is so insistent, so sincere, that his words emerge from the dark chrysalis of his mouth as bright, fluttering prophecies. In our hearts we stop asking *if* and begin wondering *when* our deeply held wishes will come true. After his sweating and shaking and cajoling he shouts another *Amen*, a word that now seems defiant, not pleading. We echo his defiance as loudly as we can, and when we open our eyes we see him pointing to the back of the church.

Our eyes follow the line of his finger, and we see the short old man hunched over in the back, two men on either side of him. Many of us have seen him before, in this very space; we've seen the old man perform miracles that were previously only possible in the pages of our Bibles. We've seen him command the infirm to be well, the crippled to walk, the poor to become wealthy. Even those of us who are new, who know nothing of him, can sense the power emanating from him.

We have come from all over North Texas to see him. Some of us have come from Oklahoma, some of us from Arkansas, a few of us from Louisiana and a couple from New Mexico. We own his books, his tapes, his holy water, his anointing oil. We know that he is an instrument of God's will, and we have come because we need miracles.

We need jobs. We need good grades. We need green cards. We need American passports. We need our parents to understand that we are Americans. We need our children to understand they are Nigerians. We need new kidneys, new lungs, new limbs, new hearts. We need to forget the harsh rigidity of our lives, to remember why we believe, to be beloved, and to hope.

We need miracles.

We murmur as the two men help him to the front, and in this charged atmosphere everything about him makes sense, even the irony of his blindness, his inability to see the wonders that God performs through his hand. His blindness is a confirmation of his power. It's the burden he bears on our behalf; his residence in a space of perpetual darkness has only sharpened his spiritual vision over the years. He can see more than we will ever see.

When the old man reaches the pulpit his attendants turn him around so he's facing us. He's nearly bald – a few white hairs cling precariously to the sides of his shining head – and he's wearing a large pair of black sunglasses. A bulky white robe falls from his neck to the floor. Beneath, he's wearing a flowing white *agbada*.

He remains quiet for a few moments – we can feel the anticipation building, breath by breath, in the air. He smiles. Then he begins to hum. A haunting, discordant melody. The bandleader tries to find the tune among the keys of his piano, but the old man slaps the air and the bandleader allows the searching music to die.

He continues to hum and we listen to his music. Suddenly he turns to our left and points to a space somewhere on the ceiling:

'I DEMAND YOU TO LEAVE THIS PLACE!' he screams, and we know there is something malevolent in our midst. We search the area his sightless eyes are probing, somewhere in the open space above our heads. We can't see anything, but we raise our voices in response to the prophet's call. Soon our voices are a cacophonous stew of Yoruba and English, shouting and singing, spitting and humming, and the prophet from Nigeria speaks once more:

'We must continue to pray, ladies and gentlemen! There are forces here that do not wish for this to be a successful service. If we are successful in our prayers that means they have failed! They do not wish to fail! So we cannot expect that our prayers will simply come true; we must fight!'

We make our stew thicker; we throw in more screams and prayers until we can no longer distinguish one voice from another. Finally, after several long minutes, the prophet raises his hands:

'We are finished. It is done.'

And we begin to celebrate, but our celebration lacks conviction – we haven't yet received what we came here for.

The prophet sways to the beat of our tepid praise. The man on his left stands and dabs his forehead. The prophet clears his throat and reaches forward with his right hand until he finds the microphone. He grabs it, leans into it.

'I have been in the US for two months now...' he begins, rhythmically moving his head left and right, 'I have been to New York, to Delaware, to Philadelphia, to Washington, to Florida, to Atlanta, to Minnesota, to Kansas, to Oklahoma, and now, finally, I have arrived here.'

We cheer loudly.

'I will visit Houston and San Antonio before I leave here, and then I will go to Nevada, and then California. I will travel all over this country for the next month, visiting Nigerians across this great land, but I feel in my spirit that the most powerful blessings will happen *here*.'

We holler and whoop and hug each other, for his words are confirmation of the feelings we've been carrying within ourselves since the beginning of the service.

'The reason I am saying that the most powerful blessings will happen here is because God has told me that you have been the most faithful of his flock in the US. You haven't forgotten your people back home. You haven't forgotten your parents and siblings who sent you here, who pray for you every day. You have remained disciplined and industrious in this place, the land of temptation. And for all your hard work, for your faithfulness, God is going to reward you today.'

Some of us raise our hands and praise the Father. A few of us bow our heads, a few of us begin to weep with happiness.

'But in order for your blessings to be complete, you will have to pray today like you have never prayed before. You will have to believe today like you have never believed before. The only barrier to your blessing is the threshold of your belief. Today the only thing I will be talking about is belief. If I have learned anything during my visits to this country, it is that belief is only possible for those who have dollars. I am here to tell you that belief comes *before* dollars. If you have belief, then the dollars will follow.'

Silence again. We search our hearts for the seedlings of doubt that reside there. Many of us have to cut through thickets of doubt before we can find our own hearts again. We use the silence to uproot our doubt and we pray that our hearts will remain pure for the remainder of the service.

'Let me tell you, great miracles will be performed here today. People will be talking about this day for years and years to come. And the only thing that will prevent you from receiving your share is your unbelief...'

At this moment he begins to cough violently, and the man on his right rushes forward with a handkerchief. He places the handkerchief in the prophet's hand, and the prophet coughs into it for a few seconds, and then he wipes his mouth. We wait anxiously for him to recover.

He laughs. 'I am an old man now. You will have to excuse me. Just pray for me!'

'We will pray for you, Prophet!' we yell in response.

'Yes, just pray for me, and I will continue to pray for you.'

'Thank you, Prophet! Amen! Amen!'

'And because you have been faithful, God will continue to bless you, he will anoint you, he will appoint you!'

'Amen!'

'Now God is telling me that there is someone here who is struggling with something big, a handicap that has lasted for many, many years.'

We fall quiet because we know he is talking about us.

'He's telling me that you have been suffering in silence with this problem, and that you have come to accept the problem as part of yourself.'

We nod in agreement. How many indignities have we accepted as a natural part of our lives?

'The purpose of my presence in your midst is to let you know that you should no longer accept the bad things that have become normal in your lives. America is trying to teach you to accept your failures, your setbacks. Now is the time to reject them! To claim the success that is rightfully yours!'

His sunglasses fall from his face, and we see the brilliant white orbs quivering frantically in their sockets, two full moons that have forgotten their roles in the drama of the universe. His attendants lunge to the floor to recover them, and together they place the glasses back on his ancient face. The prophet continues as if nothing happened.

'I do not perform these miracles because I wish to be celebrated. I perform these miracles because God works through me, and he has given me the grace to show all of you what is possible in your *physical* and *spiritual* lives. And now God is telling me: you, come up here.'

We remain standing because we don't know to whom he is referring.

'YOU! You! You! YOU! Come up here!'

We begin to walk forward, shyly, slowly. I turn around suddenly, and I realize I'm no longer a part of the whole. I notice, then, that the lights are too bright, and the muggy air in the room settles, fog-like, on my face. Now I am in the aisle, and I see the blind old man pointing at me.

'You, young man. Come here. Come up here for your miracle!'

I just stand there, and I feel something red and frightening bubbling within me. I stand there as the prophet points at me, and I feel hands pushing me, forcing me to the front. I don't have enough time to wrap up my unbelief and tuck it away.

Then I'm standing on the stage, next to the prophet.

The prophet moves closer to me and places a hand on top of my head. He presses down until I'm kneeling before him. He rocks my head back and forth.

'Young man, you have great things ahead of you, but I can sense that something is ailing you. There is some disease, some disorder that has colonized your body, and it is threatening to colonize your soul. Tell me, are you having problems breathing?'

I find myself surprised at his indirect reference to my asthma. But now the doubts are bombarding me from every direction. Maybe he can hear my wheezing? It's always harder for me to breathe when I'm nervous, and I'm certainly nervous now

'Yes sir,' I reply.

'Ah, you do not need to confirm. I now have a fix on your soul, and the Holy Spirit is telling me about the healings you need.' He brushes his fingers down my face, and my glasses fall to the ground. Everything becomes dim.

'How long have you been wearing glasses, my son?'

'Since I was five, sir.'

'And tell me, how bad is your vision?'

Really bad. I have the thickest lenses in school, the kind that make my eyes seem like two giant fish floating in blurry, separate ponds.

'It's bad, sir.'

The prophet removes his hand from my head and I can feel him thrashing about, as if he's swimming in air, until an attendant thrusts a microphone into his groping hand.

'As you guys can see, I know a little about eye problems,' he booms, and although it sounds like he's attempting a joke, no one laughs, and his words crash against the back wall and wash over us a second time, and then a third.

'And no one this young should be wearing glasses that are so thick!' The congregation cheers in approval. I hear a whispered *yes prophet.*

'I can already tell that you have become too comfortable with your handicap,' he roars, 'and that is one of the main problems in this country. Handicaps have become *normal* here.' I see the many heads nodding in response. 'People accept that they are damaged in some fashion, and instead of asking God to intervene, they accept the fact that they are broken!'

More head nodding, more *Amens*.

'Let me tell you something,' he continues. He's sweating profusely; some of it dribbles onto my head. My scalp is burning. 'God gives us these ailments so that we are humbled, so that we are forced to build a relationship with him. That is why all of us, in some way or another, are damaged. And the reason they have come to accept handicaps in this country is because these Americans do not want to build a relationship with God. They want to remain forever disconnected from His grace, and you can already see what is happening to this country.'

The *Amens* explode from many mouths; some louder, some softer, some gruff, some pleading.

'So the first step to getting closer to God, to demonstrating that you are a serious Christian, is declaring to God all of your problems and ailments, and asking him to heal you.'

A few *Amens* from the back overwhelm everything. I squint to see if I can connect the praise to the faces, but I can only see the featureless faces swathed in fog.

'So now I'm going to ask God to heal this young man who has become accustomed to his deformity. But before I touch you, before I ask the Holy Spirit to do its work, I must ask you, before everyone here – are you ready for your miracle?'

I stare at the congregation. I see some nodding. I've never thought of a life without glasses, but now my head is filled with visions of perfect clarity. I can see myself playing basketball without the nerdy, annoying straps that I always attach to my glasses so they won't fall off my face. I imagine evenings without headaches, headaches that come after hours spent peering through lenses that give me sight while rejecting my eyes.

'Are you ready?' he asks again, and I can feel the openness in the air that exists when people are waiting for a response.

I know I'm waiting for my response as well.

'I'm ready.'

'Amen!'

'AMEN! AMEN!' Their *Amens* batter me; I bow beneath the harsh blows of their spiritual desperation.

'My son, you are ready to receive your gift from God.'

His two attendants scramble from his side, drag me to my feet, and bring me down to the floor. One positions himself next to me, the other behind me. When I look over my shoulder I see the attendant standing there with his arms extended before him.

'I feel something very powerful coursing through my spirit,' the prophet yells. 'This is going to be a big miracle. Bring me to the boy!'

The attendant beside me strides up to the stage and helps the prophet down the steps. He positions the prophet before me, and I notice that the prophet seems even shorter than before. He is only a few inches taller than me. His hot breath causes my eyes to water; I resist the urge to reach up and rub them.

The prophet suddenly pulls off his sunglasses. He stares at me with his sightless eyes. I become uncomfortable, so I lean slightly to the right and his face follows. I lean slightly to the left and his face does the same. A sly smile begins to unfurl itself across his face. My heart begins to beat itself to death.

'Do not be frightened. I can see you through my spiritual eyes,' he says. 'And after this miracle, if you are a diligent Christian, you will be able to do the same.'

Before I can respond, his right hand shoots forward, and he presses my temples. I stumble backwards but maintain my balance. I turn to gaze at all the people in front of me, and though I can't see individual faces I see befuddlement in its many, various forms. I see random expressions contort themselves into a uniform expression of confusion. I actually manage to separate my brother from the masses because his presence is the only one in the room that seems to match my own. We're both confused, but our confusion isn't laced with fear.

The prophet presses my temples again, and again, and each time I regain my balance. His attendants are ignoring me now. They're both looking down at the prophet, inquiring with their eyes about something. I'm not sure what. Then I hear the shuffling feet, and I know that the people are becoming restless.

'The spirit of bad sight is very strong in him, and it won't let go,' the prophet yells.

Life returns to the church like air filling up a balloon. I see the prophet's attendants nod, and the new *Amens* that tunnel into my ears all have an edge of determination.

'This healing will require special Holy Ghost healing power. Come, take my robe!' The attendant closest to me pulls the robe from his back, and the prophet stands before me even smaller and less imposing than before. 'While I am working on this spirit everyone in this room must pray. You must pray that I will receive the power I need to overcome this spirit within him!'

I see many heads moving up and down in prayer, and I hear loud pleading, and snapping, and impassioned howling.

'That is very good!'

The prophet steps forward and blows in my eyes, and then he rubs my temples. I remain standing. He blows and rubs again. The same. He does it again, and again, and each time the praying grows louder and more insistent. The prophet moves even closer to me, and this time when he presses my temples he does not let go. He shoves my head back until I fall, and the attendant behind me eases me to the floor. I finally understand. I remain on the floor while his attendants cover me with a white sheet. Above, I hear the prophet clapping his hands, and I know that he's praying. The fluorescent lights on the ceiling are shining so brightly that the light seems to be huddling in the sheet with me. I hug the embodied light close.

After a few minutes the prophet stops clapping.

'It is finished! Pick the young man up.'

His attendants grab my arms and haul me up. I hear a cheer building up in the crowd, gaining form and weight, but the prophet cuts everything off with a loud grunt.

'Not yet. It is too soon. And young man, keep your eyes closed.' I realize that my eyes are still closed, and I wonder how he knows.

I begin to believe in miracles. I realize that many miracles have already happened; the old prophet can see me even though he's blind, and my eyes feel different somehow, huddled beneath their thin lids. I think about the miracle of my family, the fact that we've remained together despite the terror of my mother's abrupt departure, and I even think about the miracle of my presence in America. My father reminds my brother and me almost every day how lucky we are to be living in poverty in America, he claims that all of our cousins in Nigeria would die for the chance, but his words were meaningless before. Compared to what I have already experienced in life, compared to the tribulations that my family has already weathered, the matter of my eyesight seems almost insignificant. *Of course I can be healed! This is nothing. God has already done more for me than I can imagine. This healing isn't even for me. It is to show others, who believe less, whose belief requires new fuel, that God is still working in our lives.*

Then the Prophet yells in my ear: OPEN YOUR EYES.

My lids slap open, and I see the same fog as before. The disembodied heads are swelling with unreleased joy. I know what I have to do.

'I can see!' I cry, and the loud cheers and sobbing are like new clothing.

'We must test his eyes, just to make sure! We are not done yet!' yells the prophet, and nervousness slowly creeps up my spine like a centipede. 'We have to confirm so the doubters in here and the doubters in the world can know that God's work is real!'

One of his attendants walks a few feet in front of me and holds up a few fingers. I squint and lean forward. I pray I get it right.

'Three!' I yell, and the crowd cheers more loudly than before.

'Four!' I scream, and the cheers themselves gain sentience. They last long after mouths have closed.

'One!' I cry, and the mouths open again, to give birth to new species of joy.

* * *

This is what I learned during my first visit to a Nigerian church: that a community is made up of truths and lies. Both must be cultivated in order for the community to survive.

The prophet performed many more miracles that day. My father beamed all the way home, and I felt that I had been healed, in a way, even if my eyes were the same as before.

That evening, after tucking my brother and me in, my father dropped my glasses into a brown paper bag, and he placed the bag on the nightstand by my bed.

'You should keep this as evidence, so that you always remember the power of God,' he whispered in my ear.

The next morning, when I woke up, I opened my eyes, and I couldn't see a thing. I reached into the bag and put on my glasses without thinking. My sight miraculously returned.

Tope Folarin was educated at Morehouse College, and the University of Oxford, where he earned two Master's degrees as a Rhodes Scholar. He is the recipient of writing fellowships from the Institute for Policy Studies and Callaloo, and he serves on the board of the Hurston/Wright Foundation. Tope lives and works in Washington DC. This story was first published in *Transition*, issue 109, Bloomington, 2012.

Foreign Aid

Pede Hollist

BALOGUN ARRIVED IN AMERICA as a wiry-thin young man in his mid-twenties, toting one small suitcase and brimful of hope of becoming an economist. At first, he lived with a cousin and his African American wife, a nurse, and her teenage sister, in a three-bedroom condo in Baltimore, Maryland. 'Till he gets on his feet, Babe,' the cousin had assured his wife. Twelve months later Balogun had become the focus of her irritation: 'He's eating too much and spending the money he should be saving to get his own place on booze and women.' One morning, after a hectic night's shift, the wife found Balogun in bed with her teenage sister.

That evening, the cousin drove Balogun and his suitcase to the inner-city apartment of a former girlfriend. 'Marry her, get your green card, and live the American dream,' the cousin encouraged. With the eagerness of an only child on his first day of boarding school, Balogun disappeared into the grey, half-boarded apartment complex behind the chain-link fence and submerged himself in inner-city America. He flipped burgers, cleaned office buildings, and worked security for cantankerous residents in a variety of elder-care facilities – pursuing the American dream, unskilled, undocumented, and with an accent. On holidays and birthdays, Balogun called home using those multicoloured international phone cards that advertised more talk time than they delivered. His conversations were short, mostly filled with promises – to his mother that he would take care of himself and not marry a White woman; to his father that he would focus on his studies; and to his sister, Ayo, that he would one day bring her to America. But inner-city America overwhelmed Balogun. Even his occasional phone calls home stopped.

Two marriages, one to a White woman, and three child-support payments later, Logan, in his early forties, emerged from inner-city America – documented, potbellied, and with an American twang. His aspiration to become an economist had halted at 16 community-college credit hours; his promise to bring Ayo to the States had been sacrificed at the altar of financial obligations; his worldview had been framed by the lens of his two failed marriages and the tribulations of climbing his way from a daily-wage labourer to his present well-paying job as an on-call operator at one of America's biggest, most sophisticated, heavy-duty construction machine companies. And he approached life as his machines did – banging, crushing, and hauling. In fact, that was how he wooed, or maybe wowed, the ungainly, undocumented, and infertile Yamide, also from Sierra Leone: 'Am a citizen. Single. Make three child-support payments. Don't want more kids and need a wife.'

They married and lived contentedly. He removed the albatross of being undocumented from around her neck and she fed his manhood 'unlike dem gad dam Afro bitches,' Logan often observed. The addition of her salary from Maids for Hire helped to defray his financial obligations. Soon they purchased a townhouse.

A piece of America in his name and the subtlety of heavy-duty machinery in his veins, Logan was now returning to his native Sierra Leone, three super-sized Samsonite suitcases in tow, jam-packed with Dollar-Store and generic brand items. He was motivated by guilt and a desire to make up for neglecting his parents and sister for almost 20 years. When a friend cautioned he would find the country difficult and the people different, Logan scoffed: 'Bro, I graduated from ICU, Inner-City University. Ain't nothing I can't handle.'

* * *

Logan followed the wayward line of passengers toward the two-storey terminal, tapping the Louis Vuitton fanny pack with the dual water-bottle holders to make sure it was still strapped around his waist. At the immigration station, he presented his passport to a uniformed officer who peered at each page like a diviner deciphering his kola nuts. Logan exhaled and tapped his fingers against his thigh.

'Yellow book!'

Logan tossed it on the counter. The officer eyed him as would a father an impertinent child, grabbed the book, and scrutinized it with the intensity of a diviner puzzled by the message of his kola nuts. Logan's fingers tapped his thigh and his chest heaved.

'I'm from the States, bro?'

'Whether you are from America or from a septic tank, the laws of Sierra Leone say you must have the correct vaccinations.' The officer slammed his stamp into both booklets and shoved them to the edge of the counter, 'Next.' He looked past Logan.

As he stood by the conveyor belt at baggage claim, Logan recognized that the encounter had offered him a lesson, but fatigue and watching suitcases pop out of the luggage chute at the speed of childbirth aborted the little inclination he had for reflection.

Thirty minutes later, a gawky-looking man in a fading blue shirt and ill-fitting grey pants, and donning black-framed spectacles held together in one corner by soiled layers of Band Aid, hugged him. Logan returned the hug with the affection of a child instructed to greet an overweight uncle with bad breath.

'Are those your bags?' Father rippled with the excitement

of a refugee at the sight of a Red Cross relief vehicle. 'Let's hurry. We must catch the last ferry to Freetown.'

Courtesy of a gangling youth's organizational skills and an agreement that he should ride with them to their home in Freetown, Logan, his father, and one suitcase were seated in a cab on the way to the Tagrin ferry terminal five minutes later. The gangling youth and two suitcases followed them in a second cab.

'Where's your car?' Logan finally acknowledged his emaciated father.

'Garage. It needs parts.'

'I could have brought them for you.'

'Not to worry. Getting them from Brussels.'

'Okay, remind me to pay for them.'

'*Tenki ya.*'

A warm glow nestled around Father and son as the car careened on the cratered road.

Twenty minutes later, both cabs joined the line of vehicles that had just started an orderly boarding of the ferry to Freetown. Logan's taxi was two cars from the entrance gate when a terminal worker held up his palm like a traffic cop and stopped the boarding. He motioned the car straddling the gate to move back. Anxiety spread through the occupants of the stopped cars like palm oil on rice. Perhaps the ferry was full, had only one working engine, or had no fuel? Maybe the terminal workers wanted to be bribed or the ferry needed to be repositioned.

Thankfully, the speculations stopped as the noise of moving cars signaled boarding had resumed: a convoy of cars, led by a black, flag-fluttering Mercedes Benz, hurtled through the exit gate – in the wrong direction! – and sped onto the ferry.

'*Na minista so,*' Logan's taxi driver explained and promptly edged his taxi out of the lane of stationary cars and, to Logan and his father's consternation, slashed his taxi into a sliver of space in the convoy.

'Follow,' Logan's father shouted over the screeching tyres to the driver of the second cab. Unfortunately, its driver was also its owner, and he was not about to risk damage to his livelihood to board the ferry. By the time he had mustered the courage to join the metallic cavalcade now jostling to board the ferry, 10 vehicles were ahead of him.

Logan's cab galloped up the ramp and docked between a parked van and the metal wall separating the vehicle bay from the passenger cabin. Neither the driver-side nor the passenger-side doors would open to let them out. The smell of petrol hung in the cab like urine in a public bathroom. Just as their predicament dawned on them, a jeep pulled up behind and sealed them in. And, as several unfamiliar vehicles swallowed up the few remaining spots in the vehicle bay, the exhilaration of racing onboard evaporated into the sullen recognition that two of the Samsonites had been left behind in the second cab with the gangling youth.

As if to reinforce this reality, the ferry rumbled to life, jolting Logan into a frenzy. 'Stop the gaddam ferry!' he screamed, pushing his head through the window to crawl out of the cab. The van blocked his way. 'Shit!' he flopped back into the seat. The terminal receded.

'Those assholes are going to pay me for my suitcases,' he said.

'He's a minister, you know,' Father said.

'So that gives him the right to do whatever he wants?'

'No, but here…'

'I don't live here, Pops.'

With the help of a young man, the owner of the car on the driver's side of Logan's cab was found, and he manoeuvered his vehicle to create enough space for one of the doors to open. Without acknowledging his helper, Logan bruised through the tightly packed vehicles and headed toward the VIP lounge. At its entrance sat an AK-47-toting slip of a soldier.

'*Minista bizi.*' The soldier barred Logan's entrance.

He bristled like a crested porcupine.

'*Yu no yehri wetin a se?*' The soldier stood and slid his finger onto the trigger of the AK-47.

'Balogun, don't get yourself killed over suitcases.' Logan's father pulled him by the elbow.

Logan shook himself free of his father's grip, turned, and headed toward the bridge. Two at a time, he mounted the metal steps but found a rope cordoning off the glass enclosure. Inside, two men in white uniforms on either side of the wooden steering wheel peered into the onyx night, their hands cupped around the peaks of their caps. Logan stepped over the rope and stomped to the half-open door.

'Skuese me, Bro.'

The two men, one Black, the other White, turned and grimaced.

'Who's the captain?' Logan demanded with the power of a jackhammer.

'Passengers are not allowed up here,' the Black officer replied. The White officer turned away.

'I lost two suitcases because you allowed some big shot to cut the line.'

'We don't control the gates.'

'That's it?'

'Yes.'

'My suitcases got left behind?'

'They can cross tomorrow.'

'I don't know the person who has them. Can't you radio the terminal and get somebody to help me?'

'Their radio isn't working.'

The White officer grumbled. 'We have a ship to run.'

Clack! The Black officer shut the door.

'Balogun, we can replace the suitcases but not you.' The father offered perspective from the bottom of the staircase. Logan shuddered.

✳✳✳

An hour later Logan and his father walked into their home in central Freetown. A gaunt woman wearing a ratty cotton nightdress embraced Logan. 'Let me look at you.' She stepped back and appraised Logan like a shopper examining an exquisite Emilio Pucci dress. 'You're so fat.' Her face broke into wrinkles and her mouth opened onto rust-stained molars and cavities. She yanked Logan back into a second embrace. His chin rested on her shoulder bones, and his fingers tapped her rib cage.

'He lost two of his suitcases . . .' Father began.

'Stolen, Pops, stolen.'

Alarmed, the woman broke off her embrace. 'What happened?'

Father and son, like commentator and analyst, narrated the story of the suitcases. 'What is this country coming to?' The woman unfolded and refolded her head tie as if to steady her mind from the reverberations caused by the narrative.

'Don't worry, Ma,' Logan put an arm around the woman whose form had now settled into a jaded facsimile of the beautiful mother he'd once known.

'Where's Ayo? She's not able to wait up to see her big brother?'

'She is tired, works all day.' Mother glanced over at Father.

'I'll light up the mosquito coil in your room,' he said, avoiding her eyes, and headed down the dark hallway, holding aloft a candle like a miner burrowing into a tunnel.

'By God's grace, you will see Ayo in the morning.' Mother pushed Logan into a parlour chair. 'Let me get you some food.' She admired him for a few seconds more and then disappeared into the candlelit kitchen.

A smile broke onto Logan's face as Mother re-entered the parlour a few minutes later and set down on the centre table a tray laden with dishes, plates, and spoons.

'Sit down, Ma. I can serve myself,' Logan said.

'Nonsense,' she pushed him back into his chair. 'You must

be tired after all that flying.' As she served heaping spoons of rice onto a plate, Father walked back into the parlour, a young boy, uncannily similar to the youth at the airport, in his wake. He was carrying a tray of drinks. The boy handed a Guinness to Father.

'This is Tunde,' Father explained. 'He's been living with us since his parents were killed in the war.'

'Whaz up, Bro?' Logan grabbed a Star beer from the tray.

'Good evening, Uncle.'

Logan emptied half of the bottle in one gulp. 'Aaaah,' he belched softly, whipped out a $20 bill from his fanny pack and handed it to Tunde.

'Thank you, sir.' Tunde beamed.

Logan finished the contents of the first bottle in a second gulp. Tunde snapped open another Star.

'You guys must get a complete medical check-up.' Logan pointed at his mother and father with the beer bottle. 'Let me know how much it costs. And because your suitcases got stolen,' Logan reached into his fanny pack, 'this is for you.' He thrust several hundred dollar bills into his father's hand. 'And this for you,' he thrust several more bills into the pocket of his mother's nightgown.' Father and Mother shrank under the weight of his generosity. Logan downed the remainder of the beer and belched loudly, twice.

'We should go back to the airport tomorrow. That boy might have kept the suitcases,' Father said.

'Naaa. He'll keep what he can use and sell what he can't. Tomorrow I'm going to give that minister a piece of my mind.'

'A waste of time.' Father lit a cigarette.

'Maybe, but if someone does not take a stand, that kinda crap ain't never gonna stop.'

'This is not America.'

'That's not the point, Pops....'

'Time to eat.' Mother handed out two plates with massive mounds of rice doused with leafy green *plassas* cooked in palm oil. '*Sawa-sawa*. Your favourite.' Logan grabbed the plate with one hand, popped two Nexium tablets into his mouth with the other, and demolished his plate of food with a speed that left his parents aghast, both imperilled by the buttons straining against his expanding stomach.

They relaxed and attended to their plates only after Logan had finished eating and unbuttoned his shirt. His stomach rolled out like a Marabou's prayer mat.

'Darng, it's hot,' he hauled himself out of the chair and ambled toward the windows.

'Careful, they are rotten.' Father pointed to an area of the wooden floor about five feet from the windows.

'Get it fixed. I'll pay!' Logan stepped over the defective boards and opened the window. He returned to his chair and fanned the muggy night air with his shirt.

Over the next two hours, in the television-less but now mosquito-filled room, Father, Mother, and son chatted quietly, beginning with the events at the ferry terminal and working their way back 20 years, alternating stories of home and abroad, their conversation punctuated by the occasional horn from a speeding car and Mother's palms crushing hapless mosquitoes that ventured within her reach.

'We've arranged a thanksgiving service for you to thank God for protecting you and making your life a success.'

'I don't go to church,' Logan said.

'America!' Mother sighed.

'What does that mean?' Father, a lifetime chorister, quizzed.

'God was nowhere when I gat kicked outta my cousin's house, had no job, nothing!'

'Were you praying and going to church?' Mother asked.

'All I know is that I gat no one but *me*,' Logan poked his chest, 'to thank for where I'm today.' He proceeded to tell the story of his 20-year sojourn in America. They went to bed that night with smiles and handshakes, but they were like those offered through the bars of a jail cell between a prisoner and visiting relatives – well-meaning and hopeful but grounded in two different realities, and neither party fully understood the reality of the other.

✳ ✳ ✳

'Look at this American!' an uncle exclaimed the next morning when Logan walked into the parlour, his fanny pack strapped around his waist.

'Look how big your belly is.' The uncle's wife poked his stomach. Logan instinctively sucked it in, along with a bloodthirsty urge to batter her face.

'It says life is good.' The uncle rubbed his stomach in solidarity.

The aunt pointed to a basket on the floor and pulled aside a towel that covered a Pyrex dish. '*Pap!*' she said.

'Know why we made this for you?' The uncle winked.

Logan looked bemused.

'As a kid, every time you saw someone in the kitchen, you'd shout "*pap... pap...*"'

Logan mustered an indulgent smile.

'...and we would have to go make some *pap* to feed you.'

And that was how the first full day of Logan's return home started and continued – with a steady stream of people welcoming this son from America with baskets of food and stories of bygone days.

Soon after the morning wave of visitors, Mother pulled Logan aside.

'We will need more food and drinks for those who will be coming.'

Logan opened his fanny pack and counted out 200 dollars.

'Let me know if you need more.'

By sunset, visitors occupied every corner of the house and yard. Some who had come in the morning returned in the evening. Such was the crowd that Father even had to borrow chairs from the neighbours. Logan did not know most of the visitors, but all were introduced or introduced themselves as relatives. Tunde, too, invited his classmates to meet his Uncle-from-America. Besides the gift of 50 dollars, which assured they liked Logan, Tunde and his friends, like many that night, were charmed by Logan's swagger and American-accented Krio. But most of all, they loved the Americanisms – 'doggone it', 'gaddam', 'shoot', 'meh', 'dude', and 'bro' – that spiced his talk.

As darkness settled on the gathering, Logan distributed two duty-free 1.75-litre bottles of Jack Daniels and cartons of Benson & Hedges, regular and menthol. The drinkers and smokers nodded their approval. Periodically, Logan stood up, his fanny pack bulging at his side, and called out, 'Tunde!' The youth materialized.

'Get us some drinks, Bro.' Logan dipped his hand into fanny pack.

Eyes trained on him and a hush descended on the gathering.

'*Ohmos, Sa?*'

'Two dozen beer and two dozen sodas.'

'*Soda wata, Sa?*'

'Naa, meh. Soda is what we call soft drinks back in the States.'

'Why, Sa?'

'Er... er... we do things differently in America, dude.' And, with a flourish, Logan whipped out different-coloured bills, fumbled with them for a bit – feigned exasperation when one dropped to the ground – and finally slapped a fistful of notes into Tunde's waiting hand. The boy and his friends bounded off.

'What do Bill Gates and Donald Trump do with all their money?' a man asked, money conspicuously on everyone's mind.

'They spend it, Bro. They gat it and they flaunt it.' Logan tapped his fanny pack.

'But what do they buy?' another man asked.

'Clothes, houses, cars, boats...'

'And what do they do with the rest of the money after they've bought all these things?' the first man pressed.

'Kinda hard to explain. These people have... are...'

'...greedy and... (hiccup) selfish,' said a third man, who had earlier introduced himself as a retired school teacher. 'They can't... (hiccup)... spend all that money on themselves... (hiccup)... so they should share it with the homeless... (hiccup)... Americans.'

'Bro, some people choose to be homeless,' Logan said.

A disbelieving gasp shot up from the audience.

'Take me with you when you're going back, so I can . . . (hiccup) live on American streets too, Bro,' the retired school teacher said.

Many chuckled. Logan frowned.

'What's the use of a few having all that money while others don't have enough to eat or a roof over their heads?' the man who had begun this line of inquiry continued.

'They shouldn't be allowed to keep any money above a certain amount,' the retired teacher persisted.

'That's communism, Bro. Ain't the American way.'

'Well, the American way does not make sense,' the teacher shot back and beckoned for the bottle of Jack Daniels.

'It's called capitalism, free market, freedom of choice,' Logan asserted over the murmurs of agreement.

'Nonsense.' The teacher emptied the contents of the Jack Daniels bottle into his glass. 'Who in his right mind chooses to live on the streets?'

The murmurs of agreement mushroomed. Logan's heart beat fast. He felt both hot and cold.

'Capitalism works better than communism, Bro. Name me one successful communist country today?'

'And a successful country is one in which a few people own all the money that they can't use and the others choose to live in the streets?' The retired teacher downed the drink in one swoop and hissed.

Fortunately, the arrival, service, and departure of visitors interrupted the conversations about America often enough to prevent them from becoming contentious. And because every visitor claimed or was ascribed the status of a relative, Logan walked departing persons to the front gate and slapped denominations of dollars, pounds, and euros into their expectant hands. In turn, they showered him with blessings and proclamations about his American generosity.

The adulation, however, did not overwhelm Logan's ICU cynicism. On his way back from seeing off a godfather, he counted his money: fewer than 2,000 dollars left! He wiped his brow, took a deep breath, and licked his lips. 'Coast!' he muttered, recalling his grandfather's refrain when some event about the West African coast troubled him. 'What does it mean, Grandpa?' Logan asked one day.

'*Borbor*, it means Come Over And See Trouble!'

'Mr American,' the uncle who had visited in the early morning broke into Logan's reverie. 'We're running low on drinks.' He put his hand around Logan's shoulders. 'This show you're putting on is making your parents proud. They deserve it!'

***

The last of the visitors had just left when Ayo arrived home. From seven till noon, she taught full-time at a primary school. After school, she home-tutored children of wealthy Lebanese, Syrian, and Indian businessmen. Her schedule was gruelling, but the money and perks – the groceries, clothes, and generous tips – helped defray the expenses of their home. Born cross-eyed, with a mild cleft lip and a slightly off-kilter gait caused by a polio-ravaged left leg, Ayo looked like a dullard, and most people treated her like one. That was the sister Logan had left behind for America. But that sister had given way to a woman with a display-case bosom and rounded buttocks that bounced with a frivolity that inflamed dark desires in the men she met. They wanted her but did not want to be seen with her. Trapped in a body that both attracted and repelled, Ayo had come, over time, to the unassailable conclusion that, for men, desire trumped need. So she had developed a keen ability to quickly identify and work their desires to her benefit. This was the sister that sat in the straight-back chair across from Logan, who lounged on his bed.

'Open it,' he handed her an envelope. Ayo pulled out a round-trip airplane ticket and a letter of invitation to America. She smiled, but it was reserved, far from the giddy happiness Logan had anticipated.

'What's wrong?' Logan charged.

'I don't want to go to America.'

A surge of energy coursed through Logan in the way that it happened when one of his machines encountered an obstacle and he had to engage more horsepower to remove it. 'You want to spend the rest of your life *here*,' he pointed around the sparsely furnished room, 'taking care of Mama and Papa and working for next-to-nothing in a country where there's no regular electricity or water?'

'Salone has problems, Balogun, but I am old enough to know America has problems too.'

'Of course, but in America you'll be able to go to college, get a decent job, buy a house, a car, and fix your mouth. Remake yourself!'

'But I like it here. I know people. I understand the way things work. Some of my friends say they're worse off in America than here.'

'Bull spit! Look at *me*!' Logan offered his bulging stomach as evidence of American well-being.

A wry smile briefly broke over Ayo's face. Then, like a sinner about to walk into confession, she became serious.

'I'm pregnant,' she caressed her tummy.

'Congratulations,' Logan manufactured a smile. 'When are you due?'

'Five months.'

'No problem. The ticket is open. You can come after you give birth. Leave the baby with Mama and Papa.'

'They can't afford to take care of him. I'm supporting them right now.'

'Let the baby daddy take care of him.'

'Will you two come out here?' Father poked his head into the bedroom.

'Let's go and join them.' Ayo took Logan's hand. 'It's been a long time since we sat together as a family.'

'Okay, but we've got decisions to make. Who's the father?'

Ayo did not answer.

✳ ✳ ✳

They had barely settled into the milky comfort of reunion when Logan repeated his call for an estimate to repair the rotten floor boards and for Father and Mother to see a doctor. 'You too, Ayo,' he added as an afterthought. Then he announced that he had bought a ticket for Ayo to join him in America. Father and Mother exchanged concerned looks. 'I know about her situation,' he assured them, 'but she has to live her own life.'

For the next 30 minutes, Logan spoke excitedly about America's endless opportunities. He decried dependence, derided inaction, and heralded individualism and personal responsibility. 'So, let's get a court order to make sure this *Coral* supports his child,' he proposed, another step in his programme to adjust and restructure his family.

'Not necessary, and you don't have to insult the man,' Father snapped. '*We*'ll take care of *our* grandchild.'

'Dad gives me an allowance and pays for the doctor's visits.' Ayo tried to take the sting out of Father's response.

'Besides, taking him to court won't work,' Father declared. 'He'll just deny he is the dad.'

'Paternity tests will…'

'And how will that make him pay?' Father shifted in his chair.

'Gotta try, Pops. Can't move forward if y'all keep doin' things the same ol' way.'

'Yes, but before you change things, you should first know why they are the way they are.'

'So y'all gonna do nothing?'

'I know taking him to court won't get us a damn cent and...'

A surge of drumming burst forth from the radio atop a triangular stand in a corner of the parlour and drowned out Father's words.

'The news is about to start.' Mother broke the rising tension. She walked over to the radio, turned up the volume, and resumed her seat as the newscaster proclaimed.

'First, the headlines. Earlier today at State House, the president and officials from Extraction Outcomes signed a new 99-year mining lease agreement...

'Bull spit!' Logan said. 'They're just mortgaging the country.'

'But the profits will pay for all the rebuilding.'

'What profits? The very people who buy our minerals set the prices for them. Instead of just exporting, we should be making things with our minerals and diamonds. Give a dude a fish and you feed him for a day. Teach him to fish and he ain't neva gonna be hungry.'

'Except that the Salone man has no hands to fish with?'

'That's a crock, Pops. Let him get some artificial limbs.'

'Can we listen to the news?' Mother frowned.

Logan slouched in the chair and tuned out the broadcast. He replayed the events of the past 24 hours, surprised at the amount of money that he had already spent and given away but basking in the warmth of the welcome and the prospect that his efforts were going to change the life of his parents and sister. This last thought resurrected his spirits sufficiently to bring him back to the present, to the tail end of the news about the prosecution of corrupt businessmen. He noticed the concerned looks of his parents and sister.

'Why y'all look so sorry?'

The silence was palpable until Ayo spoke. 'CORRUPT has accused some well-known Lebanese and Syrian businessmen of bribing ministers to get government contracts.'

'Say what?'

'Oh, CORRUPT is an acronym for Citizens Organized to Root & Rout Unscrupulous Politicians Today.'

'About time somebody took on these corrupt ministers.' Logan sat up, energized.

'What CORRUPT is doing is wrong,' Father declared. 'They accuse people but give no evidence. It's all dem-say dem-say.'

'Based on what happened on the ferry, I believe what they say. Chuck their asses in jail and throw away the keys,' Logan said.

Father sprang from his chair and marched out of the room.

'What's up with him?' Logan looked at Mother and Ayo.

'One of the accused men is Ali Sayyar,' Ayo answered softly. 'I teach two of his children.'

'So?'

'He... he... is the father of my child.' Ayo rubbed her stomach and stared at the floorboards.

✳ ✳ ✳

Though still jetlagged and weary from playing host the previous night, the next morning Logan was in high spirits as he stood in front of the reception table outside the office suite of the Minister of Mines. 'Hey Bro,' he mustered his finest American accent, 'I'd like to have a word with the Minister.' With the bored indifference of a man accustomed to bluster, the receptionist pointed Logan to a wooden bench occupied by three other people. As Logan waited, a variety of official- and not-so-official-looking people made their way past the reception desk and into a small room blocked off by a door and a frosted louvred window. The foot traffic to and from this room was frequent enough for Logan and the other benchwarmers to know that someone important was within.

Logan walked up to the reception desk. 'Bro, a lot of people have cut in front of us. Are we,' he pointed to his fellow benchwarmers, 'gonna be able to see the minister today?'

The man at the reception desk recognized Logan's demeanour demanded action. 'Wait,' he instructed.

He swivelled around and pushed open the door, letting out a waft of smothered giggles. The receptionist emerged a few minutes later followed by an Idi Amin look-alike wearing a grey Mao-collared suit.

'Minister busy today,' he declared. Two attractive and perfume-soaked women and a black-suited man sauntered around them, barely acknowledging either the Idi Amin look-alike or the receptionist, and pushed open the door. This time, a wave of laughter and animated voices floating on perfume assailed Logan.

'You call that busy?' Logan made to follow the women.

Both Idi Amin and the receptionist barred his way. Logan thought he caught a whiff of alcohol.

'What do you want?' Idi Amin demanded.

'Two nights ago, your minister cut the line at the ferry, Bro, and...'

'You want minister for wait?'

'Hell yeah,' Logan stood firm. 'And I want him to pay me for the suitcases I lost.'

'*Luk ya.*'

Idi Amin squared up as if he were ready to unleash some terrible punishment on Logan. Then he exhaled.

'Minister always helps people,' he smiled, dipping his hand into his pocket and handing Logan a wad of Leone bills.

Logan dropped them as if he had been handed hot cassava.

'That's it?'

'Is that not what you want? Money for your suitcases?'

'Yes, but...'

'But what?'

'I don't even know how much you have given me.'

'About 25 dollars.'

'You're kidding, right?'

'My friend, people come here every day for Minister to help them. He give everybody small something. Take the money or leave here one time. Lamin!' The slip of a soldier Logan had encountered on the ferry emerged. 'Make sure this man leave now and no come back inside.'

'Yes, Sa.' Lamin shoved Logan back with the barrel of his gun.

Idi Amin picked up the money from the floor and distributed it to the other benchwarmers. They accepted the money and left with smiles on their faces.

***

On his way home, Logan plotted his counteroffensive. He would report the minister to the newspapers, radio, and TV stations, and he would begin a petition drive to remove him from office. But the indignation that had fuelled his sojourn and his anger at his treatment at the ministry quickly evaporated in sweat and bewilderment during the slow, sun-baked taxi ride home. Logan realized that he was going about his mission – to help his parents and provide a sustainable future for his sister – all wrong. Plotting to take down a minister was not the trench in which he wished to die. That trench contained his sister's virtue, her unborn child's right to support, and the dad's acceptance of his responsibility.

With a renewed sense of purpose, Logan was ready to chuck up the day as a waste until he stepped into the parlour of their home and almost bumped into a slinky, dark-skinned girl in a cotton *docket* and *lappa*, with a mid-leg slit on one side.

'See, I told you he would be here soon,' Logan's mother chided the girl. 'This is Tima, Ayo's friend.'

'Pleased to meet you.' Logan extended a handshake and broke into a smile.

'Me too,' Tima curtsied. Logan's eyes brightened.

'Can you stay?' He pointed out a chair.

'For a little bit.' Tima floated toward the chair. 'I have to take food to my grandmother.'

Logan looked puzzled. 'She's admitted at Choithram's Hospital,' Tima explained, bowing her head and refusing, like a bashful schoolgirl, to hold Logan's gaze. His heart fluttered like the wings of a caged bird.

'Tunde!'

Tunde materialized. 'Get us some drinks, Bro!' Logan dipped his hand into the fanny pack and Tunde bounded off with a fistful of notes.

'So where does a Fulani girl get a name like Tina?

'Ti-*ma*, short for Fa-ti-*ma*.' The syllables flowed with negligée lightness.

'Well, you could easily pass for a Tina.'

She raised her head, smiled, and then lowered her gaze. Logan swelled, throbbed. He had had his fill of boorish American women who demanded, contested, interrogated, threatened, and then murdered! Ti-*ma*, like Yamide, allowed him to be a man.

And so he interrogated her, and she, head bowed, answered his questions in a low, respectful voice, her fingers playing with the hem of her skirt which, in her embarrassment, lifted occasionally to reveal a leggy black thigh.

Yes, she had just started teaching… and, yes, Ayo was her mentor. They both enjoyed teaching and loved children. They even planned to start their own nursery school. That's why they tutor after school. To save up. In fact, she was the one who introduced Ayo to Ali but wished she hadn't. Well, because he's married and has several children, by several women. Oh, yes, he'll say he loves her, and he'll give her money, until he finds another girlfriend. That was what he did to…

'Tunde! Come and help Ms Ayo unload the provisions.' Mother's summons interrupted and reminded Tima of her responsibilities. She announced she was leaving and stood up. Logan also stood, simultaneously reaching into his fanny pack. 'To help with your grandmother.' He slid two crisp bills into her hand.

'Thank you.' She smiled, raised her head, held Logan's satisfied grin for a few seconds, and then surrendered to it. Logan ran his tongue over his lips. They were dry.

***

Logan began the next day in alarm. In three days he had spent more than half the money he had budgeted for ten. His alarm graduated into anger when he discovered that he had mistakenly given Ti-*ma* a $100 bill instead of two twenties. 'Bitch!' He kicked the suitcase, slamming his knee into the headboard and sending a stinging pain rippling back up his leg. He limped up and down the room like a duped Mafia boss plotting his payback.

Ten minutes later, his fanny pack strapped on, he walked into the dining room. Father, Mother, and Ayo were already at the table eating a breakfast of coffee with baked beans and sardine sandwiches – once his favourite.

'Is Ti-*ma* coming tonight?' he asked nonchalantly. Father, Mother, and Ayo froze in curiosity, suspicion, and surprise, respectively.

'Oh, she told me about your plans to start your own school.' Logan loaded his *Fula-braid* sub roll with a heaping spoonful of the baked beans and sardines mix, bit into it, and gulped from a big metal cup of coffee. 'I told her I had some ideas where you can get grant money.'

Father, Mother, and Ayo exchanged glances and then returned to their breakfast.

'Ask her to come by any evening.' Logan looked at Ayo who nodded but said nothing.

'*Wayoya! Wai! Wai!*' Logan's mother screamed, sprang from her chair, clutched her stomach, and doubled over. Ayo and Father shot to her side. Mother held them off with her right forearm but remained bent over, as if bracing herself for another assault. Everyone waited until she straightened up. Ayo and Father assisted her back into her chair.

'What happened?' Logan wiped off some of the coffee that had spilled on his shirt.

'Nothing.' His mother sighed.

'You're kidding, right?'

'It's her fibroids.' Ayo explained. 'She should take them out, but where are we going to get the $300 she needs?'

Logan dipped his hand into his fanny pack and counted $300 into his mother's hands. 'Ayo, make the arrangements for her, *ya.*'

'Thank you.' Mother smiled, picked up her plate, and walked toward the kitchen.

'Okay,' Ayo stood up. 'I'll see you tonight, late.' She picked up her handbag and walked out the front door.

Logan and his father munched in silence. In the background, Mother gave instructions to Tunde, and a rooster sounded a final wake-up call to late risers.

'Erm... erm.' Logan's father scratched his throat. 'The car parts cost $500. Plus the floorboard and doctor's fee for me and your mother, everything comes to $1,200.'

The baked beans and sardines sub suddenly felt like *raffia* in Logan's mouth. He breathed deeply twice, reached into the fanny pack, counted out the money, and pushed the notes over to his father. He folded them up and smiled gratefully. Logan pasted a smile back. Inside he screamed: 'C-O-O-A-A-S-S-S-S-T!'

Father picked up his umbrella and walked toward the front door, then stopped. 'The church restoration committee hopes you'll contribute something to refurbishing the church.' Logan nodded and pasted more smiles on his face.

'Lord 'ave mercy,' he exhaled after his father had left. He unclipped his fanny pack and counted the money he had left: $500 and some change. He re-examined the fanny pack, running his fingers through its compartments, hoping to find a folded note as he sometimes did when he searched the pockets of his clothes before doing the laundry. His fingers touched something crisp and his heart skipped with anticipation as he pulled it out: a receipt for a super-sized, double-decker hamburger meal.

Twenty minutes later, he was in a phone centre in conversation with Yamide.

'We haven't finished paying for your ticket, Balogun,' she reminded him after he told her to send him $1,500.

'Use your credit card if you have to.'

'But we agreed not to go into any more debt.'

'So you want me to stay here with no money?'

'What did you do with all the money you took?'

'You have one minute remaining,' an automated voice interrupted.

'Damn it, Yamide, my suitcases were stolen. I wouldn't be calling if I didn't need the money!'

'But...'

'Just do it! Hello... hello... hello. Daarng!'

Yamide's aversion to putting anything on a credit card was nothing new. But her refusal to honour his request was an unwelcome development. 'Watching too much gad dam Oprah,' Logan muttered as he walked out of the phone centre and stared at the city, at its drab, ailing buildings with their rusted corrugated-iron roofs; its scruffy streets teeming with traders, raggedy beggars, amputees, and forlorn office types; its clogged, bacteria-filled drains; its garbage piles streaking skyward with impunity. Logan frowned.

A few steps away from the doorstep where Logan stood, a man walked up to the building, whipped out his member, and sprayed the wall in a slow circular motion, as though he were watering a lawn with a hose. He shuffled back a couple of times to escape the splashback when his discharge hit a high orbit. After he finished, he vigorously shook the member, tucked it back in with a samba dip of his butt, and zipped up his fly. He gouged up a huge glob of spit and deposited it at the soaked base of the wall. The man turned to leave, saw Logan, flashed him a kola-stained grin, and skipped away, lightened and relieved.

Logan spat, disgusted at the man and the city, troubled by the prospect of an independent Yamide, irritated by a manipulative Ti-*ma*, but mostly overwhelmed by the neediness, the expectation of deliverance he had confronted. A gentle breeze blew the stench from the garbage pile across the street into his face. He grimaced and held his breath. A few seconds passed before he exhaled, expelling the good will of the nostalgia-driven vacationer and replacing him with the self-made man from ICU, the operator of America's biggest, most sophisticated construction machines. He regretted that he did not have the funds to splurge, but he reminded himself that he had come on a mission to assist his parents and to fulfil a promise to his sister. He was not going to let her ignorance, or anyone else's for that matter, deter him from fulfilling his objectives.

* * *

His mission clarified, Logan walked into Ali Sayyar's office later that day. He was a diminutive, black-haired, olive-skinned man made all the slighter by the huge mahogany desk he sat behind, the wall-to-wall plush carpeting, and the gravitas of the surrounding wood panelling. Logan introduced himself. Looking a little uneasy, Ali Sayyar pointed Logan to a chair.

Logan had entered the office building determined to engage Ali Sayyar constructively, but the wall of family photographs behind the businessman's head exploded the faint hope Logan had nurtured that his sister's relationship with this man was a genuine romance. Even before he'd left for America, Logan had heard stories of Lebanese and Syrian merchants mistreating, abusing, and raping their

Sierra Leonean maids. It was not enough that this man's name was involved with the corruption at the highest levels of government, but he was also sowing his corrupt seed in the country's women and had, in fact, sowed his dirty, foreign seed in his sister.

'Bro, you're the father of my sister's child, right? Well, I wanna know how you're gonna take care of *your* kid.'

Ali Sayyar leaned back and spoke quietly, slowly, confidently. 'That's between me and her.'

'Look, Jack, it becomes my business when a corrupt *Coral* like you takes advantage of *my* sister and she gets pregnant. If Salone were a serious country, your sorry ass would be in jail.'

'Take advantage!' Ali Sayyar chuckled once. 'Mister, let sleeping dogs lie. I will take care of it.'

'*It?* Jack, tell me how much you're gonna be giving Ayo per month and let's get it down in writing 'cos I don't want to end up supporting *your* family.'

'Like I have been supporting yours?' Ali Sayyar leaned forward, a cobra-like alertness replacing his deferential demeanour.

'Giving my sister chump change is not supporting my family, Jack.'

'Well, you'd better go and ask your mother who begged me for monthly provisions. While you're at it, ask your father how he got his car, who just bought parts for it, and how much provisions I send to his woman at Fort Street.'

Logan's eyes blinked like flashing lights. His cheeks and fingers twitched. He shrivelled and squirmed.

'Wha?' Wha' you saying?' Logan whimpered. He felt exposed and vulnerable like a hand in a cobra's box.

'Go figure it out, *Jack*.' Ali Sayyar struck.

'Fuckin' bastard. You think you own my family and this country, don't you?'

'Not the country. Just that fucking wooden box you call a house,' Ali Sayyar struck again as he waved an official-looking legal parchment he had yanked out of one of the desk drawers. 'You're the bastard! Now, get out of my office before I have you locked up! And by the way, I was born in Bonthe. I am a full-blooded Sierra Leonean.'

✳ ✳ ✳

Logan limped out of Ali Sayyar's office dazed, confused, like a drunk out of a bar. He walked aimlessly, bumping into people, sidewalk stalls, and tray-carrying hawkers. The heat boiled his blood. He wanted to crack the gangling youth's neck, ram the minister's Benz, haul the Black captain into the sea, wreck the ferry, crush Idi Amin, and pulverize Ali Sayyar, reduce him to pieces of lamb fit only for a Sharwama sandwich. Sierra Leone, like an *okuru* dog snarling at food from an animal lover, had bared its teeth at him.

Poda poda minivans and taxis tooted their horns at him as he lurched dangerously into their paths, perplexed by the city and country. Then he tripped and fell face-first into a mound of sand in front of a building construction site. Bystanders helped him stand and dust off the sand. He thanked them and stared at the construction site. Eureka! He recalled one of his early lessons on the job: *to destroy a multi-storey building, take out or weaken the load-bearing walls and support columns.*

That garlicky Ali Sayyar could insult him because his sister was carrying his child and because his parents had sold their souls for *coco ebeh*, a mess of pottage. They were the load-bearing walls that sustained men like Ali Sayyar, Idi Amin, the Black ferry captain, and the gangling youth, and they had to be weakened or taken down. There was no need for a full-frontal assault. He just had to change his sister and parents and change the culture and attitude of his home, which he found in a state of bliss when he finally walked into the parlour.

Ayo, his parents, and their friends were settled around

plates of food and bottles of Star Beer, Guinness Stout and soft drinks. Even he knew he could not disturb the convivial mood, at least not right then.

* * *

'I went to see Ali Sayyar today,' Logan announced when the last guest had gone later that evening.

Trepidation spread around the room as it might in a city at the announcement of an early-morning military coup. And, like citizens suddenly feeling vulnerable and exposed by their past associations and trysts with the personalities of the deposed regime, Father, Mother, and Ayo dared not venture out into the courtyard of Logan's announcement; they hunkered down to see what this new dispensation held.

'And I know everything,' Logan declared.

But, as with all coups, pockets of resistance flared up.

'Why did you go to him?' Father shot.

'Why did I go? Why did you?' he retorted. 'And you?' He turned and stared at Mother.

'You went to see Ali?' Father turned to Mother in righteous indignation. 'You went behind my back to another man? What for?'

Mother did not answer.

Father persisted. 'What is my wife going to do in a Lebanese man's office?'

'What am *I* going to do? Why do you go there every month?'

'Does he own this house?' Logan interrupted Father and Mother.

All eyes were trained on Father.

'You sold our house?' Mother pounced.

'I did not sell it. I used it as an IOU, and...'

'IOU? Sell? What difference does it make? Do you have money to pay him back?' Mother waited for a few moments. No answer was forthcoming. 'Lord 'ave maci, Augustus. After all the sweat I put into building this house, you've taken the roof from over my head. You wicked, evil man. Lord 'ave maci, Lord 'ave maci.' She collapsed into a chair.

Ayo walked over and consoled her. She turned to her father. 'How much is the IOU?'

'Five thousand dollars,' Father answered, feeling enervated, as limp as a wet dress.

Logan stood among them flummoxed. Umbrage, outrage, and betrayal occupied the house.

✻ ✻ ✻

In the days following, they avoided making eye or body contact like white-coat technicians in a bio-hazard lab. Mother bemoaned her fate and impending homelessness; Father, unable to persuade anyone that he could pay back the IOU and retrieve the deed, busied himself in church matters; Ayo left early in the morning and returned home well after she knew everyone in the house would be asleep. Logan was left severely to himself. He felt powerless, useless like a *kaka bailer* who arrives at a large family latrine with only a small *tamatis* cup, unable to and incapable of handling the crap that had been generated. He wanted to offer to pay the IOU, but he did not have that kind of money or see how he could persuade the Oprah-ed Yamide to get a loan. He bristled at the thought that he could not do what he wanted to do. Devoid of cash and a pariah in his own home, the six days until his departure seemed about as appealing as sliding down barbed wire.

Claiming fatigue, Logan spent the next few days at home. The crowd and conviviality of his first full day were never repeated, but some relatives and friends still visited, individually, at odd hours of the day, with odder stories of need and expectation of deliverance, like the faithful during a Papal visit. But Logan's fanny pack had shrunk with the rapidity of an obese person after gastric by-pass surgery, so he could lay only a firm handshake on his visitors.

***

Logan's break from the tedium of his own self-imposed house arrest came after Mother's surgery. He spent several days at the hospital, waiting for electricity to come back on so his mother could be operated on, for her to wake up from the anaesthesia, for the doctor to report on her prognosis, for nurses to give her injections and change her bandages and bed sheets. When he was not waiting, he was running to and from the pharmacy, buying medications and supplies to support Mother's recovery.

Late in the evening on the second night after the operation, Mother was sleeping soundly when Ti-*ma* came to visit. Logan had not seen her since their first meeting. Ayo said she had delivered his invitation, but Ti-*ma* had not responded, so her appearance initially irritated him, but it quickly disappeared and his confidence exploded as she listened attentively, smiled bashfully, and absorbed his presence. 'Let's do dinner tomorrow night,' he heard himself invite her. 'Seven-ish. Mammy Yoko Hotel lobby?'

Ti-*ma* nodded and bowed her head. Logan licked his lips. They were dry.

***

When Logan got home late that night, Ayo and his father were already in their rooms or asleep, but Tunde was waiting up for him.

The nephew set a tray of food in front of Logan and opened a Star Beer. 'Grandma well, Sa?'

'Gonna be fine, Bro. She's a warrior.'

Tunde smiled. Logan's frosty relations with the adults in the house had left Tunde as his only friend. He looked at the youth who was sitting on a chair on the opposite side of the table. Unlike many others who wanted something from him, Tunde never asked for anything. He came home after school, ran errands, and completed his household chores without grumbling. He listened to the world news on the BBC and VOA in late afternoon and the local news at night. In between, he studied by the light of the kerosene lamp in the parlour, if it was not being used, or by candlelight in the kitchen.

During the afternoons when Logan confined himself to the house, Tunde had taken to asking questions and listening to Logan's tales of life in America. After one such tale, Logan had concluded, 'But here, everything is messed up, Bro.'

'They're changing, *Sa*.'

'Don't see it, Bro.'

'It's like Michael Jackson said, *Sa*. You start with the man in the mirror. Ask him to change his ways.'

'Bro,' Logan chewed quickly to get his words out, 'I don't see much change taking place.'

But Tunde had his eyes closed and was reciting the lyrics to the song and scrunching his face, imitating Michael Jackson's intensity:

I'm starting with the man in the mirror,
(man in the mirror, oh yeah!)...

***

Logan spent the eve of his departure preparing for his dinner date. He considered cancelling it because money was tight. Despite a second phone call, angry words, and veiled threats, Yamide had refused to send him additional money. He would have settled for taking Ti-*ma* to a local bar and to one of the dingy guesthouses that existed all over the city, but he had no way of letting her know about the change of plan, and his resentment of Yamide's emerging independence fuelled his determination to follow through on the tryst. So he set aside money to cover his taxi and ferry fares back to the airport and for food during his layover in Amsterdam. Then, with some misgivings, he pursued the more expensive Mammy Yoko Hotel option – $75 for a room with a view of both the hotel entrance and the Atlantic Ocean, $20 for a bottle of Bristol Cream Sherry, a pack of cigarettes, and one condom (he did not have enough money to buy a pack of three and did not know where he could pick up the free condoms he'd always heard were donated to African countries to stop the spread of AIDS).

His mother was entertaining well-wishers, his father at choir practice, and Ayo at tutoring when Logan boarded a taxi for the Mammy Yoko Hotel, instructing Tunde to put the note the boy was handing him among the stack of letters he had been asked to post in Europe and America.

Thirty minutes later, he walked into the Mammy Yoko Hotel with high expectations, like an indebted gambler into a Vegas casino. His return home had taken on the feel of an investment gone bad. Ti-*ma* was his last-ditch opportunity to recoup some of his losses. At 6.45, a glass of sherry in hand, he perched on his room's balcony, closely watching the taxis that pulled up to the hotel entrance and enjoying the cool breeze and choppy blue-green Atlantic.

By ten o'clock, his eyes, strained from trying to make out alighting passengers in the darkened hotel entrance, and red from consuming more than half of the bottle of sherry, Logan accepted the fact that Ti-*ma* was a no-show and checked out of the hotel, drunk with loathing and alcohol.

∗∗∗

Disappointed with each other, Logan and his parents exchanged muted goodbyes on the morning of his departure. Best wishes. No requests. No promises. He and Ayo boarded the taxi that was to drop her off at the market and drive him over to the Kissy ferry terminal. Logan was returning light, with only his deflated Louis Vuitton fanny pack and the small plastic bag containing letters he should post or hand deliver, and a change of clothing. He had given the one Samsonite suitcase to his parents, whose suitcases were heading for inevitable collapse, like rain-soaked cardboard boxes. Everything else had been given away.

'Out here, we manage. We do what we have to do.' Ayo kissed his cheek and stepped out of the taxi by the Kissy Road Market. He followed her slightly off-kilter gait and plump form in the matching print dress and head tie until it disappeared, merged really, with the other prints and tie-dyes of the market, its bustling, rancorous energy spreading beyond the frame of the car window and his mind.

'Let's go,' Logan ordered the driver.

Logan spent the journey to the airport in irritable contemplation. He had disrupted more than he had aided his parents and sister. The irritation graduated into anger as his taxi rolled off the ferry and passed the gate where his troubles had started ten days earlier. He scanned the faces on the jetty on the off-chance that he might see the gangling youth. He did not. By the time the taxi pulled up outside the airport, he had forgotten about the youth.

He stepped out of the taxi and walked toward the check-in counter, his mind firmly fixed on figuring how he was going to handle Yamide.

'Mister, Mister!' a voice called out to him.

Logan turned and saw the gangling youth bounding toward him like a dog to a long-lost owner.

'Sonafabitch!'

The youth eased up and his face became serious. 'Over there,' he pointed. It took Logan a few seconds to locate the lone Samsonite standing majestically in front of a rickety shack. Logan scooted across the road, pulled out his keys, and opened the suitcase. From just a glance at its fullness, he could tell it not been tampered with.

'Where's the other one?'

'The taxi driver took it. He said it was his pay. I kept this one for you, *Sa*.'

Logan stared at the youth, nonplussed.

'Why?'

'It is not mine, *Sa*.'

'How did you know I would be here today?'

The youth pointed to the luggage tag. 'African Continental comes every Monday and Friday evening at 5:55 and leaves at 11:25.' The youth smiled.

'I can't take it back,' Logan grimaced. 'The stuff in it was for my parents.'

'I will take it to them, *Sa*.'

'You would?'

'Yes, *Sa*.'

'How much?'

'Fifty thousand leones.'

'Are you overcharging me?'

The youth looked indignant.

'Sorry.' Logan opened his fanny pack, counted out the money for his airport tax and secured his lone remaining 50-dollar bill. He counted the remainder into the youth's hand.

'Thirty thousand.'

'That's for one way only, *Sa*.'

Logan frowned. 'Know what? Take the suitcase. I'll...'

'No, *Sa*. Don't worry. I'll take it to them for you. Your people will be happy.' The youth pulled out a piece of paper and handed it to Logan. It read:

Lahai Kargbo

71 Hangar Rd., Lunsar, Sierra Leone

'Write to me, *Sa*. I want to know about America.'

'Do you go to school?'

'Form five.' Lahai puffed his chest.

'What do you want to do after school?'

'Go to Nigeria and study to become a pilot.'

'Nigeria! Why not *America*?'

The youth chuckled. 'I won't have the money for America, but maybe I will have enough for Nigeria.'

∗∗∗

Food had been served, two second-rate, thinly disguised propaganda movies had been shown, and the cabin lights had been dimmed. A few passengers read. Most were asleep. Logan did neither. He felt isolated – from his native land, his countrymen, and his family, especially the women – his Mother, Ayo, Ti-*ma*, and Yamide. Indeed, when he recalled how Ti-*ma* had stood him up, he bristled with resentment. So as not to think of her, he opened the plastic bag of letters and began separating the ones he would post at Amsterdam's Schiphol Airport from those he would post in America.

Among them was a piece of paper with his name on it. He opened it.

Dear Balogun,

I cannot go to dinner with you tonight. I do not date married men, but I did not know how to tell you yesterday. I am very sorry.

Tima/Tina

Logan hissed.

Pede Hollist (Arthur Onipede Hollist), a native of Sierra Leone, is an associate professor of English at the University of Tampa, Florida. His interests cover the literature of the African imagination – literary expressions in the African continent as well as in the African diaspora. *So the Path Does not Die* (Langaa Press, 2012, Cameroon) is his first novel. His short stories, 'Going to America' and 'BackHomeAbroad,' have appeared in *Ìrìnkèrindò: A Journal of African Migration* and on the Sierra Leone Writers Series website. This story first appeared in *Journal of Progressive Human Services*, vol 23.3, Philadelphia, 2012.

The Whispering Trees

Abubakar Adam Ibrahim

IT'S STRANGE HOW THINGS are on the other side of death. I fear I am incapable of describing the experience to you because I do not know what words to use. One simply has to die to understand the enigma of death.

I did not wake up in heaven as I had anticipated (for I certainly had not thought I was bound for hell, even though I had not been a saint). Instead, I woke up in a huge, seemingly infinite universe of darkness. I sensed nothing except that everything was hollow. I could discern nothing except being conscious, but, even then, I could not remember my name. The blandness of my mind frightened me to the point of screaming. My scream only echoed in the void, where it whipped itself into silence. Gradually, I reached the conclusion that my mind and my body were no longer the same entity. Then I lost consciousness again.

It came back suddenly, my consciousness. The first thing I discerned was not the alluring light of the angels, for I could see nothing. Nor was it the heavenly melody of their songs: I couldn't hear anything either. Instead, I perceived a smell, a sharp, distinct smell that my nose had known well while I had been alive. It was then that I realized that I could not be in heaven. Heaven could not smell so awful. But it took me a quarter of an eternity to recognize the smell of antiseptic in the air.

I inhaled this... air, and then it happened: I realized that my body and soul were now one, but I struggled to find my mind. Eventually, this too came back, like a thunderbolt.

It announced its return with excruciating pain all over my body, as if I had been thoroughly mangled by a ferocious beast. I heard footsteps: tired, irregular footsteps from another world. Then I heard her humming a heavenly melody. Even in my death, in a realm I was yet to understand, Faulata's voice was quite distinct. She hummed a poignant tune that did magic to my mind. It ignited my memory and challenged my mind to show me her face. Suddenly, it felt as if I were falling into an abyss, dark with still pictures, like little, incandescent butterflies gliding in the dark. They were pictures from my life, and I caught glimpses of some of them on my way down.

My frightened screams echoed inanely around me. Finally, I saw her face, with its rich tone, and her large almond eyes. Her brows were thin upturned crescents and her eyes were framed by generous lashes. Her nose stud caught the light. Her lips were small, yet full, darkened slightly by nature.

Then I saw a picture of my mother, Ummi, and I in the back seat of a small sedan with two corpulent women. I remembered the stifling heat that had pinched like soldier ants biting; I remembered feeling like a sardine in a can. I remembered Ummi's reassuring smile, then the screeching tyres, the crash of metal against metal, the shattering glass and the frightened screams. And then a blackout.

Then I saw a picture of men in black. I felt their hands on me – strong male hands, frisking my body while I lay soaked in blood. Their rough hands ran riot on my body, touching me in every conceivable place. They found what they were looking for – my wallet.

One of them said, '*Oga*, see. This one too don die.' It was as if removing my money from my body had settled the little matter of my being alive.

The *oga*'s voice was raucous. 'How much you find for 'im body?'

The first man said, 'Four thousand naira, sir.'

The *oga* grumbled, 'These ones se'f, them no carry plenty

money. Oya, put 'im body with the others but hide the money before people come.'

A third one said, 'God O! This accident bad, eh! See how everybody just die. *Chei!*'

The oga replied angrily, 'Shut up, Corporal. If them no die you go fit get this kind money wey you dey get just like that? Na this kind thing we dey pray for, no be say na we kill them.'

Ummi had been in the car with me. Was she—?

Another picture: of the same men lifting me like a sack of rubbish to God-knows-where. I heard myself mutter, 'Ummi, Ummi!'

The officers dropped me roughly to the ground and one screamed in excitement, 'Oga, this one never die O!'

It was my assumption that Ummi was dead that was my coup de grâce, and not the manhandling, as I had thought. Gradually, I faded into darkness; the curtain finally fell on my short, tragic life.

Suddenly, I felt myself crashing into the bottom of the abyss. I bounced off it like a rubber ball and struck the ground again with a thump. I felt hands holding me down. I struggled to breathe. It had indeed been a long fall. And then I heard her voice.

'It's okay now, it's okay.'

I lay back panting. Try as I did, I could not open my eyes. Every inch of me ached, from head to toe. After a while I found my voice.

'Faulata, where am I?'

Her voice was emotion-laden when she spoke, 'You are in the hospital, Salim.'

'And what about Ummi?'

Silence answered me.

***

So, I was not dead! Well, maybe not physically dead, but, otherwise, I was through for sure. My whole life as I had known it had been shattered. Abba, my father, had already been dead for long; my elder brother, Kabir, had passed on just over a year before; and now Ummi was gone. All I had left was Jamila, my teenage sister. My other two female siblings were married.

As for Faulata, our impending wedding had to be put on hold. Ummi and I had been travelling to inform my grandparents about the wedding, which was due to be held after my graduation when the accident had happened. I had two fractures on my right leg, one on my left arm and three broken ribs. But the worst damage was to my eyes. I had gone blind.

That was how I lost everything: my dreams of graduating and becoming a medical doctor were no more after seven years in medical school with just two months left to graduate. The future I was to have shared with my love, Faulata, was gone too. Everything had been blown away just like that.

My body healed in the hospital, but my mind persisted in laying siege at the gates of heaven, pleading for admittance. There was nothing more to live for. Faulata struggled to keep my mind and body from heading in opposite directions. In time, she became the only thing that was keeping me rooted to this wretched earth.

'You are not dead, Salim,' she would sob. 'You cannot leave me here.'

Her plight was understandable, of course. A woman who has lost her beloved can evoke the greatest sympathy imaginable. She made me feel guilty and I wished to put an end to our nightmare. I could not imagine her marrying the monster that I had become. Why hadn't I just died and saved her and myself the agony of loss? But I had not died, and Faulata and her seemingly undying love had forced upon my reluctant person a reason to live. So, I called my mind from the gates of heaven back to this... this forbidding world. But my mind was not very happy about this.

The flow of sympathy continued beyond my discharge

from the hospital. It was two months after the accident and my returning mind abhorred the continuous pity. Relatives, friends and coursemates kept coming with condolences, which, instead of strengthening me, made me feel exceedingly hopeless and helpless. All those who had not been able to make it to the hospital came to the house. Some, I believed, came just to see for themselves how ugly, poor, blind Salim had become! Some came as early as dawn, others in the mornings. By lunch time, the whole house would be filled. Some people would deliberately stumble into my siesta, which was the only time I could pretend to sleep; insomnia would claim me every night.

I developed a phobia for eating in front of people. I felt as if they were looking at me, shaking their heads in pity. I hated being the object of their pity. I would rather have had them laugh at me. But each time I imagined them laughing at me, I got angry and would fume. Besides, my pride would not let me eat in front of them because the exercise was tasking. I had to feel the food, like a child learning how to eat. So, when there were guests around, which was always the case, I would refuse to eat.

Visiting the toilet was something else. I needed a guide, even to shit! Often, I would miss the pit and deposit the whole thing by the side and Saint Faulata would have to clean up. She did everything diligently. She would come in the mornings before leaving for school and my house would be her first stop upon her return. I wondered how she was coping with her project and her impending final exams, which were barely a month away. With time, I began to forget to love Faulata. Instead, I relied entirely on her. Jamila, my young sister, had better things to do than to attend to me. Once back from school, she would change out of her uniform and start entertaining her array of boyfriends. She seemed to have got over our mother's death pretty fast.

I woke up one morning and came out of my room. Even with my walking cane I still stumbled over the buckets and

stools left out of place by the careless Jamila. I was in a hurry
to get to the toilet. Then I heard someone giggling. I asked,
'Jamila, why are you laughing?'

It was not Jamila but her friend, Saratu. Saratu said, amidst
giggles, 'You are wearing your trousers inside out!' Then she
cackled, very much like a hen.

Seething with anger, I said, 'Bitch!'

It vexed me to have a girl as young as her laughing at my
misfortune. In frustration, I continued my march, determined
to spite her, but not quite sure how. I failed woefully, for I
stumbled over a bucket of water and dramatically crashed
onto my scarred face. It was not so much the pain as the
cackling of the accursed Saratu that stung my heart. It rang
through the air, whipping my pride like successive lightning
strikes. She laughed her heart out and laughed her way out
of the house, inviting people to come and see.

I was so angry that I had not moved by the time the people
rushed in. Seeing me sprawled on the ground provoked
laughter from the young ones, so the older ones spanked
their butts and chased them out. Then they came to help me
up. My anger blinded my heart as well and I lashed out with
my cane. I caught someone below the cheek and he yelped.

One man said, 'Salim, we want to help you, eh?'

They tried again and I kicked out ferociously. 'Leave me
alone!' I screamed.

Another person said, 'What is wrong with this stupid boy?'

An elderly voice said, 'You don't understand.'

'We don't want to understand,' said the second. 'We were
only trying to help him and he's just hitting us!'

Some left in anger. Others stayed behind, pleading with
me to get up. I remained there until my anger forced tears
out of my damaged eyes. Some women came to plead with
me. But I remained there, unmindful of their pleas. Instead,
I thought of my mother and wept some more. I thought of
her a long time. Then Jamila started wailing. She wailed
inconsolably for a long time while I lay on the warm, sun-

baked cement floor.

Then Saint Faulata came. She said, 'Who did this?'

And the women told her. She knelt by me and touched me gently. She lowered her head to my ear and whispered, 'Salim, I am here now, you can get up, my love. Everything will be okay, by Allah's will, I promise.'

She led me to the room and cleaned the caked blood off my bruises while everyone watched in awe. Then she said, 'Wait here, I will be right back.'

She took war to the accursed Saratu's house. It was said that she fought ferociously and that she would have killed the stupid girl but for people's intervention. They rescued Saratu from her glorious claws but Faulata was not done yet. She pranced in front of the house calling for Saratu just like Achilles before the walls of Troy, demanding for Hector. But they hid Saratu. Faulata fetched some petrol and poured it on the house. She was about to set it ablaze when they seized her. She struggled fiercely and wept because they would not let her burn down the house. Later, Saratu's parents came to apologize. Neither Faulata nor I said a word to them. Then the elders came and delivered a long, boring lecture about forgiveness and reconciliation and, to get rid of them, I said it was over. So Saratu kept her distance.

But this rather unpleasant episode made me start asking questions, the type a good Muslim should not ask: *Why did this happen to me? Why should my mother die? Why must I go blind in my final year when my life should be beginning? Why, why, why?* I sought answers and could not find any. So, I grew angry. I began to blame everyone for my predicament. I blamed the driver of the vehicle for driving the way he had. I blamed the car for allowing itself to be driven into an accident. I blamed the government for everything in general and nothing in particular. I blamed the police for robbing even the dead. I blamed my long-dead father for having died. I blamed Jamila and her friend, the accursed Saratu. I blamed Faulata, at whose instance we had been travelling.

When I had finished blaming everyone I could think of, I started blaming God. It was His fault since He had decreed everything, as we had been taught. I lost faith and stopped praying.

A friend tried explaining things to me. He meant no harm really, but I took offence. He called me a 'kafir' and I called him an 'accursed son of a bitch'. He got angry and left.

Faulata was not pleased with me. She said, 'Stop looking like a soon-to-erupt volcano,' and I cursed her. She wept.

I cursed Jamila for a reason too trivial to remember: 'You stupid, fat, ugly bitch!' I shouted so loud the neighbours heard me. Jamila cried all day.

I cursed everyone I could think of, but my boldness fell short of cursing God Himself. I just could not bring myself to do it. So, I looked for something else upon which to vent my anger. I cursed everything in the house: the bed that creaked in protest each time I set my angry mass on it, the door that squeaked each time I opened it, the chairs that cringed each time I sat on them. I cursed the mosquitoes that buzzed in my ears, the flies that perched on my skin, and even the cock that crowed at dawn. I cursed Sinnoor, my cat, who kept me company when everyone else had fled my scorching tongue. 'You hairy, creepy, slimy, good for nothing son of a bitch!' I shouted. Then I seized it by the scruff and hurled it against the wall. It yowled and scuttled out. I once cursed my food and threw it away. I could not tell if I looked like a 'soon-to-erupt' volcano but I certainly felt like one. The lava of rage boiled over. I hated life, the whole of it.

I had a big row with Faulata. She had brought me an application form for the school for the blind. She was just trying to be of help, to repay a favour really. I had struggled hard to help her secure admission into the university from which she was about to graduate and she was just trying to do the same for me. But my rebellious mind did not want to understand.

I said, 'Oh, so you want me to go the accursed school for

the blind so that every son of a bitch can laugh at me, eh?'

She said, 'Oh, Salim, my Salim, what has come over you? You curse so much and you won't even pray, for God's sake!'

'Pray? Why should I pray, eh? Where was God when all this happened, eh? And like hell, don't tell me I curse. I will curse when I like. I will curse any son of a bitch I like!'

She said, 'There is a purpose in everything.'

I laughed mirthlessly. 'Of course! And what the hell is the purpose in having me blinded, eh?'

'You shouldn't question God like that!'

'Says who? I shall question whosoever I wish! Bloody school for the blind! I was on my way to becoming a medical doctor, just one damned month to go and bang, just like that, this bloody thing happened. And now you want me to go to the school for the blind, of all places!'

She said, 'I am just trying to be of help, my...'

'Damn you! Who needs your help?'

'Oh, you are such a fool!'

'Who the hell is the fool, eh? Wait until I get my bloody hands on you; I will beat the bloody devil out of you!'

'Go ahead, superman, beat me up!' But she broke down and wept. Her tears, like rain, fell on the wild fire of anger raging in my heart and extinguished it. I felt guilty and ashamed of myself. My guilt soon transformed into confusion, for I did not know how to pacify my personal saint, my Faulata. I sat there helpless and befuddled while she continued weeping.

Finally, I summoned the courage to say, 'I am sorry, Faulata.'

She wiped away her tears and sniffed. 'You know I love you, Salim.'

My heart sank further in the ocean of guilt.

'I know how you feel,' she went on, 'I can imagine how painful this is. I share your pain just as I shared your happiness, your joy and your dreams. Your dreams are mine too, just as your pain is mine. You know that, Salim. But this thing... I suppose it was destined to happen, and, besides, there is nothing we can do about it now. We can't waste forever crying over it.'

After the biggest argument of our lives, Faulata left. It seemed like she took away all the anger I felt inside and cast it by the roadside dump, never to bring it back. I was now overwhelmed by guilt: guilt for questioning God, guilt for not accepting my fate, and guilt for having caused my Faulata so much pain. With my guilt came submission – servile submission, I might add – for I felt that God had abandoned me for my insubordination and for daring to question His wisdom. I surrendered myself to fate.

From sunrise to sunset, I would sit by the window listening to children playing outside while I reminisced about my own happy childhood. I missed playing football barefoot in the dust and hopping through the grassland in pursuit of grasshoppers. I remembered dancing in the rain, praying to God to send down more rain and fried fish from heaven. I missed *chalo*, our inter-street wars, fought with maize stalks and sand bombs.

I missed the Whispering Trees, the woods down the hill from us, where we used to take refuge from our mothers' whips when we were guilty of one form of mischief or another. That used to happen quite often. We would play hide and seek there, build a tent, and imagine we were explorers from another world. We grew up amidst those trees. But that sylvan romance came to an abrupt end when Hamza, a childhood friend, fell into a shallow spring in the woods and died. Back then, it used to be rumoured that it was the resident *iskokai* that made the trees 'whisper'. It was said that the spirits took Hamza and sucked his blood. The spring was incredibly shallow, not deep enough for anyone to drown in. So we learnt to stay away from the woods.

It was in those days, when I was reminiscing about my childhood, that I started to realize how I had taken everything for granted. For instance, my good health had come so naturally that I had never thought there was anything to it.

My mother, too, had always been there; I hardly realized how important she was and how fortunate I was to have her. I had also taken for granted my dreams and hopes, all of which came so naturally with my potential. Even my sight I had taken for granted. How fortunate I had been not to have been born blind. What differentiated me from those others who had been born without sight and were no less human than I was? Now I missed all those things for which I had never once deliberately said, 'Thank you, God'.

In the ensuing depression, Faulata was the only person who understood what I was going through. Jamila, when she was not busy with her boyfriends, spared a few minutes to think of me as the lousy, pissed off, wet blanket she just had to live with.

One day, an uncle of mine, who had come to visit, said, 'This boy has gone nuts. Maybe we should take him to the psychiatrist.'

His big-mouthed wife said, 'See, *maigida*, he's downcast. Maybe he wants to start begging for alms by the roadside. That would fetch him some money, you know.'

I would sit with my loyal cat, Sinnoor, while Faulata did my laundry. She would iron my clothes, do the dishes and sweep the house. Faulata cooked my meals. Saint Faulata fed me. Saint Faulata sang my lullabies. Saint Faulata did everything. It was difficult to imagine what life would have been like without her. I do not know how she coped with her studies, for during that period she was writing her final exams.

The image of a typical blind man in these parts is of a dirty, unkempt old man with his walking stick in his left hand and his right hand outstretched. He stands begging for alms by the roadside, singing songs that, sometimes, even he does not understand. I could not bring myself to imagine myself like that. I did not want to be like that. So, one day, I mustered up the courage and said, 'Faulata, maybe I should go to... that school.'

She dropped the dishes that were in her hand and came over and hugged me. Then she sighed and began to sob.

* * *

The rains came and went. The grasses grew lush green and faded into a pale, hungry brown. I could hear the dry, cold harmattan winds blowing through the starved savannah; I could feel it on my desiccated skin. The weather grew unpleasantly chilly. Everything was cold, including my heart. Faulata was gone. She had been posted to Ilorin for her mandatory one-year National Youth Service after obtaining her university degree. I was happy for her but felt sad because, if my life had taken a different turn, I would have been a graduate too. My life, once more, became a gloomy mess.

There were periods of sunshine, of course, during the weekends when Faulata came to see me. She would come despite having called on every weekday. It was impossible not to miss her. My only solace was to throw myself wholeheartedly into my studies. I learnt well and I learnt fast. I learnt Braille and, to my surprise, discovered a universe of books for people just like me. I learnt cane-weaving and was becoming good at it. I wove a basket for Faulata and God, how she loved it! I felt pleased with myself, so I wove a handbag for Jamila, and she was delighted. When she served dinner that night, she bustled around happily.

I was rediscovering life, and the process was exciting. I managed to navigate around the neighbourhood with some success. I discovered a whole new world of numbers and was as excited as Columbus must have been when he stumbled upon America. The mathematics thrilled me. I knew exactly how many paces would get me to the street from where I would board a commercial motorcycle to school. I knew the number of paces to the toilet, to the living room, and to the kitchen, where I kept Jamila company while she cooked. I went for walks, I visited friends, but, sometimes, I just sat under the big mango tree outside and listened to children playing in the fields.

Faulata got so busy in Ilorin that she could no longer call every day. One day, she called and said she could not come over for the weekend because she had some work to do. I had, in fact, been pleading with her not to bother so much about me, but I had been looking forward to seeing her that weekend. I had wanted to show her all the wonderful things I had woven for her. I swallowed my disappointment and assured her that I understood.

The next weekend, she came. But she was in so much of a hurry that she could only stay but an hour. She sounded rather nervous and fretful. I thought it was the stress. I told her I was getting the hang of things and she didn't need to come every weekend.

She said, 'Oh, no, Salim, I am just stressed out right now, but I will be fine. Coming is not a problem, really.'

The next weekend, Faulata did not come. Neither did she call. I was so worried I called her, and she said she was just too busy. I said it was okay. The trend continued for a couple of months and I managed as best I could.

The next time she came, she had something important to say. She was restless and uncomfortable. She said, 'I... am getting married, Salim.'

I felt the stab in my heart and I gasped. I could imagine the blood gushing out, soaking my skin, my shirt and then trickling down to the floor where it collected into a pool.

She was still talking, 'I know it will hurt you, but I thought I should tell you... personally. I am really sorry.'

For the second time in my life, I died.

***

My mind climbed up to the gates of heaven once more, seeking admittance, pleading, begging, weeping and entreating. It tried everything possible to gain entry without success. So, it lodged outside the gates, just waiting and hoping. My body longed so much for a reunion with my mind (not here on this cruel earth, though, but up there) that I became oblivious to daily necessities such as eating and sleeping. Time became meaningless and my mind became shrouded in a blanket of despair. People came and left and I was never aware that they had come in the first place.

Faulata had pinned me to the world when I had wanted to die, and just when I was coming to terms with my new fate, she had broken my heart into a million fragments. I longed for death. I longed for freedom: freedom from pain, from anguish, from living. But death abandoned me in my hour of need and nothing and no one could set me free. Perhaps the only thing that reminded me of life was Jamila's constant plea by my bedside. She would talk and weep until blessed sleep stole her away.

One day my uncles came and bathed me with herbs. It was my first bath in nearly a month. They smoked me with all sorts of ritual herbs, and succeeded in smoking every miserable insect in the room dead. Still, I did not flinch. They concluded that it must be Iblis, the devil himself, who had taken possession of my soul. Next they came with a renowned exorcist, whom they called Malam Nagari, to banish the great Iblis. The malam seated me on a sheepskin and drenched me with a pungent-smelling perfume. Then he proceeded to recite the Glorious Qur'an over my head. At first, he sounded harsh, aggressive and frightening, but fatigue crept in and slowed his tempo before driving him out of breath. And still, I did not flinch.

By evening, he returned with spiritual incense and lit it all around me. He did his recitation once more until he ran out of steam. He said, 'This devil is indeed obstinate!'

His disciple then took over. His recitation was more subtle, more pleasant and more poignant. It reached out to my mind at the gates of heaven and subdued it. But as I was not possessed by any devil, my mind was not convinced to return.

From somewhere beyond my realm, beyond the gate, I thought I heard a voice, a familiar voice: my mother's voice, calling my name.

She said, 'My son, your life may be full of tribulations, but it is not a tragedy unless you make it one. Every man may stumble and fall while walking, but not all men have the courage to rise again and face the challenges ahead. You might fall once or twice, but the tragedy is in your not rising. Rise now, my son.'

The apprentice continued his beautiful recitation into the night until my body, ravaged by hunger, and my breath, choked by all the perfume and incense, gave way. I slumped.

The crowd shouted, '*Allahu Akbar!*'

***

Three days later, my rebellious mind reluctantly returned to my body and, strangely, I began to see. I could see with my mind's eye. I saw images I could not discern. They were like blurred, glowing lights that moved about. Nothing made sense, so I said nothing. I ate my meals quietly and would sit under the mango tree outside. I no longer heard the children's voices because someone had decided to build a shopping mall on their playground. The plot next to my house, previously populated by grasses and trees, was also attacked by men armed with a chain saw. I heard the trees screaming in agony as they were cut down. Each time they felled one, the children would scream in delight, drowning out the tree's death throes. Tears streamed down my eyes. I could bear the pain no longer, so I decided to go home.

In the living room, I saw those glowing-light images once more in my mind's eye: two images on the sofa. While everything was strange, I thought one of the images was especially peculiar. It looked like two images doubled in one,

one big, the other, very tiny. The second image was rather familiar.

I called, 'Jamila.'

Jamila was taken aback: it was the first word I had spoken in a very long time. I went on, 'Jamila, who is sitting next to you?'

The image I perceived as Jamila was fretting.

'Who is the strange person next to you?'

She said timidly, 'It is... Saratu.'

Ah, the accursed Saratu! That was my first encounter with her since Faulata had trounced her.

'Saratu?' I asked. 'What is wrong with Saratu?'

They looked at each other in alarm.

I said, 'Don't look at each other like that. I know there is something wrong with her.'

Jamila rose and came towards me, peering into my eyes. 'Can you... see?'

I could not, but I knew that something was not right. I just could not tell what it was immediately. Instead, I said, 'Why are you double, Saratu?'

She said, 'Double? How?'

My mind saw the image of Sinnoor, the cat, crouching in a corner of the room. I went and picked it up and then settled myself on the couch while the ladies stared at me in awe.

Jamila said, 'Oh my God! Salim, you can see!'

I said, 'Oh, how stupid I am! Of course, you are pregnant, aren't you, Saratu?'

She was pregnant. A scandal, of course, since she was not yet married. The fact that she was pregnant was known only to her and to Jamila, but how had I known? I did not understand anything any more – trees wailing, people floating about like lights... Everything seemed crazy. That night, I had a dream. Two strange men came to me and guided me to the Whispering Trees. The first one said, 'Sometimes you see better with your eyes closed.'

The other said, 'Sometimes you don't need your eyes to see.'

The first said, 'Listen and listen well.'

'Listen to your heart.'

'Listen with your heart.'

'Listen more to things than to words that are said.'

And then the trees came alive and wanted to eat me. I screamed and woke up.

Jamila rushed into my room. 'Salim, are you okay? Salim, what is wrong?'

My mind stared at her. How clearly I could see her. Her light glowed: It was a strange white light. I could see the outline of her face. I had almost forgotten what she looked like. She had grown into a fine, young woman, no longer the pimply teenager I had known. But there, where her heart should have been, was a bluish hue. It was fading by the minute. I listened to my heart and it told me it was the hue of fear. She had been frightened by my scream.

I said, 'Jamila, I am sorry I called you a stupid, fat, ugly bitch. You have grown into such a beautiful, young woman. Ummi would have been proud of you. I am sorry.'

She wept in my arms.

In that moment, I realized how much I had missed my sister.

Thereafter, my mind's eye grew sharper. I did not see things, but I saw their souls: human souls, goats' souls, chickens' souls. I was amazed to discover that even mosquitoes had souls. All these souls glowed like mild, white lights. And then I discerned that there were good and bad souls; the bad ones being in the majority. I recognized each by its unique tinge. I discovered how deceptive and hypocritical people were. I saw their faces, looking so innocent, but their souls were clearly malevolent and mean.

I listened to my mind and could tell how people felt by the hues over their hearts. Most hearts were tinted crimson because they were so full of anger: They were angry because they felt oppressed and cheated by greedy politicians and their stooges. If the police could pray for accidents and rob the dead, what else could one expect? The fat politicians made it worse. They came with their darkened souls and spat out rubbish about equity and good governance and then farted out corruption's putrid air. The hypocrisy was stark.

I spent three days exploring my rediscovered life. I saw things from a unique perspective, and that gave me insight into things that people did not ordinarily see. I saw goodness in unexpected places and I saw evil masked in the cloak of goodness. I took a new interest in people, or rather in their souls. I would go to the market, junctions and arenas: I would go to all the places where people gathered and would just look at their souls. What I saw troubled me. I grew tired and disenchanted, and so I started walking off. As I went, I felt the road with my cane because I could not see the stones – they had no souls. I kept walking until I was headed downhill and, before long, I was standing just outside the Whispering Trees, the woods of the spirits. I had not been there since Hamza's death. I turned to go but froze. Strangely, the woods appealed to me so strongly that even the recollection of my recent nightmare could not counter the appeal. Instead, my mind raced through all those memorable childhood days. I made up my mind and plunged in.

The first thing that caught my attention was the ethereal melody. There must have been a thousand birds and countless insects weaving their sublime melodies into the mysterious whispers of the trees. It was an orchestra so out of this world that for a long time I stood, lost and enchanted. Then, gathering my thoughts about me, I saw such a multitude of souls as I had never imagined possible. Birds, praying mantises, grasshoppers and myriad other wonderful insects went about their business on or around the trees and down below. I could see the souls of ants, creepers and crawlers on the ground. Butterflies drifted between tree trunks, dancing and bursting into incandescent colours, sapphire lights glinting off their wings. The souls of the trees were so pure and welcoming without a hint of evil about them. All these souls, so pure, so clean, so many, and not one stained by anger, malice or envy: no treachery, no guilt, just innocence. I began then to question man's moral justifications for lording it over all these beautiful, innocent souls. The contrast from the world I had just come from was so vivid and, somehow, I felt at home among all these pure souls. I found a fallen tree trunk and sat on it. The spirit of the Whispering Trees pacified my soul and, at last, I found such peace as I had never known.

Much later, a gentle breeze wafted through the leaves and made them rustle. It was as if the trees were whispering words meant for their ears alone. It was so easy to feel the sense of expectancy and to recognize that something was about to happen. I waited a long time and then I saw it. It was the soul of a young boy, about 15 years old. As it came towards me, I discerned that it was different. This soul was not white, but an emerald green. I had hardly had time to marvel over its strangeness when I recognized it. It was Hamza, my childhood friend who had perished in the Whispering Trees some 12 years previously. He approached me, not betraying any sign that he had recognized me. Shock held me captive.

He said, 'You have returned at last. I was afraid you might never come.' He sat down beside me on the trunk.

I said at last, 'Hamza, is this really you?'

He sighed.

I rose. 'But this can't be. You are dead. You died 12 years ago. I saw you!'

He said, 'Has it been 12 years already?' He shrugged and then looked at me and I saw that his eyes were hollow. 'You look so grown-up, Salim. What happened to you?'

'I had an accident,' I managed to say.

'I am sorry to hear that.'

'But... what happened to you? I mean... you died down there, in the stream.'

He sighed. 'You remember the day we came here, all

of us with Tanimu, Audu, Bala, you know... all of us? You remember I had taken my mother's wristwatch and that was why we had come here, to hide?'

I remembered. I could still see that wristwatch coated in gold. His mother had always treasured it because it had been a gift from her late husband. It was the last thing he had given her before he had been killed in an armed robbery attack. Hamza had taken it to show off and we had run all the way to the Whispering Trees in excitement. We had examined it as it had glistened in the sun. Then we had got tired of it and decided to play hide and seek. Hamza had put on the watch. I had made the call and they had all run to hide. He recounted to me that he and Tanimu had run towards the stream and hidden. While hiding, Tanimu had demanded to see the watch once more and Hamza had refused. They had struggled and Tanimu had tripped him. Tanimu had tried to hold on to him but his hand had been clasped over the watch, which was coming off. Hamza had rolled over on his neck and had landed face down, in the stream, breaking his neck in the process.

'When Tanimu saw that I had died already, he panicked and fled,' Hamza concluded.

I remembered that when we had found Hamza dead, Tanimu had been nowhere to be seen and none of us had thought anything of it. We had been overcome by the tragedy and the rumour that Hamza had been killed by the spirits of the Whispering Trees.

Everything had changed. Our little group had broken up and we had been forced to grow up. We had lost the capacity to look into each others' eyes. Tanimu had been the worst off, for he seemed to have lost his mind. He had looked miserable and none of us had been able to get through to him. He had merely drifted along with life and, to us, he had grown into a stranger.

Hamza and I talked some more until he rose and said, 'I must leave now. Now that you are here, I can leave. But see how beautiful this place is, see how pure and full of life it is. Yet, someday, the living will come and destroy everything.' He started off, 'Man destroys that which he claims to love.'

I did not know what to say.

'You know, Salim,' he said again, 'if you had been a doctor you would only have been able to treat the ailments of the body. But now you can treat ailments of the soul. You can understand that which most men do not. I go now, my friend.' He waved goodbye and I watched the final curtain fall on his short life.

Tears streamed from my eyes. I was amazed at how easily he seemed to have accepted his fate. In a way, I think, he was glad that his death had helped to protect the Whispering Trees by mystifying them. Men feared the spirits and had stayed away: beauty and innocence had thrived as a consequence. But for 12 long years, Hamza had lingered in those woods, waiting for someone to bear his message. It was this message that I took to Tanimu.

Tanimu's heart was framed by the yellow tint of guilt: the guilt he had lived with for the last 12 years. I gave him Hamza's message: that he should not feel guilty, for it had been an accident. His intention had not been to harm Hamza, but nature had played a trick on them. I told him that Hamza did not hold him responsible and had forgiven him.

Deeply moved as he was, Tanimu was sceptical. 'How can the dead speak?' he queried.

I said, 'He also told me to ask you to please return the watch you keep in your ceiling, the one you had taken from him. He says his mother would have wanted to have it back.'

Tanimu wept.

He eventually gave back the watch and freed his mind. He became a new man. And the joy of Hamza's mother upon receiving the watch was such that I cannot describe. Finally, it seemed, she had overcome the loss of her husband and her son.

The elation I felt at seeing all these troubled souls

liberated remains the most magnificent feeling I have ever felt. To see people in anguish and give them comfort, to free minds bound by desire, anger or guilt, to guide souls that are lost to their destinies, to reconcile souls alienated by misunderstandings – that is my life and purpose. It is what gives me joy.

I rediscovered life in serving and I discovered heavenly peace in the Whispering Trees, where I now spend hours listening to the melodies of nature and to the dead. They come once in a while, seeking to reach out to loved ones before taking their final leave.

So it was that I lost my sight to find my vision, I lost my life to find my soul and I lost my vanity to find my purpose. Now, sitting here, in the Whispering Trees, amidst all this beauty and these innocent souls, listening to this heavenly orchestra, I realize that happiness lies, not in getting what you want, but in wanting what you have.

Abubakar Adam Ibrahim is the author of the short-story collection, _The Whispering Trees_ (Parresia Publishers, Lagos, 2012), the source of this story. He is a Gabriel Garcia Marquez Fellow and has won the BBC African Performance Prize. He lives in Abuja, Nigeria.

Bayan Layi

Elnathan John

THE BOYS WHO SLEEP UNDER the Kuka tree in Bayan Layi like to boast about the people they have killed. I never join in because I have never killed a man. Banda has, but he doesn't like to talk about it. He just smokes *wee-wee* while they talk over each other's heads. Gobedanisa's voice is always the loudest. He likes to remind everyone of the day he strangled a man. I never interrupt his story even though I was there with him and saw what happened. Gobedanisa and I had gone into a *lambu* to steal sweet potatoes, but the farmer had surprised us while we were there. As he chased us, swearing to kill us if he caught us, he fell into a bush trap for antelopes. Gobedanisa did not touch him. We just stood by and watched as he struggled and struggled and then stopped struggling.

I don't care that Gobedanisa lies about it but sometimes I just want to ask him to shut up. The way he talks about killing, you would think he would get Paradise for it, that Allah would reserve the best spot for him. I know why he talks like that. He tells it to keep the smaller boys in awe of him. And to make them fear him. His face is a map of scars, the most prominent being a thin long one that stretches from the right side of his mouth up to his right ear. Those of us who have been here longer know he got that scar the day he tried to fight Banda. No one who knows Banda fights Banda. You are looking to get killed if you do. I can't remember what led to the quarrel – I arrived to hear Banda screaming *'Ka fita harka na fa!' Stay out of my business!* Banda never shouts so

I knew this was not a small matter. Gobedanisa must have smoked a lot of the *wee-wee* Banda gave him – he uttered the unforgivable insult: '*Gindin Maman ka!*' *Your mother's cunt!* Banda was bigger than him and had a talisman and three amulets on his right arm for knives and arrows. Nothing made out of metal could pierce him.

As Gobedanisa insulted Banda's mother, Banda dropped from the guava tree branch he was sitting on and punched him right in the mouth. He was wearing his rusty ring with the sharp edges. Gobedanisa's mouth started bleeding. He picked up a wooden plank and rammed it into Banda's back. Banda looked back and walked off, to the tree. But Gobedanisa was looking for glory. Whoever could break Banda would definitely be feared by the rest of us. We would follow that one. He picked up a second plank and aimed for Banda's head but Banda turned quickly and blocked the blow with his right arm. The plank broke in two. Gobedanisa lunged with his bloodied hands and hit Banda on the jaw. Banda didn't flinch. No one separates fights in Bayan Layi except someone is about to be killed or if the fight is really unfair. Sometimes we just let it go on because no one dies unless it is Allah's will. Banda grabbed Gobedanisa by the shirt, punched him twice in the face, and twisted his right arm, which was reaching for a knife in his pocket. He pinned him to the ground and, with his right fist, made the long tear across Gobedanisa's cheek.

No one holds a grudge in Bayan Layi. Gobedanisa still has his scar but he follows Banda and does what he says. It is Allah's will, everything that happens – why should anyone keep a grudge?

*** * ***

I like Banda because he is generous with his *wee-wee*. He doesn't like the way I tell him things that happen when he is away in Sabon Gari. He says I don't know how to tell a story, that I just talk without direction, like the harmattan wind that just blows and blows, scattering dust. Me, I just like to say it as I remember it. And sometimes you have to explain the story. Sometimes the explanation lies in many stories – how else can the story be sweet if you do not start it from its real, real beginning?

Banda gets a lot of money now that it is election season to put up posters for the Small Party and tear off the ones for the Big Party or smash up someone's car in the city. He always shares his money with the boys and gives me more than he gives the rest. I am the smallest in the gang of big boys in Bayan Layi and Banda is the biggest. But he is my best friend.

Last month, or the month before Ramadan I think, this boy tried to steal in Bayan Layi. No one dares come to steal in Bayan Layi. He tried to take some gallons of groundnut oil from Maman Ladidi's house. Her house is *ba'a shiga*, men aren't allowed to enter. She saw him and screamed. Then he ran and jumped over the fence. I like chasing thieves, especially when I know they are not from Bayan Layi. I am the fastest runner here, even though I broke my leg once when I fell from a motorcycle in Sabon Gari. Anyway, the groundnut oil thief, we caught him and gave him the beating of his life. I like using sharp objects when beating a thief. I like the way the blood spurts when you punch. So we sat this boy down and Banda asked what his name was. He said Idowu. I knew he was lying because he had the nose of an Igbo boy. I used my nail on his head many times, demanding his real name.

'Idowu! I swear my name is Idowu,' he screamed, as the nail tore into his flesh.

'Where is your *unguwa*?' Achishuru, the boy with one bad eye, asked, slapping him across the cheek. He knew how to slap, this boy with one eye.

'Near Sabon Gari,' the thief said.

'Where exactly?' I shouted. He kept quiet and I punched

him in the neck with my nail.

'Sabon Layi.'

Then he just got up and ran, I tell you. Like a bird in the sky, he just flew past us. We couldn't catch him this time. Banda asked us to just leave him alone. He didn't reach Sabon Layi. Someone saw his body in a gutter that evening. See how Allah does His things – we didn't even beat him too much. We have beaten people worse, *wallahi*, and they didn't die. But Allah chooses who lives and who dies. Not me. Not us.

The Police came to our area with the Vigilante group from Sabon Gari and we had to run away. Some hid in the mosque. Banda, Achishuru, Dauda and I swam across the River Kaduna, a part of which flows behind Bayan Layi, and wandered in the farms and bushes until it was late – too late to make it back across the river. Banda is not allowed to enter the river at night with his amulets. He says he will lose the power if the river water touches them at night and he cannot take them off because that too will kill their power.

* * *

Everyone is talking about the elections, how things will change. Even Maman Ladidi, who doesn't care about much apart from selling her groundnut oil, has the poster of the Small Party candidate on the walls of her house. She listens to her small radio for news about the elections. Everybody does. The women in the market wear wrappers carrying the candidate's face and the party logo and many men are wearing white caftans and red caps just like him. I like the man. He is not a rich man but he gives plenty alms and talks to people whenever he is in town. I like more the way he wears his red cap to the side, almost like it's about to fall. I will get a cap like that if I get the money, maybe a white caftan too. But white is hard to keep clean, soap is expensive and the water in the river will make it brown even when you wash it clean. Malam Junaidu, my former Quranic teacher, wears white too and he says the Prophet, peace be upon him, liked to wear white. But Malam Junaidu gives his clothes to Tanimu the washman, who buys water from the boys who sell tap water. Some day, *Insha Allah*, I will be able to buy tap water or give my clothes to Tanimu to wash and have a box where I will keep all my white clothes. Things will be better if the Small Party wins. *Insha Allah*.

I like the rallies. The men from the Small Party trust Banda and they give him money to organize boys from Bayan Layi for them. Sometimes we get as much as 150 naira, depending on who it is or which rally. We also get a lot to drink and eat.

I like walking around with Banda. The men respect him and even boys bigger than him are afraid of him. Banda became my friend about the time I finished my Quranic training in Malam Junaidu's *madarasa*. When I finished, Malam said I could go back to my village in Sokoto. But then Alfa, whose father lives near my father's house in Sokoto, had just arrived at the school and told me my father had died. I did not ask him what killed him because, Allah forgive me, I did not care much. It had been very long since I saw my father and he had not asked after me. Alfa said my mother still left the village to beg by the Juma'at mosque in Sokoto city, and I had two more sisters whose names he didn't know. So I told Malam Junaidu I was going back to Sokoto, even though in my heart I didn't want to go. I thought he would give me the fare. It was 300 naira from the park in Sabon Gari to get behind the trucks which carry wood to Sokoto. Instead he gave me 70 naira, reminding me that my father had not brought any millet this year or the last to pay for my Quranic training. I told him my father had died and he paused for a moment, then said, *Innalillahi wa'inna illaihi raji'un* and walked away.

It is not that I didn't agree that it is Allah who gives life and who takes, it is the way he said it, in that dry tone he used when teaching, that made me sad. But I did not cry. I did not cry until that evening when I heard Alfa telling some boys I was a *cikin shege*. A bastard pregnancy. I don't know where he got the idea from. They were sitting by the well near the open mosque Malam Junaidu built. I kicked Alfa on the thigh and we started fighting. Normally I would have just beaten him up but the two boys held me so Alfa could keep slapping me. I was kicking and crying when Banda passed by. Banda knocked Alfa down with one punch and flung one of the boys to the ground. I ran after Alfa and kept punching him in the stomach until my hands began to hurt. The other boys ran away. That day, I cried like I had never cried before. I followed Banda and he gave me the first *wee-wee* I smoked. It felt good. My legs became light and after a while I felt them disappear. I was floating, my eyes were heavy and I felt bigger and stronger than Banda and Gobedanisa and all the boys under the Kuka tree. He said he liked the way I didn't cough when I smoked it. That was how we became friends. He gave me one of his flat cartons and took me to where they slept. They slept on cartons under the Kuka tree and when it rained they moved to the cement floor in front of Alhaji Mohammed's rice store, which had an extended zinc roof.

Banda is not an *almajiri* like me. He was born in Sabon Gari like most of the other boys but didn't attend Quranic school. Malam Junaidu had warned us about the Kuka tree boys who come to Mosque only during Ramadan or Eid – *'yan daba*, thugs who do nothing but cause trouble in Bayan Layi.' We despised them because they did not know the Qur'an and Sunna like us and did not fast or pray five times a day. *A person who doesn't pray five times a day is not a Muslim*, Malam would say. Now that I am also under the Kuka tree, I know they are just like me and, even though they don't pray five times a day, some of them are kind, good people – Allah knows what is in their heart.

Banda is an old boy. I don't know how old but he is the only one with a moustache among us. I hate it when people ask me my age because I don't know. I just know I have fasted nearly 10 times. Some people understand when I say so, but others still ask annoying questions, like the woman during the census last year. But since the recent voter registration I have been saying I am 19 even though I have to fold the sleeves of the old caftan Banda gave me. The men in the Small Party asked us to say so and gave us all 100 naira to register and even though the people registering us complained, they registered us anyway. My head was so big in the picture on the voter card Banda and Achishuru kept laughing at me. I don't like it when Achishuru laughs at me because he has one eye and shouldn't be laughing at my head. He is so stingy he doesn't even like to share his *wee-wee*.

* * *

'We have a lot of work to do for the elections,' Banda says, coughing.

The Small Party has promised we may even get 1,000 naira per head if they win the elections. They will build a shelter for us homeless boys and those who can't return home or don't have parents, where we can learn things like making chairs and sewing caftans and making caps. Banda hasn't coughed like this before, spitting blood. I think he is sick.

Achishuru, Banda, Gobedanisa and I have been going with some boys from Sabon Gari to the Small Party office to talk about how to win the elections. No one likes the Big Party here. It is because of them we are poor. Their boys don't dare come here because people will drive them out.

Banda is coughing and spitting out even more blood. I worry. Maybe after the elections, when the Small Party becomes the Big Party, they can pay for him to see a doctor in the big hospital with plenty flowers and trees in the capital. Or, if Allah wills it, he will get better without even needing the hospital.

It is about one hour after the last evening prayer and the Small Party man's brother has just driven into Bayan Layi in a white pickup truck with the Party flag in front. He shouts Banda's name. Banda drops from the guava tree and I follow him.

'Which one of you is Banda?' a man asks from behind the truck. I can't see his face.

'I am,' Banda replies.

'And this one, who is he?'

'He's my friend, we sleep in the same place.'

'My name is Dantala,' I add.

'Well, we want just Banda.'

I am angry but I don't say a word.

'I am coming,' Banda says to me, adjusting the amulets on his right arm. It is his way of telling me he will be ok. He hops onto the back of the truck and they drive off.

✳ ✳ ✳

Banda appears just as the *muezzin* sings the first call to prayer. It is Election Day. I didn't sleep because I was anxious and I knew they would give him a lot of money for the boys.

'What did they tell you?' I inquire.

'Nothing.'

'What do you mean, nothing?' I am getting irritated. 'So they kept you all night for nothing?'

Banda doesn't say anything. He brings out two long wraps of *wee-wee* and gives one to me. We call it *jumbo*, the big ones. He also hands me two crisp 100-naira notes. I have not seen crisp notes like these in a long time.

'After prayers we will gather all the boys behind the mosque and give them 150 each. Then we wait. They will tell us what to do. Those who have their voters' cards will get an extra 200 and I will collect all the cards and take them to their office.'

I am not sure why they want the cards because I imagine they want us to help vote the Big Party out. But I want the extra 200. I am excited about the elections and the way everybody in Bayan Layi and even Sabon Gari likes the Small Party. They will surely win. *Insha Allah!*

We head for the polling centre between Bayan Layi and Sabon Gari, even though we will not be voting. The day is moving slowly and the sun is hot very early. I hope the electoral officers come quickly so it can begin. Plenty women are coming out to vote and the Small Party people are everywhere. They are handing out water and *zobo* and giving the women salt and dry fish in little cellophane bags. Everyone is cheerful, chatting in small groups. The Big Party agent arrives in a plain bus and takes off his party tag as soon as he gets there. I think he is afraid he will be attacked. He doesn't complain about the things the Small Party people are doing; he can't because not even the two policemen can save him if he does. He knows, because he used to live in Bayan Layi too before he started working for the Big Party and moved to get a room in Sabon Gari. Banda says he hardly stays there and he spends most of his time in the Capital where all the money is.

The voting is about to end and my *wee-wee* is wearing off but I still have some left from the *jumbo* Banda gave me in the morning. I am hungry and tired of drinking the *zobo* that has been going around. I can't see Banda anywhere and I turn around the corner of the street and find him bent over, coughing, holding his chest. He is still spitting a lot of blood. I ask him if he is ok. He says nothing, just sits on the floor, panting. I get him one sachet of water. He rinses his mouth and drinks some of it.

'We will win these elections,' Banda says.

'Of course, who can stop us?' We are talking like real politicians now, like party men.

'Will they really build us that shelter?' I ask.

'I don't like to think of that, all I want is that they pay every time they ask us to work for them. After the election, where will you see them?'

I am thinking Banda is very wise and I should stop

expecting anything from them. I light what is left of the *jumbo* and ask Banda if he wants some.

'I just had one before you came,' he says.

* * *

We hear screaming and chanting. The counting is over and, as we expect, the Small Party has won here. I don't think the Big Party has more than 20 votes in this place. We get up and join the crowd, chanting, dancing and beating empty gallons with sticks.

I am exhausted very quickly because I was up all night last night waiting for Banda. I slow down. I am still high and all these thoughts are suddenly going through my head – how I have hardly prayed since I left my Quranic teacher and how we only go to the Juma'at mosque in Sabon Gari on Fridays because there are people giving alms and lots of free food. But Allah judges the intentions of the heart. We are not terrible people. When we fight, it is because we have to. When we break into small shops in Sabon Gari, it is because we are hungry and when someone dies, well, that is Allah's will.

Banda disappears again. He comes back early in the morning and says we have to be out again today after the morning prayers.

'We have been cheated in the elections,' Banda says, coughing, frantic.

'They have switched the numbers. We have to go out.'

I am still sleepy, even though there is a lot of noise around. There are unfamiliar boys standing behind the mosque, shouting. I just want to sleep. My stomach is rumbling and my head hurts. This is the moment we have all been paid for. I had hoped all this would end last night. Unlike the other boys, I am not used to this breaking and burning business. Under the Kuka tree, nothing is complete without some fire and broken glass.

'These Southerners can't cheat us – after all, we are in the majority.'

I don't know the boy who is shouting but he is holding a long knife. 'There are no Southerners here,' I think, 'why is he holding out his knife? We all have knives here.' I hiss. The crowd is agitated. Banda looks like he can barely stand and is walking toward a parked pickup truck – the same pickup truck the Small Party people came in the other day. I see him bent over, talking to someone inside the truck. Banda is just nodding and I wonder what he is being told. He walks back with his hands in the pockets of his old brown jallabiya. He comes into the crowd and whispers to the boy waving his knife in the air. The boy starts calling the crowd to order.

'We are going to teach them a lesson,' he says. 'We must scatter everything belonging to the Big Party in Bayan Layi.'

I must ask Banda who this boy is.

'Burn their office!' Gobedanisa shouts.

The crowd screams. I have always wanted to enter that office. I hear they keep money there. I scream with the crowd.

Banda tells us there are machetes, daggers and small gallons of fuel in the back of the truck. We will get 200 naira each for taking back the votes that were stolen. Two hundred sounds nice. I can buy bread and fried fish. I haven't had fish in a while.

We file past the truck to get our 200-naira notes and fuel and matches and machetes. The man handing out the notes doesn't talk. He just looks sternly into our eyes and hands out the notes. He gives a hundred to the smaller boys. I push out my chest as I approach the man, raising my chin so I don't look so small. I want the 200. The man looks at me and pauses, assessing me to see if I will get 100 or 200.

'We are together,' Banda says from behind me to the man.

The man is not convinced and hands me a 100-naira note. I take it – I never refuse money – and pick up a machete from behind the truck. Banda whispers something to the man and then collects a note. He stretches it out to me – it is another 100-naira note. I am glad and suddenly the sleep has cleared from my eyes. This is why I like Banda, he fights for me. He is a good person. He gives me something rolled up and wrapped in black polythene and asks me to hold it for him. My trousers have good pockets. It is money. I am not sure how much.

The first thing we do is set ablaze the huge poster of the Big Party's candidate in front of the market. I like how the fire eats up his face. I wish it was his face in real life. The Big Party office is on my mind – I can't wait to search the offices and drawers and take whatever I can get from there before we set it ablaze.

I am the first to get to the Big Party office. The others are trailing closely behind me. They are excited, delirious, partly because we have been paid and partly because they hate the Big Party and are angry about the news we have heard.

We push the gate until we bring it down together with the pillars to which it is attached. Tsohon Soja is the old man guarding the place. He tries to struggle with some of the boys, grabs one of them by the neck and blows his whistle. Another boy snatches the whistle from his mouth.

'You are an old man, Tsohon Soja, we don't want to harm you. Just stand back and let us burn this place down,' I tell him.

This security man is stubborn. He is a retired soldier and thinks he can scare us away. He reaches for his long stick and hits one the boys on the shoulder. Gobedanisa charges forward with his machete, striking the man on the chest and on the neck. None of the boys wanted to be the first to hit the old man because they all know him. Now that he is down they strike at his body. Me, I think it's bad luck to be killing such an old man. But he brought it upon himself. I know Gobedanisa will boast about this.

I run into the building but a boy in front of me has already opened the front door. I hope there is some money in the office – there must be – why else would the security man be trying to fight a whole crowd? We all enter the place, destroying furniture, tearing papers and posters, searching drawers. We go from room to room. All I can get is a transistor radio in one of the drawers. Achishuru gets a really new prayer mat and a cap. I am disappointed.

Banda is holding a half-gallon of petrol and so is the other boy who was wielding the knife as he spoke behind the mosque.

'Get out – we are burning the place!' Banda orders.

I put my transistor radio in my pocket and it falls through to the ground. The hole in my pocket has become very big. The radio has a little rope. I hang it around my neck and pick up my machete. I am also holding the matches so I wait for them to finish pouring petrol while the other boys run out to the next thing belonging to the Big Party.

'Pour more, pour more,' Banda tells the boy.

'No, this is enough, we need it for other places. It is petrol not kerosene.'

Banda concedes. I wait for them to come out. I strike the match. The boy was right. I love the way the fire leaps out of the window and reaches for the ceiling. I remember when I was very little and my father almost beat me to death because I burnt a whole bag of millet stalks. That was before the rain stopped falling in our village and my father sent me and many of my brothers far away for Quranic training. I don't know where they are now, my brothers. Maybe they have gone back home. Maybe they have decided to stay like me.

A fat man runs out of the burning building, toward me, covered in soot, coughing and stumbling over things. He can't see well. A Big Party man.

'Traitor!' one boy shouts.

The man is running, with his hands in the air like a woman, like a disgusting *dan daudu*. I hate that he is fat. I hate his party, how they make us poor. I hate that he was hiding like a rat, fat as he is. I strike behind his neck as he stumbles by me. He crashes to the ground. He groans. I strike again. The machete is sharp. Sharper than I expected, light. I wonder where they got them from. Malam Junaidu's machetes were so heavy, I hated it when we had to clear weeds in front of the mosque or his house.

The man isn't shaking much. Banda picks up the gallon and pours some fuel on the body. He looks at me to strike the match. I stare at the body. Banda seizes the matchbox from me and lights it. The man squirms only a little as the fire begins to eat his clothes and flesh. He is dead already.

I am not thinking as we move on, burning, screaming, cutting, tearing. I don't like the feeling in my body when this machete cuts flesh so I stick to the fire and take the matchbox from Banda. At first we make a distinction between shops belonging to Big Party people and those belonging to Small Party people but, as we become thirsty and hungry, we just break into any shop we see.

As the crowd moves beyond Bayan Layi, they are stopped by the sound of gunfire ahead. I am still far behind, taking a piss, and I see the crowd running back. Two police vans are heading this way and they are firing into the air. As they get closer the policemen get out and start firing into the crowd. As I see the first person go down, I turn and run. I look back for Banda and he is not running. He is bent over, coughing, holding his chest. I stop.

'Banda, get up!' I scream, crouching behind a low fence.

Everyone is running past him and the police keep shooting. He tries, runs feebly and stops again. They are getting closer – Banda has to get up now. I want to run; I want to hope his amulets would work. But I linger a bit. He gets up again and starts to run. Then he falls flat on his face like someone hit him from behind. He is not moving. I run. I cut through the open mosque, avoiding the narrow, straight road. I run through Malam Junaidu's maize farm. There are boys hiding there. I do not stop. I run past the Kuka tree. I will not stop, even when I can no longer hear the guns. Until I get to the river and across the farms, far, far away from Bayan Layi.

Elnathan John is a full-time writer who trained as a lawyer in Nigeria. His writing has been published in *Per Contra*, *ZAM Magazine*, *Evergreen Review*, *Sentinel Nigeria* and Chimurenga's *The Chronicle*. He writes political satire for a Nigerian newspaper and his blog for which he hopes some day to get arrested and famous. He has tried hard, but has never won anything. This story first appeared in *Per Contra*, issue 25, Fall, US, 2012.

America

Chinelo Okparanta

WE DRIVE THROUGH BUSHES. We pass the villages that rim our side of the Bonny River. There are hardly any trees in the area, and the shrubs are little more than stumps, thin and dusty, not verdant as they used to be. This, Mama has told me: that the vegetation around the Bonny River once thrived. That the trees grew tall, and from them sprang green leaves. And their flowers gave rise to fruit. Of course, this memory is hers, from a former reality, one too old to be my own.

The roads are sandy and brown, with open gutters, and with wrappers and cans and bottles strewn about. Collapsing cement shacks line the roadside in messy rows, like cartons that have long begun to decompose.

A short distance from us, something comes out of the river, a small boy or girl, maybe six or seven years old. Hands flail in the air and another child joins – typical children's play. Except that it's too early in the morning for that. Except that their skin, and even the cloth around their waists, gleams an almost solid black. That oily blackness of crude.

The bus moves slowly, and for a while, as we make our way out of Port Harcourt, I worry it will break down. The last time I made this trip (about a year ago now), there was a problem with the engine. The bus only made it to the terminal in Warri, not quite halfway between Port Harcourt and Lagos. When we arrived at the terminal, the driver asked us to exit. He locked the door to the bus and went inside one of the offices in the terminal. He locked the office door too, leaving us passengers outside to fend for ourselves. We had passed no inns or motels on the way. Just splatters of small shops, their zinc roofs shining in the sun. Lots of green and yellowing grass. Clusters of trees.

At the terminal, I found a nice patch of ground on which I slept, using my luggage as a pillow under my head. Some passengers did the same. Others, I assume, wandered about the terminal through the night. The next morning another bus arrived. It took us from Warri to Lagos. I made it just in time for my interview. Lucky that I had left a day in advance. Not that leaving in advance made much difference anyway. As with the previous interview, my application was declined.

I sit on the bus again, slightly more hopeful about the engine and much more hopeful about the interview. I have not left a day early, but so long as the bus does not break down, I expect that this interview will be a success. This time I have a plan and, even if I hesitate to be as assured as Gloria is, there is a good chance that she is right, that very soon I will be on my way to her.

It was on a dry and hot day in November that Gloria and I met. The headmistress had arranged it all: I would be Gloria's escort. I would show her around the campus for the week.

That day, the headmistress stood by her desk, me at her side, waiting for this Gloria Oke. I was already one of the senior teachers at the time; I had been at the school for nearly ten years by then.

I'd expected that she'd come in like the big madam she was, 'big' as in well-to-do and well known, maybe with a fancy *buba* and *iro* in lace, with a headscarf and maybe even the *ipele* shawl. Even with the heat, the headmistress, and all the big madams who visited our campus, came dressed that way.

But Gloria entered, tall and lanky, a bit too thin to be identified as a 'big madam'. She wore a long beige gown, no fancy headscarf, no *ipele* hanging from her shoulder. Her hair was braided in thin strands and held together in a bun at the nape of her neck. Pale skin stuck out in contrast to dark brown eyes and hair. Her lips were natural, not lipstick red. On her feet, she wore a simple pair of black flats.

Even then, there were things I liked about her: the way her eyes seemed unsure, not being able to hold my gaze. The way she stuttered her name, as if unconvinced of her own existence in the world. And yet her voice was strong and firm, something of a paradox.

That first day, we spent our lunch break together, and for the rest of the week we did the same, me sharing my fried plantain with her, and she, her rice and stew with me.

She started to visit me at my flat after her week at the school was up. She'd stop by every other week or so, on the weekends when we could spend more than a few hours together. I'd make us dinner, *jollof* rice, beans and yams, maybe some *gari* and soup. We'd spend the evening chatting or just watching the news. Sometimes we'd walk around the neighbourhood and when we returned, she'd pack her things and leave.

I grew a big enough garden in my backyard. Tufts of pineapple leaves stuck out in spikes from the earth. They grew in neat rows. Plantain trees stood just behind the pineapple shoots. Behind the plantain trees, lining the wall leading up to the gate of the flat, an orange tree grew, and a guava tree, and a mango tree.

Once, while we stood plucking a ripe mango, Gloria asked me what it was like to teach science at the school. Did we conduct experiments or just study from a book? Were all of the students able to afford the books? It was a private school, she knew, but she suspected (quite accurately) that that didn't mean all the students were able to afford the texts.

I straightened up to face the wall that led up to the metal gate. Lizards were racing up and down. I told her that teaching was not my job of choice. That I'd much rather be doing something more hands-on, working directly with the earth, like in my garden. Maybe something to do with the environment, with aquatic ecology: running water-quality reports, performing stream classification, restoration, wetland determinations, delineations, design and monitoring. But there were none of those jobs during the time I did my job search, even though there should have been plenty of them, especially with the way things were going for the Niger Delta.

But even if the jobs had been available, I said, perhaps they would have been too dangerous for me, with all that bunkering going on, criminal gangs tapping the oil straight from the pipelines and transporting it abroad to be sold illegally. The rebel militias stealing the oil and refining it and selling it to help pay for their weapons. All those explosions from old oil rigs that had been left abandoned by Shell. Perhaps it would have been too dangerous a thing.

She was standing with her hands on her hips, showing surprise only with her eyes. I suppose it was understandable that she would have assumed I loved my job to have stayed those many years.

We became something – an item, Papa says – in February, months after Gloria's visit to the school. That evening, I was hunched over, sweeping my apartment with a broom, the native kind, made from the raw, dry stems of palm leaves, tied together at the thick end with a bamboo string. I imagine it's the kind of broom that Gloria no longer sees. It's the kind of broom we use here in Nigeria – the kind that Americans have probably never seen.

Gloria must have come in through the back door of the flat (she often did), through the kitchen and into the parlour. I was about to collect the dirt into the dustpan when she entered.

She brought with her a cake, a small one with white icing and spirals of silver and gold. On top of it was a white-striped candle, moulded in the shape of the number 34. She set it on the coffee table in the parlour and carefully lit the wick.

I set the broom and dustpan down and straightened up. Gloria reached out to tuck back the strands of hair that had come loose from behind my ears. I'd barely blown out the flame when she dipped her finger into the cake's icing and took a taste of it. Then she dipped her finger into the icing again and held the clump out to me.

'Take,' she said, almost in a whisper, smiling her shyest sort of smile.

Just then, the phone began to ring: a soft, buzzing sound. We heard the ring but neither of us turned to answer, because even as it was ringing, I was kissing the icing off Gloria's finger. By the time the ringing was done, I was kissing it off her lips.

Mama still reminds me every once in a while that there are penalties in Nigeria for that sort of thing. And of course, she's right. I've read of them in the newspapers and have heard of them on the news. Still, sometimes I want to ask her to explain to me what she means by 'that sort of thing', as if it is something so terrible that it does not deserve a name, as if it is so unclean that it cannot be termed 'love'. But then I remember that evening and I cringe, because, of course, I know she can explain; she's seen it with her own eyes.

That evening, the phone rings, and if I had answered, it would have been Mama on the line. But instead, I remain with Gloria, allowing her to trace her fingers across my brows, allowing her to trace my lips with her own. My heart thumps in my chest and I feel the thumping of her heart. She runs her fingers down my belly, lifting my blouse slightly, hardly a lift at all. And then her hand is travelling lower, and I feel myself tightening and I feel the pounding all over me. Suddenly, Mama is calling my name, calling it loudly, so that I have to look up to see if I'm not just hearing things. We have made our way to the sofa and, from there, I see Mama shaking her head, telling me how the wind has blown and the bottom of the fowl has been exposed.

Mama stands where she is for just a moment longer, all the while she is looking at me with a sombre look in her eyes. 'So, this is why you won't take a husband?' she asks. It is an interesting thought, but not one I'd ever really considered. Left to myself, I would have said that I'd just not found the right man. But it's not that I'd ever been particularly interested in dating them anyway.

'A woman and a woman cannot bear children,' Mama says to me. 'That's not the way it works.' As she stomps out of the room, she says again, 'The wind has blown and the bottom of the fowl has been exposed.'

I lean my head on the glass window of the bus and I try to imagine how the interview will go. But every so often the bus hits a bump and it jolts me out of my thoughts.

There is a woman sitting to my right. Her scent is strong, somewhat like the scent of fish. She wears a headscarf, which she uses to wipe the beads of sweat that form on her face. Mama used to sweat like that. Sometimes she'd call me to bring her a cup of ice. She'd chew on the blocks of ice, one after the other, and then request another cup. It was the real curse of womanhood, she said. Young women thought the flow was the curse, little did they know the rest. The heart palpitations, the dizzy spells, the sweating that came with the cessation of the flow. That was the real curse, she said. Cramps were nothing in comparison.

The woman next to me wipes her sweat again. I catch a strong whiff of her putrid scent. She leans her head on the seat in front of her, and I ask her if everything is fine.

'The baby,' she says, lifting her head back up. She rubs her belly and mutters something under her breath.

'Congratulations,' I say. And after a few seconds I add, 'I'm sorry you're not feeling well.'

She tells me it comes with the territory. That it's been two years since she and her husband married, and he was starting to think there was some defect in her. 'So, actually,' she tells me, 'this is all cause for celebration.'

She turns to the seat on her right, where there are two black-and-white-striped polythene bags. She pats one of the bags and there is that strong putrid scent again. 'Stock fish', she says, 'and dried *egusi* and *ogbono* for soup.' She tells me that she's heading to Lagos, because that is where her in-laws live. There will be a ceremony for her there.

And she is on her way to help with the preparations. Her husband is taking care of business in Port Harcourt, but he will be heading down soon, too, to join in celebrating the conception of their first child.

'Boy or girl?' I ask, feeling genuinely excited for her.

'We don't know yet,' she says. 'But either one will be a real blessing for my marriage,' she says. 'My husband has never been happier.'

I turn my head to look out the window, but then I feel her gaze on me. When I look back at her, she asks if I have a husband or children of my own.

I think of Mama and I think of Gloria. 'No husband, no children,' I say.

The day I confessed to him about Gloria, Papa said: 'When a goat and yam are kept together, either the goat takes a bite of the yam, bit by bit, or salivates for it. That is why when two adults are always seen together, it is no surprise when the seed is planted.'

I laughed and reminded him that there could be no seed planted with Gloria and me.

'No,' he said, reclining on his chair, holding the newspaper, which he was never reading, just always intending to read. 'There can be no seed.'

It had been Mama's idea that I tell him. He would talk some sense into me, she said. All this Gloria business was nonsense, she said. Woman was made for man. Besides, what good was it living a life in which you had to go around afraid of being caught? Mobile policemen were always looking for that sort of thing – men with men or women with women. And the penalties were harsh. Jail time, fines, stoning or flogging, depending on where in Nigeria you were caught. And you could be sure that it would make the news. Public humiliation. What kind of life was I expecting to have, always having to turn around to check if anyone was watching? 'Your Papa must know of it,' she said. 'He will talk some sense into you. You must tell him. If you don't, I will.'

But Papa took it better than Mama had hoped. Like her, he warned me of the dangers. But 'love is love', he said.

Mama began to cry then. 'Look at this skin,' she said, stretching out her arms to me. She grabbed my hand and placed it on her arm. 'Feel it,' she said. 'Do you know what it means?' she asked, not waiting for my response. 'I'm growing old,' she said. 'Won't you stop being stubborn and take a husband, give up that silly thing with that Gloria friend of yours, bear me a grandchild before I'm dead and gone?'

'People have a way of allowing themselves to get lost in America,' Mama said when I told her that Gloria would be going. Did I remember Chinedu Okonkwo's daughter who went abroad to study medicine and never came back? I nodded. I did remember. And Obiageli Ojukwu's sister who married that button-nosed American and left with him so many years ago? Did I remember that she promised to come back home to raise her children? Now the children were grown, and still no sight of them. 'But it's a good thing in this case,' Mama said smugly. She was sitting on a stool in the veranda, fanning herself with a plantain leaf. Gloria and I had been together for two years by then, the two years since Mama walked in on us. In that time, Gloria had written many more articles on education policies, audacious criticisms of our government, suggesting more effective methods of standardizing the system, suggesting that those in control of government affairs needed to better educate themselves.

More and more of her articles were being published in local and national newspapers, the *Tribune*, *Punch*, the *National Mirror* and such.

Universities all over the country began to invite her to give lectures on public policies and education strategy. Soon, she was getting invited to conferences and lectures abroad. And before long, she was offered that post in America, in that place where water formed a cold, feather-like substance called snow, which fell leisurely from the sky in winter. Pretty, like white lace.

'I thought her goal was to make Nigeria better, to improve Nigeria's education system,' Papa said.

'Of course,' Mama replied. 'But, like I said, America has a way of stealing our good ones from us. When America calls, they go. And more times than not, they stay.'

Papa shook his head. I rolled my eyes.

'Perhaps she's only leaving to escape scandal,' Mama said.

'What scandal?' I asked.

'You know. That thing between you two.'

'That thing is private, Mama,' I replied. 'It's between us two, as you say. And we work hard to keep it that way.'

'What do her parents say?' Mama asked.

'Nothing.' It was true. She'd have been a fool to let them know. They were quite unlike Mama and Papa. They went to church four days out of the week. They lived the words of the Bible as literally as they could. Not like Mama and Papa who were that rare sort of Nigerian Christian with a faint, shadowy type of respect for the Bible, the kind of faith that required no works. The kind of faith that amounted to no faith at all. They could barely quote a Bible verse.

'With a man and a woman, there would not be any need for so much privacy,' Mama said that day. 'Anyway, it all works out for the best.' She paused to wipe with her palms the sweat that was forming on her forehead. 'I'm not getting any younger,' she continued. 'And I even have the names picked out!'

'What names?' I asked.

'For a boy, Arinze. For a girl, Nkechi. Pretty names.'

'Mama!' I said, shaking my head at her.

'Perhaps now you'll be more inclined to take a husband,' she said. 'Why waste such lovely names?'

The first year she was gone, we spoke on the phone at least once every week. But the line was filled with static and there were empty spots in the reception, blank spaces into which our voices faded. I felt the distance then.

But Gloria continued to call and we took turns reconstructing the dropped bits of conversation, stubbornly reinserting them back into the line, stubbornly resisting the emptiness.

The end of that first year, she came back for a visit. She was still the same Gloria, but her skin had turned paler and she had put on just a bit of weight.

'You're turning white,' I teased.

'It's the magic of America,' she teased me back. And then she laughed. 'It's no magic at all,' she said. 'Just lack of sunlight. Lots of sitting at the desk, writing, and planning.'

It made sense. Perhaps she was right. But it was the general consensus in Port Harcourt (and I imagine in probably most of Nigeria as well) that things were better in America. I was convinced of it. I saw it in the way her voice was even softer than before. I saw it in the relaxed looks on the faces of the people in the pictures she brought. Pictures of beautiful landscapes, clean places, not littered at all with cans and wrappers like our roads. Snow, white and soft, like clouds having somehow descended on land. Pictures of huge department stores in which everything seemed to sparkle. Pictures in which cars and buildings shone, where even the skin of fruit glistened.

By the time her visit was over, we had decided that I would try to join her in America, that I would see about getting a visa. If not to be able to work there, then at least to study and earn an American degree. Because, though she intended eventually to come back to Nigeria, there was no telling how long she would end up staying in America. The best thing for now was that I try to join her there.

I think of Gloria as my head jerks back and forth against the window of the bus. I try to imagine her standing in a landscape like the one in the pictures she's sent. A lone woman surrounded by tall cedars and oaks. Even if it's only June, the ground in my imagination is covered with white snow, looking like a bed of bleached cotton balls. This is my favourite way to picture her in America.

I think back to my first interview. The way the man dismissed me even before I could answer why I wanted so badly to attain a visa for the USA. The second interview was not much different. That time, I was able to respond. And then the man told me how foolish I was for expecting that a job would be waiting for me in America. I held an African degree; was I unaware of this? Did I not know that I would not compare at all with all the other job applicants who would probably not be from an African country, whose degrees would certainly be valued more than any degree from Nigeria ever would?

I cried the whole bus ride home after that second interview. When I returned, I told Mama and Papa what I had done. It was the first time they were hearing about my plan to join Gloria in America. By that second interview, she had been gone over two years.

Papa was encouraging. He said not to give up. If it was an American degree I needed, then go ahead and apply to American schools so that I could have that American degree. It would be good for me to be in America, he said, a place where he imagined I could be free with the sort of love that I had for Gloria.

'It's not enough that I won't have a grandchild in all of this,' Mama said, after hearing what Papa had to say. 'Now I must deal with losing my only child, too.' There were tears in her eyes. And then she asked me to promise that I would not allow myself to get lost in America.

I shook my head and promised her that she'd not be losing me at all.

All the while, the woman I loved was there, worlds away. If I didn't make it that third time, I thought, there was a good chance she'd grow weary of waiting for me. If I were to be once more declined, she might move on and start loving somebody else. And who would I blame more for it? Her or me? All this I thought as I booked the third appointment. By then, I had already gained admission into one of the small colleges near where Gloria lived in America. All that remained was for me to be approved for the visa.

About a month before the third interview, Gloria called me to tell me the news. An oil rig had exploded. Thousands of barrels of crude were leaking out into the Gulf every day. Perhaps even hundreds of thousands, there was no telling for sure. She was watching it on the television. Arresting camera shots of something like black clouds forming in waters that would usually be clear and blue.

It was evening when she called, and mosquitoes were whistling about the parlour of my flat. They were landing on the curtains and on the tables and on the walls, making tiny shadows wherever they perched. And I thought how there were probably no mosquitoes where she was. Did mosquitoes even exist in America?

'A terrible spill in the Gulf,' she told me. 'Can you imagine?' I told her that I could not. It was the truth. America was nothing like Nigeria, after all. Here, roads were strewn with trash and it was rare that anyone cared to clean them up. Here, spills were expected. Because we were just Africans. What did Shell care? Here, the spills were happening on a weekly basis in the Niger Delta area. But a spill like that in America? I could honestly not imagine.

'It's unfortunate,' I said to Gloria.

'Something good must be made out of such an unfortunate event,' she said.

The bus picks up speed and I watch through the windows as we pass by the small villages in Warri. Then we are driving by signs for Sapele and for the Ologbo Game Reserve. The bus is quiet and the woman next to me is fast asleep, and I wonder how she can stand to sleep on such a bumpy ride. Hours later, we pass the signs for the Lekki Lagoon. We reach Lagos at about 2pm, an early arrival for which I'm very thankful, because it gives me plenty of time to make my way to the embassy on Victoria Island.

At 3pm, I arrive at Walter Carrington Crescent, the road on which the embassy is located. Inside the building, I wait in a small room with buzzing fluorescent lights. There is an oscillating floor fan in the corner, and a window is open, but the air is still muggy and stale. I think of Gloria and I imagine what she is doing. It is morning where she is in America, and perhaps she's already at her office at the university, jotting down notes at her desk, preparing lectures for her students, or perhaps even rehearsing for a public reading somewhere.

I imagine her in a gown, something simple and unpretentious, with her hair plaited in braids, the way it used to be. It's gathered into a bun at the nape of her neck, but there are loose strands dangling down her back. Just the way she was the first time I saw her.

I continue to wait. The fan oscillates and I follow its rotations with my eyes. I think of the spill and I remember Gloria's description: *something like black clouds forming in waters that would usually be clear and blue.* The waters of the Niger Delta were once clear and blue. Now the children wade in the water and come out with Shell oil glowing on their skin.

I'm imagining stagnant waters painted black and brown with crude when finally someone calls my name. The voice is harsh and makes me think of gravel, of rock-strewn roads, the kinds filled with potholes the size of washbasins, the kind of potholes we see all over in Nigeria, the kind I imagine America does not have.

I answer the call with a smile plastered on my face. But all the while my heart is palpitating – rapid, irregular beats that only I can hear. They are loud and distracting, like raindrops on zinc.

The man who calls my name is old and grey-haired and wears suspenders over a yellow-white short-sleeved shirt. He doesn't smile at me, just turns quickly around and leads me down a narrow corridor. He stops at the door of a small room and makes a gesture with his hand, motioning me to enter. He does not follow me into the room, which is more an enclosed cubicle than a room; instead there is a clicking sound behind me. I turn around to see that the door has been shut.

In the room, another man sits on a swivel chair, the kind with thick padding and expensive grey-and-white cloth covering. He stands up as I walk towards him. His skin is tan, but a pale sort of tan. He says hello, and his words come out a little more smoothly than I am accustomed to, levelled and under-accentuated, as if his tongue has somehow flattened the words, as if it has somehow diluted them in his mouth. An American.

He wears a black suit with pinstripes, a dress shirt with the two top buttons undone, no tie; and he looks quite seriously at me. He reaches across the table, which is more like a counter, to shake my hand. He wears three rings, each on its own finger, excepting the index and the thumb. The stones in the rings sparkle as they reflect the light.

He offers me the metal stool across from him. When I am seated, he asks for my papers: identification documents; invitation letter; bank records.

'Miss Nnenna Etoniru,' he begins, pronouncing my name in his diluted sort of way. 'Tell me your occupation,' he says.

'Teacher,' I say.

'Place of employment,' he says, not quite a question.

'Federal Government Girls' College in Abuloma. I work there as a science teacher.'

'A decent job.'

I nod. 'Yes, it's a good enough job,' I say.

He lifts up my letter of invitation. The paper is thin and from the back I can see the swirls of Gloria's signature. 'Who is this Miss Gloria Oke?' he asks. 'Who is she to you?'

'A friend,' I say. And that answer is true.

'A friend?'

'A former co-worker, too.' I tell him that we met years ago at the Federal Government Girls' College in Abuloma. That we became friends when she was invited to help create a new curriculum. He can check the school records if he wishes, I say, confidently, of course, because that answer, too, is true.

Next question: proof of funding. I direct him to the bank statements, not surprisingly, from Gloria. He mumbles something under his breath. Then he looks up at me and mutters something about how lucky I am to have a friend like her. Not many people he knows are willing to fund their friends' education abroad, he says.

Then the big question. Why not just study here in Nigeria? There are plenty of Nigerian universities that offer a Master's in Environmental Engineering, he says. Why go all the way abroad to study what Nigerian universities offer here at home?

The question doesn't shock me, because I've anticipated and rehearsed it many more times than I can count in the month since that phone conversation with Gloria.

I begin by telling him of the oil spill in America. He seems to be unaware of it. I tell him that it has drawn some attention for Nigeria, for their plight with the issues of the Niger Delta. I tell him that going to America will allow me to learn first-hand the measures that the US government is taking in their attempt to deal with the aftermath of their spill. Because it's about time we Nigerians found ways to handle our own.

He doesn't question me as to how I expect to connect with the US government. He doesn't ask how exactly I expect to learn first-hand about their methods of dealing with that type of environmental disaster. Perhaps, having made a life for himself here in Nigeria, he, too, has begun to adopt the Nigerian mentality. Perhaps he, too, has begun to see the US the way most of us Nigerians do, as an abstraction, a sort of utopia, a place where you go for answers, a place that always has those answers waiting for you.

I tell him that decades ago, before the pipes began to burst (or maybe even before Shell came into the area – and of course, these days, it's hard to remember a time without Shell), Gio Creek, for example, was filled with tall, green mangroves. Birds flew and sang in the skies above the creek, and there were plenty of fish and crab and shrimp in the waters below. Now the mangroves are dead, and there is no birdsong at all. And, of course, there are no fish, no shrimp, and no crab to be caught. Instead, oil shoots up in the air, like a fountain of black water, and fishermen lament that rather than coming out of the water with fish, they are instead harvesting Shell oil on their bodies.

I tell him that the area has undergone what amounts to the American spill, only every year for 50 years. Oil pouring out every week, killing our land, our ecosystem. A resource that should make us rich, instead causing our people to suffer. 'It's the politics,' I say. 'But I'm no politician.' Instead, I tell him, I'd like to see if we can't at least construct efficient and effective mechanisms for cleaning up the damage that has been done. I tell him that Nigeria will benefit from sending out students to study and learn from the recent spill in the US, to learn methods of dealing with such a recurrent issue in our own Niger Delta.

He nods enthusiastically at me. He says what a shame it is that the Nigerian government can't get rid of all the corruption. He says how the government officials themselves are corrupt. 'Giving foreigners power over their own oil, pocketing for themselves the money that these foreigners pay for the oil.'

I look at him, in his fancy suit and rings. I wonder if he is not himself pocketing some of that oil money. But something good must be made out of such an unfortunate event. And of course I don't question the man in the suit about where the money for his rings and suit is coming from.

He fusses with the collar of his dress shirt and says, 'Sometimes when Nigerians go to America, they get their education and begin to think they are too cultured and sophisticated to come back home.' He pauses. Then, 'How do we know that you will?'

I think of Mama. 'I don't intend to get lost in America,' I say, more confidently than I feel. Because even as I say it, there is a part of me that is afraid that I will want to get lost in America. There is a part of me hoping that I will find that new life much less complicated, much more trouble-free than the one here. Still, I say it confidently, because saying it so might help me to keep Mama's fear from becoming a reality. Because I know that it might break Mama's heart if I were to break my promise to her. But mostly, I say it confidently because Gloria is on my mind, and if I am to be granted permission to go and be with her, then I must give the man the answer I know he wants: an emphatic vow that I will come back home.

He smiles and congratulates me as he hands me the green-coloured card. He takes my passport and tells me to come back in two days.

The sun is setting as I make my way down Walter Carrington Crescent. I look up. There are orange and purple streaks in the sky, but instead of thinking of those streaks, I find myself thinking of white snow, shiny metals reflecting the light of the sun. And I think of Gloria playing in the snow – like I imagine Americans do – lying in it, forming snow angels on the ground. I think of Papa suggesting that perhaps America would be the best place for me and my kind of love. I think of my work at the Federal Government Girls' College. In America, after I have finished my studies, I'll finally be able to find the kind of job I want. I think how I can't wait to get on the plane.

I cross over to the next street. It is narrow, but there are big houses on each side of it, the kinds with metal gates, and fancy gatemen with uniforms and berets, and small sheds like mini-houses near the gates, sheds in which the gatemen stay.

I imagine the insides of the houses: leather couches and stainless-steel appliances imported from America; flat-screen televisions hanging in even the bathrooms, American-style.

But the road just in front of these houses, just outside the nice gates, is filled with potholes, large ones. And in the spaces between the houses, that corridor that forms where one gate ends and the next begins, there are piles of car tyres, planks of deteriorating wood, layered one on top of another. Shattered glass, empty barrels of oil, candy wrappers, food wrappers, old batteries, crumpled paper, empty soda cans.

I stop at the entrance of one of these corridors. Two chickens squirm about, zigzagging through the filth, jutting their necks back and forth, sniffing and pecking at the garbage, diffident pecks, as if afraid of poison.

I tell myself to continue walking, to ignore all of this foulness, just like the owners of the big houses have managed to do. Maybe it's even their garbage that saturates these alleyways, as if the houses themselves are all that matter, and the roads leading to them inconsequential.

But for me, it is a reluctant kind of disregard that stems from a feeling of shame: shame that all that trash should even exist there, shame that empty barrels should be there, between the fancy houses, littering the roads after the oil they once contained has been made to do its own share of littering.

Several streets down, I find a hotel, not one of the fancy

ones, more just an inn. The room to which I am assigned smells musty and stale, and I can feel the dust on my skin.

I scratch my arms with the edges of the green-coloured card. I think of the possibilities, of the many ways in which I might profit from the card. I am still scratching and making plans for America when I drift into sleep.

The story should end there, but it doesn't. A person wishes for something so long that when it finally happens, she should be nothing but grateful. What sympathy can we have for someone who, after wanting something so badly for three long years, realizes, almost as soon as she's gotten it, that perhaps she's been wrong in wanting it all that time?

My second night at the inn, the night before I am to return to the embassy for my paperwork and passport, I think of Mama, her desire for a grandchild, and I think: Isn't it only natural that she'd want a grandchild? I think of the small children emerging from the waters of the Delta covered in black crude. Their playground destroyed by the oil war. And I think: Who's to say that this won't some day be the case even in America? It all starts small by small. And then it gets out of hand. And here I am running away from one disaster, only to find myself in a place that might soon also begin to fall apart.

There is a folk tale that Mama used to tell me when I was still in primary school. She'd tell it in the evenings when there was not much else to do, those evenings when NEPA had taken light away, and there was no telling when they'd return it. I'd sit on a bamboo mat, and she'd light a candle, allow its wax to drip on to the bottom of an empty can of evaporated milk, a naked can, without its paper coating. She'd stick the candle on the wax and allow it to harden in place. And then she'd begin the story.

In the dim candlelight, I'd observe the changes that took place on her face with each turn of her thought. Soft smiles turned to wrinkles in the forehead, then to distant, disturbed eyes, which then refocused, becoming clear again like a smoggy glass window whose condensation had been dispelled suddenly by a waft of air.

The folk tale was about an imprudent little boy, Nnamdi, whose wealthy father had been killed by a wicked old man who envied his wealth. Having killed Nnamdi's father, the wicked old man steals all of the family's possessions, so that Nnamdi and his mother are left with not even a small piece of land on which they can live. And so it is that they make their new home in the bush. There, they find a two-month-old goat kid, a stray, with a rope around its neck. Nnamdi's mother ties the goat to a tall *iroko* tree. Still, they continue to eat the green and purple leaves of the plants in the bushes for food, because Nnamdi's mother decides that they are to save the goat. It will grow, she says, and when it does she will sell it for so much money that they will be able to move out of the bush, or at least build a nice house for themselves there.

But one day, foolish Nnamdi leads the goat by its rope into the marketplace, and he sells it to a merchant who gives him a bagful of what the boy assumes is money. But when he returns to the bush, to his mother, Nnamdi opens the bag to find several handfuls of *udara* seeds, some still soggy, coated thinly with the flesh of the fruit.

His mother, angry at him not only for selling the goat, but also for doing so in exchange for mere seeds, furiously tosses them into the bush. The next morning, Nnamdi finds that a tall *udara* tree has grown, taller even than the *iroko*, so tall that its tips reach into the soft white clouds in the sky.

Nnamdi climbs the tree against his mother's wishes. In the uppermost branches, he finds a large, stately house-in-the-sky. He parts the branches, those thin stalks at the tip of the tree, and pushes through the rustling leaves. He arrives at an open window and enters the house that way. First he calls out to see if anyone is home. Once. Twice. There is no response.

There is a large table not far from the window. Nnamdi walks to the table. It is covered with a white cloth fringed with silk tassels. Nnamdi runs his fingers across the tassels. In the air, there is the scent of something savoury, a little curried, perhaps even a little sweet. Nnamdi follows the scent into the kitchen and there, on the stove, the lid of a large pot rattles as steam escapes from beneath. Nnamdi lifts the lid and breathes in the savoury scent. And then he sees it, through the doorway of the kitchen, in the parlour: a lustrous cage sitting atop a white cushion. The cushion is nearly as tall as he is. Inside the cage is a golden hen, perched on the top half of the hutch. All over the parlour floor, he sees coins, glistening like the cage. Glistening like the hen.

Nnamdi goes into the parlour. He climbs the cushion and takes out the hen. By one wall of the parlour, lined on the floor, are half a dozen small bags. Nnamdi peeks into them and sees that they are filled with more gold coins. He ties some of the bags around his waist, others he tucks to the hem of his shorts. He removes his shirt and makes a sack out of it. He slings the sack across his chest and carefully places the golden hen inside.

The wicked old man returns in time to see Nnamdi climbing down the *udara* tree. He pursues the boy, catching him by his shorts just as Nnamdi leaps from one branch to the next. The wicked old man gets hold of the bags of gold coins, but Nnamdi manages to wriggle away, escaping his grasp.

Nnamdi races off, gains ground, and finally lands safely in the bush. In fact, he gains so much ground that he is able to begin chopping down the *udara* tree before his pursuer has made it past the halfway point. Feeling the sudden swaying of the tree, the wicked old man scrambles back up to his home in the clouds before the tree falls. But he scrambles back without his golden hen, and with only the bags of coins.

The story always stopped there, and then I'd pester Mama to tell me more. 'What about the rest?' I'd ask. Did the hen continue to produce the gold coins? If so, for how much longer? And what did Nnamdi and his mother do with the coins? Did they build for themselves a huge mansion right there in the bush? Or, did Nnamdi give all the coins away like he did with the goat? Did he perhaps even give the hen itself away? Did they live happily ever after?

'There's no rest,' Mama would say. Or sometimes, 'The rest is up to you.'

That night, my final night in the inn, I sit on my bed and I recall every twist of that folk tale. I think of crude. And I think of gold. And I think of crude as gold. I imagine Nigeria – the land and its people – as the hens, the producers of the gold. And I think that even when all the gold is gone, there will always be the hens to produce more gold. But what happens when all the hens are gone, when they have either run away or have been destroyed? Then what?

The next day, I collect my paperwork from the embassy, and hours later, I head back to Port Harcourt to pack my bags. The bus bounces along the potholed roads, causing my head and heart to jolt this way and that. But I force my eyes shut as if shutting them tight will prevent me from changing my mind, as if shutting them tight will keep regret from making its way to me.

Born in Port Harcourt, Nigeria, **Chinelo Okparanta** earned her BSc from Pennsylvania State University, her MA from Rutgers University, and her MFA from the Iowa Writers' Workshop. Her collection of short stories entitled *Happiness, Like Water* has been published by *Granta* in the UK and is forthcoming from Houghton Mifflin Harcourt in the US. She has been nominated for a United States Artists Fellowship in Literature and long-listed for the Frank O'Connor International Short Story Award. This story first appeared in *Granta*, issue 118, London, 2012.

The Caine Prize
African Writers' Workshop Stories 2013

Watchdog Games

Harriet Anena

HIS HIGHNESS LICKED CHARMIE'S FEET. Warm breaths staggered out of his mouth. His eyes tiptoed upwards – resting on her lean shoulders. Then they roamed around her upper body, examined the breasts that sat alert on her chest as though waiting for a command.

There was a knock on the door.

His Highness snapped out of the daydream and hesitantly took his legs off the table. He shifted his attention to Modesta, who was standing before him. He didn't say a word but leaned back in the chair, and rocked himself, as though shaking off the remnant images of Charmie.

'I'll… I'll be going to Mabira for the weekly press conference by the Minister of Potholes…' Modesta began, when she had sat down.

'So?' His Highness asked, his eyes holding her hostage.

The words Modesta had prepared a few minutes back fled to the back of her head, her mouth drier than leaves in December. Her legs shook in quick confused movements. The chair was suddenly hot and her hands became moist. Modesta could see a dozen eyes sneaking through the glass enclosure of an office to mess up her conversation with His Highness.

'Are you going to speak?' His Highness asked.

'Yes… yes. I thought you could guide me on what questions to ask the minister…' Modesta said, rubbing her sweaty hands together.

'What storyline are you thinking of? And don't tell me

you are going to ask about pothole repairs, accident figures, road tenders... those songs send me to sleep.'

'I wanted to...'

'You *wanted* to? Then what happened? Know what... go sort yourself out first,' His Highness said, ending a discussion that never really took place.

As she walked back to her seat, Modesta wondered why a conversation with His Highness always felt like a trip up a rugged mountain. Her head was a battlefield of unanswered questions, self-doubt and frustration. Across the rectangular-shaped newsroom, the people sitting in cubicles dissolved to form giant balls of eyes that kept hitting her from all sides. She walked to the left corner of the lengthy room, leaving her seat in the opposite direction. It was the emerging argument between Senior Editor – Bizzy – and Senior Reporter – Loudmouth – that called Modesta's wandering mind to order.

The two were standing near the TV stand – right in front of Modesta's cubicle. She walked cautiously towards them as they paced up and down like lost strangers. Bizzy had received a call from the Presidential Press Publicist asking how he could allow a distorted story about the President into the paper. Bizzy had insisted the story was accurate but, speaking with Loudmouth now, he was not sure what to think.

Loudmouth would have none of the reprimand. Hands on his waist, his chest heaving with heavy breathing, he charged towards Bizzy. 'How do you cast doubt over my seven years of dedicated reporting for *The Watch*? I expected a pat on the back, not a spat in my work,' Loudmouth said.

Modesta loved these moments when reporter and editor strip themselves of rank and civility; they helped offset tension over deadlines and erase conversations with annoying new sources.

Excitement filled the newsroom, as reporters listened to the verbal fight. Others left their cubicles altogether – forming a pool of bodies in the hallway.

'You are such a two-mouthed snake... praising my story

last evening and sending me to hell today. How could you?'
Loudmouth said, his voice rising above those standing.
'Look, you must know there is no room for clumsy reporting
here. If you can't get your facts right, get another career,'
Bizzy said, trying to keep his voice low.

'Give me a break! If you cannot cross-check the facts in
my story, then why are you my supervisor?'

'Come on... you are not an intern, or are you?

'Oh! I should have known that only articles by interns
grace the cover page these days!' Loudmouth retorted, as
uniform laughter blew across the newsroom.

Soon everyone was back to business – but their attention
was discreetly glued to the receding argument. Some
sat behind their computers, with fingers roaming over
keyboards – typing non-existent stories. A few walked over
to the phone booth with notebooks and pens in hand to
call imaginary news sources. Others flipped through the
day's daily, rereading the potent headline – *President Sends
America to Hell*.

Loudmouth was sure he had got the story right. He was sure
the President had said he was mad at America for sticking its
nose in the wrong place; for accusing him of vote rigging.
The President had said he had no doubt that America was
seeking to topple his government – a government led by an
elected leader. 'How can they?' the President had wondered
during the one-on-one interview.

Bold article. Copy sales shot up from 20,000 to 30,000
while Facebook and Twitter were abuzz with debate about
the implication of the President's purported break-up with
his long-time ally. 'He will soon apologize and tell them he
was misquoted,' a reader commented online.

✳ ✳ ✳

Across the newsroom, His Highness sat on the table in his
office, phone held to his ears. Some callers accused *The*

Watch of being an economic vandal by publishing a story that puts the Head of State in a bad light, while others applauded the paper for the incisive article. He was sure he had the skin to absorb the insults, threats and demands for apology, until the President himself called.

'Yes... yes Mr President... I can hear you clearly,' His Highness said.

'Why are you sabotaging my economy? What exactly do you intend to achieve by publishing a cooked-up story about me? Do you want our development partners to abandon us at this critical time of economic stability?' His Highness was asked.

'...No Mr President, no sir...' His Highness said, uttering each word with care as though they were time bombs threatening to explode in his mouth.

'I want you to fire that reporter or I'll make life really difficult in that place,' the President said.

'There's no need for such drastic actions, Mr President...' 'Of course there is. Do you have any idea of what we went through to build this country? I'll not allow rumour-mongers like you to destroy what we worked so hard for...' 'I can assure you, Mr President; we shall get to the bottom of this. If our reporter is found to have misquoted you, we shall act accordingly...'

'No, you are the Editor-in-Chief, I want that reporter sacked... Fire him!' and the President cut the call. 'Damn it,' His Highness cursed.

His head felt like a container of dry leaves and sand. He had earlier told the President's Press Publicist that 'we stand by our story and we will not apologize', but now he wondered how to deal with the situation.

He slumped back into his seat and put his phone on silent mode. He stared at his computer blankly and ignored the alert for incoming emails. When he checked his mailbox 10 minutes later, there was an email from the CEO.

As usual, the CEO cautioned him against publishing stories that can stir up political dislike for *The Watch*. 'It's not good for business,' he had written, emphasizing how the paper needed adverts from government.

But what about our mandate to inform the public? What about journalism?

His Highness had asked himself these questions several times but wondered why he could not pose the same to the CEO.

***

It was a hectic day. As His Highness looked through his to-do list to see what item fell under the 'Friday – live life' category, his phone hummed.

'I need to see you soooon and eat you up.'

His face lit up. He glanced across the newsroom through the glass of his office compartment and smiled at Charmie. She was standing at her desk, looking at her phone but discreetly glancing towards his office.

'I'm all yours to devour lollipop. At yours in 30,' His Highness replied.

He picked up the books that were strewn across the table and stuffed them on the shelf. He yanked the tie off his neck, threw it on a coat rack. He unbuttoned two buttons, displaying a portion of hairy chest. 'Exactly how she likes it!' he said, smiling to himself.

Picking his phone, car keys and the day's paper, he stepped out of office to go have a life, a life that only Charmie knew how to sweeten. She was his main office project. Fresh from university and eager to live the soft life, Charmie had tip-toed into his life like unavoidable sin. And she is hard working too – see, in just three years, Charmie had risen from being a freelance writer to Senior Reporter.

'Charmie. Oh! Charmie, my sweet wicked angel... here I come,' His Highness said to himself.

As he approached the exit, he gestured to Bizzy. 'A minute... boss,' he said in a half-whisper. By the time His Highness entered his car, an agreement had been reached. 'Give him a two-week suspension. Send a copy of the suspension letter to the President's Office... you know how these things work. We'll keep his byline off the paper during that time... and not a word to any other soul. Are we good?'

'Absolutely! I'm on it,' Mr Bizzy said, sealing Loudmouth's fate.

***

Charmie cleared her desk, a deep smile lingering on her face. She clicked the 'shut down' button on her computer as she rummaged through her handbag for a mirror, perfume and lipstick. In a minute, her lips were a coat of thick pink, her body emitted the *Catch Me* scent and her hair fell down her neck in graceful orderliness.

'I'm outa here, *gal*. I've got better things to do,' she told Modesta, who was still typing a story.

'Play safe, darling. Uganda still needs you in one piece,' replied Modesta, giving Charmie a worried look.

'Hahaha... you know me, I'm the commander... I set the rules,' Charmie said, darting out of the newsroom like a bee-stung infant.

How does she manage this office affair and work? How? Modesta wondered, a reluctant admiration for Charmie upsetting her concentration.

She knew that such thoughts always ended without answers. All she was sure of was that Charmie would take a swipe at ladies who eyed her man. Yes, His Highness was her man. It doesn't matter that he walked down the aisle with another woman just two years ago.

'That even makes him sweeter,' Charmie once told Modesta.

Sweet indeed!

***

Monday was a good day.

The lead article, exposing the theft of $40,000 by officials in the President's Office, had sent heads rolling. Those named in the investigative story were making phone calls to His Highness and Bizzy seeking to have their side of the story published. But by 4.00pm, the President had ordered the arrest of five suspected officials.

The Watch was back in the government's good books. The paper couldn't afford another confrontation with the Head of State, at least until things returned to normal.

His Highness spent most of the morning chatting with reporters and giving instructions to junior editors. Excitement was evident in his gait – one hand in pocket and another rubbing his ripe tummy. His voice rose above the expansive room once in a while, as he answered one phone-call after another – 'Yes, yes, honourable... of course... absolutely... it is our job to support nation building... absolutely... it's our pleasure...'

The article had sent copy sales up – 32,000 copies, compared with the usual 20,000. Charmie was elated. It was her story. She walked up and down the newsroom, striking her heel on the floor in a triumphant kok kok kok which gave a little more shake to her bottom. Some male reporters stared with open mouths, others simply ignored her.

Then His Highness spoke. 'Colleagues... can I have a minute of your time, please?' he said, his deep, commanding voice rising above his short, plump figure. Everybody stopped what they were doing.

'It is a good day for us today, as journalists and as a business...' His Highness said, rubbing his tummy in gentle, circular movements as though he was calming down a kicking child.

'As I've always said, exceptional and mature journalism will be appreciated but those who drag our good name in the mud through careless reporting will be shown the exit. Therefore, to the team behind today's lead story, well done ...'

The address had lasted a few minutes, followed by mild applause, chit-chat and hushed arguments.

'Why didn't he just say "well done, my darling Charmie, for the wonderful article?"' whispered Hothead to Smokie.

'We are the dream team man, so we deserve the praise too,' said Smokie, 'and I'm sure Charmie will get a special thank you later... hmmm. Patience, man, patience,' said Smokie.

The duo – both sports reporters – collapsed in a fit of giggles as they *hi-fived* each other.

'Come on... you guys are just envious. I know Charmie turned down your bids, so chill already...' said Wittie, the satirist, but the giggling duo said in unison, 'Waaa, we've been there man, been there mob time.'

*** * ***

September had come to an end but figures were not adding up for Modesta. Her pay cheque read $100. She reprimanded herself over and over again as she gazed at the payslip on her desk. *How can just one month be so difficult? Five stories and just $100? What will I tell the landlord today? What will I tell mum when she calls about the medical bill... God! This pay-per-story business must stop. I must graduate from this hand-to-mouth life, otherwise...*

'I can hook you up with a loaded *big daddy*... he's a bit old, but you need the money to spoil yourself. We live only once my friend, just once... so stop being all holy already,' Modesta's roommate Getta had recently said.

But Modesta would have none of that madness. She had dreamt about *big daddy* twice and woken up panting like a lizard that had escaped from the mouth of a cobra. She could see him walking towards her in unsteady, slow movements like the clock was under his feet. When he cupped her face in his hands, the wrinkles on his face blurred all traces of handsomeness. Modesta was sure her late grandfather was standing before her. It was a bad dream and thinking about it now, when she needed more money, made her mouth dry and bitter.

Logging in to her email account, Modesta decided to ask His Highness for guidance on how to improve her writing. She clicked on the 'compose new mail' icon and typed. 'Dear His Highness...'

She clicked 'Select All. Delete.'

She started again. 'Hallo, I know I am a good writer, but I just can't get where I want. I really need your help.' She clicked the 'send' button and closed her eyes, hoping that when she opened them, a response would have popped up on her screen. It came the next day – 'Come to my office.'

Modesta didn't know whether to be happy or scared. That office drowned her in discomfort. After a while, she started a slow walk across the newsroom to His Highness's office.

'So... what can I do for you?' His Highness asked when she had finally sat down.

'I... I need your help... I want to be a good writer,' she said, avoiding eye contact with him.

'Do I scare you?' he asked, as though sensing her discomfort.

'Yeah... somehow,' she said.

His eyes lingered over her petite frame and penetrated her insides, then he said: 'I didn't know my face was scary.' 'Nooo, you are actually... ahm, your face is ok,' Modesta said, embarrassed by her response.

He didn't reply to her comment, rubbing in the pepper of discomfort even more.

'Ok, you will bring your articles to me every time you have one and we will see how you can make them better. Ok?' His Highness asked.

The fear that had welled inside her stomach a while ago, melted in haste and her legs supported her more firmly.

'Yes, yes, thank you... sir,' Modesta said. She left the office in a hurry like a thief fleeing from the hand of the law.

***

A month later, Modesta and Charmie were competing for space on the front page. A heavy discomfort sat between the two – the situation made worse by Modesta's frequent visits to His Highness's office.

That month, Modesta had scooped a story about MPs who sleep with sex workers at their offices in Parliament while others wallowed in loan debts from commercial banks. Thereafter, she worked on investigative pieces about drug abuse among government officials, land grabbing and corruption.

Charmie itched with fury when the award for Most Hardworking Employee of the Month was handed to Modesta.

'That should be me up there, I am the star,' Charmie said, making a silent promise to reclaim her territory. She put together ideas for investigative pieces and told herself, 'His Highness will definitely like these.'

Five minutes later, Charmie wanted to speak to His Highness but she saw Modesta laughing with him in his office. The two were engrossed in a conversation she sensed was not work-related. Her temperature rose and the AC seemed insufficient. Charmie stepped out to catch some fresh air but was back at her desk minutes later. She needed to get to the bottom of this change in the wind.

A confrontation with Modesta was in order. She found Modesta at the desk, typing a story.

Charmie: 'Hey...'

Modesta: 'Heeyy... how are you, my dear?'

Charmie: 'Spare me your niceties,' she said, speaking in a murmur as she bent over Modesta.

Modesta: 'Ok, what's eating you?'

Charmie: 'I have noticed that you're getting close to His

Highness... I hope you have not forgotten that he is *my man*.'

Modesta: '*Your* man... I can see you are making an early morning joke?'

Charmie: 'Do I sound like I'm joking to you? Just back off *my guy*.'

Modesta: 'Come on Charmie... I deserve better than His Highness.'

Charmie: 'Stop pretending, everyone knows you are *chasing* him.'

Modesta: 'Oh... really? Tell *everyone* I don't *run* after married men and I don't call them my man.'

Charmie: 'This is not over yet.'

Modesta: 'The nerve!'

Charmie let out a loud, lingering jeer, picked up her bag and walked out – leaving numerous curious eyes behind.

***

December was a slow month. Most offices were closed for the Christmas holidays and big stories were hard to come by. But, determined to reclaim her dominance in the paper, Charmie started investigating allegations that some soft drinks from Ninja Bottling Company had impurities.

Disguised as a casual worker one Monday morning, Charmie eluded security at the company to start her inquiries. She interviewed workers and officials, who divulged details not only of unhygienic packaging processes, but also of inhumane working conditions.

Three weeks into her investigation, however, Charmie could not find evidence of the impurities other than confessions from unnamed company workers. She decided to take a break. Charmie walked into a bar one Friday evening and settled for a soft drink as her mind replayed events of the past weeks – especially her disappearing romance with His Highness. She realized they had not communicated in days.

'Love, I need to see you, eat your sumptuous lips...' she texted.

Where?

Asylum Bar.

I'll be there in 30.

Waiting...

Her stomach twitched in sweet expectation but a feeling of anxiety lingered. She picked up the bottle of Sip'it, raised it to her mouth but realized it was not open. 'Damn!' she muttered before shouting 'service'.

As the waiter approached, Charmie noticed something strange in the drink.

'Yes, ma'am,' the waiter said, interrupting Charmie's scrutiny of the beverage.

'Ahm... bring me water instead. I'll drink this later...' Charmie said, buying more time to ascertain what was in the drink. She made use of her phone camera and captured all angles of the floating substance.

Charmie had heard stories about rat tails, fingernails and insects being found in Sip'it soda, but what floated in her drink was a round, reddish substance with a mucus-like form.

'Eww!' her mouth became sticky and something welled in her throat, threatening to come out.

She left the bill on the counter and tiptoed out of the bar, with the bottle tucked away in her bag. 'Evidence,' she told herself as she joined His Highness in the parking lot.

He was waiting for her under the mango tree. The thick tree cover, and the darkness at 8.00pm, made it difficult for Charmie to sight his car. He saw her first and flashed the car lights. When she had finally sat in the co-driver's seat, His Highness drew the windscreen up and turned off the engine.

He cupped her face in his hands, and traced the outline of her face in the darkness. He rested his forehead on hers. Then he breathed deeply and caressed the back of her neck. He dipped his tongue inside her mouth and gently withdrew when her breathing quickened. He grabbed her lower lip with his and kissed it.

'Are you doing her too,' Charmie asked, when the kissing session had ended. 'Who?' His Highness asked.

'Modesta,' Charmie said.

He laughed, a deep long laugh that made her uncomfortable.

'Are you watching my back?' he asked, a smile still visible on his face, even in the darkness.

'I'm not,' she said, before cancelling the trip to Asylum Bar.

The half-hour drive to her house was quiet. But when he was putting his trousers back on two hours later, he whispered: 'You'll always be my special lollipop.' He left Charmie clinging onto the pillow as though it too was planning to walk out of the door.

*** *** ***

Sunday. 4.00pm.

Her keyboard went tap tap as she typed the story. Charmie knew the article would turn heads more than the corruption scandal piece. She visualized herself being patted on the back for 'exceptional journalism'. She could see His Highness praising her before everyone during the staff meeting. She grinned and laughed aloud at the thought, drawing the attention of Loudmouth, who was watching TV nearby.

'Hey, share the joy please…' he said.

'You'll find out soon, but I can assure you, this is going to be an explosion.'

An hour later, she had completed typing the story. Before she could send it to the editors, her phone rang.

New number. She picked up the call – hesitantly.

'Hello, am I speaking to Charmie of *The Watch* newspaper?'

'Yes, sir, speaking.'

'Good. This is the MD of Ninja Bottling Company. We are aware of your investigation into Sip'it Soda and we have an offer.'

'I have actually been trying to reach you for a comment. What can you say about the allegations of impurities in your soft drinks?'

'You see, Charmie, we don't want that story to run. It will destroy our business.'

'Mr MD, you know I will use that quote in the story, don't you?'

'Charmie, my daughter, let's talk about the offer…'

'I don't care about your offer. Do you have any idea how many lives you are putting at risk by selling poisonous drinks?'

'Yes, yes… I understand your concern and we are rectifying the problem.'

'Good. As you rectify the problem, I'll write the story and send a warning to consumers.'

'Ok, listen. $10,000 and kill the story…'

He cannot be serious, Charmie thought, doing a quick foreign exchange – 26 million Ugandan shillings. Wow! She could even start a business, buy a new car or buy land and leave this unrewarding profession.

'Charmie, are you taking the offer?' the MD asked.

'No. I will not trade people's health for money,' Charmie finally said.

'Ok, at least I made an offer,' the MD said before hanging up.

She reread her story and included the conversation with the MD for detail before sending it.

That night, Charmie lay on her bed and played with possible headlines that would grace her story.

Poisonous drink on the market

You are drinking sewage

Ninja selling you diseases

By the time she slept, about 10 headlines had played through her mind.

✳✳✳

His Highness read through the story twice. 'Oh Charmie, you are a thorough writer... such a darling,' he said, as he scrolled the pages up and down the screen of his computer. He picked his phone and texted her. 'Great story. I'm so proud of you.'

As he leaned back in his chair, his phone rang. 'It must be Charmie,' he thought.

It was the CEO. 'The story about Sip'it soda cannot be published. Ninja is our biggest advertiser and one mistake is not reason enough to destroy them,' the CEO said.

'We are journalists, boss, not just a business. I'm sorry but the story will be published,' said His Highness.

'We shall not discuss this further,' the CEO said and cut the conversation.

What do these VIPs take us for? We went to journalism school, pledging to be the watchdog, and they are now telling us about sales and profits? Nooooo... this is getting nasty.

His Highness reached home at 11.00pm and stayed up most of the night asking himself questions he could not find answers to. It was only when his wife coughed that His Highness realized he had entered bed without noticing her presence. He looked at her face and remembered how serene she had looked on their wedding day two years ago. Excitement had made her face glitter with undefiled innocence as she had said 'I do. I do'.

Watching her now, His Highness saw a face clothed in tired loneliness. He wanted to touch her ripe tummy and whisper to the twins that daddy couldn't wait to have them out already. He withdrew his hands before touching her. He didn't want to wake her up but he also didn't want to push aside the intruding memory of Charmie strapping her legs around his waist last night. When His Highness finally closed his eyes to sleep, the women he had conquered queued in his mind.

1   Nancy wanted a promotion. He told her all she needed was hard work and patience. But when Nancy asked him for a dance on that office day out, she dislodged

his senses as she rubbed her breasts on his chest. Her warm words dried his words of resistance. The dance ended on Nancy's bed.

2   Hella wanted to improve her writing. He helped. Her story quality improved and her byline became frequent. Overcome with gratitude, she knocked on his hotel room in the dead of the night during a retreat in Kabale. It was really chilly and saying no almost felt sinful.

3   Lisa – a half-baked journalist from those backstreet universities. She had a body that would make a man's head spin. He tried to avoid her. She asked for a lift home one rainy evening. When they reached her house, she kissed him and all details were completed in his car.

4   Viola – a hard-working and needy single mother. She refused to believe in her abilities like an atheist ignores the existence of God. He tried to lift up her spirits and the resulting esteem spoilt her. She dared him one day and swept his shaky legs off the ground onto her bed.

5   Charmie – the smart and beautiful one who runs around his mind like an excited infant. She sneaked under his skin and became a spell. He doesn't want to think of life without her.

✳✳✳

When Charmie arrived at work on Monday, the lead headline read: *Government introduces free university education.*

She struggled to push aside the disappointment creeping into her head and hoped the article would still be published on Tuesday. The conversation with the MD of Ninja Bottling Company kept replaying in her mind and she wondered whether he had offered a *brown envelope* for the story to be 'killed'.

He wouldn't dare. And His Highness wouldn't accept that anyway. He had personally told her the story was great, Charmie assured herself.

However, when the article didn't appear in the paper the next day, Charmie walked to His Highness's office and asked why her story had not been published or if it would run at all. He told her the Advertising Unit was concerned about the implication of the story on advert revenue. He, however, assured Charmie that he had made it clear that editorial decisions would not be interfered with.

'So, relax my dear. Your story will live to see the light of day,' His Highness said, giving her a reassuring smile like he usually did whenever he wanted to tell her 'you'll always be my special lollipop'.

Her head felt lighter as she stepped out of His Highness's office. She badly needed the assurance, especially since the past weeks had not been smooth for them. His Highness had ignored three of her calls, failed to reply to her texts and had not given her the weekly $40 for shopping. The thought of dumping him had occurred to her, but she threw the idea out of her mind now.

***

Wednesday. 7.40am.

Charmie walked into the newsroom 10 minutes into the morning meeting. All eyes turned in her direction as she stood by the entrance. She glanced briefly to her left, and saw His Highness in his office, reading what appeared to be the day's paper. All reporters stood next to their cubicles, noting down assignments being read out by Bizzy. She was assigned to cover homicides in the Kampala slums.

The meeting was dismissed 20 minutes later and everyone made brief preparations before running out to meet sources. Charmie pressed the start-button on her computer but the machine took its time to start. She slapped the CPU twice as her impatience grew.

She had not even looked at the day's paper but decided to check her email first. When she opened the inbox, the first email was from His Highness.

'I am sorry. That story will not run.'

Harriet Anena s a writer and editor. Born in Gulu, Uganda, she is a graduate of Makerere University and works in Kampala. Her debut poem, 'The Plight of the Acholi Child', won the writing competition of the Acholi Religious Leaders Peace Initiative in 2001. She is a mentee of the African Writers Trust and her poem 'I Died Alive' appeared in their e-anthology *Suubi* in March 2013. She is working on her short story 'The Dogs are Hungry' and a compendium of poems.

Red

Lillian A Aujo

I SEE RED. BLOOD EVERYWHERE. So many faces. Many bloodied faces looking down at me. I gasp for air but gulp blood. I swim. But my legs are heavy. If I could hold my head above the surface for just a second I would breathe. I try to rise. But the hands of the bloodied faces hold me down. Nails dig into my back, my arms. There's the pain that almost registers but dies in the shroud of sharper pain from taking in no air. The thought that was about to materialize in my head starts to go. I try to hold it but the hands stop me. I try to see it but the red high blinds me. I close my eyes and then there is black. I open them and it is still black. I close my eyes.

***

I am back at school. It is 2006 and the presidential election is all the rage. I am 17 and think about girls a lot. I wish we had girls in our school but Mom and Dad think a boys' boarding school is better than a mixed school since there are fewer distractions. But I think about girls anyway. Everyone else is in History class and, as I walk out, I curse why I have to study about dead Europeans that have long since fossilized. I walk past the flank of the Arts classrooms and half run down the stairs. Through the glass windows some equally distracted students look at me passing. They imagine I am going to the toilet and that's the direction I take. I reach the ground floor but walk past the door labelled 'washrooms'.

Instead I walk to the end of that block and cross the corridor that separates the classrooms from the dormitories. There is a six-foot wire fence that looks intact. But if you're looking for it, you see the hole where the rhombus-shaped wires have been cut. I move aside the dry and fresh twigs to pass through. When I am on the other side I replace them as carefully and as noiselessly as I can. Teacher patrol is rampant so this is a precaution we all take. No one knows who made the gate or when, but urban legend round the school is that Code is the one that possessed the courage to do it. He is a senior who has a reputation for getting things done. He is the 'go to guy' who gets you *Marlboro* or *Dunhill* when your stash runs out in the middle of the term.

After two blocks I reach the outside bathrooms. I throw a swift glance over my shoulder and take in a deep breath when there is no one. I rub my hands together in sweet anticipation but stop when I see Code leaning against the browning tile wall at the far end of the urinal. His right hand is held behind him and the left hand rests nonchalantly on his raised knee. My feet and mind have different ideas on what to do. Code notices my indecision and motions for me to come in. He holds out his right hand and there is a cigarette which he hands over. I take it without hesitation. Sharing joints is not unusual; it's a sign of brotherhood. I am flattered that Code is extending warmth to me.

I take a whiff and choke. It is not a cigarette I am used to. Code chuckles and scratches his mop of an afro and says, 'Go on, it's the good stuff, man!'

I've heard of it before but not dared to try. But this was Code asking, a guy who'd earned the nickname by knowing where and how to get things without being caught by the net of school rules. So I take a drag again, and another. And before long, I am seeing red for the first time.

***

Out of the blackness comes an image. It is a petite brown girl with long red-stained hair. She is as naked as Eve must have been in Eden. Her coloured hair falls down her chest and covers two small, firm, round breasts. She holds both hands down her middle to cover her modesty. A curly black hair escapes. I laugh and point at it. Why didn't she just dye everything red? I hear her wind-chime laugh and I stare. But why didn't she just make it red, why didn't she? If she had done that, Code would not have noticed. And I would not be seeing red. Her brown skin is the colour of bruises. I try to rub it off but the hands hold me back. I want to make her clean again but the hands with their nails digging into my skin pull me back. Into the darkness I go. I open my eyes but the black emptiness is back.

***

The Presidential election is still the rage. I wouldn't really care about it except it will be the first time I have voted. I just turned 18 and registered for my voter's card. Mom and the old man will bring it when they come over next weekend to visit me. Being Code's friend has made school fun. When class gets boring, we go through the gate and share joints. I still see red but it's not as good as the first time. He tells me there are better things to come. I have a good idea what but I don't ask since this is Code and he cannot be pushed. On Saturday night I go to Code's room and we watch movies on a laptop. I am the only one from Senior Five and the other four boys and Code are all in Senior Six. I feel important and when the movie ends, joints go round again. That night I ask when the better things will come, and all the others exchange smiles.

'It needs more money,' Code finally says.

'How much more?'

'Fifty thousand shillings, onwards.' I sigh. I haven't got that much money. I hope they will come to see me tomorrow.

The next day is Sunday. All the boys have taken showers and are wearing clean and ironed uniforms. By 11 they are all ready, hanging about the classroom blocks in clusters of six or ten. I hang back in the shadows with Code and we watch the cars coming into the school gate. I tell myself that this time they will show up in person. Soon I see the car with red number plates. I move closer and see it is his office car. When I get to the parking lot I find only Moses, one of the drivers. 'Your mother is out of the country for three months. Business. And your father is upcountry. Your things are here. And your money.' He opens the boot and I remove a carton of milk and one of juice and some other groceries. He hands me 300,000 Ugandan shillings.

'And the voter's card?'

'Oh! Your father said it wasn't ready when he went to get it.'

'Thanks, Moses. Can I use your phone to call him?' I want to ask him about my voter's card since I will still be at school by the time of the elections. I will also thank him for the money and stuff since he appreciates being thanked. His phone rings for 30 seconds then an automated voice asks if I can call back later. I hang up and hand the phone back to Moses. He says goodbye and tells me to study hard, because my father is giving me everything I need. I touch the notes of paper in my pocket. Everything I need. He gives me everything I need. I start looking around for Code. I try calling him the next day and still the same thing happens. I call my mother but of course she cannot be reached. I sulk because I really wanted to vote. Since I was born I have only seen one president and I think the country deserves a change. Those fossilized Europeans have taught me a thing or two about the franchise and voting. At a Sunday lunch last holiday, the old man asked me if I would vote and why.

'I have to vote, Dad! The Change Party Movement has a better manifesto. Besides, this government isn't doing enough.'

'It's employing your father, isn't it?'

'Yeah. But what about the rest that are not employed?
And you would still have a job, wouldn't you?'

'Of course he would.' Mom spoke for the first time. 'Only
the President leaves office.'

'That's what I thought. The ministers don't have to step
down.'

'You children think everything is easy.'

'I don't think it is easy, I just think it makes sense. Why do
we vote if incumbent African presidents never leave power?'

'Big words, my boy! Big words, Levi.'

We finish the rest of the meal in silence.

I give up on my voter's card two days before the election.
When the day comes, everyone who is above 18 casts their
ballot. That night we do some joints. The smoke swirls in my
eyes and the tinges of red dance in my view. I am happy and
I smile but it's over too soon. I am seeing my father and his
posh government cars. I am hearing the busy tones at the
end of his line. And I hate that my mother has a business trip
now. It is then I know the time is right. I fish some notes from
my wallet and hand them to Code. It is time for better things,
and he does not argue.

Two weeks later the results are announced. The incumbent
won and has another term in office. The next year is a
blinding red year. Code is done with secondary school but I
still have a year to go. I suppose I should miss him but I don't.
I have better things and better friends. I am Levi, Code's man,
I know how and when to get things done without getting
caught. I have better things that come with white fine dust,
silver spoons, bunsen burners and candles, and needles.
2006 was a year of sparkling white dust, sparkling silver,
bright yellow flames, better reds and better highs, the
beginnings of white blindness.

***

I am leaving the empty memories. I am seeing white. Like a page with invisible words. When I try to read them I fail and panic fills me. The hands with blood slap me. Their palms are sharp and they burn my cheeks. I want them to go on, so that I can feel the pain, leave the white, and see the words on the blank paper. The pain will let me see the words. But it fades and I am thrown up the white sky and into the deep blackness. An empty deep blackness.

✳ ✳ ✳

It is 2007. I am at home and my mother is there. She has gone for four business trips since the time I was in school. She comes in to tell me she will be gone to the UK for two months and asks what she should bring me. I shrug my shoulders because she has already bought me a Mac, an iPhone, iPad, the Xbox 20, and there is really nothing else that will impress me more than white powder.

'Help around the house, don't just sit here with all your gadgets.'

'Yeah, Mom.'

That day I watch the lunchtime bulletin. There is an exposé on 'How votes were rigged in the 2006 Presidential Election.' The Anchor says: 'Reports coming in show that some ministers and Members of Parliament erroneously obtained voters' cards and gave them to mercenaries who voted multiple times in the Presidential Election. According to the Opposition, this flaw casts a big shadow on the transparency and accuracy of the whole voting exercise. Implicated in these dealings are the honourable Boniface Opolot...'

I do not hear what the news anchor says next. I only hear him repeat my father's name countless times. I hurry to his bedroom and reach above the door for the spare key they keep there. I head straight for the safe. Mom told me all the important documents are in it. The combination is my birthday and as it clicks I see it hasn't changed since she told me about it. I sweep out everything with my hands. Small notebooks, papers, a stuffed A4 khaki envelope, and two passports spill onto the white rug. The papers are receipts for huge amounts of money that don't make sense to me. I tear the envelope open. There are many laminated cards in rubber-band bound bundles. My heart pounds as I count 15 more bundles of voters' cards. There's no mistaking them; it says so in the bold black print and has the national flag emblazoned on them. I find my card in the second bundle, and red rage rises to my eyes. I sit on the soft white rug for a minute or so. Then one by one, I begin putting everything back in the safe. My hands linger on the passports and I wonder why there isn't one instead of two. I open them. They're my mother's and father's. A white clarity blinds me; she has not gone to the UK. Red rage rises up in me, and lonely coldness envelops me.

***

The darkness recedes and I float in a white space. I open my eyes and see the rude colours of my world through half-open eyes. There's so much talking and shouting.

'Did you call the ambulance?'

'What should we do with him?'

'You think he'll make it?'

'God help us all. If he is dead...'

There's blood on my hands and down the front of my chequered shirt. There's a silver blade glinting white where it isn't covered in blood. Hands hold me down on the sofa and I can't move. I try to speak but blood flows from my mouth and my tongue and lips weigh a tonne. The petite girl with hair the colour of strawberries is covered in a yellow T-shirt that goes down to her knees. Her rouge mascara has run and stained her light-skinned cheeks. She looks horrified and keeps saying, 'I was naked! So naked. All these people saw me. Oh God, no! Oh no!'

I want to tell her she looked nice. Like a genie. I want to ask her where she left her pot. I want to look for Code so we can go home. Our landlady hates it when we come in late. She refuses to make a copy of the gate keys yet she locks the gate at 10 o'clock. When we left home she locked the gate behind us, and told her we'd be back on Sunday morning. Then I see a silver blade covered in blood. I know something bad has happened but I don't know what. I close my eyes and the black is back.

* * *

I replace the passports and close the safe. I stumble to my room and collapse on my bed. I call my mother. Her phone rings but does not pick up. I call her again and she picks up this time.

'Are you at the airport?'

'Just checking in now.'

'Are you going to UK?'

'Levi, I told you that a few hours ago.'

'You forgot your passport.'

'What... Are you sure?... Where did you find it?'

'The safe, Mom. The safe... So are you coming to pick it up?'

'Levi... Oh God!'

'What, Mom? Are you coming back?'

'Have you called your father?'

'No.'

'Ok. Don't call him. I am coming over soon.'

I put the phone down and wonder what kind of mother says she's coming over to her home.

Twenty minutes later, a taxi drives into the compound. She pays the driver after he has put her suitcase on the ground. She leaves it there on the gravel and hurries into the house. I remain standing by the window, waiting for her story. When she walks in, I still don't move.

'Sit,' she says. I look at her from head to toe. Her skin is flawless. Her grey slacks and yellow top are fitting but they are not too tight. She wears small gold loops in her ears and a gold chain with a pink pendant. Her dark hair is held away from her face. Her nails are a perfect red. Her ring is missing, but she still looks every part the Honourable Minister's wife. This is the best image of my mother. I relish it before I sit because I know that after that she might not look the same. Then I sit. She sits at the other end of the bed. She holds her hands then releases them.

'I wanted to tell you. But your father wouldn't let me.' Her eyes pool and she blinks rapidly.

'Tell me what, Mom?'

'I haven't told anyone...' She rubs her neck, and I feel the strain in my shoulders.

'You're still not saying anything, Mom.'

'We're not together any more.'

I bow my head and my hands hang between my knees. 'Why?'

'Your father's not the same any more.'

'What do you mean, Mom?' I look at her, I don't want to believe it.

'Remember Mary? That's why she had to go.'

'I remember that house girl, the one who always burnt the food. I thought you'd fired her 'cause she couldn't cook.'

'I was so angry. In addition to the other women, he had to add a house girl.' She stands up and paces the length of my small room. 'I can't believe him.'

'You had finals, I thought it would be too much for you, but I was planning to tell you soon.'

'So where have you been staying?'

'A small house in Kisasi – he agreed to pay rent.'

'So that's it? You just left home? What do I do now?'

She comes back and sits with me, closer this time. Her small, soft hands hold my bigger ones. 'I didn't abandon you, Levi. We tried counselling, but since last month, he pulled out.

So I think now it's over. Just remember it wasn't your fault.'

'And what about me?'

'This is your home.' Her grip tightens and so does my heart. 'Besides, if you come with me, he will think I turned you against him.'

'I am 18, Mom – I can make up my own mind.'

'I know you can, but just stay here for a while, at least until you leave university.'

I put my hands over my head as I think about coming back to that house and sitting at the dining table with him and my mother's empty seat. I think about his name coming from the news anchor's mouth. 'So did you see the news about him?'

'Yes, I heard it over the radio, I knew it would be just a matter of time before...'

'So you knew about it?' I drop her hands, walk to the door and turn the knob. I stop when I feel her hand on my arm. 'He's my husband. I don't expect you to understand.'

I don't understand. I don't want to feel the rage. 'So it's true? My father is a lying crook?'

'What do you want me to tell you? You saw what was in the safe, Levi. What can I say? He's your father. The best we can do is pray for him.'

Then it starts to happen. I feel like punching something. She shakes her head and says, 'You need to pray, Levi, it's the only thing that will help. Drinking won't help.'

Drinking! That's funny. Is that what she thinks I am on? Alcohol? Shit, man! That stuff's weak. I tell Code later that day when I am hanging out at his university hostel.

The next day, I change numbers and sneak into His Honourable's house for my clothes. The next few months I sleep on Code's one-room hostel floor. My mother sends me money. I talk to her when I am feeling low and not seeing red. I do not hear from His Honourable.

✳✳✳

The white is back and it's blindingly clear. The silver

blade is there, still covered in blood. I hear sirens and see white and red lights. I move but realize my hands are tied with something thick behind my back. I struggle but a guy wearing a shirt with green stripes holds me down. 'Where's Code? Is that the police? Why am I tied up?'

'You stabbed him, man. You killed him.' And I fall into the blackness.

✳ ✳ ✳

Now I remember everything. It comes floating to me in white clarity. It is 2013. I have no job since I dropped out of university. Code has a doctorate everyone calls 'Bachelor of Being Around'; he has been pursuing a three-year degree for over four years. Short contracts and odd jobs give him some money. My mother still takes care of my bills. We get by and share a two-roomed house.

I am with Code and we arrive at the party. I am holding the camera bag where I keep my stash. Code nods towards a long table with salads, roasted meat, chicken, sausages and roasted bananas. 'How can people eat all that?'

'I know, right! I'll never understand how people can love food so much.'

'You think they'll ever understand why you love needles and cocaine?'

'Code, don't go all philosophical on me.'

'Just saying, Levi, you're not that kid any more. Shit! You even scare me sometimes. Increasing doses...'

'Says the guy who handed me the first joint... Anyway, I see this will be some party. Where's the special cake?'

'I am sure it will come. Stuart's cakes have so much snow it gets freezing. Can't wait.'

'Says the guy who's been giving me a lecture about drugs.' At that moment Stuart breezes in with a big brown cake. A light-skinned girl who is almost half his height follows him with a cake knife and disposable white plates. She has red hair that flows down her back. The guy at the music table in one corner plays cymbals and drums. There are claps and shouts of, 'Special cake!', 'I want the biggest piece!' The petite girl and other girls pass it around.

I eat one piece and two more chunks. Soon I begin to see red. I can't stop laughing because all the guys and chicks are standing on their heads. Even the ones gyrating to D'Bange's 'Oliver Twist' are doing it on their heads. Their necks will break, I tell Code. He gives me the calm smile for when he is getting high and seeing red. Then a light-skinned body crosses my vision. Shit. It's the light-skinned girl. She is doing a striptease and is down to panties. When she takes them off it looks like they come down her neck. It is even funnier because she is standing on her head. I nudge Code, but he gets up from the sofa saying: 'No naked girls tonight. If I am not taking her home, I don't want to see her – going out for some air.' And that is the last time I see Code.

The brightness begins to fade. The people round me stand on their feet again. I begin to see His Honourable, and the pain digs deep. I want to stop it so I leave the living room. I go to the bathroom and remove the things from the camera bag. I light a candle and put white powder on the spoon. I melt it and fill the syringe. The prick is sharp but it is a sweet pain. I see the white and it's so bright that my father disappears. I float. In a beautiful high of red tinges that make everything brighter.

I walk outside to look for Code. He is seated by the fire where the meat was roasted. I see his needles and spoon so I know he is as happy as I am now. But when he turns I see His Honourable again. I am filled with a red rage and a sparkling white clarity. I know what I must do, the one thing I have been putting off all these years. I reach for the silver knife beside the tray of meat and stab him, again, and again, until all I see is red.

✱✱✱

The sirens are in my ears. Red is in my eyes. White light hurts my eyes. I cannot shield them because my hands are tied. Two police half drag and half carry me towards a police car. There's a mound in the grass covered by a thick blanket.

I sit in the car and see the other faces looking at me with horror. I smile. I smile because their faces disappear. I smile because I see my mother. Her skin is flawless. Her grey slacks and yellow top are fitting but they are not too tight. She wears small gold loops in her ears and a gold chain with a pink pendant. Her dark hair is held away from her face. Her red nails are perfect. Her ring is missing and she's my mother. Her ring is missing and she's my mother....

Lillian Akampuriira Aujo is a member of the Ugandan organization FEMRITE, and her poems and stories have appeared in their anthologies as well as in online magazines such as *The Revelator* and *Suubi*. Her poem 'Soft Tonight', which won first prize in the 2009 Beverley Nambozo Poetry Awards, appears in *Summoning the Rains*, and her short story 'My Big Toe' in *Talking Tales*.

Howl

Rotimi Babatunde

For Jack

Mo rí èmọ̀ l'Ágége
Ajá wẹ̀wù, ó rósọ
Ó gbé báági sápá kan
Ó wé gèlè sórí o
Gbamú gbamù, jigí jigì
– Yoruba children's song*

DR JACK EXITED THE WOMB howling as loudly as newborn humans bawl, unlike the other whelps littered with him that held their peace like the regular dogs they were, but Akeshe would not get to know about the circumstances of the dog's birth until after his son had fallen in love with the puppy that had a baby's eyes. There was no one who could swear they had been present when Jack was born, not even the mechanic whose bitch mothered the dog or his wife, but a lack of evidence has never undermined humankind's faith in the truth of outlandish stories. Besides, those who heard how the puppy came into the world had no reason to doubt the report because Jack was not the first animal in the neighbourhood to display traits normal only in humans.

Lady Thatcher, the late nanny goat of the postmaster who lived near the railway crossing, had been greatly respected

*I saw a grotesquerie in Agege/ A dog that wore a shirt and tied a wrapper/ The dog carried a handbag in one arm/ And crowned it all with a headdress/ Gbamu gbamu, jigi jigi

in the neighbourhood for the aristocratic airs of an English peer which she exhibited throughout her lifetime, especially when chewing grass. The goat liked wandering around town but always returned to her owner's house at the right time for her meals, three times a day with the iron certainty of death. Even that fat goat Lady Thatcher keeps to time, parents often said, using the ruminant's punctuality to admonish their children whenever the youngsters were running late for school, and many a newcomer to town had gawped on sighting Lady Thatcher raising a forehoof to knock on the postmaster's front door when her food tray was not waiting for her on the threshold.

Then there was Boogie, the depressive parrot that lived in the now-empty cage dangling from the ceiling of Palm Bar. The bird never spoke the only words he knew – Life sucks! – except if offered a thimbleful of quality liquor. Once in a while, on a good night when Boogie had taken one drink too many, the bar's patrons would look up to see the parrot nodding to whatever music was playing and sometimes, if it was a highlife number blaring out of the loudspeakers, dancing to the beats with the wild abandon of a party animal.

A drunken patron forgot to lock the parrot's cage, and the bird vanished a few months before Abacus the Great died. That monkey's grizzled facial hair, along with the tattered tweed waistcoat, black bowtie and horn-rimmed frames without lenses that he favoured, endowed him with a professorial look. More often than not, when the monkey climbed up trees, it was not to forage for fruits but to search for a suitable twig to use as a stylus. Abacus the Great spent his twilight years scratching indecipherable marks by the roadside with scholarly seriousness – equation-like squiggles that ran, as sidewalks do, from one street to the next. The monkey's owner, a half-blind retired schoolteacher who had a habit of bumping into walls and falling into ditches, claimed that those interminable doodles were mathematical calculations of the highest order.

The most remarkable case, though, was the one of the drake that fell in love with the baker's daughter. The bird had the most massive wings anyone had ever seen on a duck, and he often accompanied the baker's daughter as she went around town delivering loaves to her father's customers. One afternoon, the girl was walking past the bus stop with a tray balanced on her head and her duck in tandem when a bus conductor tried to pinch her wiggling buttocks. With all the power he could muster, the drake flew at the conductor's face, stunning him with a homicidal tornado of wings that left the man prostrate on the ground.

Onlookers at the bus stop began laughing at the conductor. The man, touching his broken nose, hissed. A match made in heaven, he said. Who else, if not a waddling duck, deserves a bucktoothed girl so dull her family had to withdraw her from school to spare themselves the embarrassment of her poor grades? The conductor coughed, spitting out blood, and the man's distress provoked the bystanders into making even greater mockery of him.

The girl's romantic walks with the drake ended soon after that incident. A fuel tanker overturned and the petrol it was ferrying spilled out, turning the roadside gutter into an instant fuel dump. Such a windfall does not come every day so the baker's daughter joined the crowd using containers of all kind to spirit away the fuel. In that frenzy of scraping and scooping, a metal bucket clattered on the gutter's edge, causing a small spark, but the girl was lucky because, unlike most of the other charred corpses, her body could be identified with the aid of her buckteeth.

In the days after, the drake kept vigil in front of the morgue to which the girl had been taken, the bird's anguished quacking more despairing than a hangman's noose, and all through the girl's interment he perched on a branch of the flame tree casting a shade on the dead in the cemetery, his head hung low. A month later, when most people had forgotten that the baker's daughter had ever existed, the drake was found floating in the pond behind the cemetery, dead.

Nothing could be more ridiculous, the neighbourhood's residents said. Just consider it. A duck drowning in a pond on a clear day. Not even the craziest writer could have imagined it.

Compared with the memorable transition of the star-crossed drake, a puppy with a baby's eyes that came howling into the world was nothing notable, so people merely wished the puppy well and hoped he wouldn't grow up stupid enough to kill himself on account of a girl blessed with a crowbar's ominous dentition and wits so dim that, even in heaven, the angels would never be able to teach her how to spell her name right.

***

The blood flowers in front of Akeshe's residence had just been planted when the mechanic with whom Jack had been living brought him to the place. Mama Junior, Akeshe's wife, said blood flowers reminded her of graveyards and carnage. She wanted them uprooted because she had lost two children already and didn't want anything connected with funerals in her vicinity. But her husband said that a blood flower was just a flower, not an omen of death.

Mama Junior told the mechanic that her husband was not at home, but the man, looking worried, insisted on waiting. Junior, Akeshe's son, was in the living room. His face was transfigured when he saw the puppy. The boy patted the puppy on the head and brought out milk from the fridge for him. Jack slurped up the milk, along with the biscuits Junior had soaked in it. Afterwards, both of them began frolicking around the living room. They rolled on the carpet, the rising decibels of the boy's laughter and the puppy's woofs reflecting their escalating excitement, and, like old friends, Jack and Junior were playing hide-and-seek behind the settees when the boy's mother entered with a bottle of beer for the mechanic. Mama Junior smiled because she could not remember ever seeing her son so happy.

The mechanic's appetite for booze was legendary in the bars he frequented. That afternoon, though, he left untouched the bottle of beer Mama Junior had opened for him. The other puppies in his house had found their mother's teats delicious enough, but Jack preferred the infant mixture the mechanic's daughter ate. His wife complained but the mechanic defended the dog because, in recent weeks, his clientele had doubled and the most miserly of his customers had stopped haggling hard with him over prices. And it was on the day of the dog's birth that he was given the lucrative offer to service the motorcycles of a food delivery company. That change of fortune could only have been caused by the dog with a baby's eyes. Don't speak ill of that puppy, the mechanic had told his wife. Without the good luck he brought us, I wouldn't have been able to afford to buy you that new necklace you have around your neck.

The woman let the matter be. A week later, the heat in their bedroom was sweltering so she took a mat out to their veranda. The gentle breeze blowing there was refreshing and she was drifting into sleep when she felt something clambering over her bosom. She screamed on seeing it was Jack.

What happened, the mechanic asked, when his wife stormed into the bedroom.

The woman began weeping, bemoaning her fall in life to a station so low that even a dog now wants to suckle at her breasts. Her husband tried to calm her down, saying that the puppy had just been pattering around in the darkness and had no designs on anyone's breasts. But the woman continued carping, bewailing the day she met the mechanic because, if he hadn't gotten her pregnant as a teenager, she could have gone to university and would have become a lawyer, and if that had happened no filthy dog would have dared to reach for her breasts because the dog would have known she would sue him all the way to the Supreme Court.

Oh, how she pitied those once lovely breasts the Almighty God in His infinite kindness gave to her alone but which had now become like a public well that everyone believed they had a right to draw from, including, God save us, that little dog that made a move for her nipples on the veranda. And, yes, just in case her husband was not sure, he should get it clear once and for all that she didn't care whether the puppy had been born with the eyes of a baby or those of a rat.

By dawn, the nonstop skewering to which the pitchfork of the woman's tongue subjected the mechanic all through the night had made hell seem like the sweetest paradise. Take that puppy away from this house, she said, or, soon enough, you'll come back from work to find out I have thrown him in the well.

A cock crowed in the distance. O Lord, into thine hands I commit my breasts, the mechanic's wife cried out. Not until then did sleep silence her.

The mechanic had learnt not to disregard his wife's threats. Some years back, she had forbidden him from talking with the old woman next door with whom she had had a quarrel. The aged widow had greeted the mechanic some days later and the man had replied, not knowing his wife was within earshot. As punishment, she had denied him sex for one long month. Jack had brought the mechanic good luck. If his wife did something sinister to the puppy, the man feared his fortunes would plummet from their glorious heights into calamity's dreadful depths. That was why he had come to see Akeshe.

The mechanic surveyed Akeshe's living room, coveting the large TV, the thick carpet and the shining leather settees which had not been there when the mechanic had visited half a year ago, before Akeshe got his new job with the local government's Environmental Department. No surprise about that, since everyone knew offenders preferred to bribe officials of the Environmental Department, the unit that apprehended breakers of the municipal code, rather than pay astronomical fines into the government's coffers. Akeshe could afford to take care of Jack well, sparing the mechanic any repercussions for letting go of the dog.

I have something special for you, the mechanic said when Akeshe returned home.

What?

There. Can't you see how lovely he is? Your son has been playing with him since I arrived.

How much do you want for the puppy?

I am giving him to you as a gift, the mechanic said.

The mechanic's anomalous kindness triggered Akeshe's suspicions. Since Akeshe began working with the local government, the mechanic had been slamming him with higher charges. That was why Akeshe had stopped taking his motorcycle for repairs at the mechanic's workshop. The man was too calculating to be trusted, Akeshe reasoned. And, if there was no catch to the mechanic's charity, why then was the neighbourhood's champion drinker ignoring the bottle of beer before him?

Why are you giving the puppy to me and not to someone else?

I know you will take care of him well, the mechanic replied. The dog has brought me good luck. I am letting him go only because raising five children is a hard enough task. I can't afford the cost of extra school fees. And I can't handle the burden of feeding another child, especially one as ravenous as a dog.

Another child? Akeshe said. What do you mean by another child?

With your new job, you're rolling in cash. The puppy eats baby food. I know you can afford to take care of him.

Since the dog has brought you good luck, I advise you to hold on to him.

I would have, if not for my wife. Last night she was sleeping on the veranda and the puppy innocently brushed her chest, but she thought he was up to something else. I don't know why she is making a big deal of that paltry incident.

Akeshe's mind went to his wife's breasts. Their heaving immensity was what had attracted her to him in the first place. His face hardened.

I am sorry, he said. I don't like dogs.

Akeshe would hear nothing more about the matter. The mechanic left with the puppy.

✳ ✳ ✳

Erelu had been to Akeshe's house only four times. The first was during Akeshe and Mama Junior's wedding, the second and third times when they lost their first two children, two years apart, and the last to attend Junior's naming ceremony. Listen, I want to promise you something, Erelu told Junior on the day of his christening. Unlike the other two that came before you, you will live, whether you like it or not. Is that clear?

The infant in her arms began crying. She didn't pacify him.

Good that you are acknowledging what I said, she said to the baby. I am Erelu. Don't forget what I told you. I always keep my promises.

The look with which she regarded the infant in her arms was enigmatic, both tender and threatening, reflecting the paradoxes in the numerous stories told about her, stories so contradictory that one couldn't be sure any more which was true and which was false.

That in her youth she was a lover of Alhaji Slender, the local chieftain of the ruling party, but had now become one of his main political allies.

That she breeds spiders in her bedroom, and that she hates all books, especially the Bible and the Qur'an.

That she never misses morning mass.

That, without her generosity, the Bishop's brand new residence would not have been completed.

That, without her generosity, the brand new car of Central Mosque's Chief Imam would not have been his.

That she was born with two gold teeth glittering on opposite sides of her mouth.

That the anointing of the Holy Ghost, not bleaching lotions, transformed her skin from sepia-dark to ghostly pale.

That she had a long-standing quarrel with the sun, which was why she never went out in daytime without an umbrella.

That she was kind enough to stop going for confession after the old priest prescribing her penance died of a heart attack in the confessional.

That the building she donated to an abandoned babies' charity was built to such high standards it will remain standing after heaven and earth have passed away.

That she executed the contract to construct and maintain the government schoolhouse whose collapse soon after completion killed 66 children, four teachers and one squirrel.

That, despite the building's collapse, the Grace of the Most High God, like the expensive handbags she fancies, continues to abide with her, even though she sometimes picks her nose with her little finger in public.

That she deserves beatification more than the venerable prostitutes in the shanty houses by the river who have to take smelly navvies to bed for a pittance.

That she loves her niece, Mama Junior, more than her own daughter but less than her favourite cocktail.

That without her influence, Mama Junior would not have been allocated a store at the best location in the municipal market.

That without her influence, her semi-illiterate in-law, Akeshe, would not have gotten his administrator's job with the local government.

That the cloud of perfume in which she moves draws butterflies to her in droves, like happy fairies fluttering around their godmother – though that information got some people so confused they wondered if butterflies meant personal servants and favour seekers.

That her necromantic skills, unlike those of second-rate witches who can fly only in the dead of night, are so top-notch that she zooms across the sky in broad daylight, her umbrella in hand, although no one has ever had the alertness or temerity to take a photograph of her while in flight.

That she doesn't travel more frequently with the emission-free technology of witchcraft, which would have earned her loads of green points, only because she prefers cruising around town in enormous jeeps like the one that roared to a stop in front of Akeshe's residence the fifth time Erelu visited.

She met Akeshe standing by the sprouting blood flowers, his eyes dark-ringed from sleeplessness. For four days now, since the mechanic took the puppy away, his son had refused to eat or drink, and Akeshe had lost so much weight in the interval it seemed it was he and not his son who was dying from starvation.

Bring back the puppy for our son, Mama Junior had screamed at her husband. But Akeshe couldn't tell her, or anyone else, that he was playing brinkmanship with his son's life because he didn't want to share his wife's breasts with a dog.

Earlier that day, Mama Junior had run into the cantankerous fellow who owned Palm Bar. The man was notorious for being an unrepentant apostate. Today is the fourth day of the boy's fast, isn't it, he asked Mama Junior. No one can survive for more than seven days without food or water. So don't be fooled by that tale about 40 days and 40 nights in the wilderness, okay?

Mama Junior was a regular in church but she wasn't ready to play Abraham with her son's life. Her decision made perfect sense, the man who owned Palm Bar said, since Mama Junior didn't want to be the Mother of Faith, only the mother of Junior. And, anyway, what else was a test of faith if not a contradiction in terms, the man quipped. Laughing, he resumed his journey towards his bar.

Mama Junior had lost two children. She wouldn't fold her arms, watching until she lost the third. She reported the matter to Erelu. A few hours afterwards, Erelu breezed into her niece's home in a glory of rustling silk, accompanied by several servants and her trademark redolence of motley fragrances.

Erelu pointed at Mama Junior. Akeshe began trembling. If that boy dies, don't you know what people will say, Erelu asked.

Yes, ma'am, Akeshe said, not daring to look Erelu straight in the eyes.

A witch who ate all her children for supper. That is what people would say.

Yes, ma'am.

And, of course, you know the name she would be called if Junior, who as we all know is a spirit child, returns to the realm of the unborn, God forbid, like the previous two.

Yes, ma'am.

Aunty, that is how your neighbours will address her if she has no child of her own. And it would be a disgrace if your wife were called Aunty, not Mama Junior, wouldn't it? Yes, ma'am.

So don't you think it would be better for everyone if that dog comes to live here so your son can resume eating?

Akeshe kept looking at the floor.

Yes, ma'am, he said.

Erelu gasped when she saw the puppy. She picked up the dog to examine him. The puppy stared straight at her painted face, with the wide-eyed astonishment of a child scrutinizing an exotic dog.

See, just see those eyes, Erelu exclaimed. This is no ordinary dog. Surely, he is one of Junior's playmates in the spirit world! He must have come to lure your son away from the land of the living back to the world of the unborn.

The puppy blinked several times. He tilted his head to look at Erelu, as if what the woman just said was the most stupid statement ever uttered in the history of the world.

You will bear a man's name, not that of a dog, she told the wriggling puppy. Jack, that will be your name from now on, whether you like it or not. Is that clear?

The little dog, whimpering, struggled harder to free himself. Erelu gripped him tighter. The precious stones glittered on the many rings adorning her fingers.

The puppy is protesting because his mission has been exposed, Erelu said. I will send my driver here tomorrow. We must take special care of him, like a child, so that he can forget about the mission on which he was sent by your son's spirit companions.

Erelu's driver brought a baby's cot for Jack. And a carpenter who constructed a fancy kennel for the dog near the budding blood flowers. And cans of baby food and children's toys which were placed along with the cot in the kennel. And a note to the town's foremost veterinarian appointing him as Jack's personal physician. And another note ordering her butcher to deliver a supply of meat and bones every week for the dog's consumption.

In line with her aunt's instructions, Mama Junior kept a close eye on Jack. Often she took him with her to her store, keeping him in the market until dusk when she closed shop for the day. And on Sundays Jack trotted along with the family to church, raising a hind leg once every few blocks to squirt some pee on the nearest lamppost or tree trunk. The dog, unlike some poorly behaved toddlers who had a habit of lurching towards the pulpit while the minister was preaching, would sit still in one place all through the sermon, his tongue hanging out of his mouth. Impressed by the dog's piety, Mama Junior's fellow parishioners often patted Jack on the head and gushed, What a God-fearing dog Jack is turning out to be!

Jack's attentiveness would earn even greater praise in the classroom. Children in the neighbourhood converged at Akeshe's house for supplementary lessons in the evenings. Whenever the home tutor visited, Jack was always the first to head for the lesson room. In the beginning the tutor tried to chase him away, but he welcomed him with gladness after Akeshe agreed to pay an extra child's fees to cover the dog's tuition. While Junior and the other children struggled against sleep, Jack, his ears pricked up, would stare with wide-alert eyes at the soporific scribbles the tutor was making on the blackboard.

The lady in the next house, who had seven children, was envious. How I wish my children took their education as seriously as Jack, she said. Instead of concentrating on their schoolwork, they find greater pleasure in playing football and stealing fruits from other people's orchards. That dog knows the value of a good education.

The tutor agreed. Believe me, Jack is the most studious pupil I have ever taught, he said. The dog will end up at an admirable station in life.

✳ ✳ ✳

So no one should have been surprised when Jack grew up to become a medical doctor. That was after Jack's buddy, Junior, fell gravely ill for the first time since the dog had joined Akeshe's household.

Junior's temperature had risen to hellish heights, and everything he swallowed ran straight through his system and out of his anus, like water through a pipe, and the boy's tongue had turned so green anyone would have been forgiven for wondering if the diminishing presence of bones and skin was not an unfortunate alien dropped from outer space onto the sickbed, his breathing coming in gasps and faltering wheezes. None of the remedies tried on the boy during the weeks he spent at the hospital had worked, and the doctors had directed that he should be sustained on intravenous fluids. But, with time, the marathon attempts to find veins not too thin for the drip feed had subjected the boy to such trauma that Akeshe decided it would be kinder to let his son succumb to whatever dread affliction was plaguing him rather than allowing the nurses to stab the boy to death with intravenous needles.

Akeshe took his son away from the hospital, against medical advice. Erelu visited her niece's home for the sixth time on the day Junior returned from the hospital. The blood flowers lining the frontage of the residence were flourishing, but they were not in bloom. The bag Erelu brought with her contained an assortment of herbs and charms with which she intended to wage war against the spells wicked people had placed on Junior.

Erelu went straight to Junior's room. She met a group of sympathizers by the boy's bed, watching him with long-drawn faces as if at a wake. Only Jack was immune to the general gloom. The dog was glad to see his pal for the first time in weeks. He pressed his muzzle into Junior's limp hand, wagging his tail and making happy sounds to draw the boy's attention.

Erelu started singing. The silver bangles encircling her arms flashed and tinkled as she danced. Jack, along with the people in the room, directed puzzled looks at her.

Sorry to bother you, ma'am, but what is going on, one of the visiting well-wishers asked.

The dog, Erelu said. Didn't you see the dog playing with the boy?

So?

The boy won't die, Erelu declared with glee. Dogs see things we can't see. If the boy was going to die, the dog would have seen it already, and the dog wouldn't have been messing around with the dead.

Jack walked out of the room, as if what the woman just

said was tripe and he had better things to do with his time than listening to such twaddle.

Erelu turned to Junior. Didn't I tell you that you will live, whether you like it or not?

The boy lived.

That dog cured the boy, the neighbours said. Whoever treated an illness so grave can treat any ailment.

The news spread. From all across town and beyond, crowds trooped to Akeshe's house to see the dog who could cure diseases that confounded even the grey-haired doctors at the hospital.

At first Akeshe, happy that his son was off his sickbed, didn't mind the crush of pilgrims that had taken over his living room. But the strangers' grimy footwear wrecked his carpet, and the incontinence of the children they brought along turned the house into a reeking shithouse, and when two women, each claiming the right to have her child touch the dog first, started a brawl that sucked in over a dozen other people and left the TV and several louvre blades smashed, Akeshe drove the crowd out of his home with a glistening machete.

The pilgrims stayed put outside the house. Their presence alerted even more people to the existence of a physician in Akeshe's home who could cure children of all afflictions. The crowd swelled. Akeshe considered calling the police, but his wife disagreed. There will be a riot and the police may kill people, she said. I don't want anyone's blood on our hands.

Mama Junior proposed that they charge anybody who wanted to consult Jack a hefty fee. Akeshe accepted her recommendation. The introduction of fees didn't reduce the demand for access to the dog, but Akeshe didn't mind now that money was rolling in.

In the week that Jack's clinic opened, the patients the dog had to see included a toddler who ate so much his parents always chained him to his bed at night, because he had made several attempts to eat his parents in their sleep after finishing all the food in the pantry. And a boy with a bat's grin who preferred standing upside down, running around the neighbourhood and climbing stairs and playing soccer with his two hands rather than with his feet. And a girl infatuated with lunar light, who was caught on the rooftop just in time as she was about to elope with the full moon. And a boy whose penis was growing so fast his family feared it would soon grow longer than his legs. And a girl whose father was willing to pay any amount to prevent her from growing up to be as ugly as her mother. And a child thief who began his criminal career in the womb, where he tried to steal his twin sister's umbilical cord. And the embalmed body of a boy, brought to the clinic in a little coffin by an old woman who wished to have her grandson's decade-old mummy cured of death.

The living room did not ensure doctor-patient confidentiality. Akeshe and Mama Junior renovated their unused garage, and they converted it into a doctor's office. The couple employed a secretary to keep accurate medical records and a nurse to assist Jack. And they erected a signboard in front of their house, which read, *Dr Jack, Paediatrician, Office Hours 9am to 5pm, Consultations by Appointment Only.*

Jack always kept mute during consultations in the clinic, regarding the world with pensive eyes, while the children ran their fingers over his fur. The children, little angels that they were, loved twisting the dog's ears, and they tried to gouge out his eyes with their fingers or with sticks, and they dragged him around his office by the tail, finding great fun in the dog's distress. Jack's response to those provocations was just silence. Even when a snaggletoothed girl bit him so hard on the tail that his eyes went red, the dog only whimpered, before sinking back into morose silence.

Once every few hours though, as if overpowered by profound gloom, the dog would sit on his haunches and howl for minutes on end. Parents who brought their children for treatment would stand up to clap in gratitude to him. What a compassionate doctor, they would exclaim. Why else would he have been howling, if not in sympathy with his patients, our children?

Jack seemed happy only after closing hours when he shook his fur over and again, and ran at a gallop through the streets of the neighbourhood. Dr Jack, people hailed him, but he would only pause to look at those fans with sad eyes before progressing on his way.

Akeshe and Mama Junior bought the rented house they lived in for an amount they never imagined they would ever be able to afford, and they refurbished it with deluxe furnishings. Mama Junior's neck rapidly disappeared into the burgeoning blubber of her shoulders as she grew fatter by the month, while Junior began strutting around in expensive designer wear, clutching high-tech gadgets that drew the envy of his peers. Not to be left out, Akeshe, who didn't care about trendy apparel and who couldn't get fat even if he swallowed a cow, wasted no time in discarding his aged motorcycle. During the party organized to celebrate the acquisition of his new car, the man raised a drunken toast to his dog.

I couldn't be more proud of Dr Jack, shouted Akeshe, his speech slurred. The investment I made in his education has not been wasted. Believe me, there's no doctor in the world half as competent as that dog!

His friends, nodding, concurred. Their merrymaking went on deep into the night.

* * *

Professional success of the magnitude achieved by Dr Jack tends to attract love, and love, as they say, is blind. One Saturday, while playing football with his friends on the pitch of the school at the far end of the street, Junior kicked the ball so hard the game had to be stopped to search for it.

The players found the ball inside an abandoned woodshed near the school's fence. They also found eight puppies in the woodshed.

Junior recognized the mangy stray that had given birth to the puppies. He had always chased her away whenever she came to visit Jack. There were many respectable bitches in the neighbourhood that Jack could have picked as a partner, and Junior couldn't understand why the doctor was dating a homeless cur. That dog is too ugly for our Dr Jack, he used to say as he drove her away with stones. But now, on getting home, Junior sang the stray's praises to his father. I didn't know she could give birth to puppies so beautiful, the boy said. They are Dr Jack's children. We can't let anyone else take them away.

Akeshe had been busy reflecting on the threat confronting Jack's medical practice. A miracle healer had just arrived in town. Unlike others of his ilk, who looked like feral beggars long marooned in the wilderness, the healer had the haircut of a hip-hop star and dressed in bespoke suits like a bank manager, and he possessed an array of dazzling wristwatches that testified to the divine presence of God in his life. There was uncertainty about what particular religion he practised, but no one doubted his spiritual powers because he barked louder than any dog when praying. Many of Dr Jack's patients didn't see any point in coming to his clinic again, since the dapper healer could not only dance and curse and roll around on the ground but he could also bark better than the taciturn dog.

The news about the puppies heartened Akeshe. Jack was a famous dog. His puppies would also be special. They would command high prices, which would make up for the loss in revenue from the clinic.

Akeshe and Junior moved the puppies into Jack's kennel. Their mother came along with them. She refused to answer to any name, except Jack. People began calling her Mrs Jack, to distinguish her from her husband. She answered to that name with the happiness of a bride on her wedding day, not minding that her husband's clinic was getting increasingly deserted because even the most faithful of the doctor's clients were finding the miracle healer's fearsome barking too charismatic to resist.

Jack now had more free time. He spent it wandering around the neighbourhood, in the company of his wife. How lovely, a schoolmistress passing by told Mama Junior. Dr and Mrs Jack! Aren't they like a couple married by a priest?

Mama Junior glowed with pride. Jack is better than those young men in the neighbourhood who frequent the brothels downtown instead of committing themselves to wedlock, she said.

Those young fellows are shameless dogs, the schoolmistress said. Frankly, between Jack and any of those wastrels, does anyone have doubts about who is the true man?

But being happily married is no antidote to the allures of infidelity. On the day of elections for the local council, Mrs Jack caught her husband pants down, locked in copulation with a younger, sexier bitch from the next street. Irate, Mrs Jack attacked the fornicators and set about separating them with her teeth.

Voters returning from the polling booths stopped to watch the curious scene, laughing and snapping pictures. But an old gentleman was not amused. The world must be going to the dogs when even dogs begin insisting on monogamy, he growled.

Jack retired from that public embarrassment to the uncompleted building near the pond, his habitual place of refuge from matrimonial worries. There were strange boxes lining his favourite room deep inside the cool building. He must have found peace there, because he was fast asleep when the first kick smashed into his ribs. The men gathered around him were holding sticks and stones, their shouting sounding like a common baying for murder.

Jack was a big, strong dog. The onset of old age had made

him less stoic. He leapt at the men. Soon they were running around in disarray, their clothes torn and stained with blood from bite marks inflicted by the dog. The wild screaming of the men drew people to the scene. Some of those who stopped by entered the building to ascertain the cause of the commotion. They were surprised to see ballot boxes earlier snatched from voting centres, and reams of fake ballot papers in advanced stages of mass thumb printing, in the uncompleted building. The crowd pounced on the men and would have lynched them if a police van hadn't turned up, its siren wailing, to take them away in handcuffs.

The news made the front pages of the newspapers, and people flocked to Akeshe's residence to thank Jack. That dog is a true democrat, they said. If elected into government he would deliver the dividends of democracy to the common man, unlike the thieving clowns currently in office.

Mama Junior and Akeshe discussed the possibility of putting Jack up as a candidate in the next election. They found the prospect tantalizing, and began developing a campaign strategy for the dog. Only dim-witted old dogs can't learn new tricks, they couple reassured themselves, but Jack was a smart geezer. The dog would easily learn how to walk on his hind legs, keeping himself upright with the aid of a golden walking stick, and he would look good wearing a bowler hat, like many notable politicians in his country.

If it was for parliament Jack would be running, his limited language skills would play to his advantage, since a capacity for intelligent debate was frowned upon in the legislative chambers anyway. He could indicate his ayes with a woof and his nays with a growl, and his performance would still be more exemplary than that of most parliamentarians, who have more important things to do than attending legislative sessions.

And if he would be gunning to be a Governor or the President, Jack would even be more qualified, considering his experience as a dog. The previous occupants of those offices had distinguished themselves mainly for their ability to stand in front of TV cameras, barking at the people that had voted them into power. That was when they were not busy wolfing down as much as they could from the national cake, and then a little more, just as Jack did whenever he was served his food.

Akeshe and his wife continued perfecting their plans. They were certain that Dr Jack's rise in politics would be rapid since an ability to lick balls, a skill which the dog had long turned into a fine art by practising it upon himself, was the critical requirement for that. Jack would have to move to the capital after entering office, but the dog would be able to cope with the relocation. On his rare trips back to his home town, the dog would speed through the streets in a convoy of siren-blaring vehicles, like his fellow public office-holders, without even bothering to wave a paw through tinted windows at people observing the passing convoy from the roadside.

Being a handsome dog, he would look dapper in a French suit or an academic gown, a wide grin spread across his snout as he received another honorary doctorate, DLitt or DSc, from a grateful university. And Jack would become a hit on the party circuit, once he mastered the tricky art of dancing on his hind legs, since it was not often one saw a dog prancing in step to complex beats, clinking champagne glasses with other political heavyweights and slapping wads of crisp banknotes on the backsides of ladies, while musicians crooned his praises to the high heavens.

Mama Junior and her husband should have known that Alhaji Slender, Erelu's political ally, would get to know about their plans for Dr Jack. Alhaji Slender was an old hound. He was much dreaded. The houses of his political opponents had the habit of bursting into flames in the wee hours. Police investigations into these fires had always turned out inconclusive, and a prominent academic loyal to Alhaji Slender had claimed that the fire incidents were the long-elusive proof of the existence of spontaneous combustion.

Alhaji Slender knew a potential top dog when he saw one.

The chieftain, Akeshe and Mama Junior should also have known, wasn't going to sit on his haunches whining while a rival dog took over his turf.

∗ ∗ ∗

The blood flowers in front of Akeshe's house were in full bloom when Erelu visited the place for the seventh, and last, time. She met Mama Junior, Akeshe and their son looking glum. Supervisors in the market had stormed Mama Junior's shop, ordering her to vacate the place because irregularities had been discovered in the manner in which the shop had been allocated to her. Akeshe had been taken in for questioning by the police over allegations he had received bribes in the course of his job with the local government. Junior had been beaten up by thugs on his way to school. And no one in the family could move freely around town again because they had all become targets of abuse on the streets. That was after the Bishop and Central Mosque's Chief Imam had railed in their sermons against a certain dog that wanted to become a man. The dog had been sent by the Devil to lead humankind astray, the clerics said, and they barred their congregations from associating with the family of wicked souls that owned the evil creature.

Alhaji Slender is very angry, Erelu said. Your dog sniffed out his men from their duty post. The dog had no business sticking his wet nose into politics, understand?

Yes, ma'am, Akeshe said.

I can pacify Alhaji Slender on your behalf. If you co-operate with us, all your recent setbacks will be reversed.

Yes, ma'am.

Erelu began shouting. Listen, I don't care if your dog is a spirit child or a tuber of yam. That dog is a dog. And a dog has no business trying to become a man, is that clear?

Dr Jack, like any man caught by his wife in the flagrant passion of adultery, merely wanted to rest for a while so he could think up a compelling excuse for his spouse. His situation was made even more delicate by the fact that his wife was a dog, so he couldn't give her the human excuse that it was the work of the Devil, because dogs do not believe in God or the Devil.

Jack hadn't rigged any election or looted the treasury of any state. He hadn't committed judicial murder, and he hadn't shot or strangled anyone to death, as the police do to innocents in their custody. The dog hadn't planted bombs in bars and markets in the name of any religion, or deployed soldiers to massacre unarmed civilians, or started a dubious war in another country. But none of that mattered because he was a dog who had been accused of wanting to become a man, and even God knows, though dogs do not believe in Him, that this alleged transgression is the greatest crime of all.

The dog must go, Erelu barked, whether he likes it or not, okay?

The living room went silent.

What do you say to that? Erelu asked.

I don't…

What?

I can't bring myself to lay a finger on the dog, Akeshe said.

You don't have to.

Yes, ma'am.

Are you giving me permission to take care of the matter? asked Erelu.

Yes, ma'am, Mama Junior said.

And you?

Yes, ma'am, Junior said.

I was talking to your father, not to you.

Akeshe thought about the matter for some seconds. His son was now too grown up to be lured by any spirit companion to the world of the unborn. Jack's clinic was no longer running. And the puppies Jack had been fathering were just ordinary whelps that couldn't be sold for great profit.

Yes, ma'am, Akeshe said.

* * *

The proprietor of the restaurant on the other side of the pond loved dogs, especially mature and well-fed ones like Jack. His establishment catered to clients with special tastes. He came to Akeshe's house with two of his employees and a cage. The employees put Jack in the cage. They placed the cage beside the petals, crimson like a murder scene, of the blood flowers.

The woman that had seven children, who lived in the neighbouring house, accused the restaurant proprietor of cannibalism. Anyone who eats a creature that bears a personal name might eat my children, she said.

The man turned to Jack. What is your name, he asked.

His name is Jack, the woman said. Dr Jack.

Let it tell me by itself. The man turned to Jack. Sir, tell me, what is your name?

Jack kept quiet. It was his first time in a cage. His dilated eyes betrayed his panic.

Can you now see that this dog has no name, the man said, chuckling. I don't eat any plant or animal that can tell me its name.

Jack began howling.

That animal sound you're making is not my idea of a name, Jack's new owner told him. Trust me, those ravenous hounds I have as customers will enjoy crushing the marrow out of your bones.

Jack's howling intensified as they carted him away, the agony of his wailing sending the neighbourhood's chickens squawking to their roosts and startling into flight bulbuls that soared screeching from treetops like an indictment of feathers to the heavens. The lament, neither human nor bestial, sounded as if it was coming not from the dog's throat but from the deepest pores of his being. It pierced walls and clothes and skin, rattling open windows through which peeped out anxious faces, and it flung ajar doors out of which stepped maids wiping their hands on aprons and drinking men suddenly gone sober and bleary-eyed children woken from their siesta and petty thieves temporarily penitent and bored housewives now alert and artisans covered with grime, with all the consternated folk composing that curious crowd, motley like the grand carnival of the world, wondering what terror could have occasioned an alarm so unearthly that it could have been the last bugle sounding to usher in the fiery doom of apocalypse.

The howling advanced down the street as the restaurant owner departed towards his kitchen with his trophy in the cage, and from Jack kept coming that gloomy and interminable wailing that recalled the dankness of dungeons and the eternal sadness of cemeteries, the dog's lamentation carrying on like the savage wind that has been haunting the universe from time's beginning, ripping death through ranks of dinosaurs burning into extinction and fanning hotter the flames dancing around hecatombs. That wind which set sail Agamemnon's plunderers and Transatlantic slave ships and blessed the Christian vessels of Columbus in whose wake conquistadores privileged new lands with the gift of gunfire and the pox, that wind which seeps in through the vents of gas chambers and sometimes blows off rooftops like terrorist bombs or whistles like missiles from hovering drones, was the same wind now wrenching trauma out of Jack's viscera.

The howling got fainter and even more dejected as the dog was ferried further away from his home, where the blood flowers were triumphantly blooming, towards death.

When the howl went silent, it kept on resounding.

Dr Jack, renowned paediatrician, died in grim circumstances. He was survived by a loving wife, several mistresses, many legitimate and illegitimate offspring, and a few well-chewed pieces of bone.

Rotimi Babatunde's stories, poems and plays have been widely published and performed. His story, 'Bombay's Republic', won the 2012 Caine Prize for African Writing. He lives in Ibadan, Nigeria.

The Book of Remembered Things

Abubakar Adam Ibrahim

I WORE MY BLACK DRESS TODAY, the one with intricate gold embroidery down the front and on the cuffs. The one scented with sweet memories. The one Shamsu bought for me. I wore it for the first time since the tragedy and didn't feel sad. My friend Hajara called me aside and said, Anisa, did you notice you are the only one wearing black to this wedding?

It was her younger sister's wedding. Her sister, who just turned 20 – as if she wasn't born right before my eyes, as if I hadn't carried her strapped to my back when she was a yowling baby. As if she hadn't doused me in her pee and baby puke. It was her wedding day and I was the only one who wore black. Everyone else wore their brightly coloured African prints. And their minted smiles. All young. Children born before my eyes.

Well, I said to Hajara, what is wrong with wearing black to a wedding?

She looked at me as if I had uttered some grave profanity. *Haba*, Anisa, it is a wedding, not a mourning, you know. You should at least pretend to be happy for my sister.

I asked her what she meant by that. Hajara, my friend, told me that not being married at 34 shouldn't make me wear mourning garbs to weddings. That was what my friend told me, Mother. And she laughed and said, Oh, Anisa, I was only joking, *wallahi*.

I said to her, Hajara, don't come here talking about marriage as if you are any happier than I am. As if your husband is not running around with those little girls at Nasarawa.

I wore a black dress today, Mother. A black dress to a little girl's wedding.

✳✳✳

I will write for you, Mother, whenever I can. I will write in this book as I sit by your bed. Some day, you will recover and want to walk these fields of scribbled memories, of things felt and things said. Seven years is a lot to miss out on in the lives of your family. Seven years you've been ill now.

I remember it like yesterday, the first time you returned from the market and said you felt cold inside. Your temperature was perfectly normal on the outside. Then it got worse. The doctors probed you and pricked you and tested every fluid in your body. Then they looked at us with baffled expressions. By then your bones had grown numb and you could only sit on the examination bed, staring blandly into the distance. We went from doctor to doctor until we had a mystified army of white-coated specialists in our wake. We walked the streets scented by the smells of hospitals, of sickness and the sorrow of loss. Then one day, the kind Dr Bala at the General Hospital said, Anisa, three years now and we still can't diagnose what is wrong with your mother. Have you thought of alternative medicine?

We went from the familiar smell of disinfectants to the heady aroma of herbs and incense and potions. They all said the same thing. Your mother is afflicted by the evil eye, by iniquitous djinns from the tamarind trees, by a horde of mystical *gwaigwai* dwarves, by a flock of riverine witches, by itinerant ghosts from forgotten times, by envious neighbours who cast curses.

But what is there to envy in you; you who had lost your husband to the call of distant winds when he packed his things and went off to fight a war he didn't understand; you who had been lying in bed for years, staring blankly at the ceiling, barely able to move even your hands; you whose upkeep is left to the struggles of your son Salisu, from his meagre salary at the ministry? When Salisu heard them say all these things, he scoffed and said, Nonsense, Mother is heartbroken because of Father. When he comes back, she will be alright, you'll see.

But the *malams*, armed with their prayer beads, recited the Qur'an over your head. The spiritualist doused you in concoctions and fed you decoctions until I feared your hair would turn the colour of leaves and bark would grow out of your skin. You just sat there and stared into the distance, the sound of your voice only a memory in our minds, the sound of your laughter gone with the seasonal winds.

So I sit with you all day, nursing you, praying that Father would return some day so you could snap out of this affliction that had ravaged your heart and soul and body. So I will write for you, Mother, in this book of remembered things.

* * *

I bleed heavily sometimes. It gushes like a freshly commissioned borehole, with the gusto of newness. Newness is not a word to associate with me, for inside, I can feel my heart ageing as the clock ticks. Tick-tock, tick-tock.

I bleed and drench my pads within minutes. I changed to ultra to contain the spirited flow so it would stop seeping out and staining my skirts. All this blood. In Father's house. If he were here he would have said, *Subhanallahi*, Anisa, we need to find you a husband. He would have said that years ago, if he had been around.

Sometimes I need to see the photos to remember what he looked like. The ones he took before he came home one day and said that photographs were *haram*, the ones you hid in your commode when he was rummaging through drawers and collecting our photo albums and feeding them to the flames.

These are things Iblis uses to deceive the faithful. May Allah curse him, he said.

He went back in and ransacked the drawers. And when he returned, the yellow-trimmed blue flames burned with the smell of Lawiza's jean skirts, our make-up things, our CDs, and dresses he did not approve of. And your high heels, too, because they made clicking sounds when you went up stairs or walked on the pavements and men turned to look. That flame that exploded with your perfume. Allure Chanel. That sweet, tender scent was you, not this smell of malady; of drugs, of herbs and of piss.

When he fetched the radios and the TV, I said to him, Father, what are you doing?

He said, Shut up, you! You are not supposed to be here. You are supposed to be married. I will find you a husband soon, *in sha Allah*.

And he cast these things, too, into the flame.

He turned to you and said, Have you seen the kind of women they show dancing on TV these days? Naked women! *Subhanallah*!

But you said nothing. You just cried.

I watched the flames devour the things we were; the things that were us. And after it had sated itself on the remains of us and put itself out, escaping in a thin wisp of smoke that gave off a rubbery smell, I felt like a stranger in my own body. And when I looked at you, I thought I saw the same emptiness in your eyes. But you turned your face away and said, Anisa, sweep away this mess and come inside before the *maghrib* prayers.

When America went to war in Afghanistan, Father came home and packed his things in the black rucksack with a red spider embroidered on it.

Muslims are being killed, he said, I am going to jihad! Jihad, I tell you.

We thought he was joking. But he walked out the door and said he would go, if necessary on foot, to Afghanistan, to kill the infidels who were bombing Muslim babies in their cribs. We waited for him to return, to walk in framed by the light of dusk. But the sun set many times and his silhouette never darkened the door. We waited, but time went past and stretched into years.

I used to think he was dead. Sometimes I wished he was. But the other day, our neighbour Mustafa the cloth merchant said, Anisa, I saw your father in Kano.

I asked him if he was sure, and he said, *Haba*, as if I don't know your father. I saw him with these two eyes *kiri-kiri*!

Well, what did he say?

Nothing. He just waved and walked away.

I wonder what Father would have said if he saw me now. If he knew how much I bleed under his roof. A woman my age shouldn't be cleaning up this mess in her father's house. Sometimes I worry, other times I don't. The state of my fertility is of little concern to me now. It is the fertility of my mind I worry about. This mind of mine; you could cast seeds of love with abundant zest in here and they would remain just seeds, for my heart, dry as hard grounds, would not yield to them. And the vagrant birds of disenchantment will come to peck at them and rid me of the bother. That is the image of my mind I have. That of dried, cracked earth. Love will not sprout here, in my heart. In my jaded heart.

❋ ❋ ❋

I let the rain wash over me, Mother. Cold rain striking my skin like cruel fingers tapping melodies of desolation out of me. I let the rain wash over me, wash away my tears as I walked through the narrow lanes, past people sheltering under the awnings, in verandas bordered by verdant hedges. They looked at me; at the wet cloth clinging to my body, at the hem of my dress fluttering in the teasing wind. They saw me, they all did. But they never saw my tears.

I walked on towards the market, where the traders and their wares had been washed away into the shelters, where the shops were crowded by customers taking refuge from heaven's cold fingers.

The rains chased everyone into shelters; everyone but the soldiers. They stood menacingly at indiscriminate checkpoints, in front of government offices pointing their guns at the streets, behind their bomb trucks parked at every other corner, before the entrance to the market with guns in one hand and horsewhips in the other. Soldiers everywhere, Mother. They terrify you as much as the maniacs who drive bomb-laden vehicles into buildings.

Salisu brought home some money from his job at the ministry. He gave me some for the housekeep because I told him we were out of provisions. No rice. No spaghetti. No groceries. No beverages. We needed new school uniforms for Lawiza and Jibreel. New sandals, too. And I really needed to get tampons for my heavy flow. When I went to his door to ask if he wanted me to get him anything, I heard them. She was laughing at first, the girl he had inside. I should have moved on then but I stayed. And then she started moaning. Faintly. And when I heard the bed creaking and their voices getting inflamed with passion, I walked away, my head filled with sounds of their sinning.

When it started raining, I never stopped. I just walked away thinking of the ardour that burned my little brother and his girlfriend, this passion I have never felt.

I clean your bedsores and change your sheets. I cook your food and feed you. I sit by your bed and write in this book. And my brother and his girlfriend make the bed creak.

I know I want it. To feel the hands of a man cup my bosom, to feel him slide into me and fill me with the fire that makes women moan and grasp the sheets like possessed oracles of the ancients. But I do not have the heart to leave you, Mother. And I do not have the heart to sin. So I walked out to the street and let the rain wash over me, wash away my tears.

***

I look beautiful today. You should see me, Mother. I went and got my hands and feet decorated with elaborate henna designs. I put on lipstick and soused myself in exquisite perfume. And I felt good. I look beautiful, Mother, but not as beautiful as you, as you used to be.

I remember how we used to walk the streets and I wished I was you. How elegant you were in your cloths – so much so that I envied you and resented myself for looking more like Father than you. How wonderful the henna designs used to look on your subtle skin. How you smelt like Allure, even when you had just come out of the bath. How your laughter used to ring in the house even when you had gone to work at Haske Insurance. How you used to sing with the voice of Celine Dion until Father pounded the dining table one night and said, Stop letting the devil use you, woman!

The sound of your laughter was carried off by the southern gales when Father changed. When he said you couldn't work any more. When he burnt the things that were us.

I look beautiful today, Mother. But not as beautiful as you used to be.

＊＊＊

The transient winds brought a man to us today. It happened in the afternoon when I was in the kitchen preparing lunch for Lawiza and Jibreel before they returned from school. Without even saying *salaam*, he walked into the living room with his shoes on. The wind brought with him the dust of distant places and the smell of foreignness. It was the smell, and the noise he made clearing his throat that drew me to the living room.

Half his face was covered in beard and his bushy hair sat on his head like an abandoned nest. He looked at me, acknowledged me with a dismissive wave and sat on the settee. He put his leg on the table, threw his head back and started to sleep with his mouth open. His snores rattled the curtain rails and shocked whatever demons tormented you.

You woke up and started whimpering. I couldn't come to you because there was a stranger in our living room, sleeping with his mouth wide open.

I walked round and looked at his face. That was when I recognized him. And that was when the smell of burnt food from the kitchen reached me.

The winds brought a man to us today. And that man was our father returning for the second time.

***

I remember the first time he returned, the first time he trundled back into our troubled peace. Lawiza, who had been a few months old when Father left, had gone out to play and rushed back to report that there was a man sitting outside the door. A strange man, she said.

It was Father, looking into the distance like one who left his shadow behind. His beard had grown wild and he had on a *pakol*, the kind of cap we had seen those gun-toting Afghans wearing on the news.

We carried him in, Salisu and I. And I cleaned his blistered feet. He sat in the chair and talked with nostalgia about the alabaster-skinned djinn who had married him.

You should have seen Zahira, he said. Her skin white like sea stone and her eyes like embers. Like embers, *wallah*.

He talked about Zahira, *chau, chau, chau*, like that. He chomped the rice we gave him and said we should learn to make *palao*, the way they cook rice in Kandahar, as if we should know anything about it. And when he talked about Zahira, he would turn his eyes heavenwards, as if he could see her face on the ceiling. He talked about how she saved him from American bullets and fell in love with him on the flowered Afghan mountains that echoed the thunder of gunshots from old and new wars.

He talked about Zahira, and didn't ask where you were. And when Salisu told him you were at a hospital, and had been there for months, he nodded and said, Ah, you know, Zahira never falls ill, *masha Allah*.

I remember the first time he returned, the first time the stranger in Father's body came back from a distant war.

He slept. That was all he did. Lawiza and Jirbeel, who barely knew him, tired of waiting for him to wake and lost interest in him. He slept, his snores rustling the curtains.

Mother, this is Salisu. I see sister Anisa has been writing lies about me, about how I bring girls into the room and do... things with them, sometimes. I see her sitting here, writing, writing, with that sneaky look of hers and now I've read everything she has written. All lies. Lies, wallahi.

I know she will make trouble with me if she sees me writing in her book of remembered things. But I will not go quietly into the night. *I think I heard that line in a movie. I like it. Anyway, I want you to read my side of the story when you get better. I pray you get better. I really do.*

You see, Mother, the problem with Anisa is that sneaky look of hers. Who would want to marry a woman whose face is cast in the mould of mourning? She has been carrying this face since Shamsu, the last man who had wanted to marry her, was killed in a bomb blast two years ago. She doesn't talk about it. But I think she loves him still. He used to buy drugs for you and story books for Lawiza and Jibreel. I liked him a lot, too. You would have liked him if you had met him, but you were ill then.

I was there the day he died. And I think Father was there, too. I never told anyone because I wasn't sure. But I think I saw him at the square two years back, just before the explosion. He didn't see me, I think. He was hurrying away, hurrying away like that, and I was pushing through the crowd to catch up with him, to look into his face, to be sure.

And then the bomb went off. Boom! Like that. You should have seen how people were running, screaming, bloodied. I lost him in the confusion. Too much shouting and blood. And bits of charred flesh. I didn't know that Shamsu was there, that he had been killed in the blast. He was a nice man. May Allah illuminate his grave. Ameen!

And now father sits in the living room, snoring like a fat bull. I am not happy he came back. He is trouble. Zallan fitina! *The last time he came, he didn't even seem to remember who we were. He was just talking about this genie he said he met. I think he is crazy, anyway. Imagine marrying a genie. Who has ever seen one? He would have been dead.*

You know, the first time he returned, he just lazed around, went out to see his friends and talked about Zahira and jihad until everyone thought he was crazy. Sometimes he would sit around for days and not say anything to anyone, even his friends. Sometimes he would disappear for days and then show up and sit down in his room, listening to recordings of fiery sermons on the radio he kept locked in there. And then when these guys in Maiduguri started making trouble, he packed his things and said, 'Masha Allah, *I went to a faraway country to fight the war. Now,* Alhamdulillah, *the time for jihad in my country has come. I am going to join my brethren in Maiduguri and together we shall impose God's law in this country. If I die, may Allah accept my soul, otherwise may He help me kill as many infidels as possible. Say* Ameen.'

We didn't say ameen.

He asked me if I wanted to go with him and I said, hell no. Wallahi kuwa.

And, four years later, he walks through the door and sleeps for three days, shaking the flower vase on the coffee table with his unbearable snores.

I am a good son, mother. Wallahi, *I try. Imagine! I am 30 now and still unmarried. My friend Dahiru got married last year. Sadi, too, who is much younger than us and still hasn't got a job five years after graduating. I was lucky I got one with the ministry. It is not easy being a civil servant,* wallahi. *The pay is not good and then you see all this money meant for schools and hospitals disappearing into private pockets. You are ok if you keep quiet. Sometimes, your boss will say, I will make you an offer you can't refuse, just like in* The Godfather. *And you get to make some money on the side.*

Anyway, I try. I can't get married and keep two families. Since dad became whatever he became, I take care of this family. I get the money for your drugs and hospital bills and housekeeping money as well. I take care of my sisters' needs and my brother Jibreel, too. He wants to be a footballer. Fourteen years old now but already as tall as I am. I pay for their school fees and all. You should know this when you get well, Mother.

So you see, I have inherited Father's family. But I am a man. I have needs, ko ba haka ba? *So, sometimes, my girlfriend comes and we fool around. Nothing serious,* wallahi. *Nothing serious. You know me, Mother, you brought me up.*

You know, I think some day I will marry her. Her name is Jamila. She is a good girl. When you get better, you will meet her. You will like her, wallahi. *You will like her.*

I have to go now. I think Anisa is back from the market. She is going to make trouble because I wrote in her book of remembered things. But you know, I think she is amazing. All that talk about her heart being like dried, cracking earth and not being able to love is nothing but babble, wallahi. *She loves you. She has sacrificed her happiness to take care of you. If that isn't love, I don't know what is.*

✳ ✳ ✳

This boy is stupid, *wallahi*. Very stupid, Mother. He just came and took my book and wrote absolute rubbish in it. Such rubbish I felt like slapping him. But I'm calm now, Mother. I am calm now.

Your son, my brother, he is very stupid, *wallahi kuwa*.

✳✳✳

He woke up today, Mother. Father woke up while I bent over dusting the chairs in the living room. He looked at me and his eyes widened. *Ya Salam*! he said, My daughter has transformed into a great cow!

The laughter of Lawiza, who had been doing her assignment on the dining table, annoyed me. I went to my room and sat on the bed. I wiped away my tears; tears that wouldn't stop coming. So I let them flow, freely down my face.

Father was not always like this, Mother. I remember seeing the world on his shoulders, when he used to carry me as a little girl. I remember when he took us to the zoo, you and me and Salisu. He took us to see the wild things that were no longer wild. Ferocious things that stared back at you with mournful eyes through the cages.

I remember, too, the incandescence in your eyes when you saw him rock us on his shoulders. I remember his smile like the moon rising over water as he told us stories of Ali Baba and the Forty Thieves. That smile was lost with the things that were us, the things the fire took. He lost his laughter when he discovered the sheikh whose voice spilled fire and hate on the radio.

And he woke up today, my Father, and called me, his daughter, a great cow.

✳✳✳

Lawiza came crying to me tonight, Mother. I was here tending to you when she came. I held her in my arms and rocked her. That was when I knew how big she had grown. Twelve years old now. Almost a woman. And she wept in my arms.

Father spent the whole day praying. He prayed and prayed. And when he was done, he sauntered into your room, startling me and standing over your bed. He looked at you and knelt by your side. Your hands looked so tiny in his, so fragile. He caressed your hand and put it to his lips. You only stared mindlessly at the ceiling.

Lawiza walked in then. He looked at her and I saw recognition in his eyes. And then he looked at me as if expecting answers from me. I looked away.

My daughter? he said, and scratched his head, screwing his face into a thoughtful mask. Lawiza?

She nodded.

He nodded, too, and said, *Allahu Akbar*! You have grown. Then he crinkled his face at the ceiling and said, Lawiza is a meaningless name. It is not a good name to bear. I shall give you a new one. Your name shall be Fatima from today. Fatima, yes.

Lawiza only gawped.

He got up and walked to the door. When he turned and scanned me, his eyes tarried here and there and I felt as if cold little fingers were running beneath my dress.

When he left, Lawiza ran into my arms and I told her it would be alright. Lawiza came to me crying. And she cried a long time.

* * *

They have all gone now, the mourners. They have prayed for you and left to tend to the bits of their lives.

You looked so peaceful, Mother, on the day you died. So beautiful it was almost frightening. You reached and patted my cheeks. Your hands felt cold and weak but it warmed my heart. I wondered then if it was tears I saw in your eyes. But you smiled. For the first time in years, you smiled, Mother.

But I didn't understand the desperate gestures you made with your withered fingers. Until you nodded when I mentioned Salisu's name. When he came, your eyes brightened with a smile. And I watched how you held his hand and squeezed it. How you waved your fingers before your eyes and he nodded. A shared code that excluded me.

You looked so small in the bed. We covered you and you

slept wheezing. We smiled and wondered if the new herbs were working. We hoped they were.

But you died, Mother, quietly in your sleep.

The first thing I felt was anger and resentment. Seven years I sat by your bed. Seven years I cleaned and scrubbed, nursed and prayed. But when you were dying, it was Salisu you wanted. It was his hand you held. It was him you gifted your last scented smile.

I still see you now, shrouded in muslin, laid out on the bed. We, children of sorrow, said prayers for you. Lawiza wailed. Jibreel, too. Salisu stood grinding his teeth. And then the tears streamed.

Through the window, I watched the men line up behind your corpse. Father was in the front row, looking up to the heavens and shaking his head. His tears rolling into his beard as they said prayers for your radiant soul.

You were mourned, Mother, you were mourned. By forgotten kith and unyielding kin. But they've all gone now. All of them. And we, the disremembered sons and daughters, are left with the burden of grief.

* * *

I write now out of habit since you will no longer read this, Mother. I write to unburden my mind. To unshackle my tongue lost in the Sahara of silence. I knocked on Father's door today. I wanted to ask him questions your death had suppressed in my mind. So I went to his door.

He was sitting on his prayer rug and the fiery voice from the radio frothed with hate. When I sat down by the door, he turned it off. Those cold fingers crawled under my dress when he looked at me. I wanted to get up and leave. But I wanted to know, too. So I asked him. Father, were you there that day, the day they bombed the square?

His eyes jumped. He sat up and his brows furrowed into a scowl. Then he caressed his beard.

I want to know the truth, Father. I want to know. Were you there the day they killed Shamsu? The day they killed all those people at the square?

Ke! What are you insinuating? he said. The fire leapt in his eyes now. But it didn't scare me. I have been burnt enough.

I never insinuated anything, Father. I just asked if you were there, I said. But did he need to say anything more than his eyes had said already?

How different are you now from those people you claim are bombing Muslim babies in their cribs, Father?

He said, What do you know about anything, you?

I looked at him caressing his beard, looking at me like that. But the rage inside seared those fingers that would have crawled under my dress. I got up and started walking. When I got to the door, he said, Anisa, may God help you understand. May He forgive you.

I will be surprised if He forgives you, Father.

I walked out the door and closed my heart to him. And I write now, Mother, to unshackle my tongue lost in the wilderness of unsaid things.

✳✳✳

He came to my room, Mother. He didn't knock. Just walked in. And I was barely dressed. He looked at me and I felt those cold fingers again. I knew what he wanted to do. I couldn't stop him. He was too strong. And no one else was home.

He came to my room, Mother. And now I feel dirty. I just want to lay down and die.

✳✳✳

They knocked on my door. They knocked and knocked. First Lawiza. Then Jibreel. Then Salisu. Three days they've been knocking. But I can't let them see me, Mother. Not like this, garbed in shame. I contemplated a razor to my wrist and realized suicide takes more courage than I can muster. So I lay in my bed, dirty and filthy, hoping to die.

Salisu talked and begged me to tell him what happened. But what can I say? That my father called me Zahira and touched me like that?

They knocked on my door. And I lay here, on this bed, begging you, Mother, to help me die.

Knock, knock, knock! Anisa, open the door! The womb of silence is warm with unremembered things. The womb of silence engulfed me.

Anisa, forgive me, please, he whispered. The accursed Shaytan made me do it, *wallahi*, Anisa, my daughter.

He sat by my door and his whispers seeped through the chinks. The gentle thuds must have been his head knocking against the door panel. I lay on my bed and wiped away my tears.

Anisa, dear. Zahira made me do it, *wallahi*. She did. Oh God! I have transgressed against myself. Forgive me!

God will not forgive you, Father, because I won't.

* * *

He bleeds. His blood drenches the sofa, drenches the rug.

'*Ya Salam!*'

That was what he said when I plunged the knife into his neck. He was sitting on the sofa then, shaking his head, muttering. I crept up from behind and stuck it in his neck. His blood is astonishingly red. And it pours like a broken tap.

I did it, Mother. I did. You held my hand and asked me to look out for my siblings. It was the last thing you asked of me. And this man, this our father, comes and lays his bloodied hands on Anisa.

I knew he had done something bad the moment I returned and found her locked in her room. And the way he turned his shamed face away from me. But she wouldn't say, not even a word. And then I heard him sitting outside her door saying that Zahira made him do it, that the devil made him do it. I did this, Mother. And the devil wouldn't have been able to stop me if he had tried. The world is a better place without him. I shall not regret this.

I just wanted to tell you, Mother. I wanted you to hear it from me. Now I need to go clean up the mess in the living room, before Lawiza and Jibreel return from school.

✳ ✳ ✳

I saw Salisu today, Mother. After two months, I saw him. He seemed so thin but his smile was reassuring. When he reached across the table and took my hands, the prison warder said, No touching.

But he won't look into my eyes. He looked down instead. We talked about the food, about the bed bugs and the torment of mosquitoes. And when we were done with the small talk, we fidgeted with our fingers.

When he said, I am sorry, Sister Anisa. I should have been there to protect you, his voice broke. The prison guard allowed us to lean into each other. And we cried. We wept, Mother.

He will be alright, Mother. He is strong. I saw him and I am stronger now. He told me you let yourself go so I could unfurl my wings and fly again. He asked me to look after the kids. And I walked out of there, sad to leave him behind, but stronger. And full of hope. I have written for you, Mother, things remembered. And now I will let the rain wash over my mind, wash away this filth. I will let the rain wash over me.

Abubakar Adam Ibrahim is the author of the short-story collection *The Whispering Trees* (Parresia Publishers, Lagos, 2012). He is a Gabriel Garcia Marquez Fellow and has won the BBC African Performance Prize. He lives in Abuja, Nigeria.

A Memory This Size

Elnathan John

Some days when I want to forget, an overwhelming guilt envelops me and, as if punishing me for daring to, comes back, fresh, clear – every painful detail. I just read an essay by Marion Winik, who wrote that she has let her stillborn son, Peewee, go because she *could not hold on to a sadness that size for very long*. It makes sense to me. I read the line over and over again. It sounds clever and practical and I try to say it to myself, to justify letting this memory go without feeling so guilty: *I cannot hold on to a sadness this size for very long*. It feels dirty when I say it.

***

I have held on to it for 10 years now. Sometimes I find myself feeling entitled to a greater sadness than anyone, including our parents. My mind lays out the reasons:

I was there when it happened. I pulled him out of the deep end of the Olympic-sized pool onto the tiled floor and put my ear to his chest and then my mouth to his mouth. Everything I had read or watched about mouth-to-mouth resuscitation came back to me, clear as day. I blew air and pumped. I rested his head against my chest and stared into his half-open eyes, pressing his cold body against mine as we raced to the hospital, willing him to live, to breathe, to smile and say 'ha! I fooled you'.

I knew him better than anyone else. He shared with me secrets he would never dare tell dad or mum, fears he would be too shy to admit to his friends, troubles he would be too scared to voice to anyone but me, the older brother he thought was wiser.

We shared things. We shared resentments against our parents. I agreed with him when he told me I was being a hypocrite because I listened to both mum and dad each time any of them wanted to complain about the other. Neither of us could wait to leave the house. We shared a love for water – river or pool, it didn't matter. It didn't matter that we had been forbidden from going near any body of water.

My family never talks about him. There is a silent agreement to erase his name from our lips, his life from our conversations. When someone mentions his name by mistake everyone goes quiet. It annoys me. It annoys me that we are rewriting our history without him, without the things that he did or said. Some days I say his name over and over in my head.

Azan.

Azan.

Azan.

* * *

His grave is unmarked and I can't find it when I go back. All I see is mounds of earth. It is not our tradition to mark graves but it hurts not to be able to tell which is his.

Apart from his photo album, all I have of him is this memory. And I am afraid to lose that. These days I try to give him a moustache and more flesh, to bring him into my present. He would have qualified as an electrical/electronics engineer and, if I knew him, he would have loved to practise his profession. I think our television was the only piece of equipment he didn't take apart. Things with little parts confuse me and make my head spin. I avoid screws like flies avoid kerosene. It always amazed me how he would take apart a piece of electronic equipment, take out what seemed like a hundred screws and parts and still remember where each one went. I think my problem is memory. I forget things easily. I always have. In the fourth year of primary school I was humiliated because I couldn't remember the words during a spelling bee. In junior secondary school, although I was among the best readers of French, I was dropped from a major role in the national French drama competition because I couldn't remember my lines and my short-tempered teacher didn't want anyone reading from a paper.

I am afraid of losing little bits of his memory – phrases he uttered, places we went, clothes he wore, his body: pronounced cheekbones, long limbs, flat forehead, big cone-shaped navel, flat tummy that he was trying to work into a six pack before he died. So I keep his photos close and do not fight the sadness. I let fresh tears drop, 10 years after.

✳✳✳

We are both in secondary school. The same height, even though I am three years older. Everyone thinks we are twins but we can never see the resemblance. His name, Azan, sounds like Hassan, the Hausa name for a twin. So this worsens the situation. We have stopped telling people that we are not twins. I think we both secretly wish we were. Everyone treats twins like members of an exotic race. I walk into the living room and he is on the landline to his friend Michael. He has taken my little book and is excitedly reading my poems to his friend. I don't like my work half as much as he does. He says, 'I hate poetry but I love your poems.' He refuses to read any other poems I recommend to him. Whatever I write, he reads, religiously. I love this faithful one-man fan club.

✳✳✳

We have both finished secondary school, him two years after me. I have accepted the painful fact that he is several inches taller than me and will probably be all-round bigger and stronger. I guess I saw it coming from the last time we fought as kids. I still ended up beating him but it was harder than any other fight we had. I knew I had to stop or soon face total humiliation. Sometimes we recall the days we used to fight and we laugh. He is a wild one, his temper worse than mine. The slightest things make him angry all day. Passing his food under sunlight, for example. In our old low-cost house all the rooms were separate and opened into a courtyard, so that to get to the kitchen you would have to come out into the open courtyard. He would shield his food from the sun with his body. 'When sun touches oil, it changes the taste. I hate the taste of sun on oil.' And somehow, even when he wasn't there, he knew when the sun had touched his food.

He hates the smell of matches and will not strike a match unless he absolutely has to. He washes his hands thoroughly when he does.

✳✳✳

Dad has bought a lot of food items. We need to offload them from the trunk of his old Mercedes into the kitchen. I am expected as firstborn to carry the heaviest item – the 50kg bag of rice. I breathe, lift one end and drag. I lose my grip on the bag and almost fall. I try again. My father watches as I struggle. Azan leaves his yams and takes the bag of rice. He heaves and in one attempt his long strong arms lift the bag. He runs with it into the kitchen, taking care to avoid the sharp thorns and branches of the dried-out orange tree before turning into the doorway. I feel shame. I look away from dad's irritated face. I feel the heavy judgement of his eyes: *you can't lift an ordinary bag of rice, look how easy it was for your younger brother.* Azan doesn't rub it in. He worships me, hangs onto my every word, trusts me. He thinks I am better than any goddamn poet. How can I feel any resentment toward him?

***

We had moved into our new house in the south of the state to escape the riots and be on the safe side. In Kaduna, as in many parts of northern Nigeria, where you live can determine whether you live or die when Christians and Muslims start killing each other. We had escaped death once and, even though our house was not yet completed, we moved in, with a mobile police escort and all our property fitting into the longest UN truck I'd ever seen.

The first time I am really scared for my brother, when I am really sure I love him to bits, is only a few months after we come here to this house where the flush doors do this scary thing of opening and closing by themselves. We sometimes make jokes about spirits invading the house. Mum says, well, there is no use running if they really are spirits. 'When they come, just dialogue with them,' she jokes, 'ask them what they want.' My brother is running, being chased by my sister after playing pranks on her. I am outside in the compound that is green with trees: orange, mango, lemon and paw-paw. The main entrance has a clear glass sliding door. Sometimes, at night especially when everywhere is lit, it is hard to know if the door is open or shut. I see him run right through the glass. It feels like someone has stabbed me in the stomach. I run to where he is. He is cut in several places. I scan his body, worried about his face and stomach. His eyes especially. Thankfully, just his arms and legs are cut. He gets up to walk and falls down. 'I can't see,' he says, 'I am dizzy.' We have a neighbour who is a nurse and has a little drug store in front of her house. We take him there for her to do something about the bleeding. I can see his veins. She stitches him up fine. We don't need to drive him to the hospital that night.

***

He is nine or so when he starts stealing. Money. I am not

sure why. He would sneak into mum's room and take his pick from her bag or purse. Mum is traumatized. When she finds out he is the one, she and dad sit him down and talk to him for hours. They need to know what the problem is. They probe and prod and threaten and cajole but he doesn't budge. They use the Bible and worldly wisdom. He doesn't speak. I wonder if someone is bullying him and forcing him to take money. This kind of bullying is common. I am scared that he will become a thief. But after a few months it stops the same way it started, without ceremony or explanation. He never steals again.

✱ ✱ ✱

I am six years older than my sister and almost 10 years older than David, the last born. My relationship with these two is not like my relationship with Azan. Some days I think they don't like me half as much as they like him. They adore him. Even though he is tougher on them than I am, they obey him without grumbling. I can barely get any of them to get me water from the kitchen. They think I like to assert my authority as firstborn too much. So I devise a way of reducing the confrontation. I ask him to do things for me, and he in turn sends them. As long as the job is done, I don't mind that he is closer to them than I am.

✱ ✱ ✱

We are in our old house and Azan walks in with a sick-looking black mongrel with brown patches above its eyes. It might have looked cute if it weren't so tiny and malnourished. It is so small he can't put a leash around its neck. He drops it at the far left of the courtyard between the tall tree with dark green guavas and the toilet. He makes a rope by tearing a thin strip of cloth from an old wrapper and ties the puppy to an iron pillar. Its bark is fierce but feeble. I am angry but

Azan is determined. It is impossible to convince him to take this puppy back to godknowswhere. This is the first dog we will have. He will be the only believer in this dog. He will name it Shanny and raise it to become a beautiful, wild dog that will terrorize the neighbours. It will outlive all but one of its own puppies. It will outlive the only one who had faith in it, who didn't let it die.

***

The one thing that is sure to make us quarrel is table tennis. One of our neighbours owns a table-tennis board and lets people pay to play. After we return from school we take off our school uniforms – sometimes just our shirts – and head off to Emmanu's house. I always win and he always gets mad because I rub it in. Typically he flings the bat and goes home as I laugh derisively. Sometimes, during the dry season, when the water is clear and the rocks are still visible above the water, we sneak off to the river to swim with mostly rough Hausa boys. There are few sins in my house greater than going to the river just two streets away. My mother would have a heart attack if she knew how often we swam in this filthy, dangerous, crowded river. Once a boy plunged headfirst onto the rocks and cracked his skull open. We take Vaseline in little cellophane wraps because our faces will look whitish afterward. We can't do anything about our red eyes. Our parents never catch us.

***

Sometimes I wish I could challenge or directly disobey my parents the way he does. I wish I had the heart to steal my father's car – he is too paranoid to let his over-18 child drive. I wish I could say no the way Azan sometimes does. I wonder what goes through his mind when he does this. I have too much fear in my heart. It annoys me.

* * *

The first time I discover death, I do it alone. I am 14 and I hear that a boy who hanged himself in the huge gully that has mango trees is to be buried in the Christian burial ground opposite my house. I have never been to the gully but, from the descriptions of Mercy, our housemaid, who knows everything about everyone, I must have passed by the place before. It is mango season and I wonder if the boy saw a ripe mango as he tied the rope, first to a strong branch and then in a noose around his neck; if perhaps he had some before he died – a last meal. He used the rope his family fetch water with from their deep well. He untied it from the metal bowl – a gas canister cut in half. Mercy tells me the details as if the suicide was her idea. My mind goes through all the processes, starting with choosing the site, a lonely gully. Would he have gone to more than one site? Did he think of another way? Swallowing something, perhaps? The gully was not too close to his house and I wonder if this means he carefully planned it so that he would have been perfectly dead by the time anyone even thought of looking for him. What went through his mind when he loosened the tight rope around the half gas canister by the well, when he folded the long rope, put it around his waist or in his pocket or in a little knapsack? Did he know how to swim, was that why he didn't just jump into the well? I wanted to see his face, look for the burn signs around his neck, look at his eyes – as shut as they may be, look at his face. For answers.

I decide to attend the funeral.

I discover my fascination with the burial ground, hurriedly built coffins, and sombre sermons struggling to rise above crying relatives. From the window of our small living room, I can see, through metal window bars, the street that separates our identical block of low-cost housing from the Christian part of the open burial ground. A burial usually starts with two or three men early in the morning with daggers, shovels and machetes. There is no readable expression on their creased faces except, after a while, tiredness, by which time their entire bodies are gleaming with sweat. They are just rounding up when the first people, usually relatives, begin to arrive, arms folded, mouth hanging down, eyes staring beyond their gaze, heaving and sighing. The first ones apart from the gravediggers come to check if the grave is the right size, if they need to increase the width or depth of the grave.

The women's arrival is my signal that I need to prepare before it becomes harder to penetrate the crowd, to see the grave, freshly dug, to see the coffin, and smell the fresh wood varnish.

Today, the diggers come and the inspectors come and the women come and the pickup truck comes and all the other cars that make our street temporarily difficult to pass. I am there before the truck but after the women. It is 4pm and dad is not due home for another two hours. I do not come in through the gate of the burial ground, but through a gap in the barbed wire fence, the point closest to our house. All the shrubs from this point on are familiar – I was here only two days ago for another burial. A child in a small coffin. Azan doesn't know. He is off playing with his friends.

The brothers look upset. They are angry, not sad. They do not nod when the pastor, preaching in Hausa, says: 'For everything under heaven there is a time. A time to be born and a time to die.' They do not hum amen when the pastor, with veins bulging on his neck, prays that God will ferry him straight to heaven. They seem not to agree with the pastor that he is in a better place. One of the brothers turns. Our eyes meet. I had been staring at him for many minutes. I see in his eyes a need to punch someone. To drag his brother out of the coffin and slap him for dying.

I do not know the words of the hymn they are singing but I recognize it from the other funerals.

I do not feel like crying. That is, until the pastor asks the family, starting with his parents, to pour the sand on the coffin. His mother fetches a handful of the damp, red laterite. Two plump women are holding her by the arm. She is sobbing as she moves forward to throw the sand into the hole. The women let go of her and, just as they do, she screams and makes to jump into the grave. The women, faster than her, catch her just as she begins sliding down the heap of laterite by the side of the grave. There is a commotion and she is carried away.

As they drag her away, my nose begins to tremble and hurt. I am fighting back the tears because I know that, once that first one rolls down, I will break down and sob like I am being whipped with a cane of thorns. Holding back that first tear is important.

I turn to leave before it starts to get rowdy. I push my way through the crowd, jog along the bushy path, kicking the broad leaves of the bright green shrubs, run past the ambulance and across the road until I reach our gate. I still have a few more minutes until my father returns. He is so predictable, my father. I lock myself in the bathroom and feel my chest swelling, about to explode. I wonder what it feels like to die – what eternal non-existence is, what it feels like. I close my eyes and try to conjure eternity. My mind travels through dark tunnels of space and time until I start to get dizzy and scared and I open my eyes. I wonder what it means when they say God has no beginning and has no end. Again, I try to imagine having no beginning and it gives me the same dizzy feeling.

Why do we have to die? This is what makes me finally break down. I cry hot, painful tears. I think of all the things that my father taught me about God and His right to rule and Adam and Eve blowing our chances at eternity just because of some fruit. I do not know if God made the right decision, letting billions of people suffer for the sins of one greedy couple. I know the answers in my head, but not in my heart. I cry for a suicidal stranger and for what I will share with that stranger one day.

I hear my brother Azan's voice and then my father's. I quickly take off my clothes, open the shower and let the water rush over my face.

***

My fascination with death and burial grounds dies when Azan dies.

***

We are back home because university lecturers across the country are on strike. I was unable to get into university for two years so we are both about to finish our first year, he in Bauchi, me in Zaria. This is the first time we have been away from each other for that long. He has grown leaner, taller. His eyes have sunk deeper. But he is still a boy. He is more temperamental, wilder, livelier. I have become more introspective, morose. I have had my first sexual experience and am struggling with religion and God and the unwieldy heaviness of a guilty conscience. He has found new friends. We are more different than we have ever been. I want quiet. He likes the loud, explicit music of Eminem. He is out more often. Once I try to walk with his friends but I find we have nothing in common.

We get into an altercation about his music. The way the house is built you can hear everything going on two rooms away. I tell him to turn down the volume again and again until he gets angry and turns it back up. It gets really heated and for the first time he threatens me. 'I will kill you!' he says. I see in his eyes someone I don't know. I am afraid but I try not to show it. I report him to our father who instantly sides with me at the mention of angry rap music. Azan and I don't talk for a month after that.

I am angry but I miss him. He doesn't want to talk to me. He is acting all tough but I can see through it a boy wanting to become a man. One day I realize he wants to go out but is broke. I split my cash in two and walk into his room. I ask him if he wants some money. He looks away and doesn't answer. I see him struggling not to talk to me. I leave the money on his table and go. When I notice he has dressed up and is on his way out I look in his room and see that he has taken the money. I smile. I have broken him. We talk later that night. I apologize. He tells me that, for the first time, I let him down. 'There is nobody I look up to like you,' he says, 'but you just disappointed me.' I swear that I will never let him down again. Then he confides in me. He tells me of some trouble at University. I feel bad that I could not see that all of it was a cry for help – the aggression, the rap songs, the fighting. I tell him we will work something out. I will travel back with him to his university if I have to.

Some of the guys in the area are going out in a few days to swim in the largest public pool in Kaduna. We plan our own trip before theirs so that we can have a chance to talk about his problems and also because we are really fed up with them. Azan is swimming at the deep end and diving from the diving board around some other boys I have never seen before. Come and dive, he shouts excitedly. I refuse. You fear too much, he teases, and dives.

A few minutes pass and although I am not looking in his direction I realize I have not been hearing his voice. I turn and I can't find him. None of the others have seen him. I put on my clothes and go out of the pool area to look for him – perhaps he went out to buy something. I am tired of swimming, and it is getting cooler. As the seconds become minutes I am increasingly afraid. He is nowhere. My heart starts to race and I take off my clothes and dive into the deep end. I search with my eyes under the water. I do not come up for air until I feel my lungs about to burst.

After coming up twice, I find him about 10 feet below the surface. With the help of the lifeguard who has just come, I pull him out. His lifeless body shows no sign of injury. His head isn't swollen and neither is his stomach. I hold his body. Put my ears to his chest. Do mouth-to-mouth. Beg God for one breath.

Just one breath. Please God, don't let him die. Don't let this happen. I can't. I won't know how to handle it.

No word from God. Just a cold confirmation of death from an impersonal doctor more concerned about a text message he is sending than the trembling young man in front of him. My father comes running into the hospital ward. I am shocked to see him. I am not sure how he has heard. He glowers at me as he walks past. A few minutes later he walks out, having also confirmed that his son is dead. He is trembling as he walks toward me.

'You are happy now, *abi*? You are happy? You have gone and killed yourselves. When we say don't do this, you think we don't know what we are saying. Look at it now. Look at it now.'

His voice floats over my head. I am sitting on the concrete floor, my back against a cold stone wall, too shocked to cry. I have no idea what has hit me. *This dream is too long, too real.* A few hours later I arrive home. I am clutching Azan's clothes. My head is about to burst. I sit outside by the water pump and hold the only thing I have left of him: a brown beach shirt, brown chinos, grey shoes that looked somewhere in between sneakers and formal shoes. Throughout that evening and the many days after, people come to the house and want to pray with us. I am tired of the prayers. I just want to block out the world with my earpiece, listen to sad songs as loudly as I can and cry.

My brother David, who is only 11, is the only one who isn't crying. 'It's ok,' he comforts my sister and mother, hugging them. I envy him.

A few months later, University resumes. The world does not end. People forget. My chest still hurts from crying. I am stuck in a dizzying loop of thoughts. *I wonder sometimes what would have happened if I had not suggested we go to the pool. If I had been swimming with him at the deep end. If we had gone to the park instead.*

* * *

I am irritating my father a lot. When I am home during breaks from University, I am unhelpful and short-tempered. I come home late and don't talk to anyone. My siblings complain to my parents about my aggression. My participation in religious activities is half-hearted. I do not hide my boredom. When my father asks me to pray after reading the day's Bible text in the morning, I mumble words they can hardly hear and end very quickly. One day, dad breaks and screams at me: 'When your brother was alive, we didn't feel the pain of your bad behaviour so much. He was a cushion...'

My entire body is hit with the same dull pain I felt the evening Azan died. Dad has peeled open the wound we had managed to keep covered, the wound we all have. It feels like he is angry that I am mourning too much, taking too much of the memory, hurting others. I walk out of the house and sit on the floor by the borehole handpump – the same place I sat because I could not take his clothes back into the house. It is cold and I am not wearing a shirt. My chest hurts. I want to go back in and say: 'When my brother was alive, I didn't feel the pain of your constant fighting with mum so much. He was a cushion.' I just shiver and cry.

* * *

On the seventh anniversary of Azan's death, I post a tribute to my brother on Facebook. Albert, who barely knows me, asks me to let go of the memories already and move on. I ignore his comment but what I really want to do is type: *Albert, fuck you! What do you know about this?*

I have gotten used to moving around with this weight and it balances me more than it pulls me down. It steadies me.

***

These days I find myself in all sorts of cluttering relationships. I think I am looking for something, only I have no clue what I am looking for. I am mostly numb and self-indulgent and end up hurting the people who are drawn to my elaborate façades. The only things I am sure about are things I have lost. Maybe I am looking for water in a store full of juice packs. Sometimes I wonder if it was really that great, what we had together. Or if I am making up this single source of joy I had for many years. At those times I stop and try to think of specific joyful events, specific bonding moments. Then it seems less likely that I am inventing things.

***

I no longer go home as I used to, even though I am now mostly self-employed and free to make the three-hour trip from Abuja to Kaduna. Dad sends me a text about how disappointed he is that I have abandoned the faith. Every bottled-up resentment comes back – the bitter words, the daily altercations, the second burial of Azan, of which we are all guilty by our silence. I send back several angry texts saying everything I have wanted to say for 10 years. Everything from the things Azan and I talked about to the numbness I now feel. About family. About God. About religion. Especially religion. I am tired of pretending around him that I can continue practising it. He tries to call me. I do not pick up. He replies. He says he knows, or at least imagined that all those years of anger must have been traumatizing. I do not know if this is enough, if I will go back home, any time soon.

When I am tempted to let go, I ask myself, not if I want to but if I can afford to. I don't know how to compartmentalize, to remember Azan and not be sad, to think only happy thoughts. I write Azan a long letter every April 1st to mark the day I pulled his lifeless 18-year-old body from the deep

end of a pool. I tell him what's going on in my life. I laugh.
I tell him who is making me smile, which relatives are
married or dead or being total assholes. I cry. I used to tell
myself: *one day I will write a nice witty story about my dear
brother, about the intensity of his life and some philosophical
interpretation about how a life lived so intensely was bound
to be short.* Crap like that. I have since killed the thought. I
hold on to this big, sad-and-happy memory because *I cannot
afford to let a memory this size disappear.*

Elnathan John is a full-time writer who trained as a lawyer
in Nigeria. His writing has been published in *Per Contra, ZAM
Magazine, Evergreen Review, Sentinel Nigeria* and Chimurenga's *The
Chronicle.* He writes political satire for a Nigerian newspaper and
his blog for which he hopes someday to get arrested and famous.
He has tried hard, but has never won anything.

The Red Door

Billy Kahora

Julius Rotiken Sayianka and Eddie Muchiri Kambo came to the small rise in the old Datsun 1200 pick up, and got off the main Narok Highway, just before Suswa, where it had all become patchwork from the '97 El Nino floods. Julius took the Datsun into free gear heading downhill to the little seasonal Rift Valley lake, now called Mwisho wa WaKikuyu after the Maasai-Kikuyu clashes. When the laga came into view, on the endless Savanna plain, a long boy lay under one of the Zebus, his mouth stuck fast on wrinkled udder, feeding like a long leech. Julius shouted Fuck! in the safety of the cabin and sharply hooted. This cleared the scene. The enjoined cow-boy sketch, canvassed against wide sky, broke into two, righting the world.

Julius glanced at Chiri, saw he had caught this piece of primal theatre, and switched off Snoop Dog on the radio. This was Leakey country, the laga once a prehistoric lake on the floor of the Great Rift. Julius saw the long boy in his side mirror recede, noting the long handkerchief over his mouth. They had passed without pause, not asking which clan he belonged to, an intended insult for the boy's animal act.

'What's with the face cloth?' Chiri asked.

Julius peered into the side mirror. 'Not sure. Maybe his family thinks they can keep him from cow tit.'

Chiri saw from his face that he was serious. A young donkey stepped away from the Datsun's quiet roar, its jaws a metronome in the plains wind. It raised its head and brayed far to the long northeast where the flat ended and the blue hills took over. They rumbled towards the other edge of the laga, a soccer field away from the long boy. Julius tipped the Datsun into the edge of the water to cool the tyres and let the makeshift blower exhaust slowly calm down.

When they stepped into the open, Julius was tall, broad shouldered, hard, thin and wiry, with a dark firm face and a small proportional head. Chiri was shorter, lighter and leant towards roundness.

They saw that the long boy had shrugged off his *shuka* and waded into the far shore. 'Definitely a badhead,' Julius remarked. 'In August, *moran* warriors should be in the forest. That idiot looks old enough.' Julius sat on the water's edge on the driver's side, stuck his long thin knees in the air, and slipped a Sportsman in his mouth, his mouth full of miraa. 'Did you see the size of him,' he said squinting against the sun glinting from the laga.

Chiri looked towards the far shore without response and squatted on his left, furrowed his palm in the water, worried the two-day grime he had picked on the road, then scooped some water into his pits. Through the wet dripping from his face, Chiri saw the long boy had now been joined in the water by his animals. From where they were, Zebu horns and humps stuck out of the laga mirror. The donkey and goat-headed sheep dipped in and out of the water as if controlled by some giant hand in the sky. Chiri spit out the taste of Zebu from the laga and cursed.

Julius and Chiri had been on the road for three days. Both were in different forms of self-exile from Nairobi. The two were close childhood friends from Buru Buru. Julius had failed in Nairobi mainstream pursuits such as education and normal middle-class behaviour, been banished by his father after his O-levels and had never been able to go back. Chiri had gone to his friend's father's funeral back in March, four months ago, and, after they started drinking thereafter, one thing led to another: Chiri walked out of his advertising job at Ogilvy & Mather, just a year after dropping out of the University of Nairobi. Chiri saw himself in limbo, this thing on the road out in the Rift Valley as good an option as any.

Chiri now watched as Julius stood up and checked all the tractor and combine parts they had bought in Nakuru, strapped to the Datsun's back. Julius slapped the bags of seed, fertilizer and insecticide, ready for wheat planting season. He then opened the bonnet, poured in water from the laga into the radiator and stepped back as water shot up in an arc, fountain-like, and then lessened as the engine cooled. He cleaned off the deposits around the battery terminals, wiped the windscreen. Chiri did not join Julius's tense ritual. Since Julius's father, Petro Sayianka, died in March, Chiri noticed and respected his friend's sudden silences, tense and abrupt. He wandered off, made sure there was no wildlife around, and peed in the open field. He watched his yellow, alcohol-heavy pee splotch in the dust, stain the earth and disappear. When Chiri saw Julius look over to him, he strolled back to the Datsun and opened the broken glove compartment. The Marie biscuits had gone soft but there was still some of the Chelsea Dry Gin. He handed over the miraa to Julius, the stems now black and curled like a small dead bird's claws. There was also some *choma* left – *mbuzi* ribs crusted with fat, crawling with ants, hours old tasty. Chiri wished aloud for some *ugali*.

'Maasais don't eat *ugali*. Spoils meat,' Julius said. Chiri did not remind him that he was half Kikuyu, a hundred per cent Nairobi Buru Buru tribe. Julius's mother, Mrs Sayianka, was Kikuyu. Chiri knew better and skinned the ribs with his teeth, watching Julius carefully pore over the miraa.

Chiri was now getting used to these small intense tutorials on what was out here, just like the silences. Lessons on wheat. Lessons on Maasais. Reflections on how shitty Nairobi, Buru Buru were. They left the dusty weed for last, lit up, got their heads going for Narok, ready for the barmaids, the fights, the ugliness, the *ujinga*. Then, they would get into planting over the next two weeks. It was July, slightly overcast, the rains would have started further south and west.

On the other side of the laga, the long boy whooped and shouted; some storks on the singular tree took off in witness. Julius, newly alert from the weed, the gin and miraa, turned like a dog studying something he couldn't quite make out.

'I have never seen a Maasai swimming,' Julius marvelled in a low voice. 'I'm not sure what that uncircumcised retard is doing here – in this no man's land, the Kikuyu on the MaiMahiu side, the Maasai on Narok side. This belongs to no one. I'm not sure whether his people know that he grazes here. This is a place of blood.'

'Maybe he just wants to play,' Chiri observed. 'A big kid.'

Julius looked at him hard and, when Chiri looked away, Julius said: 'Here on the border, the old ways are lost. Too many Kikuyus. They marry Maasais and they no longer remember the ways of the Red Door.'

'The Red Door?' Chiri asked.

Julius looked at him, smiled. 'Everything. You'll see. *Mlango nyekundu* and *mlango nyeusi* – where all Maasais come from.' Red Door and Black Door.

Chiri's eyes fell on the laga mirror, and he could just make out Julius's face – magnified and contorted, as if he were now thinking about the boy, what they had come upon earlier. But maybe also thinking of his father's death months ago. Or how to deal with Sol, his elder fuck-up of a brother, who they were meeting in Narok later. Sol had just come from the UK after seven years of doing fuck-all.

A flock of storks resettled into the small acacia tree as they saw the big head re-emerge right in the middle of the laga. Then it submerged into the water. After a few seconds, a few metres from their feet, the dog-like face with new-born baby eyes emerged from the laga, the fish mouth puckering through the handkerchief. Chiri felt the basalt age of the old plain, its prehistoric silence.

The long boy broke out of the water, hanging out for all the plains to see – tall against the Datsun's front, seemingly even longer than the car itself. Even when Julius stood up to full height, in his Safari boots, the long boy towered over him, in primal challenge. Chiri stepped back, almost bolted. Julius flicked his Sportsman in the long boy's face, reached out, tore the boy's handkerchief off his face and slapped him hard. Julius raised his hand again but the baby eyes went wider than a Friesian's. Exposed, the boy's face went flat and started gushing at the mouth and eyes. The long form cowered under Julius, who lowered his hand and let the handkerchief drop. The long boy started bawling, making star jumps into the sky. His penis, a fifth arm, jerked in all directions like an enormous hose – and then he bolted like an antelope. Julius picked up the handkerchief, went round, opened the car door, dipped his head and then came out, his face dark. Chiri remembered the childhood Buru Buru fights, the same triumphant face, the pointless violence.

'*Ero...*' Julius shouted. He hurled the Marie biscuits at the retreating figure. The packet made a long arc in the sky and then fell in the shallow water close to shore. 'Now his people will know where their milk goes.' Julius said to Chiri, picking up the white handkerchief and throwing it in the back of the Datsun.

Chiri stood there and watched the unfortunate figure dip its fish mouth in the mud of the shoreside looking for the biscuits. When Chiri entered the car, he said, 'Out here the price of milk is a beating?'

'Narok awaits,' Julius said, now relaxed. 'Time to plant.'

They chased the dying sun down, drained of energy and speech, sweeping past mostly trucks, the weed wearing off. When a Land Cruiser or Land Rover swiftly flew past them they sat up and discussed its relative strengths, weaknesses.

Outside Narok town, they came to the commercial wheat

farms, perfect like miniature Lego models, incongruous to the acacias, the open grasslands, the *National Geographic* mud huts, the scrawny Zebus, stray jackal dogs and the omnipresent goats. Inside the fence there were rows of bright red tractors and harvesters, asexual uniforms at work and calf-size Alsatian dogs guarding ploughed land dotted with young green shoots, in furrows that went on as far as the eye could see. Julius said: 'Belongs to some *mzungu* called Mike Hampstead, Minister Ntimama and Senyo. They only turn on the electric fence at night. I see they've already started planting.'

'Who's Senyo?' Chiri asked.

Julius grimaced. 'Owner of all you see ahead of you. Richest Maasai. Cows that you can't count. Land that doesn't end.'

'You make him sound like God,' Chiri chuckled.

Julius was quiet then said: 'Wait and see what's ahead of us. Problem with Nairobi and your beloved Buru Buru is that it makes you oblivious. One day I will hire a *mzungu* manager. Take my children to a *mzungu* school. That's why I'm out here.'

As they moved up the road slowly, gazing at the commercial farm, Julius explained to Chiri how wheat had roots in the Old Testament. How it was God's crop. How, unlike maize, it did not threaten the Maa sense of flatness. That a man could see and count the most important thing in life, his cows, from afar. That he could also see the dreaded buffalo coming at him. That wheat did not breed devil snakes like sugarcane, sisal. Three weeks since they left Nairobi, Chiri was still trying to know this Julius, who spoke with this old movie-preview monotone in tune with the flat roads and the long days. At times Chiri was tempted, but he knew better than to laugh. He was starting to understand that there would be more road tutorials, remembering Julius as a kid who talked up much more than he knew. He tried to understand this Julius who now lived his life around five-month cycles – in tune with the wheat, which had two crops every year. Chiri remembered his childhood friend's penchant for the fantastical when he listened to him break down the percentages. He also remembered Julius's father, Petro Sayianka, as a cold, smoothly shaven man who imposed a strict hand on his sons. Chiri wondered if any of these dreams would have been possible if Julius's father had still been alive. He could hear the new sense of freedom and possibilities in his friend's voice now that his father was no longer present.

***

When Julius and Chiri got into Narok, the strange incident at the laga behind them, the lights revived them. Narok in the evening hour was small-town alive to the evening breeze, the promise of meat, alcohol and sex. Julius did his Narok ritual, whenever they were back in town, driving around town, taking the perimeter, through London slum, around downtown Narok curved into the natural bowl that the town was built in, past the old market, the cattle sale, the Diplomat Hotel. When they came back full circle, someone shouted his clan name, Rotiken, and they stopped, waiting. Obergon, a first cousin and prosperous absentee agricultural officer, waddled up, sweating meat, full of *afya*. His broad face was all smiles till he peered into the cabin and saw Chiri. He spat on the ground and said something in Maasai. Julius grinned.

'*Habari* Kikuyu,' Obergon hailed Chiri, who ignored him. '*Habari Mudu wa House*,' he repeated to Chiri with a sneer. All of them laughed.

'Have you finished planting? Your late *mzee* was always done by early July,' Obergon asked. Julius indicated the back where all the wheat season preparations were stacked. Obergon nodded in approval, his stomach still heaving from laughing at Chiri. He looked at the purchases.

'Be careful. A lot of Kikuyus now live in Narok after being

displaced from the clashes.'

He then changed tack. 'Your brother Sol has been drinking at Agip *tangu* lunchtime,' he announced. 'The Senyo clan is there. You know what that means. *Twende.*'

The Senyo clan sat in a semi-circle flank in the open-air part of Agip restaurant, a large pride that had carved its territory in the larger Narok world, potent in its violence. Waiters buzzed around them like courtiers at a national banquet. Chiri found himself whispering the count – and it came to 27 clan members. Obergon said that this was just a peripheral side of the clan, troublemakers and idlers. The clan occupied an imperial arrangement of five tables – two doddering elders, talking with their gums with an ancient air of instruction to several men in their early thirties with hard faces. Some younger man-boys hovered around them. The women sat to the side in supplication, their cheeks ornamented with vertical scars, their litters of shy kids cowing at the men's harsh voices. Goat bones lay littered around them, spread over tables. Myriads of stray dogs had taken up station at a distance, jackals around a lion kill, sniffing.

Julius's older brother, Sol, was nowhere to be seen. One of the Senyo men in his thirties perfunctorily nodded at Obergon when the boys came in, ignored Julius and Chiri, and said something to his companions. He then glared at them as he worried a toothpick in his mouth, making deep leopard chuckles.

'Nkaiseri Senyo,' Obergon muttered, leading Julius and Chiri clear, to the other side of the bar where the bartender was imprisoned behind chicken mesh, haloed in the light of a small lamp spewing kerosene.

'See if you can find Sol,' Julius told Chiri. 'Avoid those animals.'

'Scream if necessary,' Obergon added. '*Kama mwanamke.*'

Chiri did not ask how he could spot a Senyo from afar, sensing that Obergon and Julius needed to discuss something and he was not welcome. It reminded him of moments in childhood when the Sayianka brothers would exclude him to keep him in his place.

Chiri followed the smell. Sol was not in the loo. Nor was he at the grill. Chiri went out back towards the stronger smell outside where the men peed, the grass thicket obliterated and yellowed by sun and alcohol-fuelled urine. He could see the Narok River from where he stood. Figures staggered in broad daylight, muttering Maasai expletives. He retreated hastily and walked through the tables, avoiding eye-contact with the hard men and women who sat watching him curiously in his shorts, funny hat and boots. When he made it back to Julius and Obergon, Chiri shook his head and Julius ordered him a beer. Obergon was drinking milk, his mouth ringed with white froth.

They heard Sol's laugh, crazy confident, before they saw him. When he appeared, his face was flushed – he was yet to lose all the paleness he had cultivated in England. Sol ignored Julius, acknowledged Obergon with a manly handshake. Then, showing that he had not lost any of his boxer's speed, he quickly grabbed Chiri around the neck in a headlock, grinding his knuckles into his scalp. Chiri smelled the three-day booze, realized he had missed Sol. Julius and Obergon relaxed at this and, looking over at the Senyos, signalled Chiri to finish his beer, knowing it was useless to ask Solomon to keep it quiet.

After a few hours, Sol wandered off and hit on somebody's girlfriend, one of the Senyos. The altercation was mercifully short. Chiri and Obergon arrived on the spot and Sol was on the ground, bleeding, his face swollen. He was laughing crazily. Chiri remembered all the kids the Sayiankas had beaten up – this was a sight they would have paid to see. They were kicked out and asked never to come back to Agip again. They walked outside, found Julius in a red phone booth talking to Mrs Sayianka in Nairobi, making his weekly report. When he finished they took the drinking elsewhere.

They left Narok for Nairage Ya Ngare in the early hours of the morning and were home in less than two hours. Grandma Sayianka, their Gogo, a querulous old woman, opened the door and when she saw them she burst into song. Julius would only discover in the morning that their purchases in Nakuru had been stolen from the Datsun. They could not start planting till two weeks later and so missed most of the early rains.

The Sayianka family stone house at Nairage Ya Ngare was the first of its kind in the area and had been built by Petro Sayianka in the 1980s. It sprawled with extensions, new wings, nooks and crannies, built as their father prospered and his family grew. This served as a country home, supplementing the Buru Buru house. Gogo had lived alone in the Nairage Ya Ngare house for years till Julius rejected Buru Buru and Nairobi for the wheatlands. Inside the house was a maze of corridors, cul de sacs, weirdly placed bathrooms and toilets. Most of the house did not have a ceiling and sound travelled from room to room above the walls. Only the kitchen remained a common space. Chiri and Julius took two rooms to the shaded southern side, Sol slept in their father's old room and Gogo remained on one wing by herself, oblivious of the weed and the barmaids.

It took them a few days to replenish their stocks after the theft of the wheat purchases. The wheat planting took two full weeks. After the beating, Sol only appeared once in the fields. When Julius and Chiri were done with the planting, taking a break before the weeding started, Sol declared one breakfast that he was going back to the UK, that this wheat life was dirty and not for him. He had started regaining bits of his old bravado, which even Gogo laughed at. With his face contorted, he talked somewhat recklessly of revenge. Julius remained quiet during these sessions. He had told Chiri that there was nothing to be done about the Senyos in Narok, especially now that the Sayiankas had lost their patriarch. Finally Julius, tired and dirty from another day in the fields, listened to Sol ranting away and, unable to stop himself, said: 'I just talked to Mother earlier and she is asking about you. There is a girl called Katie who keeps on calling from London, asking to talk to you. She says she has your son.' Sol looked at Julius for a long moment, seemingly confused at the mention of Katie and a son. He went into his room wordlessly.

The wheat crop was now three weeks old, susceptible to rust, which could destroy the crop in days. During this period, Julius and Chiri no longer went out nights after the long days in the fields. All day the rain poured lightly over them; in the evenings, Julius pored over his late father's papers and books – reading about agriculture, wheat farming. Chiri read some Westerns that had belonged to Petro Sayianka. Sol now guiltily retreated from them, harbingers of knowledge of his secret wife and child. Chiri sought him out, trying to remain neutral, making sure that he listened to both brothers, as he had as their childhood sidekick.

After a month all the fields Julius had leased had been weeded and it would be another three weeks before they started spraying insecticide. Julius and Chiri got on the wheat hustle, took several trips out south, past Narok town, looking for tractor and harvester work. It was now August and they were mostly on the road. They went from farm to farm, asking randomly around whether anyone needed a plough, a winch, even a tractor carrier.

On the road Julius continued his tutorials, his moods starting to swing with the vagaries of the wheat crop and the weather as the season developed. Chiri understood Julius's need to talk his farming dream into being, his voice at this stage not betraying any fear of failure. Chiri knew Julius was fighting the pious mothers of their childhood, Buru Buru middle-classness, those who had laughed when he failed his O-levels. Chiri understood that somewhere on the road he had become witness to a grand plan, that Julius wanted to go back to Nairobi triumphant, moneyed for Christmas, to show all the naysayers from his father's funeral that he had made it. When Chiri watched Julius during these first days of the wheat season, he started realizing that he had signed up for a party but was caught up in a make-or-break situation for his childhood friend. If before planting season, during the long pre-season excursions, Julius had spoken with a quiet authority, now the realities set in, with shifts in weather and crop suggesting hard times ahead.

By the end of August, six weeks after planting, it was clear that their little Narok adventure that had delayed planting would prove costly. Their crop, having missed a week's worth of rain, was 15 centimetres shorter. In remote Melilli, they had to import labour for another round of weeding. In Ngareta, their second farm, which bordered the Mau forest, wheat rust thrived and they had the crop sprayed over several times. In Suswa, the intermittent rain, driven away by strong winds, left a third of the crop stunted. That week, Julius did not call his mother, Mrs Sayianka, with the fortnightly progress report.

One morning in mid September, they received news that their Massey Ferguson Harvester had been seen stuck in the hills of Mau Narok without a driver in sight. Harvesting season had already started out there. The news came through a string of herders, just like in the old days. When they got back from Melilli, they found a Maasai herder waiting for them at the gate of the Nairage Ya Ngare house. The man said in Maasai that the machine was out in Mau Narok. When Julius asked the herder whether he could take them, he said he did not want any trouble and started walking away. Julius grinned and offered 2,000 shillings for the trouble. It was enough. The man jumped into the back of the Datsun. They stopped at the Nairage Ya Ngare Trading Centre and Julius borrowed fuel money from a Kikuyu bar owner named Johnny at 20-per-cent interest. Sol was left behind, wallowing in his post-traumatic shock.

They headed south first and caught a passing rain heading towards Tanzania. In a few minutes they were in an indeterminate land where the rain fell with such relentlessness, it was as if time had shortened or space shrunk in the grey world. Now, for two full days, they managed no more than 50 kilometres, stopping in trading centres, stuck beneath small kiosk fronts, unused cattle dips, and at times under trees in open meadows. They hardly noticed when the herder disappeared, back to the dry north. Without him, they kept at it because there was really only one road and there was little risk of getting lost if they asked along the way in the small trading centres where the event of a stranded Harvester was news.

One night, feeling as if they'd travelled almost to Tanzania, they managed to find a place to park the Datsun under a small shed up in Mau Narok. The world was a grey, stormy sea around them. With the incessant drumming of water on the Datsun's roof, Chiri could no longer remember what a dry world felt like. They were drinking heavily and Julius's eyes were glazed: he was drunker than Chiri had ever seen him. From the continuous mumble, Chiri made out that he was talking about his time in Naimenengiu. The Magic Forest. Where his father had banished him, after high school.

'Tell me about the Red Door thing,' Chiri asked. *'Mlango nyekundu. Mlango nyeusi'*. Julius looked at him.

'When I left, I ended up in Naimenengiu, in the south of the south. In the most remote place in Kenya. I remember one day I walked to smoke a cigarette, a Rooster non-filter, not far from the village, where there were some rocks that I saw every day. In that small place I did not need to be at the shop all the time. People took what they needed and left money. I wanted to read a letter I'd received from Baba. Before I reached the rocks, I looked up. There on top sat a lioness. Have you ever heard the roar of a lion next to you? Have you ever seen a snake the size of your leg?'

Chiri watched his friend's head fall to his chest. Then Julius continued, his eyes fixed straight ahead, as if something Chiri could not see was stalking him – maybe Buru Buru's need for success, memories of the wild, his father, the coming wheat harvest and the possibility of failure.

'I was there for another two months. One day the oldest man in that small village called me. I went to his *manyatta* and he said to me: "You have become one of us. Do you want one of my daughters? Do you want land?" I did not want to refuse him. When I remained silent, he asked me whether I was wanted by the government. The police. He said he could send me to his brother in Tanzania. To Mlango Nyeusi. The Black Door. I told him I had been banished by Baba. The old man shook his head and gave me five goats. He told me that I would always belong to the village. That *mzee* said that Nairobi is not for everyone.'

'St George's. Jamhuri High School. Nairobi born, man. You should have told the old man that,' Chiri said. 'All that for nothing. Sorry, but to send you out there, all due respect, what was your father thinking?'

'My father...' Julius stopped and looked at him: 'Out there, we saw a car once in two months when the Canter from Narok brought me supplies for that little shop. Out there, we ate nothing but goat. I saw *sukuma wiki* once in two months. One day I tasted a tomato, went crazy with pleasure and almost left for Buru Buru.'

'Yeah. All I'm saying is that our parents are not always right. Half of the things my Mum goes on about are crazy,' Chiri said.

'Chiri, if you'd listened to your Mum, you'd still be on campus,' Julius said.

'Yeah, and now I could do with some fries, man,' Chiri said.

He slowly slipped into the darkness and, when he woke up again, he found his head slumped on Julius's left shoulder. He could not tell in the darkness whether Julius was awake till he heard his jaws still chewing the miraa. The rain had eased up and they were now trapped in the black silence. Chiri did not dare move. His ears provided no direction or balance, so intense was the darkness. He imagined that any noise would be big enough to blow up his heart. It was a silence beyond electricity and all the other things that modernity brings – Chiri could not even imagine his mother's incessant voice. For once in his life he felt as if he was in complete nothingness. Something close to what he imagined Julius had experienced out in Naimenengiu, in the wilderness.

Julius spoke and Chiri realized his bladder was about to explode.

'When Sol and I finished school, Baba called us and asked what we wanted from life. Sol chose the UK. I was sent into the wilderness, to that shop because of what I had done. You know how wild I was.'

'We all were.' Chiri said, trying to push away the dark. 'Still are, man. Why we out here? Wheat party.'

Julius ignored this. 'Then Sol sent a letter to Mum from the UK saying that he wanted to marry this *mzungu* girl called Katie. He wrote to Baba separately and said he had a wonderful business idea but needed five million shillings for it. That he did not want to continue with school. Baba wrote to him and said that he had his blessing, asked him to come back home so that they could discuss the business venture. Baba did not ask about the *mzungu* girl.'

Chiri laughed, shaking his head. 'Sol, man. Always sly.'

'We didn't hear from Sol for one year. Baba went all the way to the UK to look for him. When he came back, he did not tell us anything about Sol. That's when he sent for me. He told me that the wilderness had been good for me and that it had taught me how to be responsible.'

Chiri sighed. 'Sure you're not taking this Sol thing too seriously?'

'Baba said wheat could be a way out for me and that I could now come back from the wilderness. I came back and Baba gave me the John Deere tractor, and the old Massey Ferguson harvester. He then leased 50 acres for me in Melilli to start with wheat.

'When Baba died, we saw Sol for the first time in seven years. He just appeared one day. We don't know whether he even got his degree. We don't know what the conversations with Baba in the UK were about. All Sol brought home was a drinking qualification and too much English. For every year Sol was in the UK, the family could have bought a Massey Ferguson. Is that serious enough for you?'

A white Zebu cow suddenly appeared out of the darkness, its horns creating a bizarre impression of a wall trophy. It peered at them through the windscreen, chewing slowly, then eased back into nothingness.

Julius continued. 'So, when I left Naimenengiu, I gave the shop to the old man. He laughed and asked what he would do with it. He said, do not go back. Stay here with us. He said: *sisi, ni watu wa mlango nyekundu*, we are of the red door and, if you ever need anything, please come back. He said that the Red Door people would always be there for me.'

Chiri could no longer hold his bladder; he opened the door quietly and started peeing on the side of the Datsun. Even before he finished, he heard Julius weeping quietly. Chiri let his friend finally grieve for his father, for his years in the wilderness, for his Buru Buru childhood and all those who had wished failure on him – his teachers; Buru Buru mothers who feared for their daughters. With no miraa, his face seemed like the Julius of old. When Chiri finally stopped urinating, Julius started again. His voice was much harder than before.

'Sol has let down the Sayiankas. He has let down our late father. He has let down...' Then Julius smiled, as if suddenly remembering something. 'You know I have never done it with a *mzungu*. And now Sol has a *mzungu* wife. And all I really have is that small shop in Naimenengiu.' The sky above them started lightening up, the darkness finally slipping away.

'That old man did not know me from the animals in the magic forest. He took me in, wanted me to marry there and said he would give me land. If anyone came looking for me, the village would protect me, say they didn't know me. All my life nobody has ever treated me with such kindness. That is the way of *mlango nyekundu*, the Red Door. You understand now.'

Chiri grinned, shook his head. 'No.'

Julius said, 'Fuck Buru Buru and Nairobi. Can't go back there. If anything, I'd go back to Naimenengiu.'

Chiri tried to picture the small shop out there in the middle of nowhere.

'I need some miraa,' Julius said as the first daylight emerged.

They found the Harvester on the hill that evening. It tilted on the hillside like a strange windmill, a small tower in the middle of nowhere. Like many other hired drivers, Edwin had taken a moonlighting gig, and, as he worked in the darkness, the harvester had somehow been caught on the large rocks of Mau Narok.

Half the wheat field had been destroyed by hailstones. They found an old man of about 70 sitting on one corner of the farm holding wheat stems and bawling like a baby in the mud. Julius watched him for a long time. He turned to Chiri. 'I don't know why he's crying. Kalenjins don't have problems getting loans. They have Moi.'

After hiring a tractor and two drivers, they dislodged the Harvester and started to tow it back to Nairage Ya Ngare. The rain had now lightened as they headed north. At every trading centre, they saw people who seemed chastened by the storm, re-emerging into their lives walking like they were in funeral procession. Chiri and the new driver they had hired took turns steering the Harvester. Chiri felt like a false king up in the Harvester cabin amid all this broken magnificence, steering through trading centres whose wheat crops had been destroyed in the storm. They passed field upon field, flattened, as if by giant hands. The Harvester had two mirrors mounted on long metallic rods and, when Chiri looked at himself, he saw how dark he had turned, how lean his face had become and how rough his forehead had grown.

Theirs was not the only Harvester the storm had rendered workless. They met other blue, green and red iron giants headed north, made redundant when the Hand Of God had prolonged the rains. The faces underneath the stoops looked up wordlessly and went back to their now-small, meaningless tasks. They finally left this funereal land and stopped in Narok, where Julius paid some cops to track down Edwin, the driver from Kisii.

When they visited a legendary mechanic called Kinuthia, he told them that the Harvester repairs would cost 200,000 shillings and could only be done in Nakuru. They left it with him and set out to look for the money.

When they got back to Nairage Ya Ngare, Chiri and Julius slept two days from exhaustion. When they woke up, Gogo told them that Sol had gone back to Nairobi. It was late September and they had 10 weeks before the first harvest in mid-December. They needed to fix the Harvester quickly.

Julius went to ask his cousin for a loan but Obergon told him that he was planning to get married and had no liquid cash. Julius could not believe he had not known of these plans but apparently his late father had already given Obergon half the bride-price. Every other week, Julius kept on unearthing the absurd amounts of money that his father had handed over to their innumerable relatives. Obergon said that there was only one person who had the money to fix their current problems: Nkaiseri Ntimama. Obergon went to see Nkaiseri and, when he came back with a report, the conditions were vicious. The money would be lent at 30-percent interest and, in case of default, Nkaiseri would auction the Harvester. Julius and Chiri received a cheque for one million shillings, paid off Kinuthia, then paid half the wages in Suswa and Ngareta. When they went to Melilli, however, the workers demanded all their money to stop them burning the wheat. It was the end of October. Julius and Chiri went to Narok and partied like it was Christmas.

✳ ✳ ✳

Early November. It is three weeks to the harvest. Julius and Chiri spend the long days in sobriety, beaten and stony broke. One Monday, Mrs Sayianka sends an urgent message with an aunt coming back from Nairobi. Julius's mother wants to hold a Christmas party for the whole Sayianka clan to thank them for all they did at her husband's funeral. She needs five goats, two sheep, one calf, one bull, five bags of rice, and five bundles of Jogoo Maize Meal. The aunt says that their mother is grateful to them and that their father would be proud. Julius escorts the aunt to the gate and, after a while, Chiri hears him laughing hysterically outside. When he comes back, Julius lets the list fall to the ground, torn and crumpled.

'Sol told Mother that everything is going well,' Julius says.

The boys now eat meat rarely and subsist on indigenous vegetables so bitter that they are an acquired taste, and on porridge for breakfast. Julius lives on miraa. He no longer waits till evening to start chewing, he starts at midday. His eyes have become glazed, his teeth and gums are starting to turn green. The only meat they eat regularly is stuffed blood sausage, goat head, tongue, spleen, pancreas – parts that Chiri did not know were edible. They buy them from this Kikuyu woman at the trading centre who at first acts shocked when they appear. Maasais do not eat innards, *mutura*, *kaigagio*, she says mockingly.

Julius insults her, tells her to go back to Central Province. She laughs. Is that where your father married? Chiri holds Julius back as he goes at her. They leave her laughing in scorn.

They no longer use shower gel, they bathe with Panga soap, then wash their own clothes with the used water. On the many nights they now sleep sober, Chiri longs for Buru Buru, even Ogilvy – to be back in Nairobi now that this adventure has turned into what he has always thought of as the life of others. At night, he listens to Julius toss and turn, talking to himself across the wall, his friend unable to sleep from his all-day chewing of miraa. On other nights, Julius tries to drown himself in sex – all on credit; payment promised to the barmaids with the next harvest. The smells of sex swirl all over the house.

During the late November days, they drive to the fields and see wheat that belongs to others turning golden like an Unga advertisement. They will be lucky if they harvest half what they had expected themselves. In the shamba in Ngareta, rust wipes out half of the harvest. In Melilli, the workers Julius paid have stolen half the field. In Suswa, there are huge gaps in their wheatfield from the scant rain. Out in Ololonga, where Julius had balked at the leasing prices but where their father had planted last season, a bumper harvest is expected.

They get back to the house one evening and Sol is back from Nairobi. Clean, dressed in new clothes. They sit outside in the evening sun and Chiri listens to Sol on how the English sun only retires at 11pm in the summer. Chiri imagines himself elsewhere, far away from here, back in school.

One quiet morning, the day after Independence Day, Julius and Chiri are in Nairage Ya Ngare. Only stray dogs, a few drunkards and some children seem awake. Everyone apart from them was partying away last night with money from the harvest. Last night, Julius paid for Chiri's first barmaid – a *Jamhuri* Day lay. Chiri was up most of the night: after every round of sex, the barmaid drunkenly repeated 'Kereti is my name, Kereti is my name'. Julius kept on banging the wall in protest at the noise, unable to sleep. The miraa has dimmed Julius's interest in sex, he no longer bothers with his barmaids. After that night, Chiri understands Julius' and Sol's penchant for these rural women. There are no anxieties, no need to please – the exchange is an uncomplicated transaction. He feels lighter.

Johnny, the bar owner, shylock, and now sometime drinking buddy, comes in, looking rougher than usual. He knows times have been tough and offers to buy them breakfast. Julius says nothing. Johnny has not started asking for the money they borrowed to go hunting for the Harvester out in Mau Narok. That request will be made just before Christmas.

As they wait, Johnny says: 'I hear there is a boy stuck in a tree at Mwisho Wa Wakikuyu. He's been accused of stealing milk from the Kikuyus and Maasais who live there. Somebody put him up a tree. Waranis, the Kikuyus are saying. His people are saying that the Kikuyus killed him. The District Commissioner will be holding a meeting at lunchtime to avoid fresh tribal clashes.'

They get to the laga in less than an hour. They have not been there since they saw the long boy three months ago, a lifetime away. On the way, Chiri keeps on glancing in his side mirror. He does not recognize himself. When they get there, the body still hangs from a leather strap tied to the acacia tree – the acacia bends with the long boy's weight. His feet are centimetres above the basalt laga shore. Chiri recognizes the fish mouth. It no longer has any teeth left, like a dog run over. The back is stripped of its skin by whip lashes. The stomach is bloated, as if filled with water. There is a black handkerchief around the neck. His animals stand peacefully to the side, grazing. The small donkey brays hard against the wind. The laga has shrunk from the dryness that December brings – they can now make out more grey basalt, volcanic foundations of the Rift Valley on the laga edges. Chiri looks into the laga; his face has become lean, he has grown darker. His teeth are yellowy brown. He looks down at his rough hands. He thinks of supermarkets, his mother's pilau, Zanze Bar, chips and sausages. He looks at the scene, the long boy, and feels a heavy weight, imagines himself sinking in the laga.

When the police finally come, they throw a sheet over the body and take it down. Julius knows one of the officers. They clap each other's hands from the time they were hunting for the driver, Edwin, who abandoned their Harvester out in Mau Narok.

'That *Kisii*, the driver,' the cop asks. 'Has he paid you?'

'Not all of it.' Julius shrugs. 'He's working for the Senyos. I can't do much.'

'Everyone works for the Senyos,' the cop says.

'The boy killed himself,' a voice in the crowd says in Kikuyu. Some of the crowd jeer at this observation. Chiri moves away from the small crowd and sits down, removes his shoes and dips them in the laga. He hears Julius ask what house the long boy comes from.

Then a small boy shouts, 'Look'. Milk flows from underneath the blanket on the basalt rock. It flows for a while from the body then it turns a bit red and stops.

Chiri and Julius watch; they want to hear the DC's *baraza*. They head to the Datsun and sit and eat *mandazis*. Then they hear that the DC will only be coming the next day. Every adult suddenly disappears when the police take the body away. They get into the Datsun but Julius remembers something. He goes into the back of the Datsun – the white handkerchief has been there all along, these long months of wheat season. Julius ties it on the acacia tree and they drive off. The young donkey brays after them and small children run after the Datsun for a few metres, panting.

'The price of milk out here is death,' Chiri says in sudden anger. Julius looks outside his window and starts laughing.

'Suicide,' he says. 'Suicide.'

That night, Chiri has dreams about the long boy from the laga.

He finds himself on a plain. The sky is white with a yellow sun. For some reason, he can run swiftly – he feels airless. He discovers he can fly – low to the ground, though. Float. Hover. He tries to take off high into the sky but something won't let him; he tries to move faster, gain momentum so that he can escape gravity. But he covers great Rift Valley distances without ever really being able to shoot away into the sky, to see whether there's anything in the white. Narok, Nairage Ya Ngare, Suswa, Melilli, MaiMahiu, the great empty plains end, the land climbs into congested Kikuyu land, Kinungi, Limuru and then teeming Nairobi in the distance.

Then he turns and there are some storks heading towards him. He feels joy. Turns to join them. When he's some distance away, he notices that the stork in the lead is larger. He slows down, unsure. Then he makes out that this is a man with wings – and recognizes the long boy's face. The boy gestures at Chiri, points towards the sky as if in challenge. When he comes close, his face is now completely fishlike, with sharp teeth. Chiri turns and flies away with the long boy in pursuit. The laga appears below them. Chiri dives deep into it and hears a splash behind him and then a voice – a grown man's voice that is not quite right.

'I want to play. I want to play. I just want to play.'

When Chiri wakes up the next morning, he feels an immediate discomfort in his shorts, a nagging feeling. He can't pee. When he feels his penis, it leaks a yellow pus. The pain is strange, small and sharp, recurs and shifts. But the leaking doesn't stop. His penis feels like a disassociated part of him. When he goes to the kitchen, Julius looks up and can immediately tell there's something wrong. Chiri tells him and Julius laughs long and loudly. Sol wanders in and Julius shares the joke. Chiri remembers this from back in Buru Buru. The two easily united when it comes to the perverse, the tragic. They now grin as if he's just passed a singular rite of passage. That he's taken another step into a brotherhood of hard-living men. They all sip tea from broken cups in the small kitchen. Chiri waits for the day's plan – whether they'll work with the tractor, harvester, or go to the shamba in Melilli to start the harvest. But then he feels the leak in his shorts come on again and knows that he will not be going anywhere. He cannot imagine being in the heat and dust in his condition. He has thought of heading to the Trading Centre to confront Kereti but does not trust Julius.

'What should I do?'

Sol laughs at the fear in his voice. Julius does not say anything. He looks at Chiri curiously, like he's learning something about him. Then he grins. The brothers know he's at their mercy. Even when they were kids, they would at times turn on him when everyone else was beaten – tease him, remind him that even if he was on their side, he was not above the Sayianka order of things. He realizes he has no money at all, that he depends on Julius for everything.

'I'll get you some pills,' Julius says.

The two brothers leave for Melilli to start the harvest. Chiri wanders in the house all morning. By midday, the pus is constant; the pain has spread to the whole organ. There is a smell around him of rot. Chiri can barely walk in the wetness; he lies down and wonders when he'll hear the familiar roar of the Datsun. When he pees, the pain is at its worst.

He is shaken awake. Julius stands over him, slightly wobbling. 'Here, Take two now and two in the morning. You should be fine.' The eight large yellow pills are wrapped in a small, grotty piece of brown sugar bag. Chiri gobbles one gratefully. In the morning Chiri's pee is sulphur yellow. The pain has gone down. The pus has reduced. But the smell remains. He feels like he could run five kilometres. He takes another dose.

When Julius and Sol head out, they look at Chiri to see whether he's coming with them to the fields. Chiri feels he could but remaining in the house alone has now grown on him. He reads most of the day. Immerses himself in the

Westerns that Petro Sayianka used to read. The medicine seems to colour the whole world in a yellow haze. At night, he cannot get the long boy out of his head but during the day he thinks of Buru Buru. He remembers the Sayianka brothers as children, and knows how hard it will be for them without their father. He goes to bed and does not hear the two brothers come in late at night, drunk.

In the morning, the pain is worse than before; the pus has streaks of red. Chiri wakes up in a blind rush. He finds Julius outside, sitting under a tree, looking terrible from the night before. The Datsun is nowhere to be seen. Before Chiri speaks, Julius looks up.

'Sol. Sol took off with the car,' he says.

When Chiri tells him about the increased burn, Julius winces.

'You need an injection. It happens at times. I'll get some money for you from Johnny when Sol gets back.' They wait for Sol till 2pm and then Julius jumps on the tractor. Chiri watches him go off, his long body bumping along the road, heading to the farm in Ngareta. Chiri sinks to his knees: the pain is unbearable. He cannot even wear shorts any more. Julius has given him a *shuka* and he ties it around himself like a skirt.

Julius comes back after a while. 'Johnny has gone to Narok for supplies,' he says. 'I left a message for him. We should be able to sort things out tomorrow.' Chiri smells maize beer on his breath.

'I had to get rid of a hangover,' Julius explains. 'You should have some for the pain,' he grins. Chiri knows that it will also kill the effect of the antibiotics. But he takes a swig and winces at the sourness. He feels lightheaded.

When Sol eventually comes back, he's even more drunk than Julius. He finds Julius and Chiri in the kitchen, eating *kunde* and brown ugali. Sol laughs. He selects a toothpick from his jeans and starts picking his teeth, flicking specks of goat meat on the ground.

'Where is the Datsun?' Julius asks. 'I need to go to finish

the Suswa harvest tomorrow.'

'Ran out of fuel,' Sol says. 'I left the Datsun in Nairage Ya Ngare. Running on empty.' He drops the keys near the small tar lamp. 'Like you, little brother.'

The tiny lamp flame throws Julius's head in a shadow dance against the wall like a genie. Julius's voice is quiet. 'You are such a fuckup. You should have stayed where you were. Dead to Baba and everybody.'

Sol grins. 'Ah, Julius, the wheat farmer speaks.' He says in a quiet voice. 'All you have done is harvest where Baba planted. Let's wait and see what happens to your crop.'

They attack each other like rabid dogs. They probably haven't fought since they were kids when Sol would come out on top. Now Julius, taller and hardened by the wheatlands, seems to have the advantage over Sol, who's been softened by England. They crash around the kitchen, smashing everything. Julius rushes Sol to try to dictate the fight, make it a wrestling match. Sol wants to keep it to a boxing contest so that he can use his speed. Even when he catches Julius with a right to the head, the momentum is still with his brother. They roll on the ground without either of them gaining an advantage. Julius, the heavier, wants to pin Sol to the ground and does for a moment, smashing his head back into the concrete. But Sol unleashes some punches to his neck. They make animal noises, curse each other.

Then an unearthly scream rends the house. They hear Gogo yell for her son, their father. Petro Petro Petro. The brothers fall apart. They look at each other with pure hatred. Gogo appears at the kitchen door. She curses them on their mother's lives and asks them to leave the house. No respect for your dead father, you children of your Kikuyu mother. They sit shocked, crestfallen at this. She relents when they ask to remain. She apologizes for calling them Kikuyus and starts crying.

The next day, two very old men appear at the crack of dawn. The boys are all summoned to the kitchen in council. The old men speak.

'We all belong to the Red Door. We raised your father when he was a boy. So, you will listen to what we have to say.'

Before they continue, they turn to Chiri and ask him where he comes from. They tell him he needs to go back there, that these are sad and strange times for the Sayianka family, and they must be borne by family alone. When the old men finally leave, Julius and Sol tell Chiri to stay out of sight. They've always been united when it comes to him. After that, the two brothers do not even look at each other. Chiri does not know what the men said but it is clear that there will be no more fights.

Julius disappears for days. Chiri cannot stand the pain that has now spread to the whole of his waist area and he takes to maize beer. Sol has stopped drinking and he seems to become the older brother that Chiri remembers when they were in their teens. Sol talks about his time in the UK and how much he missed the family, in many ways Julius most of all, who he knew would always be there for him when he came back. Chiri knows that Sol would never repeat this in front of Julius. In the end it is this sober Sol who gets some money from Gogo and takes Chiri to the clinic. The injection is excruciating but in two days the leak dries up.

After a few days, Julius comes in the deep of the night. Nobody hears him – he picks up his things and steals away again in the night. When Sol and Chiri wake up, they find his room empty, his clothes gone. Sol calls their mother but he is not in Buru Buru. Christmas is a week away. They wait for Julius for another two days but he does not come back. Just three days before Christmas, Sol and Chiri sell the wheat harvest, pay all their debts. The Senyo boy-men come for the Harvester. Sol puts all the farming equipment up for sale. Not much remains, not enough for a Sayianka clan bash. But enough for their immediate family. Mrs Sayianka, their baby sister Esther and Sol.

It is now two days to Christmas and Chiri prepares to go back to Nairobi. He wonders whether he has caught HIV from Kereti. He still thinks a lot about the long boy by the laga. Chiri now knows that he wants to go back to school – he is not sure how, but he is done with the wheatlands, the drinking, the women, the adventures. He knows he will become adept at those things that are built by Buru Buru childhoods: a university education, a formal job, a Toyota, all that Julius has rejected. He also knows he will never see the Sayiankas again when he leaves. Their childhood and what held them together has been finished by this period they've been together – by the violence, the recklessness, the struggles, the incident at the laga with the long boy.

Chiri now understands Julius's attempt to make a break with the past – to farm, to hustle, to do things foreign to a Buru Buru childhood. This has also been a time of mourning for Petro Sayianka, who tried to teach the brothers to live with each other but failed. Chiri now knows that they will not make it. That, maybe, Julius is better off in the wilderness, with the old man in Naimenengiu, the Magic Forest, where the ways of the Red Door remain alive. Chiri can see him out there by the small shop, where lionesses prowl and snakes crawl and the rules are different.

For the last time, Chiri feels the pain of the Sayianka brothers, the death of their father, the coming end of their wealth, their mother's inability to tame their wildness and, before he leaves by *matatu* on Christmas Eve, he cries for them in his room. Goodbye, my brothers.

Billy Kahora lives and writes in Nairobi, Kenya. He is working on a novel titled *The Applications*. His work has appeared in *Chimurenga, McSweeney's, Granta Online, Kwani* and *Vanity Fair.* He wrote the screenplay for *Soul Boy* and co-wrote *Nairobi Half Life.* He is also Managing Editor of Kwani Trust.

Stuck

Davina Kawuma

from: **Nandi Kamara** <kamara.nandi@gmail.com>
to: Connie Gabar <conbar888@hotmail.com>

date: Sun, Feb 3, 2013 at 1.03 AM
subject: STUCK

Connie,

What's wrong with me? 😬

Why have I granted a married man permission to court me so thoroughly? – so relentlessly?

What's happening to me? 😠

I used to be a good person. You, of all people, know this to be true. I wasn't given to stealing, cheating in exams, or sleeping around, and I only told white lies. Until recently, I possessed the unusual ability to walk a mile in other women's shoes, and I was convinced I'd sooner kill myself than have an affair with a married man.

Well, technically, it's not yet an affair since a) our lunches and dinners aren't a secret, and b) I haven't slept with him. Nonetheless, this, whatever this is, is going to be a full-blown affair by April (unless I have turned into a werewolf by then... by the way, are you Team Edward or Team Jacob?). I am unable to say no to this man (who, for obvious reasons, will remain nameless).

Even Auntie Mai (remember her? she took us to that Fido Dido ice-cream shop, on Kampala Road, one Saturday, when you came to visit), who isn't actually related to The Mummy, but is as old as most aunties are and is the only other person who knows about this man aside from Jackie (not the Jackie who room-mated with you, but the Jackie who thinks of everything; the one who surprised us, during that Rotaract Club retreat at the new hotel in Entebbe, by confessing that she'd packed a bar of washing soap, a soap dish, a toilet freshener, a pumice stone, a safety pin, a panty peg, plus a needle and black thread!)... Even my dear Auntie Mai, who has talked Henry (my brother, who outgrew his crush on you) out of several misadventures, has neither the skill nor the authority to dissuade me from seeing this man.

Speaking of which... Can you imagine that it only occurred to me last week (was it last week or this week? I forget), that the ubiquitous expression 'I am seeing someone' is derived from that urgent question (always delivered with equal parts hopeful expectation, adorable self-deprecation and desperate determination), 'So, when can I see you?'

I've heard that question a zillion times before, of course, but it was while I was in a taxi, after I overheard one of the passengers say '*Kati*, I'm dying to see you. When can I see you?' that everything fell into place.

Facepalm

I can say, without fear or favour, that I am, officially, the daftest person I know. In fact, I have taken adequate steps (the first of which is to give myself a Darwin Award honourable mention) to ensure that I never achieve this level of cluelessness ever again. The Darwin Awards, established by Wendy Northcutt, intend to 'commemorate those individuals who ensure the long-term survival of our species by removing themselves from the gene pool in a sublimely idiotic fashion.'

(Cue: 'Most of us have a basic common sense that eliminates the need for public service announcements such as, WARNING: COFFEE IS HOT! Darwin Award winners do not.)

Log onto the awards website (www.darwinawards.com)

later, and laugh yourself silly!

Now, where was I? Oh, yes, Auntie Mai. ~~(See what I did there? I rhymed. Effortlessly. Recognize game.) Now, though, seriously, back to Auntie Mai.~~ All her fervent warnings that God will punish me, and that there is a quote generational curse unquote on the women in my family, a generational curse that renders us incapable of finding men of our own, haven't transformed me back into the purpose-driven, conscience-stricken person that I used to be.

That's not even the worst part, moreover.

The worst part –

Hesitates

– is that sex with this man will kill me.

If I don't die, we will get stuck together!

STUCK like that couple I read about in the *Red Pepper* the other day (I hope it was the other day and not the other month)! See how much I've changed, and on such short notice? 😫 I never EVER read tabloids, before.

You probably think I'm making this 'getting stuck' business up, don't you? Well, I haven't. I swear. If you want proof, Google 'Couple gets stuck while having sex'.

It'll take her (we agreed that Google is a chick, right?) about 0.32 seconds to return 55,300,300 results. Don't watch any of the videos, I BEG YOU. My intention isn't to expose you to erotica. My intention is to educate you. Restrict yourself to the articles, therefore, and quickly learn that a) the getting-stuck phenomenon has a scientific name, and b) 'getting stuck' isn't confined to the African continent. Couples get stuck in, for instance, Malaysia and Australia, as well~~, where we think people don't practise as much juju as we do~~

STUCK in a room in the executive wing of the Green Ash Hotel in Bugolobi.

STUCK, Connie, in a room with a hidden camera in it.

So STUCK that the editor of a tabloid ~~(perhaps the one that published a list of Ugandan celebrities with HIV/AIDS some time back)~~ will threaten to run the photos a week later if ~~my~~ this man doesn't wire 50 million shillings to the editor's personal account.

No, the married man is not an army general, or a member of parliament, but he does have money. MPigs is how we refer to our dishonourable Members of Parliament, these days, by the way. You should know this if you a) still listen to the BBC, and b) can find time to read the comment sections on the *New Vision* and *Daily Monitor* websites. If you don't know about the MPig business, though, I'll be happy to fill you in.

They want one billion Ugandan shillings (extra) to buy themselves iPads. iPads! Each one of them earns about seven million shillings every month, of course, meaning they can afford iPads on their own. Meanwhile, they all received about 200 million shillings, a while back, to buy Land Cruisers. I'm sure they bought Premios, instead, and then kept the *njawulo* in their pocketses.

By the way, did you know that we have the second largest parliament in the world? We do, apparently. Nick (I had to settle on a fictitious name, eventually, didn't I?) told me at dinner, the other day. The second largest parliament after China! China's population is over a billion and ours is 33 million! How crazy is that? This is madness! THIS IS SPARTA!

Sorry, I couldn't resist.

Chuckles

Anyway, as if the sustenance of our MPigs' lifestyles isn't haemorrhage enough, our taxes now have to support ghosts: ghost soldiers; ghost valley dams; ghost pensioners; ghost schools; ghost electricity; ghost teachers; etcetera. Very soon, there will be ghost marriage certificates. Quote me. Uganda should get a prize for its outstanding contribution to the expansion of the supernatural realm, shouldn't it?

As if keeping ghosts on payrolls isn't enough, there's now an orgy of district creation. There are so many new ones – I'm sure there are about one hundred now – that I'm having trouble keeping up.

I guess we are back to the divide-and-rule policy, yet again. It's like the British never left 😡

How's the UK, by the way? Since you deactivated your Facebook account, it's difficult to come by updates about what's going on in your life. How is your master's degree coming along? Are the people there shocked when you tell them that we know how to drive cars, and that we don't live in tree nests like monkeys? I bet you speak better English than some of them do, and that this pisses them off.

I keep sending texts to the phone number you included in your Facebook profile, before you de-activated it, but you haven't replied to any 😳

But I have digressed. I was still telling you about Nick. We met in December last year (more details later). I won't lie – the first thing I noticed about him was his Adam's apple. It was the largest Adam's apple I'd ever seen 😟 Yet it was in no way disagreeable to look at. I couldn't stop staring at it, perhaps because I realized, suddenly, that Nick's Adam's apple conformed to an ideal of form and proportion I had no idea I held. I worried, at some point, that Nick would notice me noticing his Adam's apple. Thankfully, he didn't notice. Or, if he did, he pretended not to.

The second thing I noticed was his crow's-feet. When he smiled, they scuttled to the corners of his eyes and spread out into a delicate web. They were the prettiest crow's-feet I'd ever seen.

The third thing I noticed, albeit a bit later, was that he looked a bit like a cross between Maurice Kirya and Chace Crawford. He is very much like a Jackfruit tree, in the sense that he thinks of himself as a 'naturalized African'. He changes to 'naturalized Ugandan', though, whenever I remind him that Africa is a continent with over 50 states in it, and not one huge country. He's such a naturalized Ugandan that he now drinks beer through a straw 😊

* * *

from: **Nandi Kamara** <kamara.nandi@gmail.com>
to: Connie Gabar <conbar888@hotmail.com>

date: Mon, Feb 4, 2013 at 2.40 AM
subject: STUCK

I worry, sometimes, that The Mummy already knows. It's that new church she's attending, I'm convinced. Rumour has it that the senior pastor has an uncanny way of knowing things no one's told him, and I fear that The Mummy has acquired this talent by osmosis. The way she looks at me, these days, Connie, with a gaze like an orange-red stamen protruding from a cup of bright pale-green petals. It's her sudden interest in talking to me about sex, too. You will never believe what she said to me the other day.

She said: 'Sex is as corrosive as concentrated sulphuric acid. Just as there's a container designed for the safe storage of acid, there is also a container, known as marriage, which was designed for the proper storage of sex.'

Then, later, she added: 'Sex is spiritual, you know.'

Then she started to talk to me about STDs. Not Sexually Transmitted Diseases but Sexually Transmitted Demons – of which I know very little since, to The Mummy's chagrin, I have never read *Delivered from the Powers of Darkness* by Emmanuel Eni. *Mbu* when people have sex, they share more than body fluids. So, for instance, if Nick's great-grandfather was a witch-doctor, there is a possibility that I could become infected with, for instance, a familiar spirit.

I was, as you can imagine, thoroughly embarrassed by everything she said and extremely suspicious of every reason she gave to explain her timing. I wondered then, as I do now, why The Mummy, who had never thought it necessary to talk to my teenage self about sex, had suddenly developed an interest in my adult sex life.

I'm telling you, she knows about Nick and me. Either that, or the years she's spent teaching advanced-level chemistry have started to take their toll.

Either way, I have to end this not-yet-affair. It's what I would have wanted the woman who was seeing my husband, if I were married, to do. Right?

But I don't want to end this not-yet-affair, Connie. I don't have the strength to. I don't ever want this man to stop lavishing his attention (or money) on me. Nick is very generous.

Yet I must end this, surely, shouldn't I? I mustn't be with him, no matter how much I want to.

Shit.

I don't know what to do, Connie.

When tomorrow comes it is always today and Nick has reduced my existence to the first three chapters of a Mills and Boon novel and when I am not fantasizing about him I am re-reading his texts (there are currently 1,654 of them in my inbox, you'd best believe it, and I cannot, will not, delete any of them) and –

He reads me poetry, over the phone, you know (yesterday it was the magnificent 'Godhorse' by Kojo Laing), and says things like 'humanity is my religion' (yes, in Real Life).

This mess – this business of having Katy Perry's 'Teenage Dream' on replay for an entire month – is The Mummy's fault, of course. If she'd sent me to a boarding school where ordinary-level literature teachers taught from African poems as well as Brontë-ish novels, I'd probably be impervious to the effects of a man reading ~~African poetry~~ poems by Africans over the phone.

I badly need your advice. I've tried calling in to that late-night late-date type show on Easy FM, but the listeners give crappy advice. I wrote to the Auntie Agony in one of the dailies but she, too, gave me crappy advice. Listeners and Auntie Agony all want me to 'Walk away', 'Leave him' and so on.

'He's wasting your time,' they say. 'You can't date other men while you're with him, but he's never going to leave his wife for you. Can't you see that he's using you?'

Yadda, yadda, yadda.

Look, I'm not stupid! – OK? – and I'm not blind, either. Of course, I can 'SEE' what's going on. I've watched enough movies to know that married men never leave their wives. It just isn't done. However, knowing this hasn't lessened my compulsion to be with him, Connie.

Besides, what if I'm the one that's using him? Has Auntie Agony thought about that? Do Easy FM listeners think I'm too stupid to be getting something out of this not-yet-affair?

No, sorry, I shouldn't say things like that. I'm not using him. I like him too much to be using him. No, I don't like him. Liking is for 15-year-old girls. But I don't suppose I love him yet. He's well-read, witty, and intelligent. So, of course, I'm not using him. But, do I love him, Connie? What is love, anyway? I'm not asking about butterflies in the stomach, pseudo-menopausal hot flushes, and quickened pulses. I'm not asking about 'Love is patient, love is kind; it does not envy, it does not boast, it is not proud' (as The Mummy would say in the accent, the one that is neither British nor Gossip-Girl American, that she uses whenever she is quoting from the Bible), either.

The kind of love I'm asking about, Connie, is, I suspect, the one that is the opposite of fear. The first opposite, actually (the second and third opposites being 'power' and 'sanity').

If I do love him in this way, then what?

The other day, while Nick and I were at dinner, I made a joke about how all I would ever be to him was a side dish. He protested vehemently, said he didn't like words like 'side dish', assured me that he intended to 'make everything official'. By this, he means that he wants me to become his second wife.

No, he's not a Muslim (well, he says he isn't one) so it is not as if there are going to be two wives after me.

'I simply believe in being pragmatic,' he said.

'But what about your wife?' I asked.

'I'm an African man. Eleanor knew what she was getting

herself into.'

'What about your family?'

'They like Eleanor, but they'll like you better.'

'What about my family?'

'We'll have a *kwanjula*, of course, and I'll gladly pay bride price.'

'I want a white wedding, as well. With a reception and everything.'

'Why not? You can have that too. The whole kit and caboodle.'

'But you're already married to someone else!'

'It was a civil ceremony.'

'It's still a marriage.'

'Don't worry yourself with the details. Leave the legalities to me,' Nick said.

I actually chewed over his proposition, later that night – which, you have to admit, is crazy. I mean, I'm educated, and I have a good job. Plus, I have plenty of unmarried options.

Jason (you don't know him; he part-times as a software engineer at my new workplace), for instance, is interested in me. It would be so much easier to date him, wouldn't it? He calls to ask how my weekend is progressing, lets me borrow his car whenever I want and, since he seems to know everyone in town, always gets me unbelievable discounts on stuff. He unlocked my modem; I can now use it to hack into networks all over the world, from Luxembourg all the way to Singapore, which means I have free and unlimited internet access.

Yet I am still considering Nick's proposition.

So, again, I ask you, Connie, 'what the $*&# is wrong with me?'

What, also, did Eleanor, who has eyes like Rwanda, two Mt Rwenzoris for cheekbones, and a mint flower for lips, whom I've only ever met through the photos in Nick's wallet, and who is, judging by what Nick says about her, everything I am not (namely white, sophisticated and open-minded), ever do to me?

How is it that, at a time when my self-esteem is higher than it's ever been (when I've started taking photographs, again, for instance, and can look at the models in *African Woman* magazine without wanting to start a diet one hour later), I am seeing another woman's husband? I always thought extra-marital affairs and not-yet-affairs were for desperate women who've been emptied of all self-love.

SOS.

✳ ✳ ✳

from: **Nandi Kamara** <kamara.nandi@gmail.com>
to: Connie Gabar <conbar888@hotmail.com>

date: Tue, Feb 05, 2013 at 11.41 PM
subject: STUCK

Dear Connie,
I'm relocating to Rwanda. I'll start a new life (and a business, hopefully) there. Apparently, it is 20 times easier to start a business in Rwanda than it is to start one here.

Don't laugh.

I'm serious about moving to Rwanda. I need to get as far away from Nick as possible. Yes, of course, you'd be correct to point out that Rwanda isn't nearly as far-away-as-possible as Australia is. Don't forget, though, that:

A) I am not loaded. Therefore, the correct thing to write on the visa application form, once I am asked how I intend to support myself when I get to Australia, is 'Pass';

B) I watched an episode of *Border Security*, at work, the other day; getting into Australia is a nightmare, and

C) I am not one of those highly skilled individuals who consult for international non-governmental organizations; I don't have a PhD, and the work experience bit on my CV doesn't straddle three pages. Clearly, Rwanda is the farthest

I can afford. Zambia, possibly, if I take a loan from a bank.

I am convinced that, in Rwanda, I will not make the same series of mistakes I made, and which I outline below:

Re: The series of mistakes that led to my not-yet-affair with a married man

1: I went to that party as Jackie's +1. I don't know how she managed to get her hands on a ticket, but she did. I don't know why I thought I could go to a bourgeois event at Speke Resort Munyonyo and not be required to pay for it later, but I did. Seanice Kacungira and Fatboy had raved about the event, during their Sanyu FM breakfast show, so I knew it was the business. I'd heard that there would be a surprise Sylvia Owori fashion show, at some point, and, later, a boat cruise on Lake Victoria.

2: I didn't head straight home after Cathy's bridal shower. Instead, I let Jackie convert me into one of those aspirational types – people who read *Rich Dad Poor Dad* and think nothing of assuming the risks involved with attending bourgeois events. To my credit, I protested vehemently in the beginning. Said I had nothing to wear; pointed out that my hair needed treatment; threatened to embarrass Jackie, in case there was a four-course meal, by forgetting which fork to use at what time.

3: I tried on one of the cocktail dresses in Jackie's closet. It fitted.

4: I didn't panic when Nick walked over to talk to me. I should have talked in a random way, about non-random things (like rising sugar prices and oil), and then excused myself (since this is what I always did, as soon as I saw a wedding band on a man's ring finger; this had always been my way of 'fleeing temptation'). I did nothing of the sort (obviously); otherwise, I wouldn't be in this position.

5: When Nick asked for my number, I gave it to him. I never thought he'd actually call. I assumed that, by asking, he was simply doing the polite thing (in the same way people who say 'it was nice to meet you', even when meeting you wasn't nice, are doing the polite thing). He gave me his card, in turn – which I didn't need, since I couldn't afford a lawyer (there, now you know what he does for a living) – and I accepted it (because I, too, wanted to be polite).

6: I broke the first of many rules that had governed my phone etiquette for about a year. This rule is DON'T ANSWER THE PHONE IF THERE'S NO CALLER I.D. The first phone call lasted all of 40 minutes, and, I won't lie, I thoroughly enjoyed it. The second and third phone calls lasted longer, and I enjoyed them even more than the first (if this is possible). However, because empathy hadn't deserted me yet, I felt guilty about taking his calls. After I'd laid up enough guilt, I started to ignore his calls. (This was easy to do, since Nick called at the exact same time every evening.) Sometimes I turned my phone off a few minutes to the hour, and turned it back on a few minutes after the hour. Unfortunately, he kept on calling. I should have persisted in ignoring his calls. He'd have given up, eventually, surely, since no man is that relentless, right?

7: I talked to Edgar, one afternoon, when he'd finally found time to take me to lunch after months of a) accusing me of ignoring him, b) promising to 'catch up, one of these days', and c) complaining that his bank job didn't give him time to do anything else but get home at 11pm.

I didn't get into it right away, of course. I stalled a bit.

'Your keyboard needs an aspirin, man,' is how I started out.

Edgar frowned at me. 'Wh-at?'

I motioned towards his laptop. 'Yowa kee bohd nee deez an as pee reen, man.'

'Oh, yeah,' Edgar said. His offering, a lop-sided smile, came before his prescription. 'I'll download a tablet,' he added.

I tried, and failed, not to smile at the pun. 'You do that.'

Edgar leaned back and wiped his lips with a napkin. 'So, what's up?'

'There's a guy on my case,' I said.

'Do I know him?' Edgar asked. It appeared as if he'd addressed the last pizza slice on his plate, so I didn't bother answering.

'I want him to stop calling,' I said.

'Why?'

'Just. So, what should I do?'

'Answer the phone.'

'How does that help?'

'The more unavailable a woman is, the more interesting she becomes.'

'That can't be true.'

'I'm a guy. Trust me.'

'By the way, you'd better not be making this up.'

'As I said before, I'm a guy. I know this stuff. What you are doing, by playing hard to get...'

'I'm not playing hard to get. Weren't you listening to me? I said I want him to stop calling.'

'...whether or not it's what you intended,' Edgar continued, as if I'd never interrupted him, 'is adding value to yourself.'

'Forget value addition. This guy is married.'

'So?'

'So I don't do married guys.'

'He's a married guy, not a leper. He's allowed to talk to other women besides his wife, surely.'

'Hah. Tell that to his wife, who will probably pour acid on me because she thinks I'm trying to steal him.'

'But if you're not actually out to steal him, you have nothing to worry about.'

'That's what you think,' I said. Then I recounted a story about a girl I knew, while I was at the university, who died after an acid attack. 'She wasn't even going out with the guy. They were just friends,' I added.

Edgar cocked his head and looked at me for a while.

'Look, I've only got one face,' I pleaded.

'Then answer the phone,' Edgar said. 'As soon as you

become less interesting, I can guarantee that the dude will leave you alone.'

'Are you sure?' I asked.

Edgar let out an exasperated sigh. 'Am I sure? Trust me, I'm a guy.'

I trusted Edgar, because he's a guy, and ended up making the ninth mistake.

8: At exactly 8.00pm (BBC time), the next day, I answered the phone.

9: I continued to do so (answer the phone, I mean) for the next two weeks. The intention, of course, was to make myself available (ridiculously so) and thus 'devalue' myself. I reasoned that if I picked up the phone every time he called and replied to every text he sent (a minute after he sent it), I'd become, as Edgar had predicted, 'less interesting'.

I was relieved when, at least for a while, the plan seemed to work. The calls tapered off and the texts became less frequent. Unfortunately, that's when the lunch and dinner invitations started.

✳✳✳

from: **Nandi Kamara** <kamara.nandi@gmail.com>
to: Connie Gabar <conbar888@hotmail.com>

date: Tue, Feb 12, 2013 at 4.00 AM
subject: STUCK

Dearest Connie,
There's a ghost in Trumpet House.

Trumpet House is the newish, six-storey building in Nakasero in which the organization I work for has its head office – one of those glass-and-cement architectural afterthoughts that are choking the breath out of Kampala.

The cleaners from the first, second and third floors are on strike because of the aforementioned ghost that, apparently, will not let them go about their business in peace. There's a god-awful smell coming from the toilets because they haven't been cleaned in at least three days – it's a smell that is halfway between that of a dead dog and a wound that's turned septic.

We had a management meeting regarding the ghost situation, recently.

I sat next to Jason, about whom I have already told you.

'Where's Alistair?' I asked, at around 3.00pm. The meeting had been scheduled for 2.00pm and no one was willing to start without him, since it'd been decided that he would chair the meeting.

'*Mbu* Ali Stair has gone to town to register his SIM card. And the deadline is tomorrow,' was the explanation Jason gave.

We both reminisced about the time when meetings started on time – when Alistair was still a bona fide expatriate; when he only fraternized with other expatriates; when the entire building was wired to the atomic clock in Switzerland and 9.00 meant 9.00 (not 8.59).

'Do you think Ali Stair will call a priest to exorcise the ghost?' Jason asked, later.

Instead of replying, I thought about a time in my senior secondary boarding school. I was in the third term of my senior two, I remember, and strange things were happening in my dormitory. Some girls would wake up to find pools of urine smack-dab in the middle of their cubicles. Others would wake up to find that someone (or something) had shaved their hair and cut their nails. Whoever (or whatever) cut nails and shaved hair was always in such a hurry that the job was often slapdash; victims often woke up bleeding. We never found the razor blade (it couldn't have been a nail cutter or an electric shaver) but stumbled upon enough theories to explain what was passing off. The most plausible theory involved witchcraft (apparently, hair and nails are regular ingredients in witchdoctors' portions and concoctions).

In the beginning, the headmistress dismissed it all as a practical joke. It wasn't until one of the girls from wing B started barking (I'm not making this up, I swear. She'd get down on all fours and bark like a dog whenever there was a full moon! The chaplain had to lock her up in the chapel) that we knew how much trouble we were in. The headmistress quickly invited a priest from a nearby parish to sprinkle holy water into a bank of unused bathrooms that was adjacent to our dorm.

Anyhow, apparently, the ghost belongs to a guy who jumped to his death from the top floor of the building opposite Trumpet House. I find this theory a bit confusing; it doesn't make any sense for the ghost of that guy to haunt Trumpet House. There's another theory, though; he might have jumped because of someone here. He could have been one of those hopeless romantics who jump because they've been chucked by their girlfriends.

That's not all. There's yet another theory, based on a true story, which states that the guy jumped because he was frustrated and depressed. Apparently, he'd graduated with a first-class degree but had been jobless for five years. Two weeks before he jumped, he'd applied for a job and was shortlisted for an interview. Unfortunately, when he turned up for the interview, he found that someone had crossed out his name and written someone else's name above his. When he tried to inquire, he was told that there had been a mistake, and that he should never have been on the shortlist in the first place. The receptionist was kind enough to inform him, before he left, that the 'real reason' his name was crossed out was that he belonged to the wrong tribe. He called his girlfriend, told her that he was tired, and wouldn't be able to see her that evening. A few minutes before midnight, he jumped.

After Jason recounted the theory slash short story, I was grateful, perhaps for the first time since I'd graduated, that I had a job.

'*Bannange*, where's Ali Stair?' someone shouted.

'Call Ali Stair and find out if he's coming,' Jason said to me.

'Why me?' I asked.

'You guys are tight.'

'Excuse you. Alistair and I are not tight.'

'Yeah, right. You guys are tighter than the weave your girlfriend has on, to quote Naeto C.'

'We are not. We don't even hang out.'

'Please. I saw you two together the other week. At Barbecue Lounge.'

'It was the deputy chief's farewell party. Was I supposed to say no when he invited me? He's my boss.'

'No. He's your boss's boss.'

'Which is exactly why I couldn't say no.'

'And what about last week, at Mamba Point?'

'His friend's birthday party.'

'Some birthday party that was. What about the other weekend at Nawab?'

'Alistair and I are not tight,' I said, which is true.

To be honest, I resent Alistair. I resent the fact that, until a year ago, he was struggling to make ends meet as a new graduate. Then he comes to 'Africa' as an expatriate and, *voilà*, everything falls into place. Now, he rents a $1,000-a-month five-bedroomed house in Muyenga. Because he gets allowances for nearly everything, he never actually has to spend his salary on anything – no wonder he can afford holidays in Zanzibar and the Seychelles. He isn't that much more educated than the rest of us.

'It's their confidence and presentation skills,' Jackie keeps saying. 'Those expatriates, even when what they are saying is nonsense, always maintain an air of self-assurance. We should learn something from them.'

In any case, Alistair arrived at quarter to four, and the meeting didn't start until half past. In between, he beckoned me into the corridor and, later, into my office. The smell of his Herve Leger cologne was everywhere, and his laughter

(I can't even remember now what was so damn funny) was like a black wattle – fast-growing but short-lived. He ran a hand through his showy blonde hair (like in the movies) and stopped jawing (what I hoped was) bubble gum.

He leaned against my desk (which, apparently, is made out of the same wood that's used to make beehives), picked up my 'he wears the PANTS but I control the ZIPPER' pen and started to roll it between his thumb and forefinger.

'How's the sixth floor?' I asked, by way of making conversation, and even though I already knew the answer. The sixth floor was like a soap opera: people who worked there were always taking revenge on each other, and they were all beautiful.

Instead of answering my question, Alistair asked one of his own. 'Why are girls who don't give head trending on Twitter?'

✳ ✳ ✳

from: **Connie Gabar** < <u>conbar888@hotmail.com</u> >
to: Nandi Kamara < kamara.nandi@gmail.com >

date: Wed, Feb 13, 2013 at 13.05 PM
subject: STUCK

To be totally above-board with you, I'm acluistic about why you've bothered to get in touch. Did you honestly expect me to give you advice? Are you under the impression that we are still friends?

Like, seriously, after all this time?

Bitch, let me bottom-line things for you. I don't have the bandwidth for your BS any more.

In fact, I am surprised that, after everything that happened while I was still in UG, you have the nerve to write to me about your anecgloats and anticipointments.

Like, Oh My Gosh, why on earth would you assume that

your armchair affair or whatever it is would be of any sort of interest to me? That you and I would blamestorm together? The entire time I was reading your verbose emails, I was saying to myself, 'OK, what is the point of all this?'

I hope you are not actually subjecting other people to this sort of god-awful rambling, because, if you are, I suspect that there will be an uptick in suicide rates very soon.

It is out of the goodness of my heart, really, that I read every one of your emails to the end. I forgave the first email, and tolerated the second. After the third one, though, I figured that I had to put an end to it all, otherwise it'd all go on for forever.

Please, please, I beg you, do not send me any more emails.

PS: This is just a suggestion, and you would do well to take it. Diarize your life, OK? Just, for the love of humanity, diarize your life! If you can't do that, start a blog.

Davina Kawuma was born in Lusaka, Zambia, but grew up and lives now in Kampala, Uganda. She used to be afraid of poetry but isn't any more. In her idea of a perfect world, she writes novellas during her lunch break and publishes them shortly before she goes to bed. She has written articles and features for *African Woman* magazine, and will not be pressured into saying that she's currently working on a collection of short stories.

Clapping Hands for a Smiling Crocodile

Stanley Onjezani Kenani

GATHERED HERE ON THE SHORES of our lake were men of various ages and sizes, tall, short, fat, thin, some in torn clothes and others in new attire, such that I, in a shabby brown suit and gaping shoes, standing before this red-eyed government official, felt like a drowning man. This, perhaps, was the feeling of everyone around here, for all our faces were sad as though we had received news of a funeral. Probably it was funereal due to the possible death of our beloved lake, because, once the extraction of oil commenced, as announced by this burly government official, all the fish in the lake would likely die, and, as we all agreed, a lake without fish would be of no use to anyone.

The official, speaking through a megaphone and surrounded by about nine men in camouflage attire, all carrying guns, said: 'I greet you in the name of His Excellency the President of our Republic, with whose authority I now stand before you. He sends his greetings and wants me to assure you that he loves you all. The government is aware that you are a fishing community; that your lives depend on the lake. I am here to allay fears that arise from misinformation by those who do not wish our government well; I'm talking about opposition political parties. We have identified powerful equipment that gives us confidence to guarantee no oil spill. I repeat, no oil spill. Without oil spill, the fish will not die and neither will your livelihood. The government hopes for your co-operation. Any acts of sabotage will be met with force. Thank you for your understanding. God bless you, and also our President.'

The government official furiously drove away, leaving us covered by a cloud of dust and frustration. A few metres from where we stood was the lake, which had been a silent listener as it lay in its usual calm way, its blue waters caressing the shore with the tenderness of a loving mother. I looked at my grandfather, who was standing next to me, leaning on his stick with great difficulty, tears streaming down to his white beard as beads of sweat formed on his forehead. I feared he might collapse, the weight of the government official's words combined with the weight of his own years having become too much for him, so I held him by the hand and started walking him home. Slowly the crowd grabbed a cue from us and broke up, some walking on the long, sandy beach towards the north, others to the south, in groups of twos and threes but with hardly any conversation among them, each probably reflecting on the verbal guarantee given by the government. The sun was now about to set, its orange glow reflecting on the surface of the blue water like a torchlight in a misty mirror. Above us, white egrets or perhaps herons flew in beautiful formation, all lined up in single file. A fish eagle soared, leaving land to hover above the lake, and for once I felt a sense of brotherhood with birds as their predicament was, strictly speaking, not so different from ours, especially with regard to the fate of the lake.

We walked past the holiday resort where the rich from the cities often came at the pretext of buying fish but mostly to hide with their secret lovers – although, with the threat of oil, nothing was going to be certain even for matters of bodily pleasures, since the water would in all probability cease to be attractive for such purposes.

Next to the resort was our village where, for generations, fishing had been the only trade we had ever known. Women and children poured out of the houses to welcome us, clearly anxious to hear the latest from the government, but soon, on noticing the sadness on every man's face and the tears of my grandfather, the sorrow appeared to spread to the women and children like an airborne epidemic, dampening the spirits of everyone, such that after the sunset, as the orange glow gave way to darkness, all was quiet on the shores of the lake.

*** *** ***

Although the government was not known for putting its words into action with speed, within days several trucks appeared on the shore. Many of us from the fishing villages – men, women and children – gathered like frightened but curious sheep, watching from a distance as strange men unpacked their equipment and pitched tents. Within weeks, office blocks of the oil production centre began to take shape, while deep-water drill-ships and offshore support vessels emerged onto our waters, circling every day like flies on a wound. In the middle of the lake, where every summer we watched the sun gloriously rise over the shimmering waters, the oil company erected a giant structure that resembled an air traffic control tower, only much bigger, its two large pylons jutting out like the antennae of a grasshopper. This facility, we came to learn, was going to be an offshore oil platform which, from then on, was to forever block that part of the horizon from us. Not all the oil company staff were foreigners. There were mud engineers, pump operators and drillers who came from other parts of our country. These spoke our language and regularly came to our village to buy fish and to satisfy our curiosity by answering some of the questions troubling our minds. The actual drilling, we learnt, was still months away. A lot more work was to be carried out to lay out the required infrastructure. We mingled with these oil men to learn more. We laughed with them and made them feel welcome among us, though in truth our relationship was like that of a cow and the tick sucking its blood.

I noted, each passing day, that my grandfather was perhaps becoming the most worried of us all. As well he should, because, being the chief of the village, he carried on his shoulders a load of hopes and dreams for his people. And so, in the mornings and late afternoons, he stood on the shore and shook his head as he watched the oil men work in the waters. On those occasions I joined him, he would say, 'We must do something to stop this' – the only words he uttered before returning to his house like a tortoise retreating into its shell. Once, after standing by him in silence for a long time, staring at the offshore oil platform and the oil people working on it, Grandfather said: 'Do you know that there are spirits in this lake?' He must have seen the alarm on my frowning face as I shook my head. 'Hundreds of years ago, when slave-traders came here, many of our people opted to throw themselves into the lake to avoid being captured as slaves. Their spirits are there, because this is their grave. These spirits can sometimes be angry. I don't think the oil people are aware of this.'

On one occasion of gazing at the lake, which was in the afternoon, Grandfather said, 'Can you please take me to the oil people?' I complied and at once walked him to the office blocks of the oil company.

One of the men who often came to our village to buy fish, a tall fellow with a huge gap between his upper front teeth, rushed to greet us, as others went about their work, welding, plastering one of the office blocks, painting, or working on some machines whose names I did not know. 'Welcome,' said the man, leading us to one of the completed office blocks. 'May I offer you some tea or coffee?' he said, when we were seated in his office.

'No,' said my grandfather.

'Water, perhaps?'

'No.'

After a bit of awkward silence, the man said: 'What can I do for you?'

'Stop this rubbish and leave,' said my grandfather in a calm but emphatic deep voice, the voice only a chief such as he could carry, with a tremor reminiscent of those distant years when he had extra authority as the most powerful traditional healer in all the villages of the lake.

'Leave?' the man said, with a chuckle. 'Why? What wrong have we done?'

'Can't you see you're destroying our lake? You must stop this nonsense now. Pack your things and leave.'

The fellow laughed nervously. 'No, I don't think that is the case, sir. Your lake is not going to die.'

'That's not true. When the Leader of the Opposition held a rally here last year, he said the fish will die. The water, too, will become dirty. He said something needed to be done first, which our government has not done. I believed him and so did many others.'

'What needs to be done?' asked the man.

'Something... what did he call it?' Grandfather turned to me.

'An environmental impact assessment,' I refreshed his memory.

'That's it!' said Grandfather. 'Perhaps I need to tell you that to us, fish is everything. If you kill our lake, we are dead.'

The man looked out of the window in thoughtful silence. Clearing his throat, he said, in what came across as a carefully measured tone: 'I blame ourselves for not quickly engaging you, our wonderful hosts. No harm is going to be done to the lake. We have invested heavily to ensure no oil spillage. Please, bear with us. You would do well to understand that the world needs this oil. It has become a thirsty world, burning 13 billion litres of oil per day. You too want this oil. At night, when you're out fishing, I see lanterns in the middle of the lake. Isn't that kerosene? Now you'll have it at lower prices. Our country, too, needs it, because oil will bring a lot of money. Don't you want our country to be rich?'

My eyes strayed to a huge drawing on the wall behind the man's seat. He must have sensed that I was looking at something, as he said, pointing at the drawing: 'You see, this is where we have sunk the drilling template into the lakebed. Oil will be sucked from the earth and travel in these pipes up to the offshore platform, and you see these here? From the platform it will travel in these pipes up to this spot on land, where production will be done. So, as you can see, everything has been worked out to ensure the ecological system is not disturbed in any way.' He smiled, his eyes moving from Grandfather to me and back.

'Thank you for your explanation,' said Grandfather, 'but my mind remains unchanged. You're here to kill our lake, and I ask you to stop this and leave.'

'I'm afraid we can't stop just like that, sir,' said the man. 'We've signed an agreement with the government. We've spent too much money already. I beg you, sir, to understand us. We're already planning to buy a motorbike for every man in your village. We also plan to build a maternity clinic for your village. All these are just for a start. We will do more in future. Isn't that a wonderful thing? '

'I don't care,' said Grandfather. 'Go away. We don't want you here.'

The old man rose, and I had to hold him to prevent him from falling. He was shaking with fury. We began walking out, but the oil man stood and walked in quick strides to close the door and to stand facing us. 'Let's talk,' the man lowered his voice. 'If you promise not to tell the rest of the people in your village, we can give the two of you some money. I'm talking about good money that no fishing can make you in your lifetime.' Grandfather suddenly pushed the man with a force that shocked me, a reaction that must have taken the oil man by surprise as he staggered awkwardly and hit the door hard with his backside. As the man yelped, I jumped to stand between the two. 'Stop this, please,' I said to Grandfather, whose trembling was now intense.

'This man is evil,' said Grandfather. 'Evil, I say! How can he suggest to me to betray my people?' Turning to the oil man, who was now trying to straighten up his ruffled clothes, the old man said: 'Do you know me? Do you? Get lost! You are a dog; a filthy dog.' He spat. 'Let's go,' he said to me. We walked past the man, opened the door and closed it behind us.

To be frank, the offer of a motorbike was appealing to me. Not only because every man in the village would be given one, which sounded fair to me, but also because I needed it. I had all along been thinking about how to acquire a motorbike, yet there was no way I could afford it. With it, I could make extra money by offering transport services to areas with bad roads, where cars could not go. 'I think the motorbike idea is a good one,' I said to Grandfather as we entered the village.

'Don't sell your soul,' said Grandfather to me. 'A motorbike is nothing. It is here today, not there tomorrow. The lake will always be there if you defend it.'

'The man sounded sincere to me,' I said. 'He smiled and was polite.'

'Those who clap hands for a smiling crocodile realize their mistake when it is too late to learn from the error.' With these words, Grandfather detached himself from my supporting hand and limped into his house.

***

Weeks before free motorbikes were distributed, Grandfather asked me to call a meeting. A good crowd showed up. The old man spoke from a moored boat. The crowd looked at him and listened attentively, because, if there was any man who could do something about a precarious situation in these parts, then Grandfather was the one. He was a battle-scarred giant who had tussled with the Fisheries Department over the years and won, having compelled them to reverse the introduction of unaffordable fees for the annual renewal of fishing licences. Raising his hand for more silence, Grandfather said: 'I am aware that the oil company wants to distribute motorcycles to all men in the fishing villages. This is a trap. I ask you not to exchange your lake for the motorbikes. In fact, what we should be doing at present is to consider a protest. I ask God to join all our hearts as one, so that we should be free from fear. Let us march to the oil company and ask them to leave. Let us block their men from entering the lake. We can form a human wall and stop any oil worker from going into the lake. If the police come, that's even better, because our message will then reach the authorities.'

There was, strangely, a murmur of disapproval. Somebody in the crowd cracked a derogatory joke, something suggesting that the old man's age had made him lose his grip on reason, and the crowd laughed. In fact, even as Grandfather spoke, many people began to leave. I overheard a retired police officer saying: 'Militancy of any sort would be overboard. The government has already given its assurances that there will be no oil spill. I guess there will be a way to hold the government responsible if the guarantee is not kept.'

I said to the man: 'Beware of the government's promises. Do you remember that the Leader of the Opposition, when he addressed us last year, said an oil spill would take 700 years to clear? Even if we were to hold the government accountable, the lake would still be gone for 700 years. That is eternity, if you ask me.'

'Regardless,' said the man, 'between the old man's overreaction and a motorbike, I would choose the latter. I don't know what others think, but I am speaking for myself.'

When the meeting ended, Grandfather began to show signs of being increasingly disturbed, perhaps because this was the first time he had noticed open defiance to his authority. He spoke to himself and preferred to be alone. 'Sad,' he kept muttering. 'Nobody understands the severity of the matter.'

To be clear, I loved my grandfather, for he was the only person I considered my parent, since both my mother and father had died in a boat accident when I was in the third class of primary school. Grandfather and the now-deceased Grandmother saw to it that I grew up without lacking anything – money, clothes and the love that only family could provide. He was the one who taught me the art of fishing, and he did it well in those days when his youth and blood were warmer, before age curled his back. Over the years, therefore, any word Grandfather said to me I regarded as a commandment that could not be broken. But when it came to the matter of the motorbike, I was prepared politely to disagree with the old man, my love for him notwithstanding.

I therefore registered with an official from the oil company when he came to the village to take the names of those interested in free, brand new motorbikes. I asked other members of the family to keep it from the old man until I found ways of breaking the news to him myself.

***

Somebody must have betrayed me because Grandfather found out that I had accepted the motorbike barely a week after I received it. He called me to his house one morning and said, by way of greeting, 'How is the motorbike?' I had never felt more embarrassed in my life. All along I thought I had succeeded in staying clear of his path each time I took the motorbike and rode out of the village. Each time I kept it hidden at a friend's place, each time I pushed it way down the road to start the engine out of his sight but, no, the old man had found out my sleight-of-hand and, going by the sadness in his voice, he was far from amused. 'As you can see, not many days remain to me. I was hoping that, when I'm gone, you might lead the struggle against the oil people; but my hopes, as I can see, were misplaced.'

There was no way to describe my feeling, except, perhaps, by using clichés such as stung and gutted, none of which expressed half the guilt that consumed me at that moment. Worse, the returns I thought the motorbike might bring me weren't worth the shame, because it turned out I wasn't the only person thinking about offering transport services, which still left fishing the only realistic option of earning a living.

'Call a meeting of all those who fish in our village and the neighbouring villages,' he said.

'A meeting?' I said, arching my eyebrows in surprise.

'Yes.'

'What shall I say is the agenda?'

'Tell them it is an important meeting that cannot be missed.'

✳ ✳ ✳

Not many people came; in fact the correct way to put it was that only a handful showed up, mostly from our village. I could tell by the deepening contours on Grandfather's forehead that he was not pleased by the snub, but he showed signs of willingness to proceed with the meeting. I dutifully carried him to the boat. 'Leave me alone,' he said, and I did.

Leaning on his stick in the middle of the moored boat as usual, about 20 metres or so into the lake, he shouted: 'I'm disappointed by you all. How can you exchange your lake for these motorbikes? This lake is going to die – doesn't that make you afraid?' None of us answered him.

'If I must die to let the lake live, then I will,' he said, and I flinched, not sure what he meant by that. He continued: 'I believe that my spirit, together with the spirits of our fathers, will be angry enough to stop this nonsense. And so...' He threw away the stick he was leaning on and suddenly plunged into the water. He swam as we gasped but, instead of heading towards the shore, he went the opposite direction.

He was an agile swimmer despite his age, and in those few moments of indecision as we stood watching him swim, he went farther and farther. Then his body suddenly sunk into the water, leaving his head temporarily bobbing like a fishing float before disappearing into the water.

I dived into the water, as did many others, but I was ill-dressed for a swim. I gave up after a few metres, afraid I might drown. As I staggered back onto the shore, I turned and looked at the others who had swum to the spot by the boat. I hoped for the best while shouting and crying to attract the attention of passers-by who might help. After a few minutes everybody realized the futility of the search and returned to the shore. All of us dripping wet, we stood on the shore to gaze at the calm lake that had now become the old man's tomb, unable to comprehend why he had taken his own life. I had been aware that the matter was of great importance to him, but it had not occurred to me that he considered it an issue big enough for him to take his life.

I rushed to the police to report a suicide and to request them to help us trace his corpse.

***

The official from the government returned to address us through his megaphone. It was a week after my grandfather's death. As we gathered to listen to him, I noticed something about the water. To begin with, it had receded too far from the shore, so far, in fact, that the lake began to look like an empty pit. This frightened me, especially with the silence that engulfed the place as though we were inside a tomb. And then, just as the official ascended to his makeshift podium, I saw the mass of water rise in the distance, slowly but steadily, as if a magnetic force was pulling it from the sky. The height of the water was increasing by the second and, just as the official opened his mouth, the lake became a mountain of water, silently moving towards us. I thought of leaving, of running away, but I dismissed the thought, fearing that the gun-carrying police protecting the government official might misinterpret my actions and open fire. In his gruff voice, the official said: 'The government wants to make it clear that counter-revolutionary activities of any kind, suicides, protests, strikes, and so on, will not deter the nation from extracting oil. If there are any grievances, channel them through the appropriate authorities. We want a peaceful coexistence between your community and the oil company. Anybody planning further shows of such attention-seeking acts as suicide, self-immolation etcetera should be reported to the police. The government will also make available to your villages a psychiatrist to provide psychosocial support, as it is clear some of you are failing to cope with the reality. The President, who loves you, and sends his greetings, in whose authority I . . . .'

The water was now so high that the offshore oil platform was already buried under it, and the huge mountain was now too close for anybody to stand it. I began to run. The meeting ended at that point, as everyone, including the government official and the police, started running towards the higher ground, the latter without their guns.

It was not until I was at the top of the hill to the west that I stopped to survey the situation below. The water had gone beyond the shore and was sweeping everything in its wake. I saw the government official's vehicle tossed like a toy car before being swallowed by the angry waters. I saw our houses collapse, and the oil company's offices brought down. I saw trees uprooted and the water rise to even more frightening heights, charging towards the hill where I was. I turned and looked further west, searching for the next hill to run to. But just before I took off, the water calmed down at the foot of the hill. I looked at it in fear as I tried to comprehend it all. Surely this could not have happened without the power of angry spirits? I wondered about what had happened to other members of my family, aunts and uncles, nieces, nephews and cousins. I sat down and began to shake. 'Oh, Grandfather, your spirit is too angry,' I said. 'Please, don't be too hard on us.'

* * *

I went back to our village after a week of staying with friends from inland villages. Everything was destroyed, and the motorbikes were all gone. Various organizations, both local and international, donated tents, food, clothes and medical care to us. The only personal items of ours that survived were our fishing boats. The offshore oil platform was gone, uprooted by the angry waters like a tooth from its root canal. Since the offices of the oil people on the shore had also been destroyed, the company announced its immediate but temporary withdrawal to study a thing or two about the incomprehensible behaviour of the water before making any further decisions. There had been casualties not only among the oil people but also in every village, with 11 of the oil men confirmed dead and 16 villagers, including a cousin of mine. Whenever I walked about, I heard many people express relief for having survived, or, in some cases, sorrow for a loved one lost, but it was clear to us all that restarting our lives was going to be a challenge of unimaginable proportions.

Stanley Onjezani Kenani is a Malawian writer. He was shortlisted for the Caine Prize in 2008 and in 2012.

The Strange Dance of the Calabash

Wazha Lopang

THE SLAP CAUGHT ME just below the ear and sent me sprawling backwards into the kraal. Thankfully, I landed on the calf I had ridiculed moments earlier. There was a snort from my assailant as he leaned over the fence and took a second massive swipe at me. He missed and I was able to scramble up and lift my soggy skirt from the ground and examine the hem for damage. We were expecting important guests and the skirt was my attempt at appearing respectable.

I was cursing myself, not for the state of the skirt but because Papa's blow had caught me unawares. This monster of a man was so deceptive you would think he spent hours cooped up in his room practising his backhanded slaps against the walls. The calf I had dared to offend in Papa's presence, looked at me with large uncomprehending eyes and went to suckle from its frail mother, who had moved under the mophane tree.

'Repeat what you said,' he demanded. His voice did not quite match his bulk and, if you did not know any better, you would think somebody was hiding behind him playing him like a giant puppet. The sleeves of his khaki shirt were rolled up to the elbows. The forearms seemed larger than usual that morning.

'Repeat it!'

My ear was still ringing and so I did not immediately giggle at that voice of his. Instead I rubbed my ear and muttered, 'I don't remember.'

He spat to one side and thundered, 'That's because you are stupid!' Encouraged by the fence between us, I replied, 'No. I forgot because you hit me so hard it came out my other ear.'

Papa looked at me with his head cocked to the side as if I were some familiar yet obviously poisonous fruit dangling from a bush where one of his cows might pass. He spat again. If he continued doing that, he just might save the pastures from the crippling drought that was now into its third year. I didn't say this aloud and bit my tongue just in time, causing a tear to roll down a grubby cheek.

Papa shook his head at me, his nose flaring the way our donkey does when it sees the water barrels being loaded onto the cart. 'Why can't you be as sensible as Thabo – or your sister at least? I have no idea why anybody would want to marry you but when your in-laws arrive you had better be on your best behaviour, Pebanyana.' He trudged back up to the house in his thick boots. I knew the drought weighed on him heavily. It was crushing the seeds of joy that had once flourished in his heart. What grew there now was hurt and resentment.

I was the last-born of three children. My name was not Pebanyana. I don't think I resembled a small mouse in any way. I had pointed this out to Papa the first time he had mentioned that name and had got a bruised buttock for my troubles. My name was Tshepo and I was 13 years old.

Our farm was deep in the countryside. The nearest village, Thamaga, was an hour's travel west along a gruelling road dotted with potholes that snaked its way across parched acacia woodland before running parallel to a mountain renowned for its peculiar rock formations. It was Papa, the seven cows, and I. Just us and the drought. Neo, my sister, had recently been married to a man she had grown to tolerate. They lived in Thamaga and she visited whenever she could.

Thabo was the eldest, the favourite child and future heir to the two-room house, the cows and the drought. We hardly saw the city boy yet I lived in the shadow of his praises. Papa spoke fondly of him in rare unguarded moments of happiness. You could actually see the mamba eyes dilate when he spoke of him. Papa had a nickname for him too – Tau. I don't think Thabo resembled a lion (though he did have the appetite to match) but Papa did not value my opinions, not that I lost any sleep over this. However, it was difficult to decide whom Papa loved more: the Lion or the cows. I remember when the Lion pinched my ear after I had asked him when he would settle down and start a family. Papa had emitted a sound that resembled a laugh and said, 'I see myself in you, Tau.'

His blood coursed in Tau's city-boy veins and yet Papa was a farmer to the roots of his soul. Neo said when my mother died Papa had actually cried though it was unclear if he was crying for his wife or for the loss of a cow slaughtered in her honour. In those days he had close to a hundred cattle. 'Cattle are more important than women,' he often said with a slight tremor in his voice. 'Cattle are life. If you have no cattle you are not alive. You are simply moving in a grave with a mouth full of soil.'

People often remarked that I resembled my mother, which was obviously a lie because Papa was always smacking me about. I had never seen him lay an angry hand on the Lion. Whenever they reunited after a long absence, they exchanged playful swipes across the shoulders, and each time a paw connected with flesh the sound was like an elephant breaking off a branch. On his rare visits Tau spent hours on the sofa or, if it was not too warm, he would be on the porch soaking up the sun as I scampered from here to there on endless errands.

I slowly crawled from under the fence. Damn. I could have moved faster than that. Often when he dropped his shoulder I would already be leaning back. However, this time his hands had been in his pockets jiggling some loose change and the sound of those coins had commanded my full attention when the blow came. Next time I would steal some two-inch nails that we kept in the tool shed for repairing the rickety kraal and conceal them in my headscarf and provoke him with something like, 'How many cattle died today, Papa?' or perhaps, 'If it don't rain tomorrow, Papa, which cow are we gonna eat first?' I bet when that paw felt the nails sinking in he would bellow like a bull being castrated.

I giggled and plopped onto the ground. This was foolish because my only decent skirt was getting really soiled. But the giggles would not stop and I was trying so hard to frown as I giggled so that my heart would see that I was having none of it. Pretty soon I was hysterical with laughter. The image of my father yelling in pain and blowing on his fingers rocked my body in spasms of delight. Perhaps his hand would swell, swell and swell and then go POP! I was getting back to my feet but a crazy image of my father as a yellow balloon floating into the blue sky filled my vision and I collapsed again in whoops of laughter.

My situation, however, was no laughing matter. My father was expecting some very important guests. I was being married off to a man that I did not know and had no intention of knowing. The visit was only to confirm and pay the bride price. The actual marriage was still five years away but in essence, once the deal was done, I would be 'married'. Papa could have waited a couple of years before allowing for marriage negotiations but the drought had left him no choice. However, the fact that our guests were spoken highly of by the Lion dispelled any misgivings my father had. From the letters between Pa and our guests it was clear that the Lion knew a lot about them.

I had not met my suitor but in my mind he was a fat bullfrog with cold brown eyes. My mother and Neo were products of arranged marriages. Papa said tradition added salt to your bones. 'Your destiny in life,' he would say when

I misbehaved, 'is to prostrate yourself to your man. That is all. Always remember one thing: Every woman is beautiful until she speaks.'

In my father's opinion the thought of a girl choosing her own husband was as rare as a man with no cattle. Negotiations were scheduled for this afternoon and I had resigned myself to my fate. However, I would not be changing my dress, my suitor would have to pay for the cow dung and dirt on me as well. I did not hate marriage. It was only that the thought of getting married to someone you could not fight back did not appeal to me.

Neo was married off in much the same way; the only difference was that she was 19 at the time. Her husband regularly beat her over trivial matters. One evening, though, she boiled some water on the primus stove and casually poured it on the bed. This was in full view of the undressing husband. 'Why are you doing that?' he had asked, surprised.

'I'm just practising, my Lord. I want to see if I can empty the whole pot in one quick throw.'

The beatings had stopped. Now imagine me. How was I going to get a big pot of boiling water to the bed all by myself? Perhaps I would ask the bullfrog to assist. I could probably smile and show him the gap in my teeth... but would that gap be enough to get him to pour boiling water over himself? My laughter had dried up by now and all that was left to see was a dirty girl taking short nervous breaths.

How was I to get out of this situation? I had tried. Lord knew, I had run away three times already and each time Papa had caught me hiding in exactly the same place – the tree in the kraal. Those stupid cows kept staring up the tree despite my best efforts to shoo them off, especially the calf. This was the cause of my most recent slap. When I climbed down the tree I said, 'The only reason you found me Papa, is because that calf is a Judas! In fact, it is a Cowdas!'

My thoughts were interrupted by a car entering our yard. They were here and my time was up. Simultaneously Papa kicked the kitchen door open and roared out my name.

I rubbed my throbbing arm as I sat on the floor by Papa's feet. He had taken the trouble to put on his only blazer, a black, uncomfortable, woollen item that was two sizes too small and which had gone for quite some time without a wash. Every now and then he slyly scratched an arm as his skin reacted to the dirty fabric. There were no other relatives with us since this was just a preliminary talk. In subsequent meetings Uncle Morwesi would join Papa and I would be barred from proceedings. My sole purpose at this meeting was to smile for the guests when the time came for me to parade for them.

Across the room sat the two visitors on a low wooden stool that they had brought themselves. There was a grey sofa by the door under the light switch. Although it was as old as Papa's anger, it was still functional. It stood there unused, looking forlorn, like a tethered goat on Christmas Day. Between us was a small handmade table on which was set a pitcher of water and a small bottle of juice concentrate. Beside this were a large glass and a chipped plate with exactly three ginger biscuits.

One of the visitors was indeed a bullfrog of sorts. He was quite hairy – you could, with a bit of patience and two matchsticks, braid tiny cornrows on his forearms. His companion was slightly taller, with a pointy forehead that was sweating profusely. Every few minutes he rummaged in his coat pocket and brought out a damp blue-and-white handkerchief to dab liberally across his brow. They wore ill-fitting suits probably purchased off the hanger from Hami's General Merchandise, owned by a surly Pakistani in Thamaga. I was happy I had not changed my skirt. We continued staring at each other for a while and I amused myself by counting how many times Papa scratched at his arms and neck. Occasionally the sponge would lean over to the bullfrog to whisper something as oily drops of perspiration marked a trail between them. I wasn't looking forward to cleaning that up.

Finally, after what Papa felt to be a reasonable interlude, he cleared his throat and lifted his upper lip briefly before dropping it again. 'Gentlemen from Gaborone, good afternoon. I have been looking forward to this day. Our elders were wise when they said a home without a woman is like a kraal without cattle.' The sponge went for his handkerchief. Papa continued, 'We meet for the first time face to face and I hope that our negotiations will go smoothly. With regard to the bride price I am confident that, though money is always a difficult hurdle to overcome, eventually we will reach an agreement.' He spread his arms before him. 'All we need today is a bit of patience with one another. As the proverb goes, a cow does not void all its dung at one go.'

Our guests nodded politely while Papa took a moment to scratch his neck. He sounded calm but I knew he had one mind on the borehole, calculating how he would spend the dowry. The local Agricultural Officer had told him just last week that if his cattle did not get a regular supply of good water they would not make it through this summer. In his reflections Papa had come to the conclusion that a bride price of 12 cattle would suffice to drill and equip the borehole. This was the figure that he wanted from our two visitors.

'Mr Kgwebo,' the bullfrog croaked. 'Thank you for the warm greeting. Already the feeling of being a stranger has disappeared. However, it seems there has been a slight misunderstanding all along that was never corrected in the letters we wrote to you. The groom's family didn't actually brief us well until yesterday when we were already committed to coming here and so...'

His voice trailed off and the sponge squeezed out an opinion. 'You see, sir... er... our groom did not tell us this before but he has a... condition... you and I may find strange.'

A part of me wanted to raise my arm and ask a question but I decided to see which direction this conversation was headed. The bullfrog stuck out an arm and threw a ginger biscuit in his mouth and sucked on it. Papa was sitting ramrod straight, hands on his knees. His fingers were twitching like the whiskers of a nervous mouse. The moment I saw that, one word sprang into my head. *Pebanyana!* I muffled a giggle but I could not help my shoulders from shaking with laughter. Papa gnashed his teeth for a long second and slowly returned his attention to the two men, who had confused looks on their faces. With a strained expression, Papa removed his jacket and placed it on the sofa so carefully one would think he was nursing a cow with a fever. I believe he was just using the opportunity to think about what he had just heard because, when he started talking, his voice grew steadily with each question he asked.

'What are you talking about? Condition? You have no right to make demands to me in my own house. The strength of the crocodile is in the river. You have no right at all!'

Outside, the thirsty cows were getting restless and I could hear the bell on Matladi rattle in a way that suggested she was trying the wooden gate of the kraal with her horn. The bullfrog traced an extremely pink tongue across his wide lips. He swallowed. I had never in all my young life seen an Adam's apple move so slowly. It was like an ambitious mole burrowing through thick terrain before deciding to turn back and head for the surface.

The sponge spoke up. 'Again you misunderstand. These youth of today, Mr Kgwebo, they have... different tastes.' The bullfrog zapped up another biscuit. I was now eyeing the door, calculating how many steps it would take for my father to block it before I could escape. The words of the sponge were not comforting.

'Young man, speak up! What is the point of your visit?' His hands were still on his knees but I refused to look at his fingers. 'Is it that grown men like you are ignorant of the procedure in such matters?' He clucked softly, the way he often did when the lead cow pulled up abruptly in the field, causing the plough to lurch out of the furrow. 'Let me remind you, as the saying goes, nobody is born wise. What you do is that you identify yourselves and say "We have come to ask for a calabash of water". I then ask if you can describe the calabash you seek, which is when you identify that girl over there and give me her full names. That is the custom.'

The bullfrog croaked into life again and, as he spoke, little crumbs peppered the air. 'Mr Kgwebo, the custom is well known to us. We have not been sent here to ask for the girl's hand in marriage. I know this is what you had assumed all along and we apologize for misleading you. Our groom intends to marry another of your children.'

He was staring fixedly at the vinyl floor. The sponge had dived into his pocket again. My father and I exchanged looks. I showed him my hands and raised three fingers in front of me and mouthed off each one silently: 'Tshepo, Neo, Thabo.' I did it in reverse just so that he got the picture: 'Thabo, Neo, Tshepo.' My father was still looking at me but deep in thought. I unfolded my fourth finger at him and said, 'Papa, do you have another child that you have neglected to tell us about?'

The bullfrog had the look of a man caught doing something inappropriate behind a church. Nonetheless, he ploughed on, eager to get the weight off his chest. The sponge had almost disappeared into his suit. 'Please believe me when I say that bringing this news has been an agonizing experience for me – for all of us in fact. But in life one has to adapt to the challenges placed before one. The chameleon changes colour to match the earth and not the other way round. Our groom wants to let it be known that he is willing to pay 26 head of cattle to you but only if he receives your blessing for the marriage.' I whistled softly but, because my mouth had gone dry, what came out instead was a sharp gust of air. Papa's mouth dropped open almost to his navel. He blinked quickly and turned his head and looked out the window for a minute in the direction of the kraal, although he couldn't see it from where he sat. A very important question was still without an answer although I was not sure if I was ready for it.

'Who is being married? The girl is right here.' My father pointed a twitching finger at me and I closed my eyes and again raised three fingers. 'Papa, there is no fourth child.'

The sponge emerged like a tortoise that has waited as long as it dared in the open field and has decided to head for cover before the hawk's shadow swoops again. He spoke up with an air of resignation. 'An elephant carries his tusks no matter how heavy. Mr Kgwebo, the groom wants to marry your son. The two of them are lovers.'

The room became tense the way it sometimes gets just before an African thunderstorm. I was looking at the bullfrog. He was looking at Papa, who was looking at the sponge retreating into his suit. Thabo was still smiling on the wall. At that moment Matladi bellowed and, like a rabid dog that has chewed through its leash, Papa leapt from his chair and went for the bullfrog.

With a shriek that would have been comical in a different setting, the bullfrog positioned the sponge in front of him. As Papa grabbed him by the lapel of his suit, I was disappointed the material didn't tear right off. In the ensuing scuffle, the sponge tried to get Papa's attention by flailing his arms about and yelling, 'Mr Kgwebo, we are still here for the calabash of water! Please let's work something out.'

'The calabash you seek has no water you can use!' Papa thundered. The glass wobbled on the table but surprisingly it did not topple over. The men fell against the wall and dislodged the picture from the nail where it hung.

The Lion crashed to the ground and the fight went out of my father.

Suddenly he seemed very tired, like a stubborn old man who realizes one morning that he can no longer ignore the walking stick by his bed. 'Get out,' he said softly. 'Leave us. The words you bring are more than a man can stomach.'

The men shuffled out the door and bade dejected farewells, '*Go siame, go siame.*'

I picked up the picture and shook out the pieces of glass still lodged in the frame. I mounted it back on the wall and turned towards my father. There was a deep sadness in his eyes, a sadness that it seemed not even the bleating of a new-born calf could shake. 'What are we to do now, Tshepo? What shall become of us?'

I reached out and held his hand.

***

Six weeks passed and the cows were doing reasonably well. Papa had bought some hay and medicine for them and I must say there was a lively mood about the place – everything seemed fresh and alive. The borehole was up and running and there was enough water to sell to the neighbouring farmers who were no doubt inquisitive as to where the money had come from but had the good manners to keep their thoughts to themselves.

The important thing was that Papa's heart now had a song in it and occasionally, when he whistled an old folk tune about a hunter that had saved his tribe from hunger, I found myself thinking of my mother. He had accepted the bride price of 26 cattle after much soul searching. We never discussed the 'union'. It was as if my father had closed that door shut with his massive arms and nothing would open it. I was trying, but it would take time.

Despite Papa's wishes, Neo did go to the city to visit Tau and I was still eagerly awaiting news from her. What I wanted more than anything was for Tau to pay us a visit. It would happen some day and I guess my father knew it too. The thought of Papa and the Lion together after such a turbulent time would be a great occasion for me. I would put on my new skirt for that one! However, there was a more immediate concern for me. I was in the tree looking at the fat calf gazing intently at me. Papa was on his way to knock some sense into me. I had innocently remarked if he had ever seen a male lion without a mane and if this would explain why Thabo was what he was.

The kitchen door slammed open and I heard the heavy footsteps crunch towards me. I hissed at the calf with a twinkle in my eye. 'You Cowdas.'

Wazha Lopang is a lecturer in African Literature at the University of Botswana. He has published a short story for *Mahube*, 'As Long as it Doesn't Spoil my Appetite'. He was runner-up in the 2010 Bessie Head Literature Awards for his novel *If Mother Only Knew*. He is currently working on a novel on the occult entitled *One Thief Per Church*.

Chameleons with Megapixel Skins

Muti

The *ganja* smell hangs in the room like an expensive perfume, so sure of its very existence. The bedroom walls are a deeper shade of red, the kind seen in opium dens in Chinese flicks. From outside the large, curtainless window, light from the crescent moon hits the Bonsai plant before it filters into the room. For the last six months, I have been living with my girlfriend in this two-storeyed mansion located in the Sunnyside suburb of Blantyre, Malawi's commercial city. The house is perched right next to the 18-hole golf course of the Blantyre Sports Club. It is a prime location and this is as expensive as it gets in Blantyre's real estate. Mary can afford it because she is an expatriate medical surgeon.

Time is just after 9pm. I am lying on the bed, my dreadlocks spread across a satin pillow. Mary is kneeling between my legs, playing with my dick like a kid with a lollipop. I am pretending to enjoy it. Truth is I am numb as fuck – the last six months have exhausted just about every sexual fantasy our minds can conjure.

My mind drifts to earlier this morning. I am buying what's reputed to be the strongest ganja in the world. Ahmed, my supplier, calls it goat's piss.

'Do you know that Malawi's ganja is the strongest in the world? Even the World Bank agrees.'

'Shut the fuck up and just give me the stuff.'

With the conviction of a science professor, Ahmed celebrates its potency. 'It spends six solid months buried under a goat's kraal, sucking as much piss as possible. Like wine, this shit matures well with age. And goat urine, of course. This shit will make you forget your very own existence.'

Back in the bedroom, I draw in and cough. Mary shifts, and looks up. I smile. Over her shoulder, on the wall, the shadow of the bonsai plant has animated into an open mouth of a T-rex dinosaur. It's moving in to swallow the painting of Haile Selassie next to it. In response, Bob Marley, from below the ground, strums the Gibson Les Paul guitar and shouts 'Jah live!' Outside Marley's mausoleum, Mortimer Plano draws three times from a black coconut chalice and releases the smoke which carries Bob's message across the lush mountains of Jamaica, south-eastwards, towards Kingston. At the Palisadoes Airport, it enters via the stigma, the waving hand of Haile Selassie, who is clad in full military regalia and a Sam Browne belt. From Selassie's mind, the message is transported back to the motherland, making its entry via the Obelisk of Aksum from where it is scattered to all the four corners of the earth. The southbound message, which travels via the Great Rift Valley, gets only as far as northern Lake Malawi where, instead of reaching I'n'I in Blantyre, it is swallowed by a myriad of screaming cichlids.

HIM majestically steps out of the frame, to the window. Ghost-like, he reaches the bonsai plant on the other side and repositions it. He turns around and fixes his penetrating eyes on me, watching my fake attempts at affection with a particularly inspired disinterest. 'You are pathetic, fake Rasta,' he finally says, before walking back into his square wooden home.

I cringe with shame. Using my forearms, I lift up off the bed and shove Mary aside. Thinking it's some sort of play, she approaches again, a mischievous look in her eyes. 'I have been a bad girl, daddy,' she says. 'I need to be spanked!'

'Not now, mommy,' I say, pushing her away. She tumbles off the bed, dragging bed sheets with her.

Seconds later, she is angrily asking me to leave her house. The time is just after 9pm, a fact I point out to her. She doesn't care, she says, before slamming the bedroom door.

'Come on now! This shit is really getting old,' I shout at her.

'Get out!' she replies.

I descend the stairs, into the living room, and start watching the television. Fuck the bitch, I say, as I flip channels.

Minutes later, the bedroom door opens and Mary drops a duffel bag over the railing. It lands with a thud at the bottom of the stairs. 'Take your shit and leave, you fake Rasta.'

'Wait a minute,' I say to her. 'Can we at least talk about this?'

'No. Get the fuck out!'

'Well then fuck you too, you Scottish twat!'

'Get out!'

'You cannot even suck dick! I know African villagers who suck dick better than you do, you cunt!'

Mary did not bother to zip up the bag so several items have fallen out as it landed, including a black coconut chalice. Only now do I place my chalice in the hallucination I had earlier. Searching for the connection, I silently put the items back into the bag.

'You can keep the bag, you poor fuck!' Mary's voice continues from upstairs.

'I may be poor, but you are white trash, just like your parents!'

'Fuck you! You don't know shit about me.'

Outside her mansion, the two dogs run towards me and start wagging their tails excitedly. Lately I have been taking them for walks, mainly out of sympathy, since their owner has no such time. One of the two guards on duty walks towards me with a greeting. The younger of the two dogs barks at the guard, who takes the cue and stands back.

'*Wawa*,' says the guard.

'*Wawa*,' I answer.

'What now?'

'It is the same shit every day. But this time I have had it. Screw the bitch!'

'I see,' says the elderly guard, reflectively. 'It happens,' he says. We shake hands before he opens the thick green gate for me. I pat the two dogs and leave.

From across the gate, the fence of the Golf Club has a small opening. Caddies use this opening to fetch foul balls, a good number of which land in Mary's backyard. I enter the golf course through the opening and find myself near the green. A painted sign says 18. I cross the green and join the fairway, heading westwards. I am heading towards the river where I know there's a bridge; I need shelter. I have walked this golf course one too many times, especially with Mary. Once, I was kindly advised by a guard with a K-9, in vernacular, to take the *mzungu* home and destroy her anus. 'Make her see what that whore from Mulanje saw, after cussing at a witchdoctor.' Funny life, this. Once, I even tried to take the dogs for a walk on the golf course but the same guard flatly refused.

As I get near the bridge it starts to rain. I dash for a few yards. At the bridge, I throw myself under it, feet first, and land on a soft spot.

'Son of a monkey! Son of the donkey!' A voice shouts at me. Even in the dark, the smell tells me he is a homeless man. I take out my cheap Nokia phone and switch on the torch; it illuminates a space which is regularly used for living: an empty can here, and a torn shirt there.

'Please allow me to hide...' Before I finish the sentence, the irony of asking permission from a vagabond occurs to me. 'Wait a minute! Why the fuck am I asking you for permission, you homeless fuck?' He just grunts and goes back to sleep. I move to the far side and deposit my duffel bag on the ground. Using it as a pillow, I lie down and watch the rain trickle down from the bridge.

Now would be a good time to smoke some ganja. I then remember that, two days before, I moved the stash from Mary's bedroom to one of the drawers in the kitchen. This vain attempt at quitting just seems funny now. But, even if the ganja was still in the bedroom, Mary would not have packed it for me. She loves Malawi gold as much as I do. In any case, she would have realized, even in her angry state, that the stash was worth saving.

Two sleepless hours later, the rain is still falling. Out of boredom, I monitor, with my torch, the level of the Mudi River. For a moment, I entertain the idea that the river might flood this embankment. The intensity of this bum's sleep assures me otherwise. If there were any danger, history would have made him watch the levels of the river with me. Still, stranger things have happened in my life, especially where the rains are concerned. Turning points in my life have almost always involved the rains. A South African friend and fellow ganja dealer thinks my parents should have named me *Nomvula,* the bringer of rain. Every time I think of the rains or mud, my mind wanders back to the past, to times I would rather forget.

I am back in the past, at the Kamuzu Stadium in the middle of Blantyre. Both Malawi and I are celebrating our birthdays: I 11, Malawi 28. Kamuzu Banda, Malawi's life President, makes a grand entrance into the stadium. Behind him is a car with his official hostess and her sister named Mary. I, like everyone in the stadium, am an attentive participant in the events unfolding before me. With the concrete slab drawing thick blood lines at the back of my thighs, I am watching with the intense interest of a village boy on his first visit to the city. I am fascinated by everything, especially the opulence of the president. *That car is so expensive it can feed the whole of Malawi*, I overhear two men saying about his red Rolls Royce. Earlier, we had been bussed from St Mary's Orphanage, in the Lower Shire, and given canvas shoes and red t-shirts to form part of the decorations. Those sitting opposite us, on the other stands, read *Long Live Kamuzu, father and founder of Malawi*. We, on the other hand, are facing a menacing image of a black cockerel amongst a sea of red; Kamuzu Banda's party symbol.

As a little god in a make-believe kingdom, I am imagining that that everyone in the stadium has come to celebrate my birthday. I am having such a good time when the big gods in the heavens decide to weep their nourishing tears. The rains could not have come at a less appropriate time; July is a very cold month in Malawi. The rains go on for two successive hours, with a 15-minute break in-between.

With the rains still pouring, Kamuzu Banda rises to address us. He asks us to thank him for the rains, although not in so few words. In fact, for the next two hours, he asks us to thank him for just about everything. Every now and then, his speech is punctuated by women singing his praises.

Everything belongs to Kamuzu.

By the time he finishes his long speech, I am shivering like a wet puppy. To close the ceremonies, Malawi plays a soccer match against Kenya's Harambee Stars. Kenya wins, Kamuzu disappears to his Sanjika Palace located next to the Sunnyside suburb, and I am taken by the Red Cross people to the Queen Elizabeth Hospital where I am treated for pneumonia. Days later, I am well enough to return to my peasant life in the village.

It will take me a further 11 years to realize that Kamuzu Banda did not only piss on us, but he told us that the piss was rain.

Back under the bridge, the rain is still pouring, without signs of letting up. The water continues to rise. If it goes on for another hour, this embankment will be flooded. On the brighter side, it will give this fuck a chance to take a bath. How lazy do you have to be to live underneath a bridge and not take a bath?

Thoughts of flooding take me back to my village, in the Lower Shire area of Malawi. I am now 18. Like other villagers, I am sweating profusely while waiting for the traditional dances to begin. Earlier, the village crier announced that masked dancers, or animals, as they are respectfully called, will make an appearance to reconcile the natural, spiritual, and human forces of life and death. Proudly, I remark to my neighbour how the dances represent thousands of years of culture and society, sophisticated as it is rich.

Maliya, a parody of the Biblical Virgin Mary, takes the stage. Her softwood mask looks menacing in the sepia sunlight. Her face is broad and her rounded ears are cupped forward, placed high upon the sides of the head. Her nose is short and wedge-shaped, with eyes that are close-set. Her mouth is partially open, like she is eternally stuck in mockery stance. To warm up, she starts dance noises while intimidating the audience. The women accompanying her clap their hands.

'Her role is to instruct us through the personification of undesirable character traits,' one villager tells another.

Just as she is about to start, another villager breaks protocol and jumps from the audience, into the *bwalo* and confronts the chief who is seated nearby.

'I curse you in the name of our ancestors. You connive with the richest man in the village to take my plot of land? He bribes you and you celebrate? Where am I going to farm? My family and I are leaving this village.'

He exits the *bwalo*. The chief, unmoved, motions for the dances to start. As soon as the first drum sounds, the skies open and rain falls, scattering us into our huts, and Maliya back to the village graveyard. The rains fall for 12 hours, flooding the whole village.

The next day, with the effort of an old man, I leave home for the city. Now, years later, I still have no intentions of returning.

Outside, the rain has stopped and it is now daylight. The bum is still sleeping and will probably do so the whole day. I crawl out of the bridge and rejoin the fairway.

Fuck, I am starving! I exit through the opening and land in a puddle of mud. Mary's green gate is just across the way.

Time on my watch says 6.30. Moses the helper is not yet in but I need that sachet of ganja. I go behind the wall of the mansion and sit down to wait for him. I send him an SMS: 'Flash me when you are in the main house.'

Wiping the mud off my shoes and jeans, I cuss again. I have a particular hatred for mud. The shit conjures images of Mary-Ann, my very close friend in college. Suddenly, I am back in that period, my image of her as vivid as fuck.

Together we share dreams of changing Malawi and of fighting for equality for all. We talk of telling our own stories to invert the gaze the West uses to define us. We heed calls of the likes of Jack Mapanje, who advocate a return to the traditional life and seek inspiration in literature. We reject the way the knowledge of our ancestors has been classified as simple, and we make it our mission to show this.

We graduate and say goodbye to each other, promising to go change this fucked-up shithole. I meet Mary-Ann months later, as I am dropping my CV and diplomas at a radio station in town. She is sitting on the couch, struggling to cover her thighs with her mini-skirt. Before I can greet her, the receptionist tells her she can go in. She gets up and for the first time in my life, I see her thighs. What happened to all those long skirts? At the door, she hands over a small envelope which I am sure contains money, and disappears into the office.

After 30 minutes, Mary-Ann is still not out. I go to the reception: 'What the hell is going on?' I ask. 'How should I know?' I am rudely answered. 'Fuck it,' I say. Whatever, I am answered.

Outside, it starts to pour. I dash to the small hut located by the gate. I try the door knob but the door is locked. I cuss and exit the premises. I start walking in the rain, the envelope containing my life's achievement soaking up the rain with dedication. It slips from my hand and I do not bother to pick it up. I turn a corner and start cussing at my ancestors. A hundred metres away, a posh car splashes me with muddy water. It stops and, on the passenger side, a window rolls down. Mary-Ann sticks her head out and asks: 'Are you okay? Do you need a lift?'

'Fuck you, bitch-traitor,' I answer her.

Her face drops. She recoils into the car and they speed off.

Three weeks later, I am living in the peri-urban area of Ndirande, located in the outskirts of Blantyre city. I want to be far away from the prying and corrupt eyes of normal society. My neighbour introduces me to Rastafarianism. I am reluctant at first, claiming I am beyond believing in anything, let alone a dead monarch. Later I join the sect, especially after figuring out that the whole thing is, in a sense, a big *Fuck You* to society. It takes me five years to become a proselyte, albeit a cynical one.

In the suburb of Mandala, at a party mainly full of expatriates, my Rasta friend, a musician in a popular local reggae outfit, introduces me to Mary, who I cannot stand at first. She is beautiful and rich and educated. She is almost everything I am not. But soon I discover Mary's peculiar ability to withstand my anger and my bullshit. My tantrums, she blames on my growing up an orphan in a Third World country.

Fuck it, I eventually say. Why not? I start telling her things like 'Most nights, in a process I call mystifying ritualism, I hear a collage of voices. They scare me. I just want someone to hold, you know. Your kindness, like the rains, washes away my fears.'

Mary never gets tired of hearing such bullshit, much to my surprise. A month after meeting her, I am the best-dressed Rasta in town, and the only one who drives a sleek Mercedes Benz. With time, I get used to Mary.

Outside Mary's gate, Moses hands me the sachet. Minutes later, Haile Selassie is leading me by the hand. Like a love-struck couple, we are gliding towards the Blantyre market. 'We need to go see Ras Noah,' says Selassie. Hand in hand, we float out of Smythe Road, into Victoria Avenue.

A banner suspended above the road reads: 'Passages for the Undocumented by Massa Lemu.' Selassie smiles; I wonder.

Yards later, near the Hotel Victoria, another Lemu banner reads: 'Nihilist in search of tenure.' Again, Selassie smiles; I scowl.

On the entrance to the Blantyre Sports Club, another reads: 'In pursuit of *fulfailment*.' Selassie scratches his head; I wince.

We reach the Old Town Hall, where another banner reads: 'Those who venture there get immunized.' Selassie is now grinning; I am surprised.

We exit Victoria Avenue at the traffic lights and enter Haile Selassie Road. Selassie lets go of my hand and pushes me forward. I am gliding towards the Blantyre market. I exit Selassie Road, and enter Kaoshuing Road.

Yards later, I turn left and reach the gate to the Blantyre flea market. The bustle of the place reaches me as if from another world. Outside the door, a vendor has mounted two large speakers on top of each other. The famous Congolese song 'Maria Tebbo', by Sam Mangwana, is playing. I glide, I float, I saunter, ducking clothes on hangers and DVD covers pinned on cords in the process. I turn left and directly face a mural of Haile Selassie with the letters HIM below it.

I sit down and join Ras Noah, who is chatting with fellow brethren:

'Most people get lost in the confusion that is Babylon. It is a Rasta's duty to strive to find their place in the scheme of things. The world is full of chameleons! Seek ye salvation in things that are not only permanent but also defy meaning. That is why I advise fellow Rastas to meditate for at least three times a week at the nearby Ndirande Mountain, the so-called Sleeping Man Mountain.'

An hour later, I am disembarking from a minibus at Ndirande market. A police officer stops me for a random search. 'You won't find a thing, man,' I tell him. 'I am changed man, born again, as they say.' I take the dirt road that leads to the mountain.

'Sleeping mon montin, fe I com fe ya fe lickle smoke n' a meditation, mon', I am chanting as I climb. *'Fe I com to fil A-might-y presence. See I' n'I give tanks fe the lessons, mon!'*

I am bracing myself against the midday Blantyre heat as I make my way up the mountain. From across the road, a boy of around 14 acknowledges me. 'Yes Rasta,' he proudly says. I wave at him. After 30 minutes, an SMS finds me. I check and see it is from Mary. I ignore it.

Minutes later, my phone rings.

'What?' I shout into the phone.

'I am pregnant. You are going to be a father.'

Silence.

'Are you there?'

Silence.

'Daddy, are you there?'

'Yes, mommy.'

'Please come home.'

'Fuck yes. Yes.'

I am looking at the mountain. *Finally I see, Ras Noah.*

I dial a number:

'Hello?'

'Ahmed, my favourite Muslim, *Asalaam alekum*!'

'What do you want?'

'I think the phrase you are looking for is *Alekum salaam*.'

'I am hanging up.'

'Wait. Meet me at the usual place, at five. Bring me some. Mary and I are celebrating. And no more goat's piss.'

The voice on the other end gets cut.

I am about to say 'fuck' when I catch myself: *Give thanks and praises to the Most High,* I say instead, as I descend the road.

Muti is a Malawian author and filmmaker, born in 1980. He is the author of the funny travelogue *Walks of life, the Other Side of Malawi*. He edits *Kupeza Chambo*, an online platform promoting Malawi's heritage. This story is dedicated to Makeda.

Blood Guilt

Melissa Tandiwe Myambo

GANDHI WAS SITTING CROSS-LEGGED in the rain, plump droplets dripping off the tip of his nose. Far from his homeland, he was still proudly clad in his traditional loin-cloth, his head bowed humbly against the cold wind. There was a rotting banana and two wilted daffodils by his little toe and scattered nearby were some tea-light candles and a few hand-written notes, sodden, their ink running like mascara down a woman's tear-stained face. Without his spectacles, he could not see the cherry tree dedicated to the victims of Hiroshima.

Is that where it all began? In London, or was it in Lusaka? The 'when' and the 'where' elude me but the 'it' will be decided by posterity (what happened with Beatrix will be less important than what the world remembers as happening). Should we be judged by our actions or our intentions? Was it not Abraham who said, 'In the honesty of my heart and with the innocence of my hands I have done this'? And can't I say the same? Have I not always acted as the consummate professional in upholding the Ideals of the Revolution?

Should I begin my petition like this?

You, Sir, are known to your enemies as the Anti-Christ but I believe it is still possible for you to repair your lacerated reputation and go down in the history books as one of mankind's most illustrious Messiahs. I write to you in the spirit of Christian fellowship as one age-mate to another because the chicanery of your detractors is undermining your legacy. You have left yourself open to specious attacks on, *inter alia*, your personal integrity, political achievements and your administration's policies because of your failure to defend my profession, which I remind you is as ancient as it is venerable. (Your equivocating, euphemistic, weak-kneed defence of it makes me furious!)

Perhaps one of the differences between us is that I am a practitioner and you are a theoretician; I am a keen student of the psyche and you are merely a statesman.

Should I delete the line: 'your equivocating, euphemistic, weak-kneed…'? I do not want to offend him.

'Mai Flo, please stop knocking on the door. I am locked in my office because I have pressing business to attend to and I told you, *mwanangu*, I cannot be disturbed under any circumstances. If the mourners need more beer, send Uncle Shadreck to the bottle store. The money is in the biscuit tin on top of the fridge.'

'No, please, the beer is enough. It's State House. They say it's urgent.'

I save the email in my draft folder even though I know we will not have a power cut because we're on the special grid. I open the door a crack and Mai Flo hands me the phone. I hear the shallow breathing and I already know it is that witless oaf, the Minister of the Interior. I can see his thin, wiry body quivering with nervous energy as he struggles with his usual indecision. 'The Beatrix video is going viral, sorry to bother you at this time of personal tragedy, we are very sorry on our part but His Excellency fears the Counter-Revolutionaries will use it to incite a Counter-Revolution and start a crisis of unthinkable proportions, must we turn off the internet?'

'Take a deep breath, *mwanangu*. You sound like you're drowning. Why don't you just block access to the sites getting the most traffic?'

'No, yes, no but it's also travelling on the Facebook, on the YouTV, the blogoworld, the twitters and the emails – yahoo, hotmail, gmail, rocketmail…'

'Understood. Stop talking. Let me think.' It is possible to shut down the country's web and cellphone service but can I rely on our VIP satellite access to send this email? I must send this email at all costs, before it is too late, too late by far.

'Give me 84 minutes and then shut down all telecommunications at exactly 14:00 hours. Understood? All telecommunication networks but, in the interim, I suggest you try to trace who uploaded the Beatrix video and which one of your undisciplined staff leaked it. This type of insubordination is becoming an everyday occurrence for you. And, Honourable Minister, considering you are 25 years younger than me, why not learn something about social media.' I didn't mention that I had received news of the video's release 36 minutes prior to his phone call (he always seems to be the last to know), forcing me to withdraw from the lounge where I was receiving condolences. Why release the video now, four months later? Who filmed it? The Counter-Revolutionary Forces are gathering strength if they have placed a man on the inside. I resume my petition.

Forgive the disjointed nature of this email but it is the nature of the contemporary age. I am typing these words with my left hand on my Samsung Galaxy Tab, which my son purchased for me in Beijing just last week. There is no time to dilly-dally so I must proceed without the usual polite introductions and trust that my formidable reputation has even reached to you because I admire you and sincerely believe it will strengthen both our positions if you should find yourself on the right side of history.

We all know the old adage that history is written by the victors but we're living in a new era (I am not sure when to date the beginning of this trend – from the Enlightenment, the French Revolution?) in which history is being written and sometimes rewritten, revised and reinvented by those who believe themselves to have been wronged, either yesterday or once-upon-a-time. People like us must tread more carefully than the angels. This line of work is more noble art than sound science. It goes without saying, of course, that it is easier to break the body than the mind.

That is why I turn to you. Your country is still powerful, although in economic and moral decline (so much gun violence!), yet somehow it still provides the ethical centre for the 'international community' (distinguished by the absence of such luminaries as Iran and North Korea). I also come from what is now a pariah nation that has descended into levels of banana republicdom despite my very best efforts (Please remember that always. I am the what? The consummate professional!) and although we are more friendly with China of late and less so with you and the international community (which, let's be frank, refers to you and your allies, the former colonial powers in the cold countries as well as Japan, ancient imperial power of the East and New Zealand and Australia, settler colonies with as shameful a history as your own country's), you are still, for the time being at least, at the tiller of world opinion.

And I assure you that, if you have perchance seen the Beatrix video, you must understand that there is no blood guilt on my part. It was never a personal or political vendetta against her or her grandmother. You may have heard rumours about me and His Excellency, the President of our Revolutionary Republic. However, this is nothing but a campaign of vicious vilification unleashed by Counter-Revolutionary Forces bent on my destruction.

I sit back in my black leather chair. Seven minutes gone already and I am yet to make my case. When did it begin? Was it those rainy afternoons in Tavistock Square, or was it the day I met her grandmother in the misty mountains of our mission school days, or, years later, when we met again in Lusaka during the long war against the Settler Colonialist Anti-Revolutionaries? Looking back at a life, it's hard to put my finger on the exact beginning (my life has turned into a series of parentheses and ellipses instead of full stops and exclamation points) but what I do know is that it has begun and it is not finished. I say again, I am not guilty but I am the one who must finish this business with Beatrix, otherwise... otherwise the Counter-Revolutionary Forces will continue to grow fat like a tick on a bull.

I have always been the white egret. He is the bull. He is the People's Revolutionary Leader and it is necessary to start thinking about the leader's legacy from the very beginning. One day, statues must be erected in his image, just like that one of Gandhi in Tavistock Square. Were those notes and flowers and candles brought by his devotees, hoping he would hear their prayers? Had death bestowed divinity upon him as it had done for Julius Caes–?

'Gogo. Gogo, please come.'

'Again, you're interrupting me, Mai Flo?!'

'No, Gogo. It's Nhamo. He is pulling his hair and thrashing his body on the flagstones by the swimming pool. We're afraid he might crack his head.'

I shout through the locked door: 'Nhamo *ndiani*?'

'*Ndimwana waSisi* Shupi.'

'Shupi's first-born son? Is he having a fit?'

'No, Gogo. He has been bewitched.'

I freeze. This email must wait. I pull my prosthetic back on to my stump and move through the house heading towards the swimming pool. The mourners awaiting the funeral are draped all over every room and spilling out of the large garden into the road outside, enjoying free beer and *sadza*, but many of them are genuinely tearful. The sunlight is sharp and slices into my eyeballs and I am temporarily blinded but then I see the old men have formed a circle at the edge of the pool. Their eyes are tight, their teeth are clenched. The scent of roasting meat warms the air and the mourners encamped outside the Durawall are laughing at some joke or other but Nhamo's mother is howling loudly, her eyeballs rolling back in their sockets. Now she is screaming hoarsely. She is becoming hysterical. I quickly slap her with my prosthetic hand and move on towards the pool. They part to let me enter the circle. The little boy is frothing at the mouth but it is not rabies or epilepsy.

He is saying, 'Her eyes are bleeding black tears, her eyes are bleeding black tears, her eyes are bleeding black tears.'

Mukoma James, my eldest brother, shakes his head and mumbles in English, 'The boy is hownted.'

'He is not haunted,' I say firmly, emphasizing the correct pronunciation.

Mukoma James shakes his head vigorously, 'First your son passes yesterday but one, just like that, no sickness, no nothing, and now this... our family is under attack. This small boy is–'

'It's not that, what you're thinking. It's not that. It has come as a shock to all of us that such a young man... my son... could die so abruptly just like that but, Mukoma James, we are still awaiting the results of the post-mortem, *handiti*. Don't go spreading rumours of witchcraft.'

They all think Beatrix is responsible for these recent misfortunes... this tragedy. My son is dead, my only son, but of course, it cannot have anything to do with Beatrix... However, does that mean that even the likes of Mukoma James have seen the video and want to hold me responsible?

Nhamo turns on to his stomach, bashing his forehead against the sun-warmed flagstones, howling loudly, 'Her eyes are bleeding black tears.' Mukoma James tries to grab hold of his flailing fists but the boy is too strong. Suddenly his back arches like a cat and he somehow flips himself up and breaks through the men encircling him and flings himself into the greenish water of the pool (chemicals are in short supply because of the sanctions). Hundreds of mourners are flooding towards the pool now, screaming and beating their breasts, adding to the general commotion. They're too afraid of water to jump in because they cannot swim.

I turn to one of the younger men – whose child is he? – and instruct him to jump in: 'Push his head under water and make sure he cannot come up for air. I will time you and in exactly three minutes – no, he is too small, hold him under for exactly two minutes 20 seconds and when I give the signal, let him come up for just 12 seconds, and push him down again. We will do this until he is calmed. Shupi, stop sobbing! Bring me my bible. I will read from Romans 6.'

Shupi arrives back with my bible and hands me the cordless phone. The witless oaf is huffing down the line again: 'It is Musa! His wife's sister's uncle by marriage is the cousin of the best friend of Beatrix and we have identified him as the individual responsible for uploading the video, he didn't even try and hide it, he put it on his blog, must we pick him up?'

'Pick him up.'

'Should we bring him to Bamboo Cottage?'

'Yes, but take him through the back way because of the funeral. Make sure he has some tea and biscuits. But no alcoholic drinks. Put his wife under temporary house arrest and keep the best friend under surveillance.' I catch sight of Mukoma James' anxious expression, the wrinkles lighter than the rest of his face – the sun does not dip into those deep crevices. He did not go to mission school like me because it was established after his time and now he is a superstitious peasant and I am an educated professional. I don't believe in the things making him so dry-tongued anxious... 'Then contact the coroner and find out when I can expect the post-mortem report on my son.'

Nhamo's head comes up and he gasps for air, his eyes still rolling back in his head. I nod and the young man pushes him back under. Training as a nurse in Lusaka was mostly a cover whilst I was trained by the Revolutionary Forces in covert operations and guerrilla fighting but it formed the foundation of my subsequent work nevertheless. I was the only female who had attained the level of Commander when they sent me the parcel bomb. Fortunately, it detonated too soon and, instead of removing both hands up to the elbow, it only succeeded in slicing off my right hand at the wrist. I learnt that the most unbearable pain is bearable. It is only the mind that thinks it will break but the body will always opt for survival. At any cost. In less than 10 minutes, Nhamo is quiet, his mind quelled by the body's grasping at its most basic need: oxygen. I hurry back to my desk.

So please hear me out, old friend. May I call you that? We were both born in 1941 and although you have grown up in your country and I in mine, we have both fought wars and eaten our share, as we say. You have served your president as loyally as I serve mine. You're a staunch Christian like myself and an honourable family man. (You stood by your daughter even though your enemies attempted to turn her into your Achilles' heel – their behaviour was despicable although how she lives as a gay is a sin against God!)

My friend, you have to consider that sometimes it is *why* you do things rather than what you do that should be judged. Future generations will continue man's drive forward and focus on our legacy through a rearview mirror that will only have a partial view. We must frame that view now because it is imperative that they judge the 'why'– not the 'what'– and it is precisely here that you have gone awry, needlessly focusing on the 'how' (the details, intensity levels, duration) and not on the nobility of your intentions.

You too are an egret and your failure to properly remove these ticks plaguing your President is spoiling his legacy. Don't you see? It is because you are, if truth be told, in two minds about my profession (When you put your mind to it, you're formidable. I deeply admired your ability to persuade your country to wage an illegal war against a nation which had never attacked you. The way you hold tight to your nuclear bombs but make it unthinkable for other countries to acquire them – again Iran and North Korea take the highest honours – is another ingenious PR coup on your part!). For both our sakes, you should strive to explain that my work is not animated by malice nor sadism. It is about identifying the individual whose actions can be positively influenced to make the world a safer and more stable place.

There is another knock on the door. The meaning of 'do not disturb' seems to elude my entire extended family. It is Mukoma James, leading a shabby-looking man clad in overalls. 'This man knows a reliable *n'anga* who can diagnose the problem.'

'What problem?'

Mukoma James kneads his faded blue hat in his rough, calloused hands. He is a child of the soil, one of the benefactors of His Excellency's successful programme to indigenize the economy, returning the agricultural land to its rightful owners as per the eternally noble Ideals of the Revolution. He is a man whose hands talk more than his mouth. His words are slow and carefully chosen to sanitize them of any reference to the occult: 'We have a problem in this family.'

'What problem?'

'First, your son. How did he drown sitting in a parked car? Where did the water come from? What was that black slime covering him from head to toe? They say the doors were locked. This is not the work of a man. Now this child, Nhamo. Possessed. We cannot find the cause and the solution without help from a *n'anga*.'

I remain silent. Will he dare to speak her name?

His Adam's apple zips up and down as he gulps for air but his words seem to slow even more. Precious seconds are wasting away. 'And... people... are... saying... that... it... is... the... vengeance... of... Beatrix... She... is... a... blood... avenger...'

Silence is always the power play of the stronger party.

'...Blood... begets... blood, my sister... The... *n'anga*... can... advise...us...on... how... to... cleanse... All... our... blood... is... in... danger.'

The shabbily clad man does not even deserve a moment's notice but Mukoma James is nine years older than me. Therefore I must treat him with respect and help to dispel his primitive superstitions based on traditions of blood vengeance that I barely comprehend, a civilized lady educated by Scottish missionaries as I am, every morning beginning with the Lord's prayer. Rational facts, a dose of Christian teaching? What will quell this fear that has taken ahold of not only Mukoma James but the mourners and the nation as well? A fear that is rippling through the land, transforming whispers into shouts.

'Leviticus 19:26: "You must eat nothing along with blood. You must not look for omens, and you must not practise magic." Mukoma James, the Coroner's report has not come. The initial cause of death was thought to be drowning. The black slime I don't know but I do know that everything must have a scientific explanation. It could be the what? The Counter-Revolutionary Forces. They could be the ones responsible... but let's await hard evidence.'

The shabbily clad man suddenly speaks up, his voice cracking in terror. 'Who can save you but a *n'anga*, Gogo? They say that Beatrix is a blood avenger and she will finish all of you unless you–'

'Leviticus 19:31: "Do not turn yourselves to the spirit mediums, and do not consult professional foretellers of events, so as to become unclean by them. I am Jehovah your God."' I turn to Mukoma James and look directly at him, 'I am not a woman of blood. Blood vengeance cannot be exacted where there is no blood guilt.'

Mai Flo pushes the door open and Staff Sergeant Moyo enters, followed by two of his bodyguards. He salutes me and says 'Estimated time of arrival, seven minutes.'

'Thank you, *mwanangu*. Mai Flo, please make sure the sergeant gets some food. Mukoma James, I hope I have allayed your fears.'

The world has become more disorderly because of the breakdown of tradition. My work prevents the mass killings of the Holocaust or the Rwandan genocide. Positively re-educating one significant individual can save the lives of thousands, if not millions. You must ascertain the man's mettle before you've even begun. Those who are wedded to pure principle – not passion or the potential for prosperity or power – are the most intransigent because principle does not dissolve in boiling water. Hot irons barely singe it. Fortunately, individuals of that nature are the exception that proves the rule. The patient should never fear that death will be the outcome. Death is a relief. That is counter-productive.

I make my way through the mourners, the men clustered under the jacaranda trees drinking beer and the women in the pots, cooking, cooking, cooking. Children are pelting each other with unripe guavas and the yellow weaver birds are flitting in and out of their nests in the bamboo trees. My son is dead but the world keeps on living, breathing, dancing, singing. How is that possible? Which of us can imagine the world without our unique presence? His Excellency certainly cannot, even though he is senior to Mukoma James. He cannot imagine the Revolution will survive without him. Yet the human body must perish. It is the simple truth of all existence: the inevitable brutality of mortality... sooner or later... This is a truth which must be accepted. All that can remain behind is one's children and one's legacy. My son is dead. Now, there is only little Beverly, *muzukuru wangu*, daughter of my son. She will have to come and live with me now (her mother can go back to her own family). I will raise her up, instil in her the Ideals of the Revolution which have guided me every step of the way along with God's word.

Behind the thicket of bamboo is another Durawall, this one taller and thicker, topped with more barbed wire and electric rods. I steady the padlock with my prosthetic and unlock it with my left hand. Once through the small gate, I go straight into the little cottage. Through the window, I can see the official white Land Rover stamped with the insignia of our Revolutionary Republic. I walk into the kitchen, which overlooks a small vegetable garden. The patient is sitting there at the kitchen table, his elbows resting on the white crocheted doilies covering the table.

'Staff Sergeant Moyo, please remove those handcuffs.' The patient instinctively flexes his fingers, trying to regain circulation. He has tufty sun-browned hair, small bright eyes and a stubby nose which emphasizes the pointed chin, but physiognomy is no indicator of the seams of the mind, seams that can yield the golden ore of information, seams that can explode if the dynamite is not placed just so. In the worst-case scenario, the mind, that mine of information of infinite value, can collapse in on itself. What is this man made of?

'Moyo, make our guest some tea.' (Moyo directs one of his bodyguards to boil water.)

I sit down on the opposite side of the table. 'Ndiwe Musa, here?' He stares back at me, belligerently refusing to answer, his eyes bulging. I see he is dressed casually in a T-shirt bearing the logo of Barclays Bank and the long khaki shorts favoured by the younger generation. He must be around 35 years old, my son's age, but he is much smaller in build. I realize I have been remiss and do not even know his basic particulars like DOB. But there is no time for preliminaries today.

The capillaries in his eyes are beginning to engorge with blood, to redden. The pulse in the side of his delicate neck vibrates like that of a gecko. 'Well, I know who you are, shall we begin?' He stares me down, refusing to speak. We sit for some time. I listen to the laughing doves outside.

Suddenly he breaks his silence as if he has made a decision and he begins to recite a speech which had clearly been prepared prior to this meeting, 'And I know who you are. Gogo, grandmother of the revolution; mother of the illegitimate son of the dictator who calls himself our president; an elder who commands our contempt rather than our respect; the woman who commits atrocities in the name of the so-called revolution and calls it "treating her patients"; some even say you control the weather. That I don't agree with but most certainly you control the president and we hold you directly responsible for the utter disrespect for human rights, the subversion of democratic freedoms of the press and association and the repugnant rejection of morality and basic human decency that characterize over three decades of state mismanagement.'

When you're being vilified, it is important to look straight into the eyes of the one doing the vilifying. Will his eyes drop in shame like a daffodil wilting in the rain? Or will he draw himself up and spread his hood like a king cobra about to strike? Insult upon insult fall from his lips, I remain silent, impassive, waiting for his energy to dissipate. Finally, I see beads of perspiration appear on his forehead. Just as dew on grass signals the onset of dawn, this is my sign: 'Who is we?'

'Come again?'

'You said "we hold you directly responsible".'

His eyes flicker: 'I am referring to "we the people". We the people of this great nation who want our land but want our freedom too. You have betrayed the revolutionary ideals our parents fought for. You use land reform to camouflage your insatiable will to power! The land is soaked in blood, the blood of the people.'

I indicate to Staff Sergeant Moyo to put the tea down in front of the man. He shakes his head vehemently.

'It is lunchtime, have you eaten?'

'My stomach is queasy when I think of what you have done!' He gathers up saliva on his tongue and puckers his mouth, preparing to spit. I nod at Moyo, who grabs him in a chokehold just in time. The man begins to cough on his own spittle and I signal for Moyo to relax his grip. The man's coughing fit eventually subsides and when I hand him a glass of water he drinks it down gratefully. Janus-faced water, giver of life and death.

'Time is short, *mwanangu*, shall we proceed to–'

'Don't call me that! I am not your child!'

'Shall we proceed to the point of our meeting. Who gave you the video?'

'I refuse to answer any questions based on the obvious fact that these entire proceedings are not just extra-legal but illegal and thoroughly illegitimate. Am I under arrest? If so, which judge has ordered the warrant of arrest? Where are the police? Why are we not at the police station?'

I remove my prosthetic and massage my stump. It always remembers my missing hand like my womb from now on will always remember my missing child: '*Mwanangu*, time is not on my side tod–'

'Is this where you brought Beatrix? Beatrix, the true hero of the true people's revolution, not yours which has been corroded from the inside by the likes of you. You… you say she's a puppet and a stooge of the Settler Colonialist Anti-Revolutionaries even when you know that Beatrix stands for land and freedom. Is this where it all happened? Well, that video is being downloaded as we speak, thousands, hundreds of thousands of times. The people will be outraged, they will revolt against your tyrannic–'

'Don't overestimate the people, *mwanangu*. Never over-estimate the people.'

'Now you insult the people! When they see the video do you think they will react with the type of cynicism that characterizes your illegitimate regi–'

I see this will not be quick or easy. It could take days but I barely have 10 minutes and now this man is ranting at me, speaking half-truths, semi-facts, the apocryphal web woven around me from the very beginning by my enemies. Sadly, while we were fighting the Settler Colonialist Anti-Revolutionaries, there emerged within our own ranks those who persisted in challenging His Excellency's supremacy. Even after the Anti-Revolutionaries were defeated, the Counter-Revolutionaries remained, plaguing us like Job's boils. Why would a child bite the hand of the father? 'As I said, Musa, time is not on my side today but what you see in that video is not the whole truth.'

'I know from Beatrix's own mouth about your pathological

vendetta against her and her grandmother before her. How you doctored the facts – you are the master manipulator, merciless, mercenary, crafty, cunning. What you did was typical of your usual deceit and–'

So was that the beginning then? When I encountered her in Lusaka in 1967 at one of those *braiis* for comrades-in-exile, I remembered her well from our schooldays. Her complexion was bright as a polished penny, just like when I had first set eyes on her when we were both entering Standard Six. Her hair was fashionably coiffed in the beehive style of the era and she wore a sleeveless mini-dress that was hitched up in front because of her belly, which was growing hard and round like a pumpkin. The first thing she did was look me up and down and say: '"The Ruler"? You haven't changed at all.' She smacked her palm into mine and burst into laughter, revealing her small teeth.

A river of vituperation still cascades from his lips. The patient is becoming over-excited. 'Stop. Don't talk about things that happened before you were even planted in your mother's womb.'

'Do you deny that you fabricated "evidence" that resulted in the detention and–'

I do deny it. Or rather it was not what it seemed, just as she was never what she made others believe of her; she was never a true Christian. Her comely figure was the standard by which all the boys in the school came to judge 'womanliness' and hence they called her 'Lady Love'. By contrast, they nicknamed me 'The Ruler' because I was long and thin and straight with no waist. Her name was Rudo, is Rudo, she lives on a farm near Norton. I know this because it is my job to know the whereabouts of anyone who may pose a threat to the regime. There is no vendetta, personal or political. Yes, in Lusaka that first afternoon, she acted so superior, as if she had finally won just because she was pregnant with twins. There is always a subtle competition between females surrounding their capacity for reproduction and my enemies had spread it about that I was barren. That was given as the excuse for why His Excellency had not married me when the Settler Colonialist Anti-Revolutionary Forces kidnapped and killed his first wife. I could see as her eyes raked up and down my narrow frame that all of this misinformation was churning over in her brain but, when she was arrested by the Anti-Revolutionaries and jailed for eight years for seditious activities based on evidence provided by an anonymous source, why did they blame me? What concern was it of mine? Yes, my beak was sharp, searching out those within our ranks who displayed any signs of being counter-revolutionary, but that is because traitors cannot be tolerated. I am the egret who must remove the ticks but this has never been personal (her granddaughter, Beatrix, was in no way made to pay for the sins of her grandmother. I am, above all, a professional).

After the parcel bomb, the revolutionary forces sent me to London for treatment (despite its location in the homeland of the Settler Colonialist Anti-Revolutionaries who up until today continue to speak with a forked tongue). Since I was no longer fit for active combat duty, I stayed on to pursue a higher degree in psychiatric nursing, trying to heal my own mind, reconcile it with the lost hand. And learn more – about people, about politics, about history – so that we could learn from the past in building the bright postcolonial future. Even though the anti-colonial war was still raging interminably like a storm of lightning strikes never followed by a determining thunderclap, we began to make plans for the nation-building which would have to begin in the immediate aftermath, a nation that would be guided by the Ideals of the Revolution.

His Excellency was still in prison and I used to sit on the bench facing Gandhi on those rainy spring days in the 1970s and write letters to him, trying to lift his spirits. The letters were censored, of course, but we still managed a robust correspondence throughout those long years and, when the war finally reached its zenith, the Anti-Revolutionaries suddenly decided they wanted to settle and he was abruptly released from prison and flown to London for peace talks. I met him at Heathrow airport and I took him to see Gandhi's statue, symbol of the excellent work of the egrets.

Deification he deserved but he could just as easily have been demonized – Mahatma Gandhi lived in apartheid South Africa for over two decades from 1893 to 1914 and yet he viewed black people as one step above animals, as inferior and savage as the 'untouchables' in his native land. There were some scandals involving young girls too but the history-makers, the honers of legacy, have picked his record clean because even a bull can die of tick fever. Maybe, in the 21st century, it's more about marketing and branding. Are there just PR whizzes and spin doctors and creators of hype?

No, I don't think so. It begins with the egret, always the egret comes first.

Is that where it all began? I fear that if we can't recognize the beginning, how will we know when the beginning of the end is upon us? I need to get back to my desk.

The patient is still talking, scattering clues – clearly, he has been planning for this confrontation – and I am beginning to get a sense of the man and how deep I will have to plunge to find what I am looking for. I nod towards the pantry door and Moyo grabs the man's T-shirt. He yanks him up out of his chair and opens the door but inside is a small stone-walled room, completely empty except for a metal bucket in the corner. Inside it, the water gleams at the sudden light. Moyo shoves the man inside and orders him to take off all his clothes to prepare for treatment and locks the door from the outside.

'I'll be back in an hour.'

May I call you Dick? Dick, I must hasten to send this but please consider the gravity of the matter. Your ill-founded ambivalence towards our profession corrupts your argument to the point where it smacks of sophistry and hypocrisy. But your legacy is ineradicably intertwined with mine. Please! You must stand tall and proud like myself. Stiffen your spine before it's too late, too late by far.

The Chinese and the Russians have proved themselves miserable at PR. I wouldn't even bother with the Indians (it is a very disorganized country; I speak from personal experience, having been there thrice on official missions). I don't know anything about the Brazilians but our neighbour, South Africa, with its, *inter alia*, non-racialism, rainbow nation and truth and reconciliation are part of the reason we're in this mess to begin with. (You shouldn't think Spanish Inquisition or Guantánamo Bay. These are amateurs. You shouldn't think crucifixion or roasting alive. Not at all. The Romans were the crudest, Stalin's henchmen were little more than thugs. These are not my methods. I have developed and refined certain techniques.)

But on the other hand, your attempt at ameliorating PR by renaming a tried and true technique 'enhanced interrogation' is a euphemism that is ineffective. Your country's history is littered with them.

(I digress but what is a reservation, after all? When will your country appease the angered ancestors of the children of the soil whom you have quarantined into the small tracts of land reserved for them after the wholesale theft of the country? The indigenous native is squeezed into a reservation, no different from the Bantustan of apartheid South Africa, whilst the descendant of the original thieves frolics unfettered. Can you not see the urgent necessity of our Revolution???)

I have been thoroughly straightforward with you and hope you can recognize my sincerity, even if some of my words have been harsh. Legacy is all that will remain of either of us and all legacies must be buffed and polished. I trust that you will recognize the purity of my ideals and that is what should remain, bright as a beacon on a dark and stormy night.

I press the send button and watch my screen change. It has been sent. Now, whatever happens, I have begun to prepare for the beginning of the end. I must see to the patient but I have not heard from the Coroner's office. Five minutes remain before all telecommunications will cease. 'Hello, this is Gogo. I am still waiting.' The email comes three minutes later and consists of eight words:

Inconclusive results. Further tests required. Foul play suspected.

My son is dead. My only son. Have the Counter-Revolutionary Forces become so bold they would dare to stage this gruesome murder to frighten the population into believing these silly superstitions about blood guilt? Is this the end? The end of it all?

Yet the patient is waiting. It is essential to remain calm in this continual series of crises. I unlock my office door but, before I can step out, my son's wife lunges at me, scratching at my eyes. 'Mai Beverly, what are you doing?' I move quickly back behind the door's threshold and observe that behind her stand Mai Flo, Sisi Shupi, Mukoma James, fear making their accusing eyes luminous. Mai Beverly suddenly stops, turns and points: 'Look! Do you see what you have done? What you have brought upon us?'

Crumpled in the middle of the floor is little Beverly, vomiting copiously, her small body wracked by spasms, the black viscous liquid veritably pouring from her mouth. Mai Beverly removes her black *duku* from her head and flaps it at me as if sending her screaming words on the wings of black crows: 'It's your fault! This is your fault, you terrible witch. This is Beatrix's revenge. We have seen it, we have seen with our own eyes. Everyone has seen!' The accusing eyes form a semi-circle outside my office door and suddenly someone produces a laptop and there it is, Beatrix lying on the stone floor of the pantry, naked, a close-up of her face, mascara running in rivulets down her cheeks. Don't they see that she is unscathed? It is only tears, the floor is wet with tears. There is no blood. The camera pulls back. There I am, I am leaving. I nod to Staff Sergeant Moyo. I leave. What happens next... I am not guilty... Sergeant Moyo and his boys, they're so undisciplined. The witless oaf does not keep a tight hold on his underlings, I have said it many times. It's not just over-zealousness, it borders on sadism. There is so much insubordination in the ranks. What happens now I would never have condoned. Thuggery, pure and simple. Vengeance, vendetta.

These are not my methods.

Mukoma James is pleading with me, his hands wringing his hat to death, his words suddenly pouring from his mouth as fast as the black slime pouring out of little Beverly's mouth: 'My sister, you have to confess! Otherwise, none of us will ever be free. You have to take responsibility, otherwise Beatrix's spirit will not rest, our family is all at risk. She is attacking our children.'

'I am not guilty. Don't you see that I left? Why would I want Beatrix dead? So that her legacy can live on eternally as martyr of the Counter-Revolutionary Forces?' I try to reason with them, make them see sense. 'People say that I hated Rudo, gogo waBeatrix, but it's not true. This has never been about vengeance.'

Mai Beverly starts wailing, pulling out her hair. Mai Flo holds her around the waist. Sisi Shupi is trembling. As usual, I am surrounded by incompetence. 'Can someone please attend to Beverly. Call a doctor.'

The young man from the pool, the one who helped me quell Nhamo – whose child is he? – points to his cellphone, 'No network.'

'There must be a medical doctor amongst the mourners.' I move towards Beverly and pull her up and perform the Heimlich manoeuvre on her, expelling the contents of her stomach. She is only six. With such a small ribcage, one must be careful not to break the ribs. At first the vomiting doesn't stop but eventually after nine, fourteen, sixteen times, it begins to subside.

Her mother has recovered now, replaced the *duku* atop her head, her hands folded in her lap. I hand her the child.

I stand. I know neither where it began nor where it will end but I am, above all, the consummate professional. I head back to the cottage.

Melissa Tandiwe Myambo is the author of *Jacaranda Journals* (www.jacarandajournals.com), a collection of short stories set in Zimbabwe, and {*Parenthesis*} (www.cuppedhands.net/ melissatandiwemyambo), an electronic chapbook for charity containing stories about people on the move including 'La Salle de Départ', her 2012 Caine Prize-shortlisted story.

Chief Mourner

Hellen Nyana

There is a lot to be said about finding out that your boyfriend, Jude has died via Facebook. Or maybe there really isn't much to say because that update you have been tagged in leaves you stuck in your seat, your head reeling and your heart dropping way beneath your feet so that you are certain you are dead. Because how could it be? He was just with you three hours ago. You held onto him as you gave him your last hug and jokingly told him he really didn't have to go. 'You can be late for work tomorrow. No one will notice,' you said as he got onto the bus. He told you everyone would notice because he is always the first one in office and he squeezed your hand because he has grown accustomed to the hesitant goodbyes that always mark the end of his weekends with you at your upcountry home. The squeeze tells you that he also does not want to go but he must.

How could it be? That three hours since your last 'I miss you already' text from him, there are 20 people tagging you in gushing comments about how sorry they are and how he is gone too soon?

There is a lot to be said and yet you sit still, willing your mind to stop messing with you. You sit still, remembering his silly imitation of Usher's moves on the dance floor last night and remembering his miserable attempt at an omelette when he made you breakfast just this morning. You tell yourself that they have the wrong person and the wrong name.

'There are no words to tell you @Solome at this time.

Jude will be missed RIP,' reads one update from a Chris ILikeTheBad Gonza you do not even know. The Judas, Jude's Facebook name, is rarely updated but you decide to check it just to see if he has been included in the stupid prank. It is awash with 'we'll miss you's, 'how can it be's and 'we are gutted's. You scroll down the page to see who could have started all this.

'Man, lyf widout you won't b d same,' writes another. These must be the idiots who, even after Facebook has done them a favour and reminded them of your birthday, simply say HBD as if spelling it out correctly is such a bother. The same idiots who act like they have known you all their lives just because you have given them a glimpse of your life on social media. The same idiots who get insulted when you don't invite them to an event in your life and harass you with, 'I thought we were friends' messages. The same idiots who are always so excited by the notion of citizen journalism that they rush to be the first to break news like international media channels.

You feel anger rising within your chest, smouldering like a heartburn and threatening to be spewed out like sea sickness, and you tell yourself not to get bothered because you would have known if what they are saying had actually happened. You call Jude's number but it cannot be reached and you tell yourself they must be in Mabira Forest where there is poor phone reception. Besides, people just don't die like that. Not young people anyway. And you have made promises to each other. You have a future planned out and he knows how you hate it when people make promises and do not fulfil them. Just last night at the disco he whispered in your ear: 'I should wife you soon, babe. Look at the way all these men are looking at you like I am not even here.' You playfully slapped him because he knows you are not ready for marriage, as you believe both of you still have individual dreams to achieve before you can settle down.

You keep scrolling down his wall till you find the first message from Ray, his housemate:'Just received news of the death of my housemate Jude in an accident at Namawojjolo. Shocked! Shocked! Shocked! Details l8r.' You want to laugh out loud at the absurdity of his knowing this and your not knowing but, before you do, your phone starts ringing and it is Jude's cousin. He is crying uncontrollably on the other end of the line and then everything in your head gets mashed up.

A few hours later, your sister is holding your hand and calling your name gently. Her husband is standing beside her. They are both looking at you like you are a puppy caught in a thunderstorm being coerced out of hiding. You ask what time it is and they say it's midnight and that they came as soon as they heard. They tried to call you several times in vain and even when you opened your door to them, you continued to stare at them as if they were not there.

'It's for real then, isn't it?' you ask your sister.

'I'm so sorry,' she says, and tries to embrace you. You hold her at arm's length and ask her to tell you everything.

Jude's bus collided with a fuel truck in Mabira. No one survived. A stranger called Ray and told him: 'The owner of this phone is dead.' A confused Ray called the man back just to be sure and, 30 minutes later, news on the radio confirmed the accident. Your sister had received a call from Ray. Unknown to everyone, your phone battery had died at the time and they went on to send their condolences the only way they knew how.

You give your sister a long empty stare, tears stream down your face and you tell her you want to go home. She says your bag is already packed and that she will call your boss the next day.

You try to numb your brain by telling yourself that whatever you think is happening around you is not happening but the potholes you keep hitting won't let you sustain that thought. The Mbale-Kampala highway is a road you have been travelling for the past three years and, to get your mind off things, you challenge your brain to guess which towns you are in as you drive through. You use the same trick to try to ignore the incessant craving to lick clay that has been nagging you all day. As you approach Mabira Forest, your stomach turns and you hold your sister's hand. The smell of fuel hangs in the air and you fight the wave of nausea that hits you. Traffic has been slowed down and the police cars and a mob of people working through the carnage are blurred by your tears. You reach for the door lock but your sister sees you just in time before you throw yourself out of the moving car.

'I killed him. I killed him. I killed him,' you cry hysterically. 'If he hadn't come to see me... If I had convinced him to stay longer... If he had taken another bus... I killed him.' You are now bawling, hitting your head on the back of the seat before you. By the time you get to Kampala, your cries have been reduced to little whimpers and you feel drained.

In the morning, before you go to Jude's home where people are gathered for the vigil, your sister asks you to put on a long dress. 'You are meeting the in-laws. You have to be decent,' she says.

'No one at his home really knows me,' you tell her. 'Do I introduce myself to his family when I get there?' you ask her. She doesn't hear you, as she is more intent on the sartorial presentation and her long, black dress is found the most suitable – sombre and respectful. She slicks back your hair in a little ponytail. You slip on your brown knock-off Ray Bans, your eyes heavy, swollen and dry.

When your sister does not take the Naalya turn off the Northern Bypass, you ask her whether she knows where she is going. 'His parents' house is somewhere in Kyambogo,' you tell her.

'Ray gave me directions to a house in Kirinya. That is where everybody is gathered,' she explains slowly and patiently, as to someone who may have lost their mind.

The house, four or three bedrooms, looks like it has been recently completed, the paint that trendy orange-brown that all new Kampala houses have now. In the compound are the dying embers of the ceremonial funeral fire. Around it are men in oversized coats clutching onto their mugs of porridge. Through your shades you can see people huddled in groups according to how they knew Jude.

You can recognize Richard and JT, the guys from his workplace who took him out for drinks when he was promoted to head of section. That night, JT had teased Jude about his ability to land a hot babe like you. 'You must really like him a lot if you fell for his weak jazz,' he had teased, Jude laughing uncomfortably. You wonder if Simon, the one whom he referred to as 'my ass of a boss', was there somewhere.

You see his childhood friend Stano, the one he told you he had played *dul* with and snubbed girls with when they hit puberty. He is talking to Jude's cousin; the one you met once at a random house party in Naalya long before you ever even defined what it was that you two had together; the same one who called to break the news to you. And there is Johnnie with another group of friends they were with in school. Johnnie often refers to you as 'our wife' because, according to him, there is no way Jude could land a better chick than you.

They all look up when you enter the compound, their pity glaring and ugly like an open wound. Your sweaty palm tightens around your sister's. You hear people wailing inside the house and you tell her you do not want to go in there. She says it is better for you to be in the house when they bring him. You take note of how she has carefully not referred to him as a body and you hang onto the hope that this may be a bad dream after all.

'*Nga kitalo nnyo ba ssebo*,' you hear her condole with the men in the house.

'*Kitalo nnyo. Nyiike*,' they respond in chorus, shaking their heads with sadness and disbelief.

There is hardly any space for you to sit in the sitting room but the older women gathered there make room for you. Most of the women are dressed in *gomesis*, their hair is wrapped in scarves and turbans, and they are so overcome with grief that they keep sneezing into hankies attached to their bras and sashes. Their red eyes tell you they have been at this for a while. Scattered at their feet are vernacular hymn books from which they must have sung all of last night.

Suddenly, as if the news is just breaking to her, a woman, maybe a relative, breaks down and wails about how Jude has 'died too much'.

'Juudi banange ofudde nnyo! Otulesse n'ani?' she asks, raising her hands in the air. You wonder whether you are expected to scream out loud like this – after all, you are asking yourself the same questions this woman is asking. Whom has he left you with? How can he leave you like this? And why so soon?

In the corner you catch a glimpse of the girl whose picture you once saw in his wallet, his sister. She is offering some water to their mother, seen in a photo on his phone, asking her to please take something. You have never met his mother because the one time he asked, you reasoned it was too soon, 'What if we don't work out? I would have to break up with your family as well.' When you said that, Jude said he was insulted that you believed your relationship had such a short life span. He said you made him happy enough for him to tell his mother, his only living parent, about you but you said it would put too much pressure on you to be the perfect girlfriend. His reassurances that you were indeed the perfect girlfriend fell on deaf ears. You would meet his mother when you were ready, you promised and he never brought it up again.

She must have felt your eyes on her because she looks up at you, her eyes swollen, red and pained. You drop your stare, ashamed that you have turned into the people outside who stared at you with pity. You wonder whether Jude could have told her about you and whether she knows that Jude had been on his way from seeing you and whether she blames you for his death.

But if his own mother is crying softly in the corner, what is the proper way for you to mourn? You wonder. Had you been his wife, you would probably have rolled on the ground and wailed that this was the end of your life with your husband gone and no one would have felt it was inappropriate. You would have broken down every time you looked at your children because they would most likely have been carbon copies of him and you wouldn't have been able to stand the painful reminder. People would have held you and beseeched you to be strong. '*Munange gguma. Beera mu gguma,*' they would have tearfully entreated you. But here you are, a girlfriend only known to a few of his friends, not even his Facebook official – what is the right way for you to mourn?

One of the older women next to you turns and asks whether 'she' has woken up. You tell her you do not know because you have no idea what she is talking about or whom she is referring to. She turns to the other women and they just shake their heads, sigh heavily and cast down their sorrow-laden eyes.

A few minutes later, all eyes in the sitting room turn towards the corridor. You can hear the sniffles of a woman approaching from the side of the house where the bedrooms should be situated. When she comes into view she is crying laboriously like she has been crying for days but cannot stop even if she wanted to. Two women support her on each side and help her move towards the corner where Jude's mother is seated. She is wearing a green and brown *gomesi*, her hair is wrapped in a polka-dot scarf and a huge cloth, the sign of a chief mourner, is tied around her waist. Jude's mother has a similar cloth around her waist as it is believed that her stomach, having carried her now-dead son for nine months, must be in some sort of turmoil from the loss.

She lets herself down with a thud and Jude's mother starts to cry again. A little girl comes in after the woman, tugs at her *gomesi*, and, failing to get the attention of the crying woman, sits down at her feet. She has her back to you but, from her height, she could not be more than four years old. This reminds you of the time, perhaps a month ago, when you told Jude that your relationship was now a three-year-old, ready to go to a prestigious kindergarten in the playgroup class. He laughed at your reference and said it seemed like just yesterday when he fell for the girl that was teetering in her heels.

You met him at your friend Claire's graduation party. You had been on the streets looking for a job for a little under a year and you were starting to be bothered by never having your own money and having to watch TV all day. This invitation to your friend's party was one of the best things to happen to you because you would meet most of your other friends there and it was the one time you could actually go out without your parents asking too many questions. Most importantly, all you had to worry about was transport to the party as the food and drink would be taken care of.

You asked the *boda boda* man to drop you a bit away from where the party was so you could use his side mirror to check your lipstick and wipe off that layer of dust that clung onto your face from the ride. You fidgeted as you took off the shawl you used to cover your off-shoulder dress, a bit too revealing for 3pm on a Saturday. You tried to remove the dust that had collected on your black patent pumps but you gave up on it. The heat and the fussing were making you sweaty and more nervous about making your entrance. As you teetered to the gate, you heard a hoot from a car that you had not heard approach and stepped aside and mouthed a sorry to the driver. You met him again at the gate as he came in after parking his car and he said hello. Later, when you found your group of friends, they could not stop asking you about the mystery man you entered with and you desperately tried to convince them that you did not know him. Claire later exonerated you with the revelation that he was actually one of her elder brother's friends and there was no way you could have known him.

The driver, who later introduced himself as Jude, offered to give your lot a lift from the party, your teetering to the gate obviously ingrained in his memory.

As he dropped you off, he heard you curse under your breath. 'My *siso* just texted. Our *zeeyis* are home and they asked for me,' you explained when he asked what was up. You profusely thanked him for the ride as you took off your shoes and tiptoed barefoot into your gate. He drove off, the giggles of tipsy girls in the back of his car in his wake.

It was another two or three months before you ran into him again. This time at Mateos, where your girlfriends, most of them already working, were buying you farewell drinks. You had finally landed a job with a bank but they were unfortunately posting you at their upcountry branch in Mbale. While you were happy finally not to have to depend on your parents, you mourned the loss of your social life and whined about how you were ever going to manage to live so far from home. Your friends, having grown tired of your missing out on hanging out with them because you never had money, were relieved, 'We'll hang out whenever you are in Kampala and we'll definitely come visit every so often,' they offered. 'Yay road trip!' screamed Fifi, her Long Island Iced Tea making her shriek even louder.

By your third Sex on The Beach, you were already offering everyone in sight a hug and Jude caught an overly tight one when he came by your table to say hi to Claire and you girls. He congratulated you on your new job and you gave him an earful about the death of a social life that had never even begun. He said it would be good for you to leave the noisy big town and you told him your concerns about having nowhere to go to entertain yourself. He said you were a big girl now and it would help you save and you moaned about how you would miss the Ban Café vanilla milk shakes. And then he asked for your number: 'In case I ever happen to be that side of the country.' He was a surveyor with one of the firms in town and the chances of being that side were actually not that slim.

Your move upcountry cost you some of your friends. Keeping in touch became a bit costly and, the few times you were in town, they always had something to do. It made your other friendships stronger though, Jude being one of them. With each phone call, chat and email, he became less of the dude you ran into occasionally and his presence moved into your life, made itself at home and made you want to pay attention to it and ever so gladly.

You tried to spend as much time together as you could spare, spending more weekends at your home upcountry than at the apartment he shared with Ray in Kampala. Their apartment was very male; sparsely furnished and very lacking in warmth. When he led you to his room, you sat at the edge of his bed, feeling like it had just been put together a few minutes earlier to allow for human occupancy. For one, the bed had no blanket and the closet barely had any clothes in it. Jude tried to brush off your worries and said he hated blankets and it was laundry day that day.

You tried to ignore your discomfort and were relieved when you noticed that Jude liked travelling so most times he opted to come to you in Mbale. While you were in Kampala you made it a point to introduce him to your friends and your sister who had started to think that you were making him up.

'Mummy, is he coming back from his trip today?' the little girl asks her tearful mother, her small voice laced with so much panic that it draws you out of your reverie. This makes the woman cry harder and mother and daughter get into what looks like a crying competition.

Outside, there is a sudden rush of feet and several women wail loudly as a crowd moves towards the main entrance of the house. Six men, their faces blank and purposeful, carry a coffin, gently asking that people move out of the way so they can find a place to put it.

The women in the house break down as if on cue and you feel your body taken over by another wave of grief. Amidst the wailing, an older man announces that there will be no viewing as it was a bad accident. You turn around to your sister and weep into her lap. You tell yourself over and over again that this cannot be true. You have been certain you would see his face again to wake him up. You would get a moment to tell him to cut the crap and that it was a bad joke and he should stop. To tell him that you were sorry for not sharing news you should have shared because you were still not sure how you felt about it. You should have told him before he left your house. You should have explained why you said the smell of alcohol on his breath that morning turned your stomach. You should have explained why you had insisted that he made you an omelette even if he knew you never really cared for eggs before. And yet now, with no viewing, even that had been taken away from you.

After what seems like forever, the wailing of the women around you subsides and you manage to pull yourself together. You sit up and you find the young girl now looking at you. And she looks exactly the way you have been imagining the child you are carrying would look like.

Hellen Nyana has worked in the media industry since she was a student at Makerere University, as a freelance reporter, sub-editor, reporter and columnist. She has been nurturing stories in her head, and leaving the gruelling Ugandan newsroom environment a little over a year ago has given her more time to put these stories onto paper and share them with other people.

Rules

The prize is awarded annually to a short story by an African writer published in English, whether in Africa or elsewhere. (The indicative length is between 3,000 and 10,000 words.)

'An African writer' is normally taken to mean someone who was born in Africa, or who is a national of an African country, or whose parents are African.

There is a cash prize of £10,000 for the winning author and a travel award for each of the shortlisted candidates (up to five in all).

For practical reasons, unpublished work and work in other languages is not eligible. Works translated into English from other languages are not excluded, provided they have been published in translation and, should such a work win, a proportion of the prize would be awarded to the translator.

The award is made in July each year, the deadline for submissions being 31 January. The shortlist is selected from work published in the five years preceding the submissions deadline and not previously considered for a Caine Prize. Submissions, including those from online journals, should be made by publishers and will need to be accompanied by six original published copies of the work for consideration, sent to the address below. There is no application form.

Every effort is made to publicize the work of the shortlisted authors through the broadcast as well as the printed media.

Winning and shortlisted authors will be invited to participate in writers' workshops in Africa and elsewhere as resources permit.

The above rules were designed essentially to launch the Caine Prize and may be modified in the light of experience. Their objective is to establish the Caine Prize as a benchmark for excellence in African writing.

The Caine Prize
The Menier Gallery
Menier Chocolate Factory
51 Southwark Street
London, SE1 1RU, UK
Telephone: +44 (0)20 7378 6234
Email: info@caineprize.com
Website: www.caineprize.com